THE DRAGON'S HONOR

Omnibus Including Book 1-3, The Princess Knight and selected short stories

C. H. Smith

Swamp Island Words

For all of those that seek refuge within the pages of a book....

CONTENTS

NOTHING MORE THAN ZERO

MAP OF KEALQUA

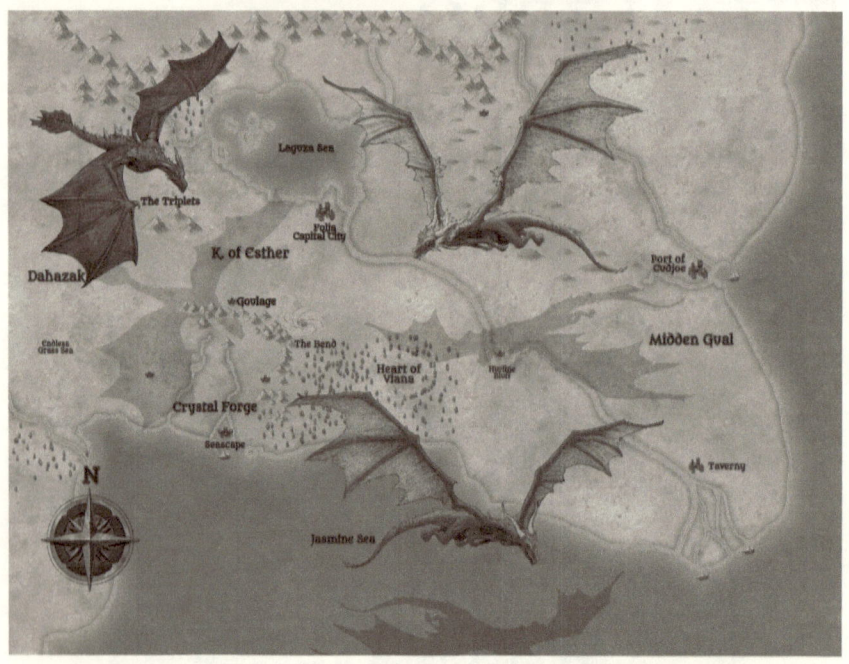

CHAPTER 1

The empty quiver dangled from Jaxson's sweaty back as he scanned the southern and western sky for any still in pursuit. He and his dragon, both exhausted, could see for miles from the top of this ridge. To the east, the sun had finally crested the tallest of the peaks in the Dragon's Spine. To the north lay uncharted territory.

"Think we finally lost them," he said, still searching the skies.

It had been a long night attempting to evade the large group of steam drakes. Zero would have no problem taking on a single drake, or even four, but they had been pursued by multiple dozens at least. Their long, slender bodies were built for bursts of speed. Jaxson had never known of this many eagle-sized drakes working together, and their sustained pursuit wasn't typical of their hunting style.

"Let me have a look at that wing," Jaxson said to Zero. "You keep your eyes sharp."

Zero extended his left wing as he gazed south, watching for any sign of the drakes. It didn't take Jaxson long to find the slash in the thin membrane between the long bones of Zero's wing. There was very little blood, and the cut was straight. *Thank the tiny gods for that,* thought Jaxson as he rummaged through his pack, looking for something to mend the wound.

As he finished sewing up his dragon's wing with a fish hook and line, he noticed a pool of blood around one of Zero's back legs.

"Oi, what happened there?"

What happened where? asked Zero in Jaxson's thoughts.

"Your back leg is all bloody! Did you not notice that?"

Zero swung his barrel-sized head around to see for himself. *So it is,* he said in Jaxson's mind, before turning his attention back to the south and west.

"And when did that happen? You been bleeding all night?" asked Jaxson.

Zero allowed him to tend the wound but offered no further insight into the cause of the injury. He just kept sentry, waiting for the relentless steam drakes to appear.

After mending the wound as best he could, Jaxson leaned on a rock overlooking the valley that wasn't the same valley he had spent most of his life in. After years of waiting for word from his father without a clue to his whereabouts, an old man, Dreknoxious, had shown up at his door with a hint of where to look. They had agreed to travel together to the Kingdom of Esther, but on the way, Dreknoxious had departed on urgent business. He promised to return and help their other traveling companion, the Princess of Seascape, face a fearsome battle. Jaxson decided to help too.

It was in that battle, facing terrible odds, that Jaxson and Zero fought against the Goat Head Sorcerer for the Princess. The steam drakes, vast in number, had forced Jaxson and Zero to flee the field. As long as the drakes were pursuing them, they couldn't fight against the Princess's army. But unlike other steam drakes, this horde did not get bored and give up. They had pursued Jaxson and Zero through the mountains and the night. Jaxson knew that he and Zero needed to find a place to rest safely, but this was unfamiliar territory. To the south, he thought he could see the triple peaks that towered over the Red Dragon Castle. That would place them almost at the point where the mountain range swept west and dangerously close to the Bend.

His father had taken great care in warning Jaxson about the strange things that occurred this far north. Creatures straight out of legends and nightmares roamed the mountains and the skies. An unnatural sea storm swirled over the land constantly, never moving away. The high winds from the storm spun out menacing clouds and frequent lightning. It was no place for man or dragon. Jaxson told Zero they had best avoid going farther north.

We need to find shelter and get some rest, said Zero in Jaxson's thoughts.

Aloud, Jaxson responded, "Yeah, we do… first time we leave the comfort of our little valley, and all this happens."

Zero looked at him and chuckled. *At least it's not boring.*

They both laughed. Jaxson's shoulders relaxed, and he rolled his head in large circles. Eyes closed, he felt the adrenaline seep away and weariness start to take over.

CHAPTER 2

The sun burned through Jaxson's eyelids, forcing him out of his deep sleep. He shook his head slowly to clear it, then looked out over the valley. The ground was rocky beneath him, and he could feel the rhythmic, deep breaths of Zero at his back.

Suddenly, his eyes widened. They should not have slept in the open, exposed.

He bolted to his feet and screamed for Zero to wake up. His head jerked from side to side as he searched the skies.

Zero rose quickly, though he stifled a yawn.

"How could we be so stupid?" said Jaxson.

Zero did not respond, but only moved to the edge of the ridge.

"Do you see anything?" asked Jaxson. His eyes were still wide and his hands had yet to calm. He shuddered at the thought of what would have happened if the steam drakes had found them in so vulnerable a position.

I do not see pursuit from the south or west, said Zero.

Jaxson's shoulders relaxed, and his hands stopped quaking so violently. "Thank all the tiny gods… Maybe we lost them for good."

His gaze shifted to the east. He half-expected to see a wall of steam drakes bearing down on them, but all he saw were blue skies and a lone eagle riding the current of the wind. The noble one circled high above, either in search of a meal or just enjoying the wind through his feathers. Seeing this was a good omen, and Jaxson liked good omens.

A small smile crept onto his face. It had been a long and frightful night, and there had been several moments when he had been sure the steam drakes would be their end. In the warm light of day, however, watching the noble eagle own the skies above him, a sense of peace overcame him. He was on his way to find his long overdue father. Thanks to the old man, Dreknoxious, he even had a place to begin searching.

His smile faltered as he thought of the old man. They had intended to travel to the capital of the Kingdom of Esther together. Circumstances Jaxson did not fully understand had caused Dreknoxious to depart quickly with only a promise to return. Jaxson had no idea how the old man would find him now, after their terror-filled flight through the mountains. *But if anyone can find me, it's him*, thought Jaxson.

He was brought out of his daydream by a strange grating sound. He looked all around but could not see anything that might have caused the noise. Zero had not seemed to notice, his gaze still locked on the horizon. Jaxson thought he might have imagined the whole thing, until he heard it again. The sounds of large rocks scraping together was closer this time, coming from on top of the ridge above them. Jaxson walked towards the sound and noticed a large, crevice concealed by a slight rise. The sound stopped just as Jaxson peered over the edge, down into the dark. The deep shadows concealed everything beyond a few feet. He nudged a small stone off the edge and heard it strike the wall on the way down. He waited patiently, expecting it to hit the bottom at any moment.

There is movement to the south, said Zero.

Jaxson didn't respond, still staring into the inky black darkness. He waited for the sound to come again; in each moment that passed a tiny trickle of fear filled more of him. A strange thought tickled the back of Jaxson's mind. *Something was down there.* Something darker than the deep crevice itself.

More urgently this time, Zero said, *There is significant*

movement to the south, and it's headed our way.

Jaxson waved a hand, then bent closer to the crevice. He strained his eyes for any sign of movement.

We need to go now! said Zero in his mind.

Jaxson had started to turn away from the crack when he saw a blink.

"What the—" he yelled as a giant petridrake burst up from the crevice.

Pebbles and dust rained down as the gray drake rose high into the air, unfurling his wings and bellowing a fierce challenge. Zero was at Jaxson's side in an instant, urging him to mount. Jaxson only stared slack-jawed at the ancient beast. With skin rougher and harder than stone, the petridrake was larger than its cousins, the steam drakes. It was larger even than Zero. Still stunned, Jaxson watched as the beast locked eyes on Zero and started to dive.

Without hesitation, Zero sprung up to meet the attack. Jaxson recoiled from the shock of their impact that reverberated deep in his chest. The heavier petridrake drove Zero back towards the ridge. Fresh blood dripped from Zero's back leg and wing.

"Get away from it!" yelled Jaxson. He started running to the edge of the ridge. Zero wheeled from underneath the petridrake, skimming the rocky ground as he soared away from the immediate danger. Jaxson reached the end of the ridge and watched as Zero slowly gained altitude once more.

I've got an idea, said Zero.

"Don't do anything crazy," said Jaxson. Even though the distance was great, Zero heard him and laughed.

Watch this. Look south, the dragon said in Jaxson's thoughts.

Jaxson looked in that direction and saw their persistent pursuers, the steam drakes, approaching quickly.

Zero banked hard directly at the petridrake. The stone-skinned beast snarled and leapt towards Zero.

The moment before impact, Zero veered away. The petridrake shot past but recovered quickly to give chase. Zero led him towards the steam drakes, always staying just out of reach. Jaxson could do nothing but watch as his friend turned his head and blew dragon's fire towards the petridrake, then suddenly went into a sharp dive. The petridrake, temporarily blinded by the fire, kept due south – straight into the eager steam drakes.

The piercing cries of the steam drakes filled the air as they were forced to engage this new enemy. Zero, flying close to the mountains, circled back to the ridge undetected.

Jaxson climbed onto his back, and the pair made their escape. To the east laid the Heart of Viana, where men and dragons alike were rumored to enter and never return. West or south would mean risking an encounter with the victor of the steam drakes and the petridrake. The only option was north... towards the Bend.

CHAPTER 3

A gentle tailwind helped keep Zero aloft as the duo made their way slowly towards the Bend. The mountains below grew more hostile. There were no longer green trees or plants, or any other signs of life. Jaxson could see no place where they could land and rest comfortably.

At least the bleeding from his leg has stopped, and his wing is holding up, thought Jaxson.

It is. I think I will be fine," Zero responded.

"I didn't realize I was talking to you," said Jaxson.

No matter. You are exhausted. Let's rest.

"Not yet," Jaxson said, looking at the wall of clouds ahead.

Black, gray, and white clouds swirled. The vortex was an impenetrable barrier. Silent lightning from within the clouds flashed sporadically across the horizon. The unnatural storm, constantly spinning and dancing, never opened to reveal what lay beyond. Jaxson thought it looked angry.

Zero banked to the left, traveling parallel to the storm. Jaxson tore his eyes away from the clouds to look for a likely spot to rest. The jagged rocks below were uninviting. Still, he kept looking for a smooth stretch of ground or a nice overhang that would hide them while they recuperated. The empty quiver on his back reminded him how vulnerable they were out in the open.

"I don't believe it!" he said suddenly.

What do you not believe?

"Approaching from behind us," replied Jaxson.

A large group of steam drakes – albeit smaller than it once was – loped haggardly on their tail.

Will they ever give up? asked Zero.

Jaxson sighed. "We won't survive another encounter. There are just too many for you, and my bow is useless."

I see no other options, said Zero.

Despite Zero's best efforts, the steam drakes gained on them steadily until Jaxson could see the wounds from their battle with the petridrake. The charcoal-gray leader was missing one of his hot-ember-colored eyes. Several others had gashes or torn wings. They maintained pursuit relentlessly.

"Zero! They're getting close. Into the clouds..." said Jaxson. "It's our only chance."

Zero tensed beneath him, but hesitated only a moment before turning straight into the storm of the Bend. *Hold on tight, Jaxson.*

The storm pulled them in with amazing force. Jaxson's head was thrown back, and he struggled to remain in the harness. He gripped with both hands as his dark hair whipped into his face. Through the strands, he saw the remaining steam drakes follow them into the storm and promptly get obliterated, the wind hitting them with such force that they were torn apart. Jaxson would have smiled if it had been possible.

There was a tremendous pain in his head as if it was being smashed between large boulders until nothing existed except the sound of the wind and his tenuous hold on the harness. He couldn't hear Zero; he couldn't even hear himself think.

Then the hair on the back of his neck stood up. Zero tensed once more, his wings straining. A flash of blinding white light engulfed them, followed by the crushing sound of thunder. The hurricane continued to rage. So loud. Jaxson's hold on reality slipped. He attempted to call out to Zero, but no words came. His vision blurred. The pressure on his head was too much, and he slid slowly into the nothingness.

CHAPTER 4

Jaxson floated blissfully along in the deep nothing suspended in the inky darkness for an amount of time beyond reckoning. He had not heard any sound or seen anything at all in the comforting darkness. He was relaxed and free. He thought he heard something – a voice, perhaps. Then he heard it – really heard it, this time. Definitely a voice. He couldn't make out the words, but he was sure the voice was familiar.

A troubling thought occurred to him. *Where am I?* When nothing came to mind even as he strained his eyes and ears and racked his brain, he was disquieted for the first time in the dark. *Who am I?*

Jaxson! Jaxson! Are you well? screamed Zero across the black expanse.

As if swimming up from the depths of a warm pool, Jaxson followed the voice. Slowly at first, then with more urgency. His eyes blasted open and light flooded him, threatening to consume him just as the darkness had. He was dazed by the brilliance of a warm, sunny afternoon sky.

He blinked rapidly, and slowly his vision adjusted. A concerned Zero towered over him, but Jaxson barely saw him. Instead, the green, fertile valley took his full attention. Tall, evergreen trees lined the outer rim of the valley, giving way to large oaks. To the west, a rumbling waterfall cascaded from a mountain into a large pool, with several streams branching out. The sight of the falling water reminded Jaxson of his intense thirst. He stood up and, for the first time, he noticed the castle at the far side of the valley. It was huge, and Jaxson was drawn to it… drawn to a pulsing power coming from the ancient stones.

Are you well?

"I'm fine. Where are we?"

Zero took a long, slow look around the valley before he said, *Within the storm.*

Again, Jaxson looked up at the blue sky. He was going to object, but then he noticed that above the mountains all around them swirled dark clouds. They were in the eye of the storm.

"That's odd."

That is not all that is odd. Look up there, said Zero. He indicated the ridge just behind them. Sitting perfectly still, watching them, was a smokey dragon. It was twice as large as Zero, and even from this distance, Jaxson could tell something was off. The smoke dragon did not look solid. It shifted, and its edges were difficult to distinguish.

"How long has it been there?" asked Jaxson.

I have been able to differentiate a total of three, and at least one has been visible at all times since we arrived. They fade in and out but have not come any closer.

"What do you think they want?" asked Jaxson.

Zero shrugged.

Jaxson looked back down into the valley. He had to make an effort not to look at the castle. Instead, he followed the path of the longest stream east across the valley floor. They needed water and something to eat. The stream passed through trees that he thought may bear fruit. He glanced back up at the smokey dragon. It faded away just as another started to take shape several feet away.

"Come on, let's go have a drink," said Jaxson as he climbed into the riding harness.

CHAPTER 5

He looked over his shoulder and was shocked to see not one smokey dragon but all three perched on the ridge behind them. Zero pushed off the ground with his powerful legs as he unfurled his wings. They were off. Jaxson smiled as the breeze hit his face. Again, he looked behind them. The smoke dragons were in pursuit but keeping their distance. One was directly behind and one on each side.

"We have company," said Jaxson.

Zero just snorted and kept flying at a leisurely pace.

"Head toward the waterfall."

Zero tried to angle to the west but was cut off by the smokey dragon on that side. He tried again and the dragon from the rear appeared, keeping them from turning.

Let's try the other direction.

With a quick snap of his wings, Zero dove down and to the right, under the third smoke dragon. The rear dragon gave a piercing cry as all three turned quickly in pursuit, and then vanished. Jaxson looked over his shoulder but could no longer see any of the dragons.

"Nice move, Zero! They seem to have lost interest—"

Fire erupted in front of them. Jaxson could smell the heat as Zero turned sharply from the inferno. Through the flames and waves of heat, Jaxson saw all three smoke dragons billowing dragon's fire, creating a barrier not dissimilar to the clouds of the storm around the Bend. With no options left, Zero angled toward the structure in the distance and set a deliberately slow pace. Jaxson, still singed, did not like their destination being forced upon them but could think of no alternative.

The smoke dragons resumed their escort positions, appearing content to leave Jaxson and Zero alone if they flew in the direction they chose. As they approached the large structure, Jaxson could see more details. It resembled a castle, but everything seemed too large. The towers were easily twice as tall as any structure Jaxson had ever seen. The stones that made up the towers were jet black and as large as the mountain cottage he had called home for years.

"Land well before the gate," he said. "Let's get an idea of what we're getting into."

You think the smoke dragons will allow that?

"As long as we don't stray, I think they'll leave us be. They didn't bother us earlier."

We'll see. Zero slowed and started a soft descent well before the large gate.

Just before Zero touched down, the smoke dragons disappeared. Jaxson dismounted and walked to Zero's head. Both stared at the immense structure in front of them. Seven tall towers shot up above a large central structure. It was encircled by a wall fifty feet high and just as thick, but the gate was what caught Jaxson's attention. It was as imposing and almost as tall as wall itself, with seven metal bars thicker than his legs. On each bar hung a huge sigil which appeared to have been carved with painstaking care. The top sigil depicted three small circles on the tracks of a larger circle within a larger circle still. Within each of the three smallest circles, detailed scenes were carved.

One such scene showed a king wearing a crown and with rings on all of his fingers. He was walking up a flight of stairs which were actually peasants bent over in varying degrees of supplication. Despite the distance between them and the gate, Jaxson had little trouble seeing and understanding the scene of the greedy king. The sigil slightly lower and to the left appeared at first to be simply a wavy line crossing the large metal circle. Then Jaxson noticed it wasn't a solid line. Instead, the flowing line was formed by naked, interlocking bodies. The details made Jaxson blush.

Each sigil was elegantly simple in design but intricate and precise in form. One showed an eye above a pyramid, and another depicted a five-pointed star created by jagged, sharp lines. There were others, and Jaxson tried to etch each one into his mind. They seemed powerful and important.

Our guides are back, said Zero, bringing Jaxson back to situation at hand.

The smoke dragons again positioned themselves in such a way as to force them to the gate. Jaxson looked at Zero and nodded. As they stepped toward the castle, the gate began to swing inwards slowly. As soon as they were beyond the wall, the smoke dragons dissipated once more. Jaxson and Zero were alone inside the vast courtyard. When the gate closed behind them, a chill ran up Jaxson's neck. They were here now; what that was worth, he had no idea.

CHAPTER 6

From where they had first landed, the castle had appeared to be directly behind the wall. Once they had passed through the gate, Jaxson realized the castle was actually much larger and much farther away. A path lined with evenly spaced elms and oaks before them led directly to one of the seven tall towers. Jaxson looked up to the top of the tower and was amazed to see it was just as large at the top as it was at the base. Beyond the tower loomed the ancient castle.

"I guess we should have a look around?" asked Jaxson.

Zero nodded, and they set off down the path toward the tower. *It's strange. These trees are thriving. The grass is green and lush without weed or bramble.*

Jaxson could not see a brown leaf nor vine or weed in any direction. "That is no more strange than anything else," he replied.

Yes and no. That fact alone is not that strange, but couple it with the fact we have not seen another living being of any kind in this valley... and it starts to feel odd. Who is maintaining these grounds? Why have we seen no animals? Not a single bird? Something is just off—

Jaxson stopped in his tracks and turned his head to the right. "Do you hear that?"

Zero turned and brought his head lower to be on Jaxson's level, in order to see under the trees. Then he laughed. *And I see the source!*

Both sprinted to the sound of running water. A stone, three-tiered fountain below a statue of a dragon flowed with crystal-clear water. After they had filled their bellies to the bursting point, Jaxson stepped back to admire the artistry of the fountain. The pool was oblong and longer than Zero and was cut from a single solid stone. The bottom tier of the fountain was midnight black and about half the size of the pool. The middle tier was fire-ash gray stone, flat like the bottom and about half the size. The top stone, from which the water flowed, was solid white. The flying dragon statue in the center of the white stone had a single back claw resting upon it.

"That statue has horns like you," commented Jaxson.

I am quite certain horns on a dragon are commonplace.

"I don't think so. I've never read about any dragons with horns like yours, and the only dragons we have seen didn't have them either," said Jaxson, looking at Zero's two crescent-shaped horns on the top of his head. The same dark green that covered his back also adorned the horns, which arched toward each other and almost touched at the tips.

It is of no consequence, replied Zero.

Jaxson opened his mouth to continue the debate, but then a dark shadow blocked out the sun. For a moment, he thought a storm must be rolling in, although they had seen no clouds within the storm of the Bend. A dragon more than twice the size of Zero flew overhead, angling to the first tall tower to which the path led. It was darker than night and seemed to swallow the light around it. It circled the top of the tower and flew back in their direction.

Let's go!

Jaxson scrambled onto Zero's back, and before he was set in the harness, Zero sprang from the ground. With three powerful beats of his wings, they were above the giant elm trees. The black dragon quickened its pace and was on top of them in an instant. Zero attempted to veer left but the giant dragon stopped in the air above them and beat his wings to send a powerful gust of wind down. Zero could not withstand the gale. He was forced to retreat to the ground or risk being blown into a tree.

Satisfied, the black dragon circled high and then slowly made his way to the ground near the fountain. Jaxson expected the ground to shake when he landed, but he was surprised how gently the black dragon set down. He was massive, long and thick, solid black with a hint of gray along the belly and around the face. He had a pair of crescent-shaped horns atop his head, their tips almost touching just like Zero's. When his gaze fell upon them, Jaxson was bare as though the black dragon saw him completely, right down into his soul. He locked eyes with the ancient dragon and then could not look away.

Finally, the black dragon spoke. *Is he your rider? Or is he your captor?*

Zero glanced at Jaxson, then back to the dragon. *I am not his prisoner, if that is what you are asking.*

What is your name, young one?

Zero is the name I am called. But my hatching name is Zerrophidious. I do not know why I have told you. Only I and he know it.

It is an old name, a strong name. It suits you. Zero bowed his head as the black dragon continued, *You may call me Forseti, though that is not my hatching name nor my fire name. Now, what are you doing with this weak one?*

Until that moment, Jaxson had sat quietly, in awe of Forseti's size and majesty. "What makes you think I'm weak? Because I'm small or because I'm human?"

Forseti turned quickly at the sound of Jaxson's voice. His mouth hung open as he looked from Jaxson to Zero and back again. Then he threw his head back and roared with laughter, long and hard. When he caught his breath, he said, *Bless the Seven Gates! We have much to discuss.*

CHAPTER 7

The second floor of the castle was open and airy. Every two hundred feet, colossal columns rose from the floor to the ceiling, their tops almost out of sight. Their number was hard to determine. Jaxson could see seven in one row, but he couldn't see the far side of the chamber. They had followed Forseti around

to the rear of the structure back and through an open gate larger even than the gate in the outer wall. He led the duo to a fire ring close to one of the columns on the left side of the chamber. Zero settled on the side opposite to the black dragon and watched as Forseti blew dragon's fire onto the rocks within the fire ring. Jaxson shielded his eyes from the blast of heat. When he looked back, a pleasant, albeit large, fire was crackling in the ring.

Now, we are all settled. I must ask, how did you pass through the Taufan?

"You mean the storm? I'm not completely sure, but I think we just flew through it." Jaxson glanced at Zero, who gave a slight nod.

Flew through it? What would cause you to even attempt it?

"It's not like we had much of a choice. Steam drakes have been hounding us for two days, and then we almost landed on a petridrake," said Jaxson. Each word he spoke came quicker than the last. "We thought we'd lost them when Zero put the petridrake in the others' path. He is hurt; I am exhausted. And still we had to use the storm, the Taufan, to finally escape them!"

Jaxson's chest heaved and sweat beaded his brow. There had not been time to really think about the dangers they had only narrowly escaped. He knew they were lucky to be alive and – more or less – in one piece. The steam drakes had pursued them much farther than was typical of their kind. And the petridrake... he had never seen one before, or even heard of one living in the Dragon Spine Mountains.

And the sentinels? How did you avoid them to gain access to the gate?

Jaxson started to reply, but Zero talked over him. *The smoke dragons? They were on us from the moment we broke free of the clouds. If we stopped, they stopped. If we moved, they guided us. Guided us here.*

Interesting, replied Forseti. He turned to the column and studied the intricate carvings. There were words, but not of a language Jaxson could read.

"So, what is this place?" asked Jaxson as he moved closer to the column.

Forseti glanced at him but did not answer. Jaxson shuffled his feet and looked around the chamber. The silence stretched on. Zero stared intently at Forseti, then abruptly turned away.

"What's wrong, Zero?"

This is a strange place, but I am not sure I believe everything he tells me.

"What has he told you? What have you told him?" Jaxson demanded. He moved quickly to Zero's side, never taking his eyes from the black dragon, Forseti.

I have told him nothing he did not need to hear, though it may be difficult to comprehend, said Forseti. He turned from the column to face them fully. *Zero insists that I speak with both of you from here on, and I will honor his wishes. You asked what this place is. It is the Temple of Greeti and home to one of the seven portals linking all parts of this world together. I am its guardian and have been for the last age. You are the first outsiders I have spoken to in a very long time.*

"That does not seem hard to believe, given everything we have seen so far," said Jaxson.

I do not believe that is the part Zero is struggling with, said Forseti, looking at Zero. *Perhaps he should tell you.*

Zero's eyes widened, and he looked back and forth between Forseti and Jaxson. He took several steps away from Jaxson, shaking his head.

"Zero, it's fine. Tell me what he said that bothers you."

He told me that he is old – very old. He told me that his time on Kealqua is passing, and that I am... Zero trailed off and looked at Forseti. *I won't do it!*

"Won't do what?" asked Jaxson.

He says I am to be his replacement as guardian here. It is what I was hatched to do!

CHAPTER 8

A constant breeze blew through the second floor of the castle overlooking the lush valley. They had entered on the opposite side, and now they were nestled up next to the mountains again. The storm clouds of the Bend – or the Taufan, as Forseti had called it – shifted and spun around, ever changing and yet always the same. This was the first time Jaxson could study the unnatural storm up close, without being in the midst of it or being chased by steam drakes. He found it to be beautiful yet terrifying. Zero had been silent since Forseti had told him of his new responsibility. Jaxson did not understand exactly what it meant, but he knew Zero was completely against it.

"Why are you pouting?" he said.

The green dragon's nostrils flared, and Zero responded, *I do not pout. I am just thinking.*

"You want to fill me in?" asked Jaxson, watching the Taufan rage on.

Zero was silent for a long time. Finally, he said, *I am not sure how much to believe. Forseti says he can show me the truth, but I need to be willing to see it. Everything he tells me is cryptic. You know he is old, but not how old. He is ancient, older than the Bend itself. He flew over these mountains before elves arrived, and before men. But none of that matters. What matters is that he claims I am a descendant of an ancient line of dragon kings, for lack of a better word. He is of the same line.*

"That's amazing. He told you all that?"

Yes and no. He did not speak to me, but something more. He opened up his memories to me – or more accurately, he pushed them upon me.

"That's amazing! But does that mean we will have to stay here? What would we be protecting? This old castle? It's nice and all, but I'm not sure it needs full-time security. Nobody can get through the Bend." Jaxson began to pace back and forth along the wall overlooking the valley.

Zero watched Jaxson walk in little circles.

I saw something in the memories... I am not sure if he intended me to or not. It could explain some of it, I think.

Jaxson stopped pacing and looked at Zero. "Well?"

I caught only a glimpse before the memory moved on, but I think what I saw was important. It was an archway in the middle of a stone room – big, like everything else here – but I couldn't see through it. It was midnight black, but not solid. It rippled like water with a breeze on it. I could see to either side of it, but within it... nothing.

Jaxson resumed his nervous walking. "And you think this archway is important?"

Zero nodded.

Jaxson continued, "And it's here in the castle?"

I believe it is. Zero rose to his feet as Forseti glided around from the side of the castle toward the duo. He angled his body slightly and came to a rest just outside of earshot.

"Now we'll get some answers," said Jaxson. "Come on."

As Zero followed Jaxson, he muttered, *To get answers, we need to know what questions to ask.*

CHAPTER 9

Forseti flew out of the large opening and into the sky guiding them to the uppermost level of the castle. After they landed beside him on the open balcony, Forseti talked about an age before men and elves, about the seven great dragon kings that ruled the world with honor and balance. He told them about the seven portals that linked all of Kealqua together, which were created by the first wizards. He spoke of grand cities which featured places of learning and spirituality. The world had been connected and thriving. Elves came first to the island region of Nebur, then other places. Men followed afterwards, in Specerin and Crystal Vale. The dragons nurtured both infant races, and eventually the dragonriders of vast magical powers came to be. All of this was before the Blank Years.

"What are the Blank Years?" asked Jaxson. "I'm sure I've heard that phrase before, but I don't know what it means."

Forseti gave a deep sigh. *The Blank Years are not a time forgotten or lost, as the name may suggest. It was a time of no advancement and even serious regression. The study of magic took a dark turn, making some dragons regret ever teaching elves and humans the art. Wars broke out on a scale unseen before. New races that thrived on destruction entered the world. The numbers of orcs and goblins multiplied rapidly. Every aspect of the world the dragon kings had attempted to build took a step backward. It was at the end of the Blank Years, after a terrible war that I will not discuss now, that it was decided by the elders of my race to seal the portals from each other and from the world.*

You have been here alone all this time? asked Zero.

I was not alone at first... but it has been only me for quite some time now, responded Forseti.

"I'm sorry," muttered Jaxson. "My dad left me and Zero a few summers ago, to go and battle the people that would seek to hurt Zero. I know it's not the same, but I miss him terribly."

Dusk came quickly in the valley. The sun had already fallen behind the mountains, and the shadows lengthened rapidly and grew darker. Eerie stillness settled across the valley, and all was still on the top floor of the Temple of Greeti. Jaxson was lost in thoughts about his father, the reason they were in the mountains in the first place. Zero stared out at the coming night, as perfectly still as a statue.

Forseti broke the silence first.

I settled with my grief long ago. It is still there, a piece of me. But it is rare for it to catch me unprepared. It does happen from time to time, though, and in those moments, I have found it best to allow it to run its full course. Shutting it down within me never did any good. Now, I understand you are not dealing with grief but with uncertainty and fear. But you have already taken the most important step. You are moving forward and not allowing the fear to paralyze you. I commend you for that, Jaxson.

Jaxson nodded, unsure how to respond. Since they had left their little mountain home to search for his father, nothing had gone to plan. He had left with Dreknoxious, an old family friend that Jaxson suspected was something other than he claimed to be. Then the perilous flight through the night, and the next day's attempt to escape the steam drakes and the huge petridrake. They had sought safety in the Bend, and as amazing as this place had turned out to be, now Forseti was telling them Zero had to stay, to be a guardian. They hadn't even left the mountains yet, and everything had gone wrong.

Forseti, in the vision you showed me, I saw a large doorway filled with darkness, said Zero. *Was that the portal you spoke of earlier?*

It is... and it is the reason you must remain here as guardian of this temple, replied Forseti. *Let me show you.*

He turned away from the valley and walked into the long, narrow hall. They walked in single file for a time, lacking enough space for both dragons to walk side by side. The hall ended abruptly at a stone wall. Forseti turned his massive head and whispered, *Believe there is no wall.*

He stepped directly into the wall.

Jaxson's mouth fell open as the black dragon appeared to melt into the stones with each step. When he was gone, Jaxson walked up to the wall and raised his hand to strike it. He expected his hand to pass straight through the stones, but was surprised when his hand smacked the surface, hard. A pained welp escaped his lips, and he waved his hand rapidly.

As Jaxson shook his throbbing hand, Zero laughed.

"What's so funny?"

You look like a chicken flapping its wing, said Zero.

"Well, it hurts! What are we supposed to do now?"

We need to believe there is no wall, replied Zero.

He took a deep breath and stepped forward, passing Jaxson and walking through the wall.

"Zero – are you all right?"

Yes. Just focus on your next step and know *nothing is going to stop you, said Zero.*

Jaxson took a deep breath. The wall looked and felt solid. When he took a step forward, his head smacked solid stone with a thud.

"Well, that didn't work," said Jaxson as he rubbed the rapidly swelling knot on his head.

Here, said Zero, and his tail appeared through the wall beside Jaxson. *Grab my tail. We will do this together.*

Jaxson rested a hand on the tough scales and allowed

himself to be pulled through the wall.

CHAPTER 10

I did not believe you would be able to pass the barrier. You surprise me, and that is not easily accomplished, said Forseti to Jaxson. When Jaxson did not respond, he continued, *There is more to you and your relationship with Zero than I first thought.*

"What is that supposed to mean?" asked Jaxson.

All in good time, replied Forseti. *But first, Zero, you and your rider need to see this.*

Jaxson looked past the ancient dragon, and he saw the doorway Zero had mentioned earlier. It was taller than even Forseti, and easily wide enough for both dragons to pass through side by side. Its frame was made out of a stone that Jaxson did not recognize. It looked smooth and rough at the same time, depending how the light touched it. At the top of the frame were three rubies the size of dragon eggs. The precious stone on the left glowed with inner fire. As interesting as the frame was, the black, rippling surface suspended within it was doubly so. Jaxson couldn't tear his eyes from the shimmering portal. It was pulling at him, wanting him to come closer.

Zero cut between him and the massive doorway as he circled to its rear. Jaxson was finally able to look around at the rest of the room. Although still huge, it was the smallest chamber they had been in thus far. He looked back at the wall through which he had passed, and was surprised to find it was no longer there. Even the hallway was gone. Instead, only a wide-open chamber that ended at the far landing. Zero completed his pass around the doorway and settled beside

Jaxson.

It is a free-standing structure, said Zero. *The only difference is there are no red stones on the back.*

"So strange," replied Jaxson.

Forseti circled the doorway, and once behind it, Jaxson could only see a ghostly shadow through the door. When the black dragon returned to the front, he stopped near the glowing red stone.

It has been an age since one of these stones glowed. The only difference in all that time is that now you two are here, said Forseti. Jaxson started to speak, but Forseti talked over him. *Now is the time for listening. I will tell you all you need to know. And if you still have questions after I am finished, I will do my best to answer them.*

****

With the history beyond history already explained, Forseti launched into a more personal account of the past. He explained how he and his dragonrider had been chosen to guard the portal as it was sealed away. No one – neither him or the elders – thought it would be for an extended period of time, much less the thousands of years that had passed. His dragonrider had given up hope long ago and succumbed to his own depression.

Forseti dealt with the passing of his closest friend as best he could. And nothing changed. The Taufan blew around the valley, and no one came to relieve him of his duties. The only change in his routine was when he ventured out of the valley for food, when no roaming elk herds passed through. Even that grew tiresome over the years, when he failed to encounter any other dragons near the Bend.

Still, he fulfilled his responsibility. He guarded the empty portal and the impregnable valley.

Then, fifteen years ago, one of the rubies on the portal began to glow again. Forseti knew that could only mean a dragon of royal descent and his bonded rider were nearby. He had been watching the empty portal as the black, traveling void returned within the archway just yesterday, coinciding with Zero's and Jaxson's entering of the Taufan. But when another ruby did not start to glow, he had lost heart. It was merely a coincidence, or perhaps the magic was failing after so many years. The sentinels had allowed them to pass, however, meaning that Zero, at least, was supposed to be here.

So, these were the reasons Forseti took Zero to be the new guardian of the temple and the portal. He had given up on Jaxson from the first moment, because he did not resemble the dragonriders of old. He was too young and too scrawny. Forseti had not seen a weapon or a staff. Then Jaxson had passed through the last barrier protecting the portal, surprising Forseti again. Still, the remaining two rubies were dormant. Now, Forseti was unsure if Zero was indeed intended to remain.

CHAPTER 11

The fire crackled as the fat dripped from the elk's hindquarters. Beside the temple, Jaxson rotated the spit quietly under the stars. He drank deeply from his skin he had filled at the well, but it did nothing to sate the hunger in the pit of his stomach. Still, the one thing living alone with Zero in the mountains had taught him was patience. He would not rush it and risk burning the meat – or worse still, his mouth. He would wait for the dragons to return. Zero had flown with Forseti toward the mountains to the north just before sundown, at the older dragon's request. Jaxson had attempted to ask where they were going, but had not received much information in reply.

He took another swig from the waterskin and found it empty. As he strolled through the trees along the path to the well, he tried to decide how he would talk Zero into getting out of here. He needed to find his father, and it was obvious he wasn't here within the Taufan. The original plan, before being chased for a day and night by the steam drakes, had been to travel into the Kingdom of Esther with Dreknoxious in search of any sign of his father. That had all gone wrong. When Forseti had told them that Zero was to be the new guardian, Jaxson's heart had sunk. He would not leave Zero no matter the cost, but he also couldn't abandon his search for his father. He didn't want to admit it, but he was worried about his father. He could think of no reason for him to be away for so long.

He was thinking in circles. He had been worried about his father for a long time, so why was it bothering him so much now? Perhaps he was actually worried about Zero wanting to stay, wanting to connect with his past. Jaxson didn't know the full story of how his father had acquired Zero as an egg. He didn't know any part of the story, really. Although Zero had never asked, Jaxson knew he was curious about his origins. Dragons stay with their young until the little ones are able to fend for themselves, so it was unlikely he was abandoned. Now Forseti had offered a clue to his past, and Jaxson was concerned that the allure would prove too much for Zero to turn down.

He filled his waterskin and decided not to think about it again until he had talked with Zero. He turned to return along the path toward the fire where the mouthwatering meat was cooking.

Jaxson looked left and then right, but there was no path in sight. He walked around the well, thinking that maybe he had gotten himself turned around while deep in thought. On the other side, three paths appeared where he was sure there had been none moments before. The first was wide and smooth, but went to the south, well away from the temple. The middle one was worn but overgrown. It had not been trod by anyone in quite some time. It led directly away from the well – if indeed he had was turned around, it should lead him straight back to the temple. The final path was shrouded in shadow more profound than the starlight should cause. Limbs, barren and twisted, from gnarly trees reached over the dark and broken path.

In every fairytale he had ever heard, the easy path was a trap, and only a fool took the most forbidding path. He pondered the middle path that seemed not to have been taken by any for a long while as maybe being his best option. He looked at each path again and took a deep breath. He could smell the grass and the scent of the coming rain, but underneath these was the pleasing aroma of crackling meat over a fire. He focused on the intoxicating scent and turned away from all three paths. He followed his nose all the way back to the fire and the two waiting dragons.

I told you he would return before daylight, said Zero as he rose to greet Jaxson.

Well before daylight... which path did you choose? asked Forseti.

Jaxson looked from one dragon to the other. "Was this some type of test?"

When neither dragon responded, he looked at Zero and asked, "Were you in on it? What was the point?"

I wanted to prove— Zero began.

Forseti cut him off. *Which path did you choose?*

"I didn't take any of the paths. I followed my nose back here!" said Jaxson. "Now what was the point?"

You may not have picked one of the three paths, but you did choose, said Forseti. *And again, you surprise me. Zero is right. You are worthy.*

"Worthy of what?" asked Jaxson.

All in due time, said Forseti.

It is of no concern, said Zero. *We should eat, then sleep. Tomorrow we will be on the path to find your father.*

Jaxson smiled. Finally, they would be on their way.

CHAPTER 12

The flight back through the Taufan seemed easy compared to their hectic trip only two days earlier. Jaxson hugged Zero's back as he flowed up and down on the strong winds, always moving toward the outside of the Taufan. Forseti had spoken with Zero briefly about not fighting the storm winds to instead use them to his advantage, and it worked. Jaxson did not feel the force in his head threatening to send him back down into the depths of blackness. A full belly and some rest helped.

The sun dazzled him as they broke free from the clouds, low to the ground in between two colossal mountains. The Dragon Spine Mountains ranged to the south and the west. Foothills filled the landscape away to the north, and there was a large forest to the east. There was not a cloud in the sky.

Zero shot straight up into the air, gaining speed as he climbed. Jaxson let out a joyous yell as Zero pulled up and immediately started to plummet back to the rocky ground. Jaxson reveled in exhilarating freedom, his hands in the air and wind blowing through his hair.

There was no need to stick close to the mountains, as the steam drakes had been obliterated on their way into the Taufan of the Bend. Now the pair could go in any direction they wanted – which presented them with a new set of problems. Jaxson knew he needed to go north to the Kingdom of Esther, but he wasn't positive what he would do once he got there. What was more, he knew to go to the Kingdom, but not *where* in the Kingdom. And it was big, stretching from the Dragon Spine Mountains to beyond the

Laguza Sea.

However, Zero surprised him, turning to the east to fly alongside the forest.

"Where are we going?" asked Jaxson.

Forseti told me this forest is called the Heart of Viana, home of the elves, replied Zero. *We need supplies not available within the Taufan. We can trade for them here.*

"Trade with what? We don't have anything."

I have a plan, but when we get there, you need to do the talking.

"Why?" asked Jaxson. When Zero gave no answer, he asked again. "Why? What does that mean?"

Zero kept flying, still not answering, so Jaxson settled in and started making a mental inventory of everything they would need. He needed arrows to begin with, and a backup bow string. New clothes wouldn't hurt. He had water, but very little food. Without a pack to carry anything in, the list couldn't be too long.

Still, without anything to trade, making a list seemed pointless. After a time, Zero filled him in on the plan Forseti had given him. Jaxson thought it was a long shot at best.

****

They flew for hours along unchanged forest. The grassy hills to their left were endless. Jaxson spotted a change in the landscape immediately. Two large stone pillars stood just beyond the forest, on level ground where the trees met the hills. A road ran from the pillars onto the rolling plains to the north, where it faded into the horizon.

Zero dropped lower and reduced speed. As they passed the pillars, Jaxson saw nobody. Zero turned slowly and circled back to the pillars once more. The lonely stones did not seem inviting to Jaxson.

The dragon touched down softly on the hillside beyond the pillars. He gestured with his head for Jaxson to approach them. Before he was halfway there, three figures appeared between the pillars. He was sure they hadn't been there moments before, but there was no mistaking the three elves that stood there now. He raised his hand in greeting as he continued to walk forward. The stoic elves, who wore clothes in natural hues of brown, green, and tan, did not respond, waiting as motionless as the pillars beside them. Jaxson continued his approach, still unsure about Zero's plan but beyond the point of backing out. They did need supplies before going into the Kingdom, and before the next leg of their journey to find his father.

"Hello there," he said as he finally came within earshot.

"Greetings from the forest," said the middle elf. "Do you come seeking to trade?"

Jaxson nodded and came to a stop before the elves. The middle elf, the one that had greeted him, was tall and slender, with green clothes and a large eagle feather in his hair. The two on either side were shorter and stouter. One wore tan clothing and wore a small deer antler on a cord around his neck. The final elf wore brown and black clothing and was the only one with his arms exposed. At first, Jaxson thought he saw intricate tattoos from wrist to shoulder, but on closer inspection they appeared to be a second skin fitting snugly in place.

"We are in need of several items, if you have them," said Jaxson.

The elves exchanged glances, and the antler elf said, "You do not appear to come from the north, and therefore you are not one of our regular trading partners. Also, you do not have much to trade, unless your barter remains with your dragon."

"I'll show you mine after you show me yours," said Jaxson.

The middle elf stared at Jaxson, but Jaxson didn't look away. Finally, the elf laughed and gestured for Jaxson to follow as all three of the elves turned and entered the forest.

CHAPTER 13

Once inside the forest, Jaxson noticed there were many more elves than he had expected. Some were traveling along the branches of the trees, and others were busy weaving baskets or tending small gardens. They were lively and spoke with each other quickly but quietly. No one spared him a second glance as he followed the three elves to a circle of rocks around a small fire. He was offered a glass of clear, yellow liquid which he sipped politely. His head danced with visions of spring, flowers and gentle sunlight, and the scents of new grass and the crispness of an early morning frost jolted his senses. The laughter of the elves nearby startled him. Jaxson looked down at the small cup with the clear liquid in amazement.

"First time drinking the drop of the sun?" asked the first elf.

"Yes. It's amazing," said Jaxson. He took a larger mouthful.

"We often forget how the things we find so simple and boring are in fact a wonder to the other races," said the elf. "My name is Grothum, and I will be your trading partner. And your name?"

Something tiny flew directly above Jaxson's head, a blur of green with a spot of red. He tried to follow it with his eyes but couldn't keep up. "Uhh, my name is Jaxson. What was..."

Grothum looked in the direction Jaxson was staring. From the lowest branch of a tall oak, a vine laden with purple flowers cascaded down. Flitting from flower to flower was the tiniest bird imaginable, no bigger than Jaxson's thumb.

"There! What is that thing?"

Grothum laughed again. "It is called a bee bird or, as you humans call it, a hummingbird. Beautiful little creatures that drink the nectar of flowers, and, like bees, help to spread and propagate those same flowers. Have you never seen one?"

"I have not. Most of my life has been high in the mountains. We have fairies but not bee birds," replied Jaxson. "So tiny and its wings are a blur."

"Yes, yes. But perhaps now it is time to get to business," said Grothum.

"You're right, of course. How do we begin?" asked Jaxson.

"Simple. You tell me what you want from the trade. I will tell you if we have it or how long it will take to bring it here," said Grothum. "Then we will discuss what you have to trade for value."

Jaxson looked around but did not see any place to store goods. He didn't think anything would be on hand. "I need some food. Something filling but portable, about five days' worth."

"Have you ever eaten elven food? It is simple fare but, as with that drink, it is all natural. We can provide the food."

"Next, I will need arrows. My quiver will hold about a dozen and a half. And do you have bowstrings? I like to have a backup." Each request was easier for Jaxson to make. If Zero's plan worked and the elves had everything they needed, they would be set for supplies for a good while.

"We can do arrows, and a backup string is always a good idea," commented Grothum.

"Do you happen to have any clothes that would fit me? And shoes?" asked Jaxson.

"The clothing will be no problem as long as you don't

mind natural hues? We would normally have plenty of human clothes, but our trading partners to the north traded for nearly all of it last week," said Grothum. Jaxson nodded, and he continued, "The shoes may be more problematic, but I will send a runner to another camp. Perhaps he will be able to acquire suitable footwear for you."

Jaxson listed several other items: a pack, an extra waterskin, and a small knife to replace the one he had lost recently. Grothum did not raise any objection even when the list grew long. He simply sent one elf or another to procure the items. When Jaxson ran out of things to ask for in trade, the runners had already gathered quite a pile behind Grothum.

"Is that all that you require?" asked Grothum.

Jaxson looked at the goods with hopeful glee. Replacement clothes and even shoes sat beside arrows and packages of food. He could not think of a single thing to add, until a flash of feathers zoomed up to the hanging flowers above his head. He said, "One more thing... I would like a feather from one of the bee birds."

Grothum's head flew back in laughter. "What a request! We do not take feathers from our bird friends, but if they are freely given, we carry them. I'll ask one of our tiny friends for you, but do not truly expect any results. Never has one outside of our forest received a feather."

He turned from the fire, and Jaxson heard a low whistle that warbled slowly, then more quickly. As the tune danced, Jaxson imagined one of the small hummingbirds in a sea of flowers, flitting from one to the next, taking in its fill of sweet nectar. Grothum's tune changed, becoming slower and sweeter. A tiny ball of feathers darted down and hovered directly in front of Jaxson's face. Grothum's whistle changed tune again. He extended his hand gently, and the hummingbird lit on his finger. Jaxson saw the long, needle-like beak of the hummingbird bob up and down, and then the bird shook. After the bird flew back to the flowers, a tiny, iridescent feather remained in Grothum's hand.

"This is truly special," said Grothum, almost to himself.

CHAPTER 14

Other elves started to gather around Grothum. He held the feather in his cupped hand, his eyes never leaving it. Jaxson saw the other elves talking quietly but urgently. He saw their furtive glances in his direction, though he never saw anyone looking directly at him. It was plain even to Jaxson, with his limited elven knowledge, that a bird giving a feather in this manner was different and noteworthy. The elf with the full arm sleeves that looked like another skin spoke quietly with Grothum, then approached Jaxson.

"Greetings again. My name is Belhie – we met earlier at the pillars," said the new elf.

"I remember. I thought your sleeves were tattoos at first. They're quite striking," said Jaxson as he studied the diamond shapes that intertwined and flowed up Belhie's arms.

"They are not tattoos, but they are not sleeves either. They are the skin from a mighty tree snake that calls this forest home. He gave them to me many years ago," said Belhie.

"That's amazing! Why did he give them to you?"

"Under normal circumstances, we, the Elves of Viana, would never discuss this with any outsider. These are not normal circumstances, however." Belhie motioned for Grothum to approach, then continued, "This feather was given by one of the bee birds to you. It is an honor, and not one bestowed on anyone outside of the forest of Viana... until now."

"I don't understand," said Jaxson, reaching his hand toward the feather.

"We do not fully comprehend what this means either," replied Grothum. He allowed Jaxson to grasp the feather gently.

A need to make a great journey overcame Jaxson. He knew in his heart it was time to migrate north towards... something. He was thirsty, so very thirsty. A craving for sugar came over him. Slowly, all these urges slid away, and he was once more just Jaxson grasping a tiny feather. He looked at Grothum, then Belhie, with wide eyes. Both elves seemed relieved, and they laughed.

"Quite a rush of emotions, isn't it?" asked Belhie.

"I'm not sure what it was. It was as though I was flying, and then I became thirsty for something sweet. All the while, I had a desire to be moving north," said Jaxson.

"Listen carefully, the bee bird has offered you a feather, and you have accepted. This means you will forever be linked not just to this bee bird, but all of them," said Belhie. His gaze was intense, and Jaxson dropped his eyes. "You must learn to control when you allow the urges and thoughts of the bee bird to enter your mind."

"How is that possible? I was completely overwhelmed by it," said Jaxson.

"The tree snake whose skin I now wear, and the noble one, the eagle, whose feather Grothum has in his hair, are like the bee bird to you. We are linked, and that link is invaluable. If you were an elf, we would guide you on your spiritual journey with the bee bird. Since you are not, we will warn you to guard the feather. When a bee bird is close, the emotions and thoughts of it will be stronger, but you can control how much you it affects you," Belhie told him.

Jaxson wasn't sure why or how this was happening. Even now, he felt the pull to travel north and a thirst for something sweet. "Why did it give me a feather?"

"We may never know," said Grothum. "But I think the primary reason is that you asked."

"And the bee bird sensed something in you. Some sort of kinship," said Belhie.

"Maybe it's because we both desire to go north?" said Jaxson with a shrug of his shoulders.

"It is more than that," responded Belhie. "The bee bird travels north every year only to return later. It goes when its nature pushes it."

Jaxson looked up at the bee birds flitting around the flowery vines. Again, he was almost overcome with their thirst and their desire to move north. He closed his eyes and concentrated on Zero. The strange sensations of the bee birds left him, replaced by the comfortable connection with his dragon. Zero's curiosity about the bee birds was in Jaxson's mind as well as the dragon's impatience to move the trade along. It still wasn't a certainty that his plan was going to work.

"I think I will be able to control it to some degree," said Jaxson. "It's not all that different than when I open up to my dragon."

"That is possible," replied Grothum. "Now, should we discuss what you have to trade for everything else? The feather was freely given, but arrows, clothes, and food have a price."

"We can do that," said Jaxson. "Do you mind if Zero – that's my dragon – joins us?"

CHAPTER 15

Zero walked slowly with his head held high and his wings pushed straight back. He did not look at anyone or anything, but remained the picturesque vision of a dragon. Jaxson was impressed with his friend's stature and bearing. *His plan might work after all,* he thought.

The elves, although they studied Zero scrupulously, did not seem overly impressed. Grothum walked out to greet Zero first. "Welcome, dragon guest. Please, settle by our fire."

Zero looked down at the elf briefly, then passed the fire to stand beside Jaxson. Grothum shrugged and walked back to join the rest of the elves.

Belhie addressed Jaxson. "Your dragon is here, and we have shown you all the requested items in trade. We have provided arrows, clothing, shoes, and even a pack to carry all the food. Now, what do you offer in exchange?"

Here goes nothing... Are you ready, Zero? Jaxson said in his mind to Zero. "Well..."

My name is Zero, Dragon of the Greeti, descendant of the dragon kings of old. I request an audience with the Elven King Rhomius, said Zero.

Jaxson heard him loud and clear, but the elves made no indication they did. His brow furrowed, and he glanced at Zero. The dragon remained stoic, looking straight ahead. All of the elves had stopped chatting or working, the first indication they had heard Zero loud and clear.

Finally, Belhie stepped forward. "You claim to be a Dragon of the Greeti. But I wonder if you even know what that means?" said the elf loudly. When Zero did not acknowledge him, he continued, "Of course, you would attempt to invoke the name of Greeti when you have nothing to trade for the goods we have provided. And you demand to speak to our great Cyren Rhomius? How bold!"

Jaxson edged nearer to Zero. He wanted to be close in the event that a quick departure became necessary. The other elves laughed at Belhie's outburst. Some said that Zero was no Dragon of the Greeti. He was too small and too young. Even Grothum found it amusing.

All of the elves laughed, except one. He was a tall, slender elf who had only recently arrived and had hovered near the edge of the deep forest. Now he walked up to Zero, chin held high and shoulders back. His fine white hair was braided loosely down his back. His presence silenced the elves.

"Zero, claimant of the title Dragon of the Greeti, can you prove you are what you say?" asked the new elf.

For the first time since making his proclamation, Zero moved. He lowered his head level with the newcomer. They locked eyes for a long moment. Once again, Jaxson became nervous. The plan had been simple. Claim Zero was a Dragon of the Greeti, and when he was asked how he could prove it, he was to say Forseti's name. Zero locking eyes with a powerful elf was not the plan.

The new elf lowered his head and closed his eyes. Zero resumed his stoic stance once more, but his eyes remained on the elf.

Finally, the elf spoke. "This dragon's claim is true. I swear it by the tiny gods and my father's throne. Zero is a Dragon of the Greeti, and the first to enter our forest in thousands of years. Let us rejoice."

The other elves stood with open mouths, staring at the new elf. Then almost as one, they gave a triumphant yell. Grothum threw his arms in the air and danced around.

Belhie sank to his knees with tears in his eyes.

Jaxson looked on with utter shock. This was not the reaction he had been expecting.

Forseti warned me this might happen, said Zero, speaking only to Jaxson.

Quietly, Jaxson responded, "Did he? I didn't realize you two had this all planned out."

The elves that dwell in this forest, in the Heart of Viana, have ever been allies to the Dragons of the Greeti, said Zero. *I have just told the tall elf the answer to a question that is thousands of years old. The elves desired to use the portal to return to the other side of Kealqua, but were shut out once the Taufan went up. Forseti is going to allow them to be the first to return to the temple once the Taufan falls.*

The tall elf approached and extended an arm to Jaxson. After a brisk handshake, the elf said, "My name is Calin, Prince of the Heart and heir to its throne. This is truly a special day for us. Anything you need is yours. Zero told me that the two of you will be eager to continue your journey. But know that you are always welcome in the Heart. A Dragon of the Greeti and his rider that was bestowed a feather are always welcome."

CHAPTER 16

The wind blew through Jaxson's hair, forcing it back over his shoulders. He smiled as Zero soared over the rolling plains, with the forest in sight near the horizon. They were backtracking, which would normally bother Jaxson, but after all that had happened the last few days, the sun on his face and a full complement of supplies allowed him to relax. Soon they would see the Taufan of the Bend on their left as they flew into the southern regions of the Kingdom of Esther. One step closer to finding his father.

The encounter with the elves had left Jaxson perplexed. Zero knew more about the Temple of Greeti and the portals than he had let on. When Jaxson asked him about it, Zero said that Forseti had left impressions in his mind the day he had shown him the memories. He knew things now that he had not before. The elves' desire to enter the portal within the temple was one such piece of knowledge, which had circled up to the surface of his mind when its need became obvious. Forseti had sent them to the elves for supplies, understanding that the knowledge within Zero would be of great help.

"What other useful things are you hiding in your head?" asked Jaxson as they flew lazily to the west.

I don't know. At least, I won't know until I do... if you understand, replied Zero.

"Not really. How did you know about the elves wanting to get to the portal? And the elven king's name?"

The horizon tipped up as Zero banked slowly to remain

in the favorable wind. He rarely had to move his wings if the wind held up.

"Did you hear me? How did you—"

I heard you. It is not easy to explain. When we first landed and I urged you forward, that was all on the advice of Forseti. When the elves appeared between the pillars, I knew them, and knew them well. But that was impossible. So, I started thinking about all the things I knew about elves. Their desire to return to their homeland through the portal, and their king's name, was simply in my head. I don't really know how to explain it any better than that.

Zero leveled out and continued to glide. Jaxson hesitated, then said, "Is everything normal other than these extra memories? Are you well?"

Yes, yes. I am fine. Better than fine, actually, said Zero. *I have always wondered where I came from, and now I have an inkling. After we find your father, I intend to find out more. We need to find him.*

"I agree. I'm just not sure where to start. Dreknoxious was supposed to be with us. He would know," said Jaxson.

They fell into a comfortable silence. Though they weren't sure where Jaxson's father was, Dreknoxious had told them he was in the Kingdom of Esther. The duo was flying in the correct direction, and for now, that was good enough.

****

After passing the Taufan at the Bend, they flew for several hours before finding a likely spot to camp in the foothills below the familiar Dragon Spine Mountains. A small stream bubbled on the far side of the glade, but it was blocked from view by thick undergrowth. Tall trees with long, green needles obscured a view of the mountains behind them. Jaxson started a small fire and snacked on some of the elven food from his pack, and Zero left in pursuit of his own meal. Clouds, lit red and orange, filled the horizon as the sun sank slowly. Night birds were starting to call to each other, and crickets sang their songs to usher in the night.

Jaxson leaned his head back against a large rock and lazily watched the sky for Zero's return. His eyelids were heavy, and he tried to stifle a yawn. He lost that battle and stretched his arms wide. When his mouth closed, so did his eyes.

He awoke to the familiar sounds of wind produced by wings and leaves rustling, as a dragon landed behind him. Without rolling over, he asked, "Did you find enough to eat?"

He could hear Zero move along the edge of the clearing, circling to the fire the long way round. Slowly, Jaxson came fully awake. The stars above and the lack of moon meant he had slept longer than he thought. He sat up. He could hear Zero's low snores as he rested on the other side of the fire.

Then what just landed behind us? thought Jaxson.

A twig snapped behind them. Jaxson whirled around, but the starlight didn't offer much of a view. He strained his eyes and ears, but all he could see was the gentle swaying of the trees against the backdrop of stars and the only thing he could hear was the running water in the creek.

"Zero! Wake up," said Jaxson urgently. He didn't shift his attention from the direction in which he had heard the noise. He backed away slowly until he was beside the fire, and he bumped into Zero's side. He tapped on the rough hide. "Wake up! I think something is out there."

Being this close to the fire ruined what little night vision he had. He made his way to Zero's head, and to his surprise, he saw that the dragon's eyes were wide open and looking in the same direction.

"Do you see anything?" whispered Jaxson.

Not anymore. I thought I caught a glimpse of a red tail, but it is gone now, replied Zero.

What is gone now? boomed a voice in Jaxson's head.

The duo whirled around to find a massive, red dragon standing over them. His head was bent down, and its hot breath blew into Jaxson's face. Before they could make a move, the dragon said, *I wouldn't leave so soon. It has taken me days to find you!*

CHAPTER 17

After the initial shock of a giant, red dragon sneaking up on them had worn away, Jaxson found himself relieved to finally have some direction. Tollison had been sent to locate Jaxson and Zero by none other than Dreknoxious. There had been some back and forth concerning how Tollison knew the old man, but Jaxson was satisfied that Tollison's claim was true. Jaxson didn't feel the need to divulge all that he and Zero had seen recently, and Tollison did not ask.

On your way, and even once you arrive, you need to be on guard, said Tollison.

"For what?" asked Jaxson as he shoveled more of the elven food into his mouth. It was late and, after the scare, he found himself to be starving again.

Bounty hunters, of course! Did Dreknoxious tell you nothing of what you are flying towards? responded Tollison with wide eyes.

"The last time we spoke, there were other things to worry about," said Jaxson.

Zero moved away from Jaxson a little, apparently no longer believing Jaxson needed protection. *So, what are we expected to encounter?*

I have no idea! But on your way to Goulage, be on the lookout for bounty hunters. They will travel in small groups of three or four. Most will be armed well and be upon armored mounts. Only occasionally will with they be in the company of a dragon, said Tollison.

"Bounty hunters? Why should they be interested in us?"

Tollison sighed, and the wind from his breath almost tipped Jaxson over. *You really are ignorant of the world. Riding a dragon is a capital offense in Esther. And of foremost concern, Zero is an unregistered dragon. That will draw attention in itself. You would be wise to be more stealthy when you camp at night, for the remainder of your journey.*

"We hear you. Tell us about Goulage," said Jaxson. Zero and Jaxson listened patiently as Tollison talked at length about the small town of Goulage.

In years past, Goulage had been a bustling town on the verge of becoming a major city. Two major trade routes passed through the town, and the townsfolk spent much of the money made from the three mines with the passing traders. However, with the decline in travelers coming from the south out of Crystal Forge and tensions with the people from the west, fewer and fewer traders came through the town. The mines were mostly bare, and the people were too tired to keep digging. Goulage was a shadow of its former glorious state. Still, Tollison said there were some good people left, although many had "lost their way."

"Aren't dragons common in the Kingdom of Esther?" asked Jaxson.

Even though it was dark, Tollison turned and looked in the direction of Esther. *Not as common as we once were. I have not been over the plains of Yallwen, as we dragons call it, in many years. I refuse to wear the mark required by the king now.*

What is the mark? asked Zero.

No matter. Meet Dreknoxious in Goulage near the great fountain on the north side of town," said Tollison. "*He will explain anything he thinks you need to know. As for me, I am set to depart. Good tail winds to you.*

Zero bowed his head, and Jaxson waved.

"It was an honor to meet you!" Jaxson said. "I hope our paths will cross again soon."

Tollison chuckled. *So wonderful to talk to a human other than Dreknoxious. Though I am not sure he is really human. Regardless, you two be careful.*

Tollison left their camp as the sun rose. Jaxson yawned and looked at Zero. Without a word, they both settled down for a nap before starting the trek to Goulage. Jaxson's father would have told him to never go to a strange place tired or hungry.

CHAPTER 18

Jaxson and Zero decided to follow Tollison's advise on a more cautious route for the next few days. They moved back into the mountains that ran almost due west. No fires after dark made their traveling days shorter but safer. They still did not stand watch all night, but did take effort to find sheltered areas to rest. One night they slept in a shallow cave, and the next in a thick stand of evergreen trees near to a ridge. The extra precautions weren't ideal but worth the hassle if they could make it to Goulage unscathed.

Jaxson had to convince Zero it was best for him to go into town alone first, to determine the lay of the land. The dragon found a small cave that overlooked the path from the mountains to the farms on the outskirts of the town. Jaxson figured if he left at daybreak, he would make it into Goulage by midday.

The next morning came quick and bright. As Jaxson made his way down the path, he stayed in constant communication with Zero. They needed to test how far they could be from each other and still communicate. Even when Zero was out of sight, they could hear each other. The farther he went down the path, however, the fainter Zero's voice in his mind became. By the time he had passed through the farms and into the outer edge of the wall-less city, Jaxson could only gauge the dragon's emotions, rather than actual words. He could understand Zero's anxiety and tried to send calming sensations back.

It was difficult for Jaxson to send Zero happy thoughts as he looked at the state of the town. Large ruts lined the roadways. The wooden tiles on the nearby roofs were warped and splintered. Each step he took provided new evidence of slow decay. Weeds littered what had probably once been a spice garden outside one home. Trash filled the alley between two larger buildings. Everything from the buildings to the streets and from the peoples' clothing to the wagons they maneuvered was worn down and neglected. Even his travel-worn clothes were better than the attire of the few residents moping around. They kept an eye on Jaxson without making direct eye contact. Each time he passed a townsperson, the back of his head tingled with their stares.

Worry wormed its way into his head, and Jaxson, out of fear his dragon would overreact, had to send reassuring thoughts back to Zero. As he approached the center of the town, he heard a crowd ahead. He stepped around a corner to enter a large, cobblestoned square. Like everything else in Goulage, it was clear that it had seen better days. Stones were cracked or missing. At the edges of the square were displayed pitiful goods on ragged stalls. But what caught Jaxson's attention fully were the people. Most were on his left-hand side, fewer on his right. The two groups were separated by a single, empty gallows. The wooden frame appeared to have been cobbled together using anything easily obtained, and it seemed to Jaxson that the whole thing might tip over and collapse at any moment. Shouts came from both sides, but the majority drowned out the smaller group.

"Death is justice! Hang him! Death is justice!" the majority chanted.

The smaller group yelled back. "Freedom! Not guilty! Freedom!"

Jaxson concluded that the two groups were one spark away from exploding on each other, and he didn't like the smaller group's chances. *I don't need any part of this,* he thought, and ducked backwards into an alley, still keeping an eye on the crowd behind him. Suddenly, he was flat on his back, struggling against flailing arms and legs on top of him.

"Hey! Wait, slow down," yelled Jaxson as he struggled to rise. The young man that he had plowed into rolled off of him, and was quickly on his feet.

"This way," yelled the man. "Follow me!"

Jaxson was unsure why he did it, but he followed the man into an abandoned warehouse and up the stairs. On the second-floor balcony overlooking the large bottom floor, they stopped, their chests heaving. Jaxson put his hands on his knees and followed the man's gaze to the door through which they had entered. When it became clear that no one had followed them, the man turned and stuck out his hand.

"Sorry about that, pal. Name is Tam."

Jaxson shook Tam's hand. "Jaxson. Who were you running from?"

"I wasn't running from anyone," said Tam with a chuckle, but again his eyes scanned the bottom floor.

"Who are you looking for, then?"

"What? No one. I'm just looking," replied Tam.

Jaxson nodded. He pointed behind Tam to the bottom floor. "Then who is that?"

Tam didn't hesitate. He was running again. Jaxson laughed but followed. When Tam stopped, Jaxson said, "Not running from anyone, huh?"

"Well, I guess I wouldn't mind avoiding the sheriff or anyone from the McNair family, for the time being," said Tam.

"Any particular reason?" asked Jaxson.

"Let's just say the spot of trouble Lil' James McNair is in right now might be my fault."

Jaxson shook his head. "I don't know what you're talking about."

Before Tam could reply, a large, muscular man grabbed him from behind. Jaxson turned to flee, only to see three more men dressed in uniforms similar to the first coming up the stairs. Jaxson turned in a circle, then put his hands in the air.

"You look awful spry for a dead man, Tam," said the big man.

Tam smiled and shrugged his shoulders as best he could while being restrained. "I feel pretty good too, Sheriff."

"Let's get you to the old barracks. No way we're going anywhere near those gallows," said the sheriff. He pointed at the men behind Jaxson. "And bring his friend there. If Tam here is dead, no telling what that fella is up to."

CHAPTER 19

Water dripped constantly onto the stone floor of the long-abandoned barracks. The only fixtures in the windowless room were four cots filled with semi-fresh straw, two sconces with burning torches, and one bucket for relief. The solid wood door had a sliding plane which the sheriff pushed aside to check on them from time to time. Jaxson paced while Tam slept. He had tried to plead his case to the sheriff; to tell him he was new in town and had never met Tam before they crashed into each other in the alley. Although the sheriff had seemed to believe the story, Jaxson was still no closer to getting out of the barracks cell.

Jaxson pressed his ear to the door. After a few moments of silence, he crumpled to the ground. His hands cradled his head, and his foot stamped rapidly. He had no idea how or why he was in this temporary jail, but he knew he had to get out.

"Is it all quiet?" asked Tam, one eye peeking through his long, disheveled hair. "Good, I can quit faking now."

As Tam sat up, Jaxson's mouth dropped open. He shook his head without taking his eyes off of Tam. "Why were you faking sleep?"

"Didn't want to answer any questions."

Jaxson snapped to his feet and took a couple of steps toward the lounging man. "Well, you should have kept faking, because I have a few questions myself."

Tam sighed and rolled smoothly into a sitting position. "Guess I owe you that much, friend. Shoot."

"Why did everyone think you were dead?" asked Jaxson.

Tam chuckled to himself then rose to his feet with exaggerated effort. "You get right to it, don't ya? I guess most everyone around here thinks I'm dead cause that's exactly what I wanted them to think."

"Why?"

"I am not sure I need to answer that one," said Tam with a smile.

"Fair enough. What does that have to do with the family you mentioned? The McNairs?"

"You were paying attention," mumbled Tam. "Let's just say the McNairs and my people have never really seen eye to eye. So, when I died, I made it look like one of them did it."

"But you aren't dead," yelled Jaxson as he turned and paced the small room.

"Being dead would put a damper on my ability to keep on having fun," said Tam. He threw his head back and cackled wildly.

"What in the tiny gods' kingdom is wrong with you?"

This only made Tam laugh harder, doubling over with the strain. Jaxson turned to beat once again on the door. His patience with this whole situation had reached its limit. There was no reason for the sheriff to be holding him. One conversation with both of them would prove there was no way Jaxson would be associated with Tam. He beat on the door again but could hear nothing on the other side.

What is the problem? asked Zero in his head.

Jaxson started. Zero's voice in his head was really weak. Zero must still be a good distance from him. He closed his eyes and thought only of his dragon. *Nothing. Everything is fine.*

Where are you, then? I have sensed you are nervous, persisted Zero.

I'm in jail, but it's nothing to do with me, replied Jaxson. *I expect to be out of here soon.*

Jail? Do I need to come get you? asked Zero. *I can be in town in moments.*

No. At least, not yet. What do you mean, you can be here in moments? You're supposed to be in that little cave.

I am flying above the clouds. No one will see me. And if they do, they will probably think I am a noble one.

A noble one! Ha, said Jaxson. *Just stay out of sight.*

Tam's eyes narrowed and he leaned closer to Jaxson. "What are you muttering about eagles for?"

"What? Oh, didn't realize I was talking out loud," replied Jaxson. He looked down at his shirt and busied his hands with flattening out the many wrinkles of the elven clothes.

"Maybe... But you were talking with something. Talking with your head," said Tam. "Is it eagles? You can talk to birds?"

"You're crazy," said Jaxson, sure he could not trust the young man who had faked his own death for whatever reason.

"I know that look you had," said Tam, standing up. He started pacing. "Personally, I don't like talking with birds. Their minds are so... different. Small animals – now, them I get. Always looking for a meal."

Jaxson stared at Tam for long moments as he worked through what he was saying. "You can talk with animals? You?"

"I can speak with most animals, but rats are the easiest for me," replied Tam.

"No way."

Tam stared at the far wall. It was the first time since he had stopped faking sleep that he had been still. The cell became eerily quiet. Jaxson shuffled his feet, and even that noise seemed muted.

Then a scruffy, long-tailed rat popped out of a tiny crack in the wall. It scurried straight to Tam and hopped on his knee. Tam leaned close and gave the rodent a seed from his pocket. He whispered something to the rat, and it raced back to the crack and disappeared.

"Wow! I don't... I didn't even know people could..." said Jaxson, still staring at the crack in the wall.

"I've just always been able to talk with them. I don't know anyone else that does it. Well, until now," said Tam. The young men locked eyes. Jaxson looked away first, and Tam gave another belly laugh. "Never a dull moment in Goulage!"

CHAPTER 20

The ceiling of the makeshift cell stayed the same no matter how long he stared at it. The water dripped, and Jaxson stared without seeing. Minutes felt like hours, hours like days. Time became insignificant. The only interruption to the doldrums came from Zero, who checked in on several occasions, always insisting it was time to get involved. Jaxson finally had to promise to "scream" at the first sign of trouble, to make him gain altitude. They didn't need anyone seeing a dragon flying over the town.

Tam slept. *Or he is faking again?* thought Jaxson, for at least the tenth time. When the door to their cell banged open, Jaxson nearly hit the roof, but Tam slept on.

Jaxson met the indifferent eyes of the sheriff with a silent plea. He wanted to get out of here. He *needed* to get out of here. He had done nothing wrong, and still he was in the cell. So, when the sheriff spoke, Jaxson clung to every word, eager to please.

"You don't know Tam?" asked the sheriff. When Jaxson shook his head indicating he certainly did not know Tam, the sheriff continued. "So, what are you doing in Goulage?"

"I am just looking for a friend, sir. His name is Dreknoxious, and he is old with a long beard. A really long—"

The sheriff held up his hands, stopping Jaxson short. "No one by that name is in this town. Nor have I ever heard of such a man."

Jaxson's shoulders slumped, and his head hung low. He had hoped that Dreknoxious had been waiting on him, and perhaps had left word with the sheriff about where he could be found. It was a ridiculous thought, a crazy hope, but the time spent staring at the ceiling had put many strange thoughts in Jaxson's head.

"We were traveling together and became separated. But I'm meant to meet him here, I'm sure of it," pleaded Jaxson.

"This place is more dangerous than a drake's nest with fresh hatchlings. I expect you to be moving on, and moving on soon," replied the sheriff, crossing his arms. Jaxson concluded that no amount of reasoning or pleading would affect the man.

"I imagine I will," he replied weakly.

"Stay put for a moment, and I'll get you on your way," said the sheriff. He nudged Tam with his boot. "Come on, boy. There are several people that need to see you still breathing... for the time being."

The sheriff exited the cell with Tam in tow. Immediately, Jaxson heard raised voices. Even though the door was cracked, he couldn't make out exactly what was said. There were multiple new voices, and the conversation quickly became heated. A shrill voice cut over the rest, demanding that "something be done about this nuisance." A loud cackle followed, and Jaxson smiled despite the circumstances. Tam did seem to enjoy the craziness he created.

The voices in the other room dwindled, and then Jaxson heard a door bang closed several times.

The sheriff returned with a scowl. "I'm gonna be straight with you. You need to be very careful getting out of here right now. Like it or not, you were seen with Tam when we brought you over, and that boy has set this whole town against itself."

"I'll be fine, sir. Just let me have my bow and be on my way," replied Jaxson.

"I will, and I'll guarantee your safety to the main road north of town," said the sheriff.

"Thank you—"

The sheriff spoke over him. "If you take Tam with you wherever you're going."

Jaxson cocked his head to one side and looked at the sheriff. He thought for a moment, then asked, "Why would I want to do that?"

"Look, Tam is a good kid, but trouble follows him. Truth be told, he's the start of most of it. But he's my nephew, and if he stays here, he's a dead man."

"That still doesn't concern me," said Jaxson. He didn't need anything that would slow him down or cause a distraction. If he couldn't locate Dreknoxious, he would go to the capital of the Kingdom of Esther. His search had to start somewhere.

"You're right, of course, but I believe Tam ran into you in that alley for a reason. I don't have a clue what that might be. I just don't think that it's something you should abandon."

Jaxson sighed. He had no reason to take on the burden of a troublesome traveling companion, but perhaps Tam could be useful. His talent with animals could help Jaxson figure out how to use the hummingbird feather effectively. And besides, he didn't want to see the jovial Tam get hurt.

"When do we leave?"

****

Sticking to back alleys and cutting through abandoned buildings, the sheriff led them to the outskirts of the town in short order. The road to the north wasn't surrounded by farms; instead, a thick forest choked out the sunlight. Jaxson told Zero they were moving north and to stay out of sight for the time being.

They had been walking for less than an hour when Tam asked, "Why don't you carry a blade?"

Jaxson glanced at the short sword at Tam's hip and replied, "Never needed one. They aren't very good for hunting."

"There are dangers on the road besides animals," replied Tam. He attempted to pull out his sword, but it stuck in the sheath. He pulled harder, and the blade popped free. Tam reeled and fell into the ditch beside the road.

"Looks like that sword is more dangerous to you than anyone else," snickered Jaxson.

Tam brushed himself off and put the sword away. "I still think you should have a sword, or at least a big knife. Where we going, anyway?"

"I'm headed north to the capital—"

"You have people meeting you out here?" asked Tam. He grabbed Jaxson's arm, bringing them to a stop.

Jaxson peered ahead. "No. Why?"

"My furry friends tell me three fellas are hiding in the bushes just ahead," said Tam.

As the words left his mouth, the bounty hunters stepped forward out of the brush with swords drawn.

CHAPTER 21

Jaxson put his hands out and backed away slowly. Tam pulled out his sword again and kept pace with him.

"We need to get out of here," said Tam.

The bounty hunters laughed. All three appeared to be veterans of many fights, with scars visible on their arms and faces. The two on either side of the tall, bald-headed bounty hunter were shorter, with long, greasy hair. One was missing teeth, and the other had an open wound on his arm that was festering. The only things that didn't look beat up and misused were their weapons. The swords were all clean and straight. There was no filigree or embellishment, just quality, serviceable weapons.

The leader said, "Don't go running off just yet."

"What do you want?" asked Jaxson. Tam had stopped backing away and was a step in front of him. The bounty hunters had stopped as well.

"See, we've been in that little hellhole for quite a while," said the bald hunter. "We know everybody and all the little secrets. It's good to see Tam raised from the dead!"

The bounty hunters all laughed again, and Tam's cheeks reddened. Jaxson slowly slid his hand near to his quiver.

"What does that have to do with me?"

"We've been seeing this dragon circling high above town – trying to go unnoticed, I'm sure," said the hunter. "The only thing I know of that keeps a dragon near this many people is either her eggs have been taken, or its rider is there. No one has any eggs… woulda heard about that. And you're the only new fella in town."

The two men on either side started to slowly encircle them.

The leader continued, "So, we're just gonna take you to the regiment over that way. They pay good money for a rider there."

"If I am a rider with a dragon, how are you lot going to deal with it?" asked Jaxson.

"We'll be gone with you before the flying lizard even knows," said the hunter. "Tam, you should get lost. This don't concern you."

Tam adjusted his grip on his sword but made no move to leave.

"Well then, grab them both."

Jaxson fumbled with an arrow but couldn't get it nocked before the long-haired bounty hunter was within sword range. Tam sidestepped in front of him and made an awkward block. His sword hit the dirt road with a puff of dust. Instead of pressing their advantage, the bounty hunters stepped back to laugh at Tam and Jaxson again.

"Boy, you should have run while you still had the chance," the leader said as he stepped forward.

Without waiting for them to remount their attack, Jaxson pulled back on the bow string and loosed his arrow that he had finally seated. A loud *thunk* sounded, followed by the agonizing scream of the leader. The other two bounty hunters wasted no time and charged once more. Before they closed the distance, three large deer crashed into them from the side.

"We need to go, now!" yelled Tam. He pulled Jaxson by the arm into the underbrush, away from the road and the bounty hunters.

"What were those stags doing?" asked Jaxson in between breaths. The boys were moving quickly but Jaxson knew the bounty hunters would be on their trail quickly.

"I told the deer that the bounty hunters were trying to hurt a fawn," said Tam. "They didn't like that."

They stopped to rest and listen for pursuit. Tam had sheathed his sword and stood with both hands on top of his head, breathing hard. Jaxson leaned against a tree and closed his eyes. He let Zero know they were fleeing to the east, and that he thought they had lost the bounty hunters.

Before Zero responded, an arrow struck the tree inches from Jaxson's face.

Zero, we could use some help!

Already on the way.

"We need to find a clearing!" said Jaxson.

"What? No. We need to get into the bush and try to circle back to town," replied Tam.

"Trust me. We need the space."

Tam looked at Jaxson for a moment, then said, "This way. It's a fair piece, so don't dawdle!"

Jaxson stayed on Tam's heels as they pushed through the thick bushes. Brambles and thorns ripped at their clothes, but they kept moving. Jaxson looked over his shoulder for signs of pursuit, and wasn't looking where he was running when a large root tripped him. He sprawled face first just inside an open space in the thick forest littered with old rock. *Ruins of some kind,* thought Jaxson

Tam urged him to the largest rocks at the center of the clearing.

"Well," he said through labored breaths. "Now what?"

"You'll see," Jaxson said simply.

A few minutes passed before he saw movement in the trees near where they had entered the ruins. The leader of the bounty hunters, his shoulder hastily bandaged, emerged from the forest, obviously tracking them. Moments later, the other two appeared on either side.

"Nice try! Now come on out," said the bounty hunter.

Jaxson closed his eyes and stood with his hands raised. Tam pulled at his shirt in a fruitless effort to get him back behind the large rock.

"You caught us," said Jaxson. "I don't want to run anymore."

"I should let Mac put an arrow through your shoulder to even the sc—"

The bounty hunter never finished the threat. Zero landed hard directly on top of him, then spun immediately and slashed with a razor-sharp claw at the bounty hunter holding the bow. The bowman took two staggered steps before collapsing. He did not rise again. The final hunter didn't need any further reason to hit the trees running.

Tam stood up and gaped as Zero walked over.

"Tam, meet my friend."

CHAPTER 22

Jaxson sat laughing at Tam's inability to rationalize Zero's appearance in the glade. Tam watched Zero lounge near the tree line, as far from the bounty hunters' bodies as possible. He started to ask a question for the fifth time, but it sputtered out, again.

"How... Is he *your* dragon?" Tam finally managed.

"Not really mine. More like a really good friend – a brother, really. We grew up together." Jaxson smiled and motioned to Zero. "A really big brother."

"Your *brother*... Is he dangerous?"

"Not to you," replied Jaxson.

Abruptly, Tam bolted to his feet. He paced around for a bit, then muttered something about checking- the bounty hunters. Jaxson had no clue what he was checking them for, but he was glad Tam seemed to have finally snapped out of his daze.

Tam rolled the leader over and searched his vest, then his pants. Jaxson saw him pocket whatever he had found, grab the sword, and move on to the next bounty hunter where he repeated the process. He was quick and thorough. Then he stood and looked around. He walked to where the third bounty hunter had escaped into the woods.

"Where is the third? He should be right here," Tam said, indicating where he was standing.

Jaxson shrugged and then pointed to the trees. "I think he ran that way, screaming in terror. We don't have to worry about him anymore."

Tam ran to the tree line. He threw his hands in the air and kicked at a clump of dirt. "You let him go? YOU LET HIM GO?"

Zero raised his head, and Jaxson held up his hands. "It's fine. He's long gone."

"That's precisely the problem. He'll be back, and he'll have friends with him!" yelled Tam.

"No way he's coming back, not with Zero right there," said Jaxson.

Tam shook his head and muttered to himself. He took a couple steps into the trees, then turned and looked at Zero, then back to Jaxson. "You know, some bounty hunters have dragons too…"

This took Jaxson by surprise. Why would a dragon work with a bounty hunter to track down dragons and their riders? He couldn't fathom it.

"I had no idea," he said doubtfully.

"Really! We need to get out of here. You and your dragon go that way," Tam said, pointing north, "and I'll circle around and go back to the mountains. No way I can keep up with you two."

"Calm down," said Jaxson. "We're not leaving you."

I can carry both of you, but not for very far. Back into the mountains is the closest shelter, said Zero in Jaxson's head.

*That's the wrong way, but I don't have a better plan,"*replied Jaxson.

Tam shook his head when Jaxson suggested they both ride Zero into the mountains. After some convincing talk and Zero nudging him playfully, Tam finally relented. Just before Zero launched them into the air, Tam said, "After we find a place to hide out, I can sneak back into town and grab some things. Maybe even *procure* a couple of horses. The sheriff really should've given us some anyway, so it's his fault."

Jaxson let out a yell, happy to be free of the town, free of the jail cell, and on Zero's back in the sky. Tam said nothing else until well after Zero had landed outside a cave that looked livable, at least.

****

The sun was quickly escaping to the horizon when Jaxson, Zero, and Tam entered their newly-found hideout cave. Just inside and lining both sides stood tall pillars of glowing glass. Jaxson stared at the different colors as they danced up and down the flowing glass. He was reminded of a campfire flickering, jumping, possessing a life all its own.

"What is this?" asked Jaxson as he reached out to touch one of the glass pillars. His hand recoiled quickly, then he laughed softly. "It's cool. I expected it to be burning hot... warm at least."

He could see a distorted picture of Tam through the semi-transparent glass as the young man slowly walked around it. Tam, too, reached out to brush his fingers against a pillar.

"Amazing," he muttered. "Never in my wildest dreams..."

"What? Do you know what they are?" asked Jaxson.

The pillars pulsed and flickered, creating colorful light within the cave, which was larger than Jaxson had assumed. Zero was ahead of Jaxson and Tam, but he turned to listen for Tam's reply.

"They must be dragon glass, but I've only ever seen shards and tiny pieces," said Tam. "Even those are very valuable. These must be worth a king's ransom. A dragon first, and then dragon glass unlike any I've ever imagined. What will I see next?"

"I don't know. But we could stay here, or explore a bit," replied Jaxson.

With the dragon glass lighting the way, there was no need for a torch. Jaxson started moving deeper in the cave.

C. H. SMITH

Tam sighed, but followed.

CHAPTER 23

The cave widened as they moved slowly deeper into the mountain. The pillars of dragon glass became taller but more spread out, though their burning light still more than sufficed for Jaxson to see where he was going. Zero led the way, keeping a steady pace.

Ask Tam what he knows about dragon glass, said Zero.

"You seem to know a bit about the pillars. Can you tell us?"

Tam shrugged. "I know the same as everyone else, I suppose. Let's see... Dragon glass glows for a long time – lifetimes, even. And, of course, it's very valuable. I can't even imagine how much all this is worth. I guess several castles, maybe even a whole kingdom. More. I really don't know."

Jaxson stopped and stared at Tam. "That much, really?"

Tam nodded and gestured at the nearby pillars. "I can't even figure it, really, it's that much. Some people say sorcerers and witches seek it for their spells and such. I've never encountered one looking for dragon glass, but that's what people say. And..."

"Go on," Jaxson encouraged him.

"Most people, myself included, believe that it's made by dragons, which is why it is called dragon glass," said Tam. He looked at his feet and turned away from Jaxson slightly.

You should tell him, Zero said to Jaxson.

Jaxson made eye contact with his dragon, then gave a slight nod in agreement. "My dad told me about dragon glass once, years ago. He said he had held a piece the size of a melon while trading in the Jasmine Sea. He said as amazing as the green, glowing glass was to see, more amazing still was the fact he could *feel* the dragon that had created it. Feel it within him… I wish I'd asked him what he meant."

Tam gave a low whistle. "Well, I don't kn—"

Zero stopped suddenly and lowered his head, peering into the darkness ahead. *Something is not right.*

Jaxson nocked an arrow and inched forward.

In front of Zero, several pillars had been toppled, and there were shards and chunks of dragon glass littered about. Glass crunched under Zero's massive claws, and Jaxson slipped more than once. There was a bend in the cave ahead, and Jaxson motioned for Tam to stay quiet. Zero extended his neck as far as possible to peer around the corner. Before he could report what he had seen, Tam tumbled to the ground and let out a yell of pain.

"What's happened?" asked Jaxson as he helped Tam to his feet. Zero didn't turn back to watch the commotion, focused instead on what lay ahead.

"Slipped on the glass," said Tam as he brushed himself off. A large blood stain grew rapidly on the sleeve of his shirt.

"How bad is it?" asked Jaxson.

Tam rolled up his sleeve to reveal a long, deep gash running from the back of his wrist clear to the elbow. Blood poured out even as Tam attempted to squeeze the wound closed. Jaxson called Zero over and positioned himself on Tam's opposite side. Before Tam could even ask what they were doing, Jaxson grabbed his wrist gently but firmly. He closed his eyes and focused on the wound. The warm blood oozed out of the cleanly cut skin and lacerated muscle beneath. His breathing slowed and then a tickling sensation began at the back of his mind. He focused on that and sent it through Tam to Zero. Moments later, the sensation returned through Tam's arm, back to him.

Tam watched in awe as the laceration healed rapidly until it was just a thin, aggravated line. The puffy redness around the wound slowly receded until a ghostly scar was all that remained.

Jaxson hung his head and drew ragged breaths.

"Wow. That is amazing," said Tam.

Jaxson struggled to his feet. "It'll be tender for a few days, but other than that, the wound is healed."

"Thank you. Even though I'm not real sure what just happened... thank you."

You need to rest, said Zero.

*Not here. Do you think it's safe ahead?"*Jaxson replied, speaking only to Zero. The dragon nodded his large, green head, so Jaxson said aloud, "Let's get around this bend. I need to find somewhere to rest."

****

As soon as they cleared the corner, the smell hit Jaxson. His head spun, and his stomach threatened to spill its contents onto the cave floor. The odor reminded him of the time his dad had brought home two large turtle eggs in a sealed case. The case had been designed to protect the eggs in transit, and his father was delivering them from a rich merchant to a client. When he had opened the case to show Jaxson the rare eggs, the putrid, rotting stench had struck him in the face. The eggs had been broken for quite some time without his dad's knowledge.

This smell was similar, but far stronger. Tam lost the battle with his stomach and retched loudly. Zero, the only one seemingly unaffected, kept moving forward.

Jaxson, stay back there. You don't need to see this.

See what? said Jaxson, stumbling towards Zero.

He instantly regretted his choice. In a nest of smooth rocks and rounded dragon glass sat two large, broken dragon eggs. Both must have been very close to hatching, because the decomposing remains of the two tiny dragons were hanging out of the shells.

Jaxson turned and barreled back along the cave. He passed the broken pillars and through the beautiful glow without seeing either. He didn't stop until he had passed through the opening and stood under the stars. A light breeze of fresh air hit his face, and he felt better. Then his mind went back to the broken shells and tiny dragon bodies, and he, too, lost the battle with his stomach.

I told you not to look, said Zero as he and Tam exited the cave.

I didn't think... What happened to them?

Nothing natural. I wonder where their mother is right now.

I don't know. But I'm sure we don't want to be here if she comes back to find her eggs broken," said Jaxson.

"Are you talking about the mother dragon?" asked Tam. "She has to be long gone. Those eggs have been busted for quite some time."

"You're probably right," said Jaxson. "And besides, I'm in no condition to try traversing these mountains at night. Zero probably shouldn't try to carry both of us either."

"We'll camp right here, then," said Tam. He started to set up a meager camp.

Jaxson just spread out a blanket and fell down on it. The last thing he remembered was Zero taking off to "scout the area," and Tam attempting to spark a tiny bundle of twigs, before darkness overwhelmed him.

CHAPTER 24

Jaxson was last to wake. Tam tended a small pot over an even smaller fire. Zero stood near the edge of the ridge, looking out over the foothills toward Goulage. Jaxson's head still hurt, though the intense pounding of the day before had lessened to a dull ache.

He sat up, and regretted it instantly. After a couple of deep breaths and with immense effort, he made it to his feet. Zero turned to look at him, then resumed his watch. Jaxson walked gingerly over to the fire and sat slowly on the ground. Tam smiled and offered him a waterskin. The water was warm but satisfying. He accepted a bowl filled with a runny stew. Each bite of the stew and sip of the water made Jaxson feel a little more like himself. His head cleared enough to replay yesterday's events.

"Let me get this straight... Yesterday we were in jail, released, attacked by bounty hunters, fled to find a fortune of dragon glass, and finally discovered busted dragon eggs?" asked Jaxson.

Tam kept eating his stew. He nodded. "'Bout sums it up."

"What a day," said Jaxson.

Tam placed his bowl to one side, and looked Jaxson in the eye. "I don't know what to think. I'd never met a dragon before yesterday, and then all this glass..."

He pulled out a handful of the dragon glass shards and chunks. Even in the sunlight, their fiery glow of green, blue, orange, and red was visible. Both young men stared at the glass.

"Can you ask your dragon why they make it?" asked Tam.

Jaxson looked at Zero and tilted his head. "He says he doesn't know, but he had a brief connection with the dragons that made the pillars inside which doesn't seem possible. Some were very old and some newer."

A soft, shuffling sound came from the cave. Jaxson scrambled over to his bedroll to find his bow. Zero flared his wings and moved closer to the mouth of the cave as Tam pulled his short sword.

The group waited quietly, then the sound came again. Jaxson nocked an arrow and drew back the string. He could see movement deeper in the cave.

"Ho there! Don't shoot!" came a familiar voice from farther within the cave. A long, grey beard attached to a frail, old man came shuffling out of the cave. His gnarled staff clicked on the stone and his feet made soft scraping sounds with each step. "I said don't shoot. I am of no threat to you, Jaxson Alpine."

"Dreknoxious? What are you doing here, old man?" said Jaxson with a laugh as he put his arrow back in its quiver.

"Looking for you, of course," replied Dreknoxious.

Jaxson grinned from ear to ear, and even Zero seemed relieved that it was the old man and not something more sinister emerging from the cave. Tam, on the other hand, did not sheath his sword immediately. Instead, he circled behind Jaxson to put as much space between himself and the newcomer as possible.

"Tiny gods! You found me," said Jaxson. "Though I have no idea how."

"The how is quite simple," said Dreknoxious. "We were set to meet in town, and when you did not show, I began searching. I was fortuitous enough to see Zero descending into the mountains late yesterday evening. It has taken me quite some time to locate exactly where, but here you are at last."

Jaxson thought he could detect a smile through the long beard and returned it eagerly.

"Here we are, for sure," he replied. He studied the old man who had visited his father so often in their secluded mountain home. He looked the same as always: old but vibrant wearing his flowing robe with his wooden staff, the same. Then Jaxson frowned. "Dreknoxious, how did you get in the cave without us seeing you?"

"My boy, there is more than one way into the caves of the Dragon Spine. In fact, most are connected," said Dreknoxious. "Now, is there any of that delicious-smelling stew left? I'm starving."

CHAPTER 25

After Dreknoxious had polished off the remaining stew and chewed on a hard piece of bread produced from inside his flowing robes, proper introductions were made. He asked many questions about where Jaxson had been and what had kept him from their rendezvous for so long. Jaxson avoided talking about entering the Taufan at the Bend, or their meeting with the ancient dragon there. He wasn't sure he was ready to reveal those things to Dreknoxious, and definitely not to Tam, who was almost a stranger. Once he had answered all the old man's questions, he had a few of his own.

"You left us abruptly back on the other side of the Dragon Spine Mountains. Did you ever make it back to the group? I was chased off by a whole mess of steam drakes, so I'm not sure what happened."

Dreknoxious's shoulders sagged, and he let out a long sigh. "Bad business. It did not end well, but I am glad you are safe. I was worried."

"And how do you know a dragon?" Jaxson asked, aware that he was peppering the old man with questions. "Tollison is the one that set us on the path to Goulage."

A hearty laugh rose from the old man, and he said, "I have known Ol' Tolly since he was fresh from the shell. There is no one in all of Kealqua I trust more than that overgrown lizard."

I can't decide if I want to call him Ol' Tolly or an overgrown lizard the next time we see him, said Zero to Jaxson.

Jaxson chuckled. "I don't think I'd call him an overgrown lizard. He doesn't seem like a dragon I would want to offend."

"Perhaps not, but I am too old to worry about such things. I have plenty of other things to keep my mind spinning," said Dreknoxious.

"Like what?" asked Jaxson.

Tam had settled down and watched the two old friends banter, uncomfortable and out of place. He started to rise, but Jaxson put a hand on his shoulder.

"If you're sticking with me for a bit, you might as well hear what he has to say. I think it's going to be about where we're headed next."

"Right you are," said the old man. "I have begun to fear for Alan, your father. It is not like him to be out of contact with me for this long, but especially not with you. The good news is that I have confirmed his last known whereabouts to be the capital of the Kingdom of Esther."

Jaxson sighed. The capital, bustling with the chaos of a large city, was nothing like he had ever experienced, having spent most of his life in the mountains and trading in small villages nearby. He worried that he wouldn't not be able to locate his dad in such a mass of humanity.

"At least we know where we're going," he concluded.

"Yes. You have a destination, but I must warn you. Things are not at all good in Esther, and even worse in the capital," stated Dreknoxious. "The Demon Lizard Death Cult is growing rapidly and is no longer hiding in the shadows. I fear their leaders have the ear of the King, and they are probably why all the bounty hunters are targeting dragons and their riders."

"But some of the bounty hunters ride dragons," said Tam quietly.

"They do, and I don't claim to know how they have convinced the dragons to join their cause. Even the DLDC has dragons, and its purpose is to eliminate dragons from the world of men," said Dreknoxious. "But that is not your only concern. Getting to the capital will itself be a challenge. Goblins are no longer keeping themselves to the mountains. Reports have indicated they have roamed as far as the Triplets to the north. And, of course, you have to evade the bounty hunters, bandits, and even the King's men if you wish to arrive at the capital intact."

Zero lifted his head and peered down the mountainside. Jaxson asked him what was amiss.

Zero told him it was nothing. *Ask him if he knows what befell the dragon eggs inside the cave.*

"Zero wants to know if you have any idea what happened to the eggs in there," Jaxson said.

"The DLDC and their bounty hunters – that is my first thought," replied Dreknoxious. "Where the mother dragon is, I have no idea. I am going to seal the cave before I leave so whoever committed this foul deed cannot profit from the dragon glass."

"Seal it? How?" asked Jaxson.

"Block the entrance with stones or something. Never you mind that, boy. You should be thinking about how you are going to get to the capital," replied Dreknoxious.

"Which way do you think we should go?"

"I have given some thought to the route you should take. Despite goblin activity near the Triplets, I think you should head to those isolated peaks and then descend to the capital from the west. Zero is less likely to attract attention out there, and perhaps you can come up with a way for him to enter the capital with you," said Dreknoxious. "I assume you have a healthy education in the geography of the region? Yes, I knew your father would insist upon it."

"And once we're there…"

"I will meet you in the gardens of the palace. Check there

each morning as the sun rises," said Dreknoxious. Before Jaxson could protest, he held up his hands and continued, "I know I am always leaving, but there is much that requires my attention. My business, which is not your concern I might add, is vibrant and ever changing. If I am as late to arrive to the capital as you were to Goulage, meet with my friend at the castle."

"Who is this friend, and how will I make contact?" asked Jaxson.

"The gardens surrounding the castle are a good place to start. Ask any of the gardeners where the yellow moon flowers are located. My contact will find you soon after."

Once again, Zero raised his head to peer down the mountainside. A tree branch snapped, and Dreknoxious pushed Jaxson toward the cave.

"Everyone behind me!" the old man screamed.

"What is it?" asked a nervous Jaxson.

"Could be goblins or a petridrake. Or it could be the bounty hunters have tracked you all the way here."

A large stag bounded up the mountain toward the group. It was lathered, and one of its antlers had been torn away. Three wolves broke from the trees in hot pursuit.

Tam rushed to the edge of their camp and closed his eyes. All three wolves stopped and looked at him. He pointed behind him and then back to the trees. The wolves turned and escaped into the forest, leaving their meal to bound away without further harm.

Tam turned and saw that Dreknoxious's mouth was open. "The wolves think there are four full grown dragons up here."

"You are a Ottewn? These are strange times indeed. A human that speaks with animals..." Dreknoxious's words trailed away and he began pacing up and down. Finally, he said, "Jaxson, that is all you need to know. Go find Alan – I fear he may need our help. Tam, I think you would do well to accompany him. I have so many questions for you, but that will have to wait. I must be on my way. Much to do."

Without waiting another moment, Dreknoxious turned and walked into the cave. As he passed, Jaxson thought he could hear him muttering.

Then Dreknoxious shouted, "Step back, boys!"

Jaxson and Tam moved to the edge of the camp, along with Zero, as a large stone fell down the mountainside, coming to rest directly in front of the cave mouth. After the dust had settled, Jaxson could see no way into the cave at all.

CHAPTER 26

The wind carried a chill even this high up Mount Fornessor, the largest in a group of three peaks known as the Triplets. The other two were Fillen and Mijon, both smaller and more rugged than their older counterpart. It was said by the people of the Kingdom of Esther that Fornessor was home to the very first dragon. As the two smaller peaks rose from the land, Fornessor had paid the price. A large crack rose up each side of the older mountain, coinciding with the climb of the smaller peaks. It was the smoothest of the three aside from the cracks and had the most trees. Several small springs flowed down its sides connecting at the base to form a creek that fed into the larger Rillorium River to the east.

Fish and game were plentiful, and the last of the blackberries clung to their vines in defiance of the upcoming winter. The mountain also provided excellent views of the surrounding landscape. The Laguza Sea, which was not really a sea but rather a large lake, was visible to the north. To the west, the lands of the Dahazak stretched well beyond the horizon. Finally, to the east, only an hour's ride by horse and less than half that by dragon, stood the Folja, capital to the Kingdom of Esther. Jaxson stood beside Zero, gazing towards the capital, thinking about all it had taken to get here.

Weeks earlier, Jaxson and Tam had been riding their horses that Tam had procured, heading north along an ill-maintained road. Zero had warned of something unusual ahead, so they slowed. Jaxson nocked an arrow, and Tam pulled out his short sword. What they found though, was carnage. The exact number of bodies was hard to quantify with bits and limbs strewn about. Fifteen to twenty of the King's men and bounty hunters, littered the road and a small clearing beyond a ditch – all slain. As Jaxson and Tam moved through the field of death, Jaxson spotted the large body of an icy blue dragon, just past the clearing. It was obvious that a great struggle had occurred, but Jaxson couldn't see any bodies of the opposing force. Either they had carried their dead away, or they had come through the battle unscathed.

The young men soon discovered that nothing useful had been left behind. All the bodies had been pillaged. Jaxson studied the dragon's body as Zero landed behind him.

What do you think happened? he asked Zero.

A battle, but against what foe, I cannot say. And what killed the dragon?

I have no idea. Let's go find out, Jaxson responded. Then he said out loud, "Tam, you want to have a look?"

On the armor of the harness attached to the dragon's lifeless body they found an engraved sigil. It was the same as the brand seared into the captured dragons they had seen – and it was Zero's ticket into the city.

From their current camp on Mount Fornessor, it was only an hour's ride by horse and less than half of that upon Zero. Though Folja had seemed so foreign and intimidating on the start of their journey from Goulage, days after finding the dragon's sigil they had encountered an inviting group of traveling traders who had eased some of Jaxson's fears.

Jaxson had seen them first, just off the road before dusk, their wagons circled around a roaring fire. He glanced at Tam, and both angled their horses to the pleasant smell wafting their way. After brief conversation with a foul-smelling guard, Jaxson and Tam were escorted to the fire circle and introduced to a larger-than-life man named Bruton who wore lavish clothing, gold chains, and rings, and who talked loud and laughed louder. It was from him that after several days the duo gained useful information about

Folja. But that was after they had made a trade or two.

CHAPTER 27

"First and foremost," said Bruton with a flourish of his hands, "and before we go any further, our trade is to, well, trade. So, if you have something you wish to offer, we can start negotiations."

Jaxson took stock of what they had in their possession. There was nothing they could spare, unfortunately. He reached out to Zero to see if he had any ideas, and Zero reminded Jaxson of the time his dad had dealt with a similar band of traveling traders.

That might work. Thanks, Zero. Now find someplace to get some rest, Jaxson told Zero, who was circling high above.

"Before I show what I have to offer, I will tell you what I desire," said Jaxson.

Bruton roared with laughter, and all the others in the caravan joined in. Even Jaxson smiled as he waited for a reply. Tam, quiet and watchful, smiled but did not laugh. Bruton looked at Jaxson with a wry grin and said, "That is not how we usually begin, son. But go on now... Tell us what you desire."

"I desire to help keep your Forever Pot plentiful," Jaxson said as he revealed a freshly taken pheasant that had been intended for their supper that night.

"And what do you seek in return?" asked Bruton.

"A bowl to fill our bellies and conversation that leads to friendship," replied Jaxson. His father had said those exact words years ago.

Again, Bruton's laughter rumbled. "There is more to you

than there seemed at first glance. Sure, you can help fill the Forever Pot and sup with us around a warm fire tonight!"

The young man stirring the stew that produced the mouthwatering aroma took the pheasant with a slight bow. Bruton guided them around the fire and introduced them as "friends of the dust." After meeting everyone, Jaxson and Tam sat on a log near the fire and listened as the traders bantered with each other before the meal was served. The stew was hot and satisfying, and the bread was white and only slightly stale around the edges. Jaxson laid his head back against the log and looked up at the few stars just appearing in the twilight.

"How does a young man like yourself know how to greet folk such as us?" asked Bruton.

"My dad and I came across a caravan once, years ago," replied Jaxson. "We were just outside of goblin territory, and the traders were very wary. I was amazed at their change in attitude after dad offered them some carrots for the Forever Pot."

"Wonder where he learned it?" asked Bruton.

Jaxson shrugged his shoulders, and the camp became quiet again. The horses, picketed behind the wagons, rustled the grass, and the fire popped sporadically. Even those sounds were subdued by a full belly and a sense of safety that Jaxson had not realized he had missed until that moment.

"You said first we needed to trade. What comes next?" asked Tam from the other side of Jaxson.

"Straight to the point, huh?" said Bruton with a chuckle.

"I don't see the need to tarry when we have places to be," responded Tam.

"Fair enough. Typically, our business would conclude after trading, but young Jaxson here has proved to be a friend of the dust. You can stay with us on the road as long as you would like, provided you pull your own weight. Or you can leave any time you desire."

"We didn't see your wagons all morning, so you must be headed north as we are," said Jaxson. When Bruton nodded, he continued, "I don't see why we shouldn't join you for a time."

"It's settled, then. We will break camp before the rising of the sun and we won't stop until the evening site has been found," said Bruton. "Shake the dust from your clothes and rest well. You are with friends."

****

Over the next few days Jaxson watched the seven-wagon caravan with growing wonder. It was a small group of people: Bruton, his wife Sherrin, and their two adult sons, one of whom was married with a small child. There was also a hired hand and his wife, along with three guards. Each morning before the sun rose, the wagons were packed, the horses hitched, and the camp cleared. Each evening before the last wagon came to a stop, the first was already setting up that night's campsite.

The first wagon contained daily supplies such as pots, pans, dry and preserved foods, and water, among other things. The second was strictly for the horses, filled with feed, oats, extra tack, and harnesses. The next wagon contained cots, bedrolls, extra clothing, and family needs. Jaxson never saw anyone enter or even open the next three wagons, and he assumed the goods intended for trade were stored in them. The final wagon was home to the guards and was in the worse condition by far. When Jaxson asked Bruton about its rough appearance, the large man grunted and shrugged. He made a comment about no one in his family neglecting a wagon like that.

Days later, several hours after sunrise, the caravan came to a fork in the road. Bruton and his family were heading east, so Jaxson and Tam departed their company, though not before some brisk trading.

"We've been together for days! You have nothing of value to trade besides your friendship, and that will not be worth much in goods," said Bruton with a laugh.

Early on just after coming down from the mountains, Jaxson had discussed with Tam that they may need to trade a small piece of the dragon glass Tam had packed away. The air was turning cold, not just due to their trek north but also the coming of winter. Their horses could also use some oats instead of the tough grasses found alongside the road.

"How about we tell you what we are seeking, and if you have any of it, we'll make an offer," said Jaxson.

Bruton opened his hands, palms up, and swept them wide, indicating he was open to trade.

Jaxson nodded. "We have quite the list."

"We are in need of winter coats, traveling food, oats for the horses, and feathers for arrows," said Tam.

Bruton's belly bounced as he chuckled. "And what do you offer in trade?"

"Before we show ours, do you have what we seek?" asked Tam.

"We could accommodate the request easily. But it would tally a gold mark, or at least fourteen silver pieces," replied Bruton with a frown. "Sorry, lads."

"Is that all?" asked Jaxson. "In that case, we also seek information, which can be much more expensive."

Bruton raised an eyebrow. "Indeed. Certain information can be very expensive, but the wagons need to push on. What do you have to trade?"

The large man's eyes bulged when Tam pulled out a hand-sized piece of red glowing dragon glass. His mouth moved but no words passed his lips. Jaxson and Tam smiled.

Tam said, "You think this will do?"

Once Bruton could finally speak, he gestured wildly.

"Open the wagons – we're trading today! Boys, all you asked for will be yours, and the finest we have. And any – and I mean *any* – information I can provide. It will be done."

"We want to know about Folja," said Jaxson. "Everything you can tell us. We need a general layout of the city. Where can we go to locate someone within the city? Where do the King's dragons stay? We have many questions."

"We'll travel no farther today. After you select your goods, I will give you my complete attention..." said Bruton. "Once the glass is in my hand, that is."

CHAPTER 28

Much had happened in the five weeks they had been on the road north. Jaxson had spent more time in the saddle of a horse than ever before. They hunted and fished for food, though Tam seemed to favor foraging for berries and edible fruits more with each passing day. Tam had said his taste for meat had not completely gone, but his willingness to hunt for it was slowly seeping away. For the first time in Jaxson's life, he had whiskers. Tam had a full-grown beard, and teased Jaxson about his facial hair from time to time. After another round of his jovial remarks, Jaxson said, "Looks like you're turning into the animals you talk to, with your furry face!"

Tam laughed for the first time in days, and offered to teach Jaxson that night how to shave. Then, as they sat at their little campfire, Tam opened up about his past, something both had avoided doing during their time together.

He was the eldest son of an old and powerful family in Goulage. At one time, the family's reach had extended from the great river in the east to the capital, and down to Goulage. With the town's decline, his father's interests are now closer to home. Tam was expected to take over the family business one day, but he could never see himself sitting behind a desk looking at figures and messages for the rest of his life. So, he spent as little time learning from his father as possible. Most in the town considered him a slacker and a bit of a prankster, though the latter label seemed warranted. Tam told Jaxson that this trip had proved to him that he was meant to be on the road and in the wild, rather than in a town pushing papers.

In turn, Jaxson revealed more about his own past. He spoke of his father, Alan. How he was a courier of sorts, a seeker of rare items, and a jack of many trades. His father had made powerful friends plying his trade across Kealqua. He also had some strong enemies. Jaxson's mom had died a few years ago from a weak heart. Jaxson didn't elaborate, and Tam didn't push what was a tender subject.

Jaxson had spent most of his time alone with Zero. His dad had travelled extensively and would be gone from their mountain home for weeks or even months at a time. When he came back, he would stay for a while, then go again. Jaxson had no idea where or how his father had acquired Zero's egg. He was just glad that he had. His mom had wanted to be rid of it. She thought a dragon would bring unwanted attention upon them, and that it would eat them out of house and home. She saw no reason to keep a dragon around – until Zero hatched. There had been an instant connection between Jaxson and Zero that his mother couldn't deny. Jaxson didn't talk about his most recent adventures that had spurred him onto his current path, but he did elaborate briefly about Dreknoxious.

The old man was a friend of his father's and had stopped in on them many times over the years. Jaxson always assumed he was a seeker and trader of rare items, like his father. However, the more time he spent with Dreknoxious lately, the more he realized that there was something different about him. He knew things no one should have a right to know and could do things that defied logic. He traveled quickly and never tired. He had a limitless knowledge of almost any subject Jaxson had asked him about. Jaxson couldn't pin down exactly what Dreknoxious was, but he was sure the old man was more than he seemed.

****

"What is your plan?" asked Tam for at least the fifth time in the last few hours.

Jaxson and Zero continued to look out over the Kingdom of Esther from their camp on the ridge high up Mount Fornessor. Even with all that Bruton had told them about Folja, there was so much they didn't know. Dreknoxious had told Jaxson that his father may be in the city, but was concerned he may have been in trouble. Should Jaxson start by looking in the prisons? What if he was dead? How would he know?

Too many questions. His shoulders sagged. "I don't know."

"We can't stay up here forever. We came to find your father... let's get to it," said Tam.

He is correct. We cannot help your father from here, said Zero.

"Both of you are right, of course," said Jaxson. "Tomorrow. We will go into the city tomorrow."

"And..." prompted Tam.

"I'll try to locate Dreknoxious's contact in the palace gardens. Perhaps he can tell us where to start," said Jaxson. "And Zero, I want you to stay up here. I'll check out the dragon keep and make sure all we need is the crest."

Zero's large nostrils flared.

"I know you don't like it, but it's easier for me to blend in riding a horse rather than an almost full-grown dragon!"

Tam studied Zero for a moment. When the dragon settled down, he said, "Tomorrow it is, then."

CHAPTER 29

The horses' hooves clomping down the dirt path were the only sounds in the predawn stillness. Jaxson and Tam had left the camp on the mountainside hours earlier, striking south in order to approach the city on the main road and not from the direction of the Triplets. Jaxson strained his eyes but could see very little as the stars were shrouded, and the sun provided only a faint glow on the horizon. He focused instead on listening for anything unusual, but that too proved fruitless, as all he could hear was the steady cadence of the horses.

Unlike most major roads leading to other major cities, the thoroughfare to Folja had no merchants and was not lined with inns. There were no bazaars or open markets. There was nothing to distract travelers from the view of the castle and the older and larger dragon keep behind it. The sun had risen fully by the time the duo had passed the farms and saw the capital of the Kingdom of Esther for the first time.

Jaxson, wide-eyed and mouth open, stared toward the black and blood-red stone of the castle. He saw the sweeping walls, impossibly high and dotted with archer's nests and the occasional tower. Behind the castle, sat the enormous, smooth dragon's keep. The buildings, which did not rival the Temple of Greeti within the Taufan, were not what caught Jaxson's full attention, however. Throngs of people moved in all directions. Lines of people streamed into the palace. Another steady flow of bodies moved out of the castle's gate, walking toward the market. Guards, dozens and dozens, marched along the tops of the walls. Men guiding carts with vegetables, hay, and scraps jockeyed for position along the road leading to the city. There were more people in Jaxson's view now than he had ever seen in his whole life.

"I know the plan was to split up, but..." began Tam. "If you aren't sure?"

Jaxson pulled his eyes away from the masses and looked at Tam. "No. No, I'll be fine."

Tam shook his head. "Then I'm headed to the market. News and rumors flow like water in places like that."

Jaxson didn't respond. Instead, his eyes followed a group of armored soldiers as they marched out of the castle gates and beyond view along the wall.

"Look, come with me until we get a grasp on what we are dealing with in the city," said Tam.

"I guess," replied Jaxson. He raised his chin and straightened his shoulders. "First the market, and then to the gardens to meet Dreknoxious's contact."

"I'll do all the talking," said Tam.

Jaxson rolled his eyes, but was secretly relieved. "Just remember, we're here for my father... His name is Alan Alpine, and he has a long scar on his neck."

****

After the chaotic swirl of bodies, sounds, and smells of the marketplace, Jaxson enjoyed the tranquility of the palace gardens. Lanes and paths wound through a maze of spectacular flowers and budding trees. The rich and vibrant colors were second only to the pleasant, mingled aromas of the flowers, grasses, and fertilizers, which massaged the nose instead of punching it, like the smells of the marketplace.

Jaxson closed his eyes and reached out to Zero. Over the period traveling north to the capital, they had worked on maintaining contact over longer and longer distances. Despite this training, all they could communicate to each other this far apart were feelings. As soon as Jaxson reached out for Zero, impatience and boredom crashed into him. He laughed out loud and sent back safe and positive thoughts.

Tam walked beside him as they ambled along the lanes.

"What did that last merchant tell you?" asked Jaxson.

Tam snuck a peek at Jaxson from the corner of his eye, then laughed. "If your face hadn't been buried in that pot of rice and greens, maybe you'd have heard." He smiled, but Jaxson could see no mirth in his eyes. He had heard something that troubled him, that much was clear. Jaxson was only unsure why Tam didn't share his findings.

He stopped suddenly as a sweet, nourishing sensation washed over him. He turned and was drawn into a circular courtyard surrounded by high walls. Vines, covered in tiny pink and yellow flowers, grew thickly from the ground to the tops of the walls. Smells of spring and honey and fresh grass filled the small space. The air buzzed as hundreds of tiny hummingbirds darted along the vines, getting their fill of nectar.

A giggle escaped Jaxson's lips. Here within the courtyard, he was renewed, strong, ready. He threw his head back and his arms out, and twirled around, soaking in the energy the tiny birds passed to him.

"What did you say?" he said, coming out of his revelry.

Tam shook his head. "I said... Remind me how we are supposed to find this contact of Dreknoxious's?"

"Oh, right. We need to find a gardener and ask where to find the yellow moon flowers," replied Jaxson.

Tam pointed at a small woman tending the vines on the other side of the raised platform in the center of the courtyard. "What about her? Looks like she works here."

"She will do," said Jaxson.

CHAPTER 30

The baggy robes of the gardener tending the vines did little to hide how small she was. Jaxson approached her from behind and cleared his throat. She whirled around quickly, her spade held like a knife to defend herself. Jaxson noticed she appeared older than he had at first thought. She was closer to Tam's twenty years than his sixteen. The dirt smeared on her cheeks only added to the threat presented by the spade.

Jaxson raised his hands and backed away slowly. "Whoa now! Didn't mean to scare you," he said.

The gardener looked down at the spade and blushed. She quickly put it away and said, "Why were you sneaking up on me like that?"

"I wasn't sneaking," said Jaxson. "In fact, I came seeking help."

Her eyes narrowed. "What kind of help?"

"We – myself and my friend over there—" Jaxson indicated Tam, "—are interested in seeing the moon flower. We hear this garden has some?"

"Is this some kind of joke?" said the woman. She looked around expectantly. "Did Rockus put you up to this?"

Jaxson and Tam exchanged confused glances. "No joke," Jaxson said. "We're looking for the moon flower."

Her smile was replaced by an impatient scowl. She pointed to the platform behind them. "The moon flowers are in the raised bed on that platform there. You walked right past them."

Jaxson looked back to the small platform. In a stone bed grew a lush green bush which spilled over the edge. On each side, blossomed the largest white flowers he had ever seen, easily bigger than both of his hands put together. They were snow white, a darker cream color near the center. Even from this distance, Jaxson could see the outline of a star within each flower.

"You got any yellow ones?" asked Tam from behind Jaxson.

"Not many people come to the royal gardens seeking a fairy tale," said the woman. "Why do you?"

Jaxson took a step closer. "An old friend told us to seek them out in this garden."

"Does this friend have a name?" she asked.

Jaxson glanced at Tam, who nodded. "Dreknoxious."

The woman made no indication that she had heard him. She stared at Jaxson without moving. Just before Jaxson was going to repeat the name, she said, "Finally! You must be Jaxson, and that makes you Tam. My name is Aleera."

"Great to meet you!" said Jaxson.

"Yes, well met, but I thought it would be more difficult to find our contact," said Tam.

"I have stayed near the moon flowers since Dreknoxious told me to expect you two," replied Aleera.

Jaxson nodded. "That makes sense. So, where is the old man?"

Aleera sighed. "Dreknoxious passed this way over a week ago. He did not stay long."

It was Jaxson's turn to sigh. He ran his hand through his long hair. "I can never find the man when I need him."

"He expected your arrival weeks ago. He thought he was the one showing up late," said Aleera.

"It took us longer than we would have liked," said Tam. "What's our plan now, Jaxson?"

Before Jaxson could reply, Aleera interjected. "I have no idea when Dreknoxious may return, but he did tell me some about your search. I know you seek your father, Jaxson. I may be able to help you."

"How can you help?" asked Tam.

"Do you think a man like Dreknoxious would trust me if I had no skills of my own?" asked Aleera.

"That doesn't really answer the question," replied Tam. Aleera glared at him, and Tam stared right back.

"Come on. Everybody can help," said Jaxson. "What do we do now?"

Aleera pulled her gaze away from Tam. "I have a few ideas."

"I do as well," said Tam, though he never took his eyes off of Aleera. "I'm going to start by checking the dungeons."

"And I can gain access to the palace. I'll start there," said Aleera.

"Now we're getting somewhere," said Jaxson. "I'm going to look around the dragon keep. I need to learn everything about the place, so I can bring Zero back with me."

"How are you going to get into the dungeons?" asked Aleera.

Tam sneered. "Don't worry about it. I'll get eyes down there."

"I hope you don't find him down there," said Jaxson. "Aleera, my dad's name is Alan Alpine. He's tall and thin, like me. He also has a rough scar on his neck. I don't want to talk too much about why he was here, but I know he doesn't like everything that's going on, especially with the dragons."

Jaxson didn't notice Aleera start at the mention of a scar, but he saw Tam looking in her direction. He seemed to have been watching Aleera closely, as if to gauge her reaction to Jaxson's description. *It doesn't matter. Stay focused,* Jaxson told himself. The sun had crossed the midday zenith, but there was still plenty of time in the day.

"Where do we meet after?" asked Tam.

Jaxson shrugged and looked to Aleera.

"There is an inn near the docks, known as Sea Critters," said Aleera. "Its real name, which is on the sign, is The Turtle, the Seahorse, and the Octopus. It has adequate enough rooms, and sailors from the ships are always in and out. They're loud and haven't bathed in weeks... You two should fit right in."

CHAPTER 31

As he walked out of the gardens and around the castle's outer wall, all the way around to the dragon's keep, Jaxson imagined many ways to get into the keep. Each scheme was more elaborate and ridiculous than the previous one. Even while he was planning his entry, he devoted part of his attention to avoiding large, uncomfortable crowds. He stayed close to the castle wall, as most seemed to give the castle a wide berth. He was deep in thought when he rounded a corner and found the dragon keep looming over him.

The stone keep predated the castle by hundreds of years. It was from another time when dragons and their dragonriders were revered, and in turn, the dragonriders and their dragons kept the kingdom safe. There were no dragonriders now, only people that rode dragons by force or by controlling them somehow. Jaxson often wished he had the magic of the dragonriders of old. They were said to rival even the great wizards of their time.

The large stones were interlocked tightly without mortar. Age had turned them dark black on the lower levels, fading to a lighter gray above. Large, gateless openings encircled each floor, offering safe landing places for dragons, except at the bottommost floor, which was solid stone, with the exception of the service entrances and one conventional gate not large enough for a dragon to squeeze through. Jaxson stared in wonder as a large crimson dragon, riderless, landed on the third level and scampered inside, head low.

Guards wearing the colors of the King of Esther circled the keep and stood watch at the gate. After watching for some time and still no closer to finding a way in, Jaxson decided to take a closer look at the gate. He tiptoed along the rubble alongside a dilapidated building, approaching the gate slowly.

Then he heard sounds of a chase from behind him. He saw the guards first, then a scruffy, small boy of twelve years shot past him. The boy tried to turn toward the keep but slipped on some loose rocks. The guards would be on top of him within moments. Without thinking, Jaxson rushed to the boy and shoved him behind a pile of broken barrels. He waved at the guards and pointed back towards the castle, yelling that the boy had gone that way. The two winded guards turned and jogged in the opposite direction.

Moments later, the brown-haired boy popped up. "Thought my goose was cooked for sure that time."

"Why were they chasing you?" asked Jaxson.

"I thought they had too many apples in their sack," said the boy, revealing two large, red apples from somewhere in his loose shirt. "What made you help me?"

Jaxson thought for a moment. "I saw no risk in it. If I hadn't helped you, they would have caught you, no doubt. But… by helping you, I could find out why two guards were so eagerly pursuing a small boy. If I needed to, I could turn you in myself."

"And are you going to do that?" asked the boy. He slowly started inching behind the barrels again.

"I don't see any reason to get all worked up over a couple of apples. My name is Jaxson. What's yours?"

"My friends call me Mica. Thanks for the help, but I have to be getting to work," said the boy as he brushed off his pants.

"I won't hold you up then," said Jaxson. He backed up and allowed Mica to return to the dusty street.

"Great! I can't be late again. Griz'll whip me and let me

go this time. Mucking out the dwellings isn't much fun, but it puts coin in my purse." Mica started walking toward the dragon keep, and Jaxson fell in step beside him.

"Do you work at the keep?" he asked.

"Of course, I do. Where else are there any dragon dwellings that need tending?"

"I'm not sure what a dwelling is," replied Jaxson.

"I guess they're big stables for the dragons," said Mica. "But everyone knows that. You aren't from here, are you?"

"I am not," said Jaxson. "Think ol' Griz would hire me to help around the dwellings?"

Mica looked Jaxson up and down, then smiled. "Probably. There's always more work than hands to get it done. Come along, and we'll find out."

****

Jaxson followed the boy through a service door of the keep and into a low-ceilinged, crowded room. Boys and young men shuffled around, waiting to receive their assigned dragon dwelling to clear out and service. Everyone grew quiet as a short man hobbled into the room from a doorway at the far side. He walked with an odd gait, and Jaxson noticed he had one wooden leg. Half of the man's face was a melted scar, except around his lips, which were perfect as his teeth when he gave the group a large smile.

"That's Griz," said Mica quietly. "He'll be giving out the orders. Some of us will help bring up food for the dragons. Some will be assigned to the riders' area cleaning, cooking, and stuff. I'm hoping to draw one of the dragon dwellings. Afternoons are easy if the dragons aren't here, and most of the time they aren't."

"What do new guys get to do?" asked Jaxson.

"Mostly cleaning duty. You'll sweep the halls, or something like that."

Griz turned his gnarled head towards Jaxson and Mica. "You new, then?"

Jaxson nodded. "I am—"

"Fine. You don't know better, but keep your mouth shut while assignments are being given," growled Griz.

"No need for all that, Griz," said Mica.

Griz focused on the small boy, and Mica wilted. "*You* should know better, boy! No easy job for you today. You get Blackthorn's Dwell."

A collective gasp came from the boys in the room. Now everyone was looking at Mica with a mix of fear and dread.

"You wouldn't," replied Mica.

"Might teach you some respect," said Griz with an impish smile. "Oh, and the morning crew didn't make it up there. The dwell hasn't been mucked in a couple of days. Should be ripe."

Mica's face turned white, and he appeared to be sick. Jaxson leaned close and whispered, "Are you unwell?"

Griz's attention snapped to Jaxson. "You don't learn too fast, do you? You can join him!"

Before Jaxson could respond, Mica pulled him to a stairway at the back of the room. They were halfway up the stairs before Mica said, "Bad luck, but we should be all right. Maybe Blackthorn won't be in the dwell. We'll muck it good and get out. With two of us, it shouldn't take long."

"Why is everyone scared of Blackthorn?" asked Jaxson.

"He's a nasty, protective dragon. He don't like folks in his dwell, ever. But he's pleasant compared to his rider, Grayton. That is one foul fella," replied Mica.

"That doesn't sound good," said Jaxson.

Mica shook his head and kept climbing. "Nothing for it but to do it. We'll get through it. Just keep our heads down and hurry. Like I said, maybe Blackthorn won't be around."

CHAPTER 32

Jaxson's chest heaved and his boots felt as though they were filled with water as he slogged up the final steps to the top of the dragon keep. Mica, unlike Jaxson, appeared unfazed by the climb. He put his hand on the door handle leading to Blackthorn's Dwell, and his shoulders tensed. When he opened the door slightly, Jaxson didn't have to see inside to know it was empty: Mica's shoulders dropped, and he let out a deep sigh. He turned to Jaxson and giggled. "Come on, let's get to work."

The spacious dwelling was surprisingly clean. Jaxson looked all around the room for something to "muck," but he only saw a large pile of stones along the far wall. Near the back of the dwell, wooden doors were set into the floor, and he saw a small area filled with items such as buckets, mops, and brooms.

"Mica, I thought this place would be messier, the way everyone talked about how disgusting mucking a dwell can be," said Jaxson.

Mica looked around for a moment, his brow furrowed. Then he smiled and said, "You're thinking of horse stables, right?"

"Yeah, I guess," replied Jaxson.

"Dragons aren't as simple or as dumb as horses. They do that type of business outside their dwell."

"So, what are we to do?" asked Jaxson.

"We have quite the list. Follow me, and we'll get started. With the tiny gods on our side, we'll be long gone before

Blackthorn or Grayton come back."

He led Jaxson to the rocks and around the rear. Even before they turned the corner, Jaxson's nose filled with the stench of rotting and charred flesh. Bones, cracked and burnt, littered the floor behind the stone barrier. Although there was very little meat, what was left had clearly been sitting there for days. Worms and bugs crawled all over it. Jaxson turned away quickly.

"Come on, it's not that bad. I've seen worse," said Mica, giving him a pat on the back. He pointed toward the far wall. "Take this broom and start sweeping the stuff that way."

Mica walked over to the trapdoors and jerked on a thick rope attached to the wall. The doors dropped open with a loud bang. Jaxson started shoving the remains of the dragon's meal toward the opening in the floor. Mica grabbed a wheelbarrow filled with a bluish powder and followed behind, dusting the floor liberally. Several smelly, sweaty trips later, the remains were down the hatch, and the floor was covered in blue powder. *Smells better already,* thought Jaxson as he leaned heavily on his broom.

"No rest for the weary," said Mica. He held two mops and a bucket filled with water. "Still quite a bit to get done."

"Can we take a break?" asked Jaxson.

"After we clear this cleanse powder."

After an hour of work, mopping and slogging the bucket back and forth, the floor was clean once more. Jaxson sat on one of the rocks and laid his head back. Mica put away their cleaning supplies and came to join him.

"We might just get finished in time," said Mica.

Jaxson nodded. After a moment, he asked, "Mica, how do dragons get a dwelling?"

Mica had pulled out a hard piece of bread from somewhere in his ratty clothes. He replied, "Don't know. Don't care."

"Do you know if there are any empty ones?"

Mica looked at Jaxson out of the corner of his eye. "A few. Why?"

"No reason."

"Break's over, question boy. Let's sweep out Blackthorn's landing," said Mica.

****

Hours later, drenched in sweat, both boys leaned against the outer wall overlooking the Laguza Sea. A cool breeze danced across Jaxson's tired body and tickled his sweaty neck. The orange sun was almost touching the horizon to the west. He was tired and knew he was going to be sore in the morning.

"All we have to do is get the dragon's meal up here, and we'll be finished," said Mica.

"Are you ready?" asked Jaxson.

"Not just yet… This view almost makes it worth it. You ever been to the mountains on the other side of the Laguza?"

"No. I have been in mountains, just not those," replied Jaxson.

"I want to see the mountains one day. See 'em really up close."

"Mica, does the keep ever get dragon visitors? Dragons that don't live here?"

"Some riders live way off and only come by occasionally, if that's what you mean," said Mica.

"Where do those dragons stay?" asked Jaxson.

"You ask a lot of questions…" Mica sighed. "The other three dwellings on this level are empty. They say it's to have room for guests, but I think no one wants to be near Grayton and Blackthorn."

"Why is everyone so scared of those two?"

"I hope you never have to find out," said Mica. "Come on, let's get the meat up here and then get out."

The boys turned and walked back into the dwell. Halfway to the trapdoor, the room went dark. Jaxson turned and his mouth dropped open. In the opening stood Blackthorn, larger than any dragon Jaxson had ever seen, blocking the fading sunlight.

"That's not good," said Mica.

CHAPTER 33

Mica grabbed Jaxson's shoulder and whispered in his ear, "Stay quiet, and come with me."

Jaxson followed the scruffy boy back to the trapdoor and then beyond it. For the first time, he noticed other doors in the wall, of varying sizes. Mica opened one of the small ones at eye level. Jaxson saw it was filled with taut ropes running up and down.

"Was Grayton with him?" asked Mica as he yanked on several of the ropes.

"I think there was a rider. That would be Grayton, right?"

"Tiny gods help us," said Mica. He tugged several other ropes, some twice and others just once, then back to the first for two more tugs.

"What are you…"

"No time to explain. It's how the people in the kitchen know to send us meals for both a dragon and a rider," said Mica.

His eyes bulged as he turned to look back to the landing. Blackthorn, large and charcoal black, walked into the dwell. He looked around and then dipped down to allow Grayton to slide from his back. Once Grayton was on the ground, Blackthorn turned and laid on the landing, looking out at the sunset. Jaxson was impressed with Grayton's light but ornate armor. A silver breastplate over a supple leather shirt offered some protection but great mobility. He carried a longsword at his belt with a large emerald at the end of the hilt. His weapon and armor were immaculate, but Jaxson thought Grayton himself looked like he needed a bath. He wasn't exactly dirty but greasy.

"Where's my food, boy?" boomed Grayton.

Mica bowed low. "On the way now, sir."

Grayton grunted and walked through a doorway. Beyond, Jaxson saw a small room with a sitting chair and a table with only a bench. Mica followed and poured wine into the only glass. After the bounty hunter was seated at the table with glass in hand, Mica came back out to check for the food. He opened another small door next to the one with the ropes. It was empty. Mica stuck his head inside to look down the shaft. Then he started yanking the ropes again, now with more urgency. After a few moments, the ropes jerked in response. Mica wiped his brow and smiled at Jaxson.

Jaxson moved beside the boy and looked into the second door. The smell of roasted meat wafted up the shaft. He could see a plate laden with meat, potatoes, and bread rising up to meet them. Mica pulled the plate through the door and turned to deliver it to Grayton.

"Oof," said Mica with a start. Grayton stood right behind them with his arms crossed.

The plate tumbled out of Mica's hands and landed on the tall bounty hunter's boots.

A smile flashed across Grayton's face just before his hand slashed out. Mica's head jerked to the side, and he tumbled to the floor, holding his bloodied cheek. Jaxson saw Blackthorn raise his head and his nostrils flare, but then he simply turned back to the sunset.

Grayton pulled back his foot to kick the fallen boy. Jaxson jumped in between them.

"My apologies, sir! Let me clean your boots while Mica gets you a fresh plate," he said. He knelt and started unlacing Grayton's boots before the bounty hunter could object.

"Fine. But be quick about it," said Grayton. He kicked off his dirty boots, then strutted into the sitting room.

Jaxson helped Mica to his feet and wiped the blood away. "The cut isn't bad, but you're going to have a whopping black eye."

"Don't worry about it," said Mica, swiping Jaxson's hand away. "Be quiet and get to work, or it'll be worse."

He returned to pulling on ropes, then cleaned up the spilled food. Jaxson saw Mica eat as much as he threw down the shaft. Footsteps behind Jaxson made him double down on the boot cleaning.

"Never seen you around here before, boy," said Grayton.

"No sir. I'm not from the city," said Jaxson without rising from his work.

Grayton grunted and paced around. "At least you show some respect. You aren't as dumb as this one," he said, pointing at Mica, "or the dragons. They have to be made to show respect."

Jaxson snarled but kept cleaning the boots. Grayton ambled off just as the ropes started jerking again. Mica pulled out a fresh plate of food and delivered it to the bounty hunter, who wasted no time in tearing into the steaming meat. Jaxson finished the boots, and as he placed his hands on the floor to help him stand, there was something squishy under his fingers. Maggots squirmed out of a chunk of putrid meat that they must have missed while cleaning up. Without a thought, Jaxson jammed the smelly meat deep into one of Grayton's boots.

As Mica exited the sitting room, Grayton yelled, "Bring my boots here, boy!"

Jaxson brought the boots to the bounty hunter, bowed, and exited as quickly as possible. As he passed Mica, he whispered, "We need to go, now."

The boys were almost to the stairs when they heard

Grayton scream.

"Run!" yelled Jaxson.

"I'm gonna kill you, boy!" Grayton yelled as the boys fled down the stairs as fast as they could.

CHAPTER 34

Jaxson followed closely as Mica raced down the stairwell, sometimes taking two or three steps at a time. Mica was faster than him, but Jaxson was determined not to get left behind. When Mica came to a sudden stop on a landing just above the bottom floor, Jaxson crashed into him at full speed. Both boys hit the ground hard but were on their feet in seconds. Jaxson started down the stairwell that led to the room where all the boys gathered to get their assignments, but Mica stopped him.

"We can't..." he said, still taking in haggard breaths, "go that way."

"What? Why?" asked Jaxson, bent double with his hands on his knees. "Isn't that the way out of here?"

"It is. But if Grayton hopped on Blackthorn, that's right where he'll be waiting," said Mica.

"You're probably right. Where to, then?"

Mica looked around. "There aren't many routes to choose from, and each has its own risks. I think we should go out by the kitchens. We can cover ourselves in flour or something. But to get there, we have to go right beside the armorer."

"Is that bad?" asked Jaxson.

"It's where the dragons' armor is made, and if rumors are true, where sorcerers imbue it with magic," said Mica. His eyes were wide, and his head was twitching from side to side. Jaxson thought he looked like a startled deer. The slightest noise would make him bolt.

"Is that still the best way to avoid Grayton?" he asked.

Mica nodded.

"That's our plan, then. We can do this. Now, lead the way."

"Well, we can't go down," said Mica. "This way. Follow me."

He ran along a hall with no doors, stopping frequently to listen for trouble. Jaxson stayed close, but not as close as he had on the stairs, his head still thumped from their collision. As they approached an intersection, Mica indicated they should stop.

"I've never been this far, but I'm fairly confident we need to go right," he said.

"Let's do it, then," said Jaxson, starting down the hall to the right.

Mica grabbed his shoulder and pulled him back.

"Not so fast. We need to be careful. The armorer is down that hall. Stay quiet, and if we're seen, run."

Jaxson nodded. It would be a dreadful way to end his quest to find his dad: caught by some magic armor-makers in a place he should never have been. He hoped Tam and Aleera were having better luck than him. Calming his mind, he sent a nervously confident thought to Zero.

Why are you nervous? Zero said in his head.

Why are you so close? Where are you? asked Jaxson.

Don't worry. I am above the thick clouds above the city. No one can see me, replied Zero. *Now, why are you so nervous?*

No time to explain. We, Mica and me – he's a boy I just met – have to sneak past some magic-wielding armor-makers to escape a pissed off bounty hunter in the dragon keep.

Do you need me?

I do. But right now, I need you to stay out of sight and be safe. I'll let you know if things get out of hand.

"Jaxson! Can you hear me?" asked Mica.

"I can. Sorry, I was just thinking," said Jaxson.

"Come on," said Mica as he started down the hall.

The hall was straighter and narrower than their previous path. Doors lined the right-hand side and every twenty steps on the left was a small window. They were halfway along the hall when Jaxson first noticed a tingling running all through his body. It was the familiar sensation he knew from the times he and Zero had used their skill to heal someone. Yet, this time it was foreign in a way that was difficult to describe. It was cold and wrong. Each step he took, the sensation became stronger until he couldn't take it anymore. He had to see what was causing it.

The door was a single solid piece of wood interrupted only by a circular handle. His hand vibrated when he grasped the handle and pulled. From somewhere far behind him, Mica pulled on his shoulder, and he heard him pleading for them to keep moving. When the door finally cracked open, Mica fled.

Jaxson was horrified. Inside the room was a young dragon strapped down with many heavy chains – though, in its pitiful condition, the restraints seemed unnecessary. Robed and hooded figures stood around the dragon, chanting in a language Jaxson did not understand. Two others were holding a sigil – like the one Jaxson and Tam had found in the forest – beneath a wound in the dragon's side. The final robed figure pulled a long dagger, expanding the wound. As the blood of the dragon landed on the sigil, steam rose and a hissing sound filled the room.

Jaxson locked eyes with the dragon and deep anguish and hopelessness washed over him. He tried to tell the dragon he would help, and opened the door wider. Suddenly, the dragon's head snapped up and he looked right at Jaxson.

"RUN!"

And Jaxson ran. He ran from the robed figures. He ran from the plight of the dragon. Most of all, he ran because he was not ready to confront that type of evil; he could barely comprehend it. Using dragon's blood in magic to control other dragons – that was the only way the bounty hunters could control their dragons. Jaxson felt ill as he stumbled into the kitchen. Mica braced him and led him through the doorway into the night air.

"Sea Critters Inn," he mumbled to Mica before passing out.

CHAPTER 35

Dusty cobwebs stretched between the wooden rafters of the low ceiling. Jaxson watched a spider scurry quick as lightning across its web to trap a fly. Nothing in his head was working so fast. His thoughts were jumbled. The last thing he remembered was the overwhelming crush of dread and defeat coming from the chained dragon in the keep. The edges of his vision started darkening again.

"You back with us?" asked Tam.

Jaxson tried to turn his head to see Tam, but settled back on the bed instead. "I guess," he said.

"What happened?"

He forced himself to sit up. After opening and closing his eyes several times, his head cleared. "I was able to get into the keep," he said, looking around the room. "Where's Mica?"

"The boy? He dropped you off and ran," replied Tam. "Haven't seen him since."

Jaxson took tiny sips from the cup Tam offered. The water was cool. The bread had been fresh two days ago, but still Jaxson attempted to nibble at it. His thoughts strayed back to the captured dragon. He could never imagine Zero being held in chains and drained of his blood like that.

ZERO!

Are you nearby? asked Jaxson.

I am still high above you, replied Zero. *Are you well? I have been worried.*

I'm with Tam now. I should be fine, said Jaxson.

Good. I need to rest. I will be back at Mount Fornessor. Stay well.

Jaxson smiled. At least Zero was unharmed and hadn't tried to storm the keep.

"How long have I been asleep?" he asked Tam.

"Through the night and most of today," replied Tam.

Jaxson was amazed that Zero had stayed aloft for that long. With his head cleared and strength returning, he asked, "Did you find anything about my dad?"

Before Tam could answer, a long, furry worm with legs leapt into his lap. It was wiggling and moving rapidly, causing Tam to laugh and shout. "Move off now, Sugar. I'll get you a treat in a minute."

"What in the name of the tiny gods is that thing?" asked Jaxson with a smile on his face.

"This here is a ferret. She's crazy about the sugar cubes horse trainers use on their mounts. Hence her name. She's rambunctious, but sweet and helpful. She even helped check the dungeons for your father."

"And…" Jaxson trailed off.

"Your dad isn't there," said Tam.

"That's great! Have you heard from Aleera?"

"I have. She should be back any minute. I know she didn't find much – but Jaxson, I need to tell you something." Tam put Sugar on the ground with a few sugar cubes to keep her busy. "I saw the leader of the Death Cult. They're the ones controlling the dragons. I overheard him telling some rough-looking guys to bleed the winged beast dry, and then get rid of it."

"That's horrible. And I think I know what he was talking about," said Jaxson.

"Hold on. The man, the leader, he was tall and thin, with —"

There was a soft tap at the door, then it opened slowly.

An old man with a gnarled, wooden staff slowly entered the room with Aleera in tow.

"Dreknoxious!" exclaimed Jaxson. "You're here."

"I found him nosing around the gardens looking for you two," said Aleera with a smile. "So, I brought him straight here."

"We have much to discuss... much, much to discuss – but first, do you have anything to eat?" asked Dreknoxious, eyeing Jaxson's bread and licking his lips.

After consuming anything edible in the room including some of Sugar's horse treats, Dreknoxious settled on the end of Jaxson's bed and looked at the group before him.

"I am so glad to see that you boys are safe. When you did not arrive in Folja before me, I feared the road north had become more dangerous than I had anticipated," he said. His warm smile spread to the others. "And you met Aleera! The little tip about the moonflowers played out, I see. Now, is there any word on Alan?"

Tam looked at Jaxson and started to speak. Jaxson beat him to it. "No, we have been able to ask around with the merchants, check the dungeons, and Aleera checked the palace today. You didn't find anything, did you?"

Aleera shook her head, so Jaxson continued, "Not even a whisper."

Dreknoxious's brow furrowed, and he closed his eyes. When he opened them again, he looked at Jaxson. "I am truly sorry I could not wait for your arrival. There were pressing matters to the west that needed my immediate attention."

Jaxson tilted his head. "What kind of pressing matters?"

"It is a humorous but sad tale for another time, I am afraid. I do need to impress something upon the three of you," Dreknoxious leaned in, looking at each of the three young people in turn. "The problems facing the dragons, the people of Folja, and the Kingdom of Esther are just a glimpse of a bigger issue. I don't have all the answers yet, only bits and pieces, but it's enough to indicate that something drastic is happening right under our noses."

"What do you mean by that?" asked Tam.

"I have said all I am going to say before I hear from you two. Aleera filled me in on all she knew on the way here," said the old man. "Tam, you searched the dungeons? Anything turn up, besides human suffering and depravity?"

Tam looked from Dreknoxious to Jaxson and back. "Nothing out of the ordinary in the dungeons. I did see the leader of the DLDC, and he was talking about torturing dragons or something."

"That is troubling news. Jaxson?"

Jaxson recounted all he saw in the dragon keep, from how Mica had helped him get in, to Blackthorn, to Grayton, to his eventual escape after seeing the chained dragon. Dreknoxious asked many questions about the captured dragon and the room in which it was held. As the old man asked more and more probing questions, Jaxson realized he had seen more than he had realized. Dreknoxious seemed particularly interested in the robed figures.

"Could you see any part of their bodies?"

"I told you I couldn't," replied Jaxson.

"What about the hand holding the blade? Did you see it?"

Jaxson thought back to the dagger ripping down the side of the chained dragon. "No, all I can remember is blood."

"Did their heads seem to be shaped like normal heads?"

"Their heads? They were in full robes! But yes, I guess they were normal," said Jaxson, throwing his hands up. "What does that have to do with anything?"

"This is important. Think. Think only about the robed figures... Did anything seem different about them?" asked Dreknoxious.

Jaxson replayed the whole scene in his head. He attempted to avoid focusing on the dragon. The three standing around him seemed off. Why was that? They had their hands raised, but their arms were too long, and their elbows bent the wrong way.

Jaxson relayed this to Dreknoxious. The old man sighed and sagged heavily onto the bed, bracing himself with one hand.

"Vile sorcerers from the Isles of Creptin. The rumors are true," said Dreknoxious.

"Who are they?" asked Jaxson.

"Beings to avoid," he said with a dismissive wave. "Anything else?"

Jaxson looked at his feet for a few moments then up at Dreknoxious. "Well, I think I have a plan to rescue that dragon, and with you here, it might just work. I'll have to go get Zero, of course. He will need a rider to be allowed into the dwellings even with a sigil."

Dreknoxious, Tam, and Aleera listened to Jaxson's plan. After a spirited debate with input from all three, and alterations to the original plan, they had a course of action. Dreknoxious told them to wait one day and then strike that night. Jaxson agreed, as he needed time to rest and contact Zero. The old man left with a promise to return the next day at sundown.

"But what about the search for your dad?" asked Aleera. "If we do this, we'll have to leave – it doesn't matter if we are successful or not."

"My dad saved Zero as an egg," replied Jaxson. "I know he'd want me to save this dragon too."

CHAPTER 36

The cool air blew through Jaxson's hair as he soared high above Folja. Zero slid effortlessly from wind current to wind current as they waited for the signal that it was time to enter the keep. Zero wore the sigil they had found in the woods in the hope that it would keep anyone who might notice them from becoming suspicious. Neither of them liked how it had been made, but it didn't seem to effect Zero at all.

Jaxson had left the city early that morning to meet Zero near Mount Fornessor and inform him of the plan. By now, Tam and Aleera should be in the keep, and Dreknoxious should be preparing the distraction about which he seemed so giddy. Jaxson chuckled as he recalled how the old man's eyes had lit up when he said, "Don't worry about it. I have a few ways to turn some heads."

What exactly did Dreknoxious say about the sorcerers? asked Zero for the third time.

He didn't say anything, really, replied Jaxson. *Just that they were bad. I think that he suspected they were here. Are you ready for this?*

I am. When the signal is lit, we wait for Dreknoxious's distraction. Then we go in.

That's it. Pretty simple – until we get in there.

We will worry about that when the time comes," said Zero. "Are you sure we should be doing this?

I don't see any other choice.

But what about your father?

Jaxson looked down to the keep and thought of all that

had happened since he and Zero had left their mountain home in search of his missing father. He was still no closer to finding his father than he had been when he started.

It's the right thing to do, he said.

Moments later, Zero said, *There's the signal.*

Jaxson looked down, but all he could see was a tiny orange dot near to the bottom of the dark keep. *I'll have to take your word for it.*

What will Dreknoxious do now? asked Zero.

He said we'd know when we saw it, replied Jaxson.

To the south, over the farmland beyond the city walls, dragon's fire erupted across the sky, illuminating dozens of steam drakes flying toward the city. Jaxson could hear their piercing shrieks even from this distance. The sound reminded him of their perilous escape from the large pack of drakes, which had eventually forced them into the Bend.

Again, the dragon's fire lit the sky. Alarms sounded within the castle and the keep. Soldiers spilled out of the barracks to line the walls. Dragons and their riders took off from the keep to meet the drakes.

This was the distraction, and it was working beautifully. Jaxson had no idea how Dreknoxious had accomplished it, but the keep was emptying and all eyes were looking south.

Zero started his descent as dragon's fire lit the sky once more. Tollison, the huge, red dragon, was chasing the drakes toward the city. Jaxson thought he saw Dreknoxious on his back, waving his staff. Then he heard clearly, although the distance should have been too great, Dreknoxious yell, "To arms! Defend the city!"

Their angle of descent was steep, and when Zero's feet finally struck the landing outside the room in which the chained dragon was being held, Jaxson was relieved. The gate had been opened, and Tam greeted him as he slid off Zero's back.

"No problems?" asked Jaxson.

"None. It was just like Dreknoxious said," replied Tam. "No one on the bottom floor stopped us, and we haven't seen anyone on this floor."

"Where's Aleera?"

"Over there, working on the chain," said Tam. "This dragon's in rough shape. I don't think it can fly even if we get him free."

Aleera jogged over. Her face was pale, and her lips were thin lines. "It's only one chain wrapped around it several times. I've picked the lock, but I need help moving it. It's so heavy."

"You can pick locks?" asked Tam.

Aleera was looking back at the dragon and didn't respond.

"Aleera, are you well?" asked Jaxson.

She shook her head. "Yes. And yes, I can pick locks. We need to hurry."

"I can help you with the chain," said Tam. "Jaxson, you and Zero do your stuff."

Jaxson approached the injured dragon slowly, his hands held out, sending out calm thoughts. Zero walked to the other side.

The dragon knows we are here to help, said Zero.

Let's get to it, then.

Jaxson placed both hands near to the long wound on the dragon's side. Zero placed a wing over the dragon's back. Jaxson extended his mind to Zero. The hair on the back of Jaxson's neck stood as Zero gathered energy and held it. Then his fingertips started to tingle as Zero slowly released the energy, through the other dragon, to Jaxson. Jaxson's arms buzzed with energy, then his whole body, until he was about to burst with the magic contained within him. He concentrated and willed it to flow back to Zero. The wound on the dragon's side closed until only a thin, red line of a scar remained.

The healed dragon lifted its head, then stood slowly. The heavy chain that Tam and Aleera had been struggling with fell away. It unfurled his wings and stretched its neck out. The purple scales along its back shimmered as the dragon shook out the stiffness from being held captive by the restraints.

It turned to Jaxson and then to Zero. Finally, it looked at Aleera as she stepped forward.

"*She* says thank you, and her name is Soaren," said Aleera with a blank face.

Jaxson's eyes widened. "Amazing! I've never met a female dragon and.... you can hear her?"

Aleera simply nodded and placed a hand on Soaren's head. Tears fell down her face, and her body shook. Tam's eyes were wide; he was clearly as shocked as Jaxson.

A voice from behind them brought everyone out of their surprised stupors.

"Jaxson? What are you doing here?" said a tall man wearing the uniform of the DLDC and holding a large ring of keys.

"Dad?!"

CHAPTER 37

Jaxson thought back to the last time he had seen his father. The early spring dew was on the grass as the sun crested over the Dragon Spine Mountains. There was a chill in the air that warned that winter may have one more storm to send their way. They were outside the cabin, and his father was dressed for traveling. It had been a great three months, but like always, his dad had a job that needed doing. Jaxson sat on the big rock beside the cabin, with Zero right behind him, and watched his dad disappear along the path that led west into Crystal Forge.

Now, here he was, right in front of him. Just as Jaxson had agreed the search was less important than the life of the captured dragon, his father had appeared. But he was wearing the uniform of the Demon Lizard Death Cult. Something gnawed at the back of Jaxson's mind.

"Jaxson, you can't be here," said Alan. Then he noticed Zero near the gate. "For all the tiny gods' tears, Zero's here too! Out, now! Even I can't protect you in here."

Tam stepped forward. "It's him. The one I told you about. He's their leader!"

Jaxson looked back and forth between his dad and Tam. His mouth hung open and his eyes lost focus. "What the…"

"It doesn't matter right now," said Alan. "You have to go. All of you."

Aleera didn't have to be told again. Quickly, she was on Soaren's back, and they disappeared out of the gate. Jaxson saw the purple dragon rising and then banking to the east.

Tam stepped in between Jaxson and his father. "Jaxson, get on Zero and get out of here. We have what we came for," he said, pulling out his short sword.

"Listen to your friend," said Alan.

Jaxson started to object, but Tam pushed him toward Zero. The dragon nudged him gently with his head, and Jaxson climbed into the harness just as a score of soldiers broke down the door. Alan's eyes widened as he saw them stream into the room. He shouted, "Rebels! They released the dragon. Take them alive – I'll have questions for them to answer."

Zero didn't give them the chance. He was through the gate and in the air before the soldiers took another step.

Jaxson looked back over his shoulder to see Tam surrounded, his sword still ready. He feared his friend wouldn't be taken without a fight. The next moment, they were too high to see Tam any longer. Jaxson scanned the skies for signs of Aleera and Soaren. Then it struck him that Aleera and Soaren were like Zero and him. He didn't know how it had happened, but it was true. But in the darkness, he couldn't see them anywhere.

Dragon's fire lit the sky to the west. Dreknoxious and Tollison were still causing a ruckus. Jaxson thought he caught a glimpse of a purple dragon headed south, away from the city. He hoped it was Aleera and Soaren escaping, even if it was in the wrong direction.

"Stick to the plan. Circle wide over the Laguza and head back to Mount Fornessor," said Jaxson.

Zero didn't respond right away; he simply flew faster and higher, away from the keep.

Perhaps Aleera is going to circle to the Mount from the south, said Zero.

Maybe. More than likely, she'll go wherever Soaren leads her. It's what I would do in her place, replied Jaxson.

Do you want to talk about your father? asked Zero.

Yes. But not now. We need to get somewhere safe.

They flew farther north than they had ever been, through the night and into the early morning sun. Somewhere over the Laguza Sea, when Jaxson thought they were in the clear, Blackthorn and his rider, Grayton, crashed into them, hard.

CHAPTER 38

Zero tumbled toward the sea below. Jaxson gripped the harness with every bit of strength he possessed, and even that was barely enough. Just before splashing down into the sea, Zero righted himself and flew straight across the surface of the water, gaining altitude with each beat of his wings. As he reached for his bow, Jaxson spotted Blackthorn high above them, keeping pace. He nocked an arrow, and Zero banked hard right. Blackthorn shifted, then dove down towards Zero once again.

This time, however, Jaxson warned Zero, who was able to turn away without taking the full impact of the black dragon's strike. Still, he took a mighty blow just behind his rear legs. Blackthorn was above them again in moments. Each time Zero veered one way or the other, their enemy mirrored him. The islands in the distance were too far away to be of any help. There was no cover over the flat water.

"We have to change this up. We are at his mercy down here," shouted Jaxson.

Take the shot at Grayton this time, said Zero. *Whatever happens, take the shot, and do not miss.*

He angled toward the islands and slowed down, feigning a more severe injury than he actually had.

Blackthorn dove, but stopped short of impact and flew directly above them, just out of bow range. Grayton's head appeared over the black dragon's shoulder, smiled wickedly, and yelled, "I see you boy! Nowhere to run to now."

Just as his laughter reached Jaxson, Blackthorn dove

sharply. Zero waited until the last possible moment, then turned and flew straight up, exposing his vulnerable underbelly but giving Jaxson a clear shot. The arrow was at Jaxson's ear and released before he even realized it.

A scream of pain from Grayton let Jaxson know he was on target but had missed a fatal shot.

Blackthorn abandoned the attack and whirled away. Jaxson let out a whoop as the bounty hunter retreated.

I need to rest, said Zero.

"Head for the islands. I think we bought ourselves some time," said Jaxson.

****

From the top of the ruined tower on the deserted island Jaxson and Zero had a commanding view in all directions. No one would be able to approach without being seen. It gave them time to address Zero's wound and make a new plan.

"What's next?" asked Jaxson as he cleaned the last of the blood from Zero's back.

Perhaps Aleera or Dreknoxious have already arrived at Mount Fornessor. We should go there as the original plan dictated.

"That's one option," said Jaxson. "But we need to find a way to get Tam out. There's no way he could have fought his way through all of those soldiers. He was definitely captured, or worse."

If he was captured, he may have revealed our destination. Mount Fornessor may not be the best place to go.

Zero gestured with his head, indicating for Jaxson to look back in the direction from which they had come. Dragons were flying directly above the water, slowly weaving back and forth. They were searching for Zero and him. Grayton must have told them of Zero's injury.

"How many do you count?"

There are three searching the water and one well above, replied Zero. *It might be Blackthorn, though I cannot be sure at this distance.*

Jaxson sighed. He didn't want to leave, even though that was the safest course of action. It would mean going away from Tam, his only friend. Away from Aleera and Soaren, a pair like him and Zero. Away from the father he had sought for so long. Away from the only connections he had in life, other than Zero. He simply had no idea what came next.

"What do we do now?"

A familiar voice came from behind them. "First, I think you need to tell me exactly what happened."

Both Jaxson and Zero started violently before turning to see Dreknoxious standing near to the edge of the ruins.

"Where did you come from?

CHAPTER 39

"Are you hurt? No? Good. Let's have a look at Zero then, shall we?"

Dreknoxious wasted little time in assessing the wound on Zero's back. Jaxson had cleaned it well, and the old man gave him a nod of approval.

"It's so frustrating that we can heal others but not ourselves," said Jaxson. Dreknoxious raised an eyebrow and Jaxson shrugged. "I do have some secrets, you know."

Dreknoxious snorted. "Not as many as you might think. Now, tell me what happened."

Jaxson launched into the tale of the daring rescue the previous night. He left nothing out. When he recounted the part about Aleera and Soaren, Dreknoxious interrupted, guessing what had happened next. The old man appeared very excited that Aleera had bonded with the dragon, but he didn't seem surprised. Then Jaxson had to tell the part about his dad's betrayal. His eyes burned, and his stomach rolled violently as if a rabbit was hopping around in there.

Dreknoxious allowed Jaxson to release all of his pent-up emotions, then pulled him into a strong embrace as Jaxson sobbed. Suddenly, Jaxson remembered the dragons and bounty hunters that were searching for them. He pushed himself away from Dreknoxious and searched the skies.

"What are you looking for, Jaxson?" asked the old man.

"We saw some dragons searching for us, just before you showed up," replied Jaxson. "I just don't want to be surprised again."

"They are gone."

"How do you know?" asked Jaxson with a frown.

"Because I told the dragons they needed to search elsewhere," replied Dreknoxious. "So, they did."

After some hesitation, Jaxson stammered, "Who are you? Really? I know you were dad's friend, but who are you?"

"Perhaps it is time you know. You are going to be stronger and more important than me soon, anyway," said Dreknoxious. "I am the last remaining Wizard of Greeti, and I have long awaited the day that dragonriders once more rule the skies with might and magic. Finally, the day is near. Who I am is not as important as who you will become... Dragonrider Jaxson."

EPILOGUE

Zero stood beside Jaxson as they looked into the portal within the Temple of Greeti inside the Taufan. The ancient dragon, Forseti, stood near to the end of the long hall, eagerly waiting to see whether the young dragon and his dragonrider would brave the portal in search of the tools needed to reach their potential. He had not been surprised when they had returned days ago. It had been quicker than he anticipated, but there was never any doubt they would return.

Forseti had told them they needed training if they were to become dragon and rider together, for Jaxson to become a dragonrider. He explained there was no one alive that could guide them, but there was a way to gain the necessary training. Through the portal, they could enter the land of their ancestors and seek a book – a book that, if read correctly, would help them prepare for the journey ahead. They did not know it, though Forseti thought Zero had an idea, but their destinies were intertwined not only with each other but with the destiny of the whole of Kealqua.

Zero looked at Forseti before turning back to the portal. As one, Jaxson and his dragon stepped forward into the shimmering void. Then they were gone, and Forseti sighed. It had begun. There was a chance.

"It is done, then?" asked Dreknoxious as he materialized beside Forseti.

It is as you said it would be, replied Forseti. *But is it the way it should be?*

"You know what we face. We need dragonriders," said the old man.

Need them? It is because of them we are in this position to begin with, but you are too young to have experienced that, said Forseti.

"I am old... But you are right. Too young for that," sighed Dreknoxious.

Will he find it?

Dreknoxious thought back to all he knew of Jaxson, Zero, and Alan, Jaxson's father. "I would be surprised if he did not. He has a great ally in Zero – his only ally, really. But people do the most unlikely things at times. Still, the only reason he agreed to go is because he *felt* isolated, alone. He had nothing left here. Nothing but Zero."

You saw to that, said Forseti.

"I did what I thought I must," said Dreknoxious. "Now it is up to Jaxson and Zero to bring back the knowledge we need. I think he will succeed. He has to... Or the world as we know it will cease to exist."

WORTH LESS
THAN ZERO

CHAPTER 1

Hauntingly beautiful lightning streaked out from the black clouds, always staying parallel to the horizon. The clouds, which held life-saving water, never let a drop fall over the sandy dunes in front of him. With his face covered except for a tiny slit for his eyes, Jaxson watched the storm roll to the south with a faint smile on his lips. If he had seen those same clouds a month ago just after he had come through the portal, he might have chased them over the horizon in hopes of conquering his thirst. The desert was a brutally efficient teacher, however. He now knew better than expending that much effort chasing the ghost of water.

He stood on a rocky ridge overlooking the dune sea that stretched out before him. The sun was almost to the horizon, and though a sandstorm dulled its glow, the reddish evening light that did peek through added to the beauty of the dark clouds and lightning over the windswept dunes. He liked the desert just before dusk. It was as if the whole world was holding its breath waiting for the coming night. The heat leached away slowly at first then more quickly. Just as the sun touched the horizon, Jaxson looked to the east.

"There they are again. It has to mean something," he said.

You know what it means. You know what the first step has to be, said Zero in Jaxson's head. *We both have our own tasks ahead. You just don't want to admit it.*

Jaxson turned back to the lights on the tops of the temples in the distance. Every day at sunrise and again at sundown, they lit up with dazzling light. He and his dragon,

Zero, had ventured out to the temples several times knowing they were important to their quest. They were impressive, if not old and neglected, at least from the outside. The three temples stood side by side with the two outside temples dwarfing the middle. On top of the giant structures, a large assortment of dragon glass of varying colors and sizes was arranged to catch the sunlight at dawn and dusk. The normal-sized entrance for the temple on the left was way too small for Zero to follow Jaxson into it. The temple on the right had a circular entrance forty feet up the smoothest side. Zero assured Jaxson he would fit even if it was tight, but he doubted that Jaxson could make it through on his back. They spent two days flying around the much smaller, middle temple but found no visible entrance.

Jaxson shook his head. "All we really know for sure is we don't want to be on the ground near the temples for any extended period of time."

That is certainly true. Those bug creatures are formidable, replied Zero.

"Do you really think it is that simple? You go in one temple, and I go in the other. Then a magic door appears for the final temple that holds the book we need?" Jaxson glanced at Zero.

I do not think any of this is simple, said Zero. *If it was, Forseti would have explained it to us.*

"But he didn't because he didn't know," said Jaxson.

The two friends had been over this a dozen times. Jaxson knew deep down that Zero was correct. He just did not want to split up. After his father's betrayal back in Folja, he was not sure who or what he trusted. His father being the leader of an organization bent on enslaving or killing all of the dragons on Kealqua was a truth he could not grasp. And the ancient dragon that sent them through the portal to find a training book for dragonriders had not mentioned anything about splitting up to go into different temples. His head was tangled with so many confusing thoughts.

We have waited for weeks with no change. We need to do something different if we want to find the resources we seek, said Zero.

Jaxson watched the colors of the three temples. The one on the left was sky blue and brilliant. It dazzled and flickered in the waning sunlight. The light from the temple on the right was yellow as a sunflower. But the real show was on top of the smallest tower. The light started as blue, then changed to yellow and back to blue. It cycled the two colors until the last rays of the sun hit it for the day, then it exploded into vibrant green light shooting out in all directions.

"You are correct, of course," said Jaxson. He sighed deeply. "Let's do it tomorrow, at first light. Hopefully we will be out again before the midday meal."

CHAPTER 2

The night's chill spread across Jaxson's arms as he mounted Zero. They were leaving the small temple the portal was housed to enter the larger temples. They were the only other structures the duo had found in the weeks since coming through the portal. As they flew, Jaxson thought of their one encounter with the bugs that seemed to guard the temples.

It was during their first few days after stepping through the portal. Jaxson and Zero had found water over the dunes to the south in a little growth of scrubby trees amongst the rockiest terrain they had seen. On that day, they ventured farther from the portal temple than they had the previous days. It was almost sundown when they spotted the three temples in the distance. As they approached, Jaxson knew this is where they were supposed to be. Zero circled high above several times, but they saw nothing threatening so they landed in front of the smallest temple.

Sand stretched as far as Jaxson could see behind them. It even piled up along the base of the temple. In the air the middle temple had seemed so small, but from the ground, it was huge and only small in comparison. Jaxson's feet did not sink into the sand the way it did on the dunes as he approached the grand stone structure. He looked at Zero and said, "Beat your wings hard. I don't think the sand is very deep."

The wind caused Jaxson to stumble back a step. The sand stung his hands and face, but it was working. The dark brown flagstone beneath the sand was slowly being revealed. Jaxson moved behind Zero to escape the fury of the wing beats. With each gust of wind, more flagstones in varying colors were unearthed. An elaborate design had been hidden beneath, a winding river with its origins in the mountains within the flagstones. Then the three temples with color exploding from their pinnacles took shape.

"That is amaz—" Jaxson started before something crashed into him.

He slid across the sandy flagstones, turning as he went. He came to rest before a tall slender bug. It had six long legs and two segmented body parts. Its head, several feet above the ground, was long and thin with two antennae at the very top twitching wildly. It reared back on its hind two legs before charging on all six directly at Jaxson. Frantic, he tried to scramble away but could not get to his feet on the sandy ground. Just before the giant bug reached him, he closed his eyes and put his arms over his head. He braced for the attack, but instead, he was met with a loud crunching sound.

He peeked through his arms. Zero stood over the crumpled mess that was the bug creature moments before. "Thanks, Zero. What is that thing?"

I have no idea. Its body is hard though. When I struck it with my tail, it tried to get back up. I pounced on it before it could get upright again, said Zero. The dragon looked side to side. *Did you see where it came from?*

Before Jaxson could reply, four more of the huge bug creatures emerged from the sand and started running toward them. Jaxson did not hesitate. He was lucky to have survived the lone bug; four was way too many. He hopped on Zero's back and they launched into the sky. When Jaxson looked back down at the flagstones, he saw a beautiful mosaic of the temples and surrounding landscape from back when this area had been lush and green. Then the mosaic was covered with hundreds of the bug creatures streaming out of a hole in the desert not far from the temples.

Jaxson chuckled as he remembered that encounter with

the bugs. If it wasn't for Zero, he knew he wouldn't be here today. They had not seen the bugs since then, but they also hadn't stayed on the ground near the temples for any extended period of time either.

The wind blew his hair away from his face as the lights on the tops of the temples were activated by the morning sun. The middle temple started out green with the early morning rays, then changed to the alternating blue and yellow light—a reversal of how they were displayed at sundown. Though they flew high above the temples, the lights were no less brilliant.

"Are you ready for this?" asked Jaxson.

I am ready to try. I see no other option, replied Zero as he started his descent. *I'll drop you off first. Do not delay; enter the temple immediately so the bugs cannot locate you.*

"I'll go in my temple as soon as I see you go in yours," said Jaxson.

Jaxson felt Zero roll his eyes, but the dragon remained silent for the remainder of their descent. As Jaxson's feet sunk into the cool sand in the shadow of the temple, Zero said, *Be safe. We have no idea what is in these temples, but stay on guard. The dragonriders of old possessed great magic, and some of it may have survived to this day.*

Jaxson nodded and watched Zero take off and circle the other large temple. The sunlight spilling over the large buildings caught his scales, and a flash of green eerily reminiscent of the smallest tower's color flashed across the sky. Zero made one more pass, then twisted and dove straight to the hole in the side of the temple.

Hope there is room for you to slow down, thought Jaxson.

Before Zero could reply and just before he entered the temple, two smaller dragons struck him from above simultaneously.

As the shock wore off, Jaxson hurried toward his dragon and best friend that was currently tumbling to the sandy ground. When he approached the end of his temple, a dragon smaller than Zero but larger than the two that assaulted his dragon cut him off. On the new dragon's back was a grizzled, chubby man with a large patch covering his left eye. The dragon roared in Jaxson's face, causing him to turn away with his hands over his ears. The next thing he knew, something struck the back of his head. As darkness overtook him, he saw Zero climbing back into the sky slowly as the two dragons spun off away from him.

CHAPTER 3

Light streamed in softly through the bedroom window, letting Jaxson know he had slept in longer than normal. It bounced off the cave rocks on his bedside table, throwing different colors all over the room. He picked up the shiny rocks from anywhere he could, but there was one cave at the top of the valley that held the most interesting ones. The rocks seemed to grow together from the cave floor to the ceiling. Zero's large size kept him from going farther than the main cave, but Jaxson could squeeze through a crack that opened up to another large cavern filled with sparkling green and pink and white rocks. The light from his torch had made the rocks glitter and dance just like the sun now.

He threw his wool blanket to the floor and stretched the tightness out of his arms. He yawned as he got to his feet and made his way to the kitchen. The crackling and popping bacon could only mean his father had gotten a late start too. *My dad?* Something felt off, but the aroma of fatty bacon dissuaded any further pondering.

After sitting, he poured a glass of fresh spritemelon juice and strummed his fingers impatiently. His dad turned with a hot skillet and said, "Well look who decided to join the land of the living!"

"Good morning, Dad," replied Jaxson as he stifled a yawn.

"Best to eat it while it's hot. This isn't the best bacon, kinda fatty, but it'll do."

Jaxson filled his plate with bacon and sourdough bread. There was even butter on the table that he applied liberally to his bread. The first bite was warm and thick. The butter ran down his chin and splattered on the table.

"Slow down, boy," said his father, chuckling quietly. "It'll still be there in a minute or two."

"I can't," Jaxson muttered through his full mouth. After finishing that bite and nibbling on the toast, he continued, "Where did you get butter? And this bread seems fresh this morning!"

"Some of us have been busy... and *some of us* slept most of the morning away."

Jaxson grinned in spite of his overfull mouth again. He couldn't believe his luck. He was able to get some much-needed rest, eat hot bacon, and even enjoy butter on fresh bread. No time in his life could he remember doing all of these, at least not on the same day.

They both laughed and ate well past the time they should have stopped. Jaxson had never been so full. His father was home from his many travels and the day was still young. They could go fishing or explore some more caves. Perhaps they should go to the village on the far side of the mountains to stock up on supplies. *Either way, it's gonna be a day to remember*, Jaxson thought to himself. Then he silently said to Zero, *Have you eaten yet? Looks like we are gonna have a busy day! Dad's home.*

When Zero did not immediately answer, the uneasy feeling in Jaxson's gut he had buried sprang forth. Again, he thought something was off. "Dad, have you seen Zero this morning?"

Alan, his father, sat up from his lounged position on the large sitting chair. He glanced out the window then back at his son. "Why, sure I saw him! I'm sure everything is fine. He might just be busy."

His father's smile, which was always comforting, did nothing to assuage Jaxson's anxiety. Zero never went out of talking range without first letting him know. He hoped nothing was wrong with his dragon. "I think I'll go check on him."

As Jaxson rose, so did his father. Just before Jaxson pulled the door fully open, his father's hand slammed it shut. "What are y—"

"Before you go out there, son, there are some things you need to know."

"Like what?"

"First," Alan said as he guided Jaxson back to the center of the room, "I want you to know I love you very much, and everything that I do is for you and your future. Second, and perhaps more important, is that I am not always right. I have made mistakes in this life, but at least with my most recent, I have been given a chance to correct it."

"What are you talking about? Does this have something to do with Zero?" Jaxson asked, tearing away from his father and running for the door. He burst out into the dazzling morning sunlight but could make no sense of the scene before him.

There directly in front of their little mountain home lay Zero. He was bound to the ground by several thick chains, thicker than Jaxson's leg. His side was bleeding profusely, yet there was no struggle. Finally, Jaxson spotted the large, thick helmet that had been strapped onto Zero's head. Across one side were strange letters Jaxson was sure he had seen before etched in bright red. Zero blinked, and Jaxson breathed for the first time since seeing him in this position. *He's alive!*

"See, this beast will not have control over a son of mine," said his father from right behind him. "I have made sure of that."

"What happened to him?!" Jaxson yelled as he ran to his friend. Zero noticed Jaxson for the first time and immediately started struggling against the chains and helmet. He could barely lift his head with all the extra weight. The stakes holding the chains to the ground pulled, but held tight.

"Lizard, stop straining, or you'll get the knife again," yelled Alan.

"Zero! I'm here; I'll get you out of this!"

Just as Jaxson reached his oldest friend, he was struck from behind. His father leered down at him.

"I was afraid of that... You disappoint me, boy." Alan motioned with one hand, and several armed men Jaxson had not noticed trotted over to Zero's neck. "The only thing to do now is eliminate the demon lizard."

The armed men raised their axes as one, and Alan cackled loudly. Jaxson screamed and struggled to get to Zero, to throw his body in front of the axes. But he wasn't going to be fast enough. The axes began their descent, and he saw the recognition in Zero's eyes. Zero knew it was pointless to struggle any longer.

The world slowed. A butterfly danced past Jaxson's face. His father's maniacal laugh cut through his ears, just like how the rocky ground cut into his hands and bare feet. The first executioner's arms bulged under the strain of swinging the giant ax. Then he smelled smoke...

That doesn't make sense. There shouldn't be smoke, Jaxson thought as the world around him dissolved.

CHAPTER 4

His eyes stung even before he opened them. Jaxson could taste the thick smoke as he struggled to come fully awake. He was lying near a fire on rocky, barren ground but could see nothing else. When he shot up, his head swam, forcing him to close his eyes once more. The memory of his father hurting Zero in his dream threatened to overwhelm him. *It was just a dream*, he reminded himself. Deep down, however, the truth of his father's betrayal back in Esther weighed heavily on his heart. He reached out to Zero and was pleased when his dragon responded that he was unhurt.

"Go slow, boy. You suffered quite the whack on your noggin," said a scruffy voice behind him.

Jaxson turned, slowly this time, and saw only the one-eyed man from the temple. The temple where he was attacked. "You would know. What did you hit me with anyway?"

The large man looked down and shuffled his feet. He reached behind his back and pulled out a chunk of smooth wood that was attached to a long cord. "About that... Sorry, I didn't mean to put that much juice on it. But we were kinda in a hurry. You and your dragon seemed intent on committing suicide. We didn't want that to happen."

"Suicide? What do you mean?"

"No one that goes in the Desert Temple of Skree ever comes out again. We lost one of ours that way. Just didn't want to see you suffer the same fate..." The one-eyed man paused, and when Jaxson did not argue, he continued.

"Name's Mannix. What do you call yourself?"

"Jaxson. Where is Zero? My dragon?"

"He flew down to the cove with Tephra and Salvia for some water and a chance bite to eat. He is fine."

"Yeah, he told me," replied Jaxson. His head was feeling better with each non-smoky breath.

"Did he? That's quite the distance for you two to be talking," said Mannix with a chuckle. "Quite a long distance indeed."

"I don't have to explain myself to you. You should be explaining instead. Why did you attack us?"

Mannix took a deep breath and stared off across the desert. "I told you already. It's suicide to go in the temple. We came here to stop one of ours from entering in search of the treasure, but I fear we were too late. Not for you, however; we still saved you."

Jaxson rose to his feet and looked the older man in the eye. "I didn't ask to be saved. I am not here searching for lost treasure. What I seek is more important."

His breathing was heavy, his fists clenched. He continued to stare at the meddlesome man wondering what gave him the right to mess with him and Zero. Mannix raised his hands in mock surrender. "Whoa now. We saved your life. It might be too much to ask for a little gratitude, but I definitely don't deserve your anger."

Jaxson threw his hands in the air and stormed away from the fire and Mannix. As he paced around, he tried to get his bearings. Dunes in all directions; everything looked the same. He could not see the ridge he and Zero had camped on in the past few weeks, nor the three temples. He tried reaching out to Zero again but could only get the sensation that he was not in danger and nothing more. He did not know what to do. But as his options were limited, he decided to play nice.

"You are right, of course. If the temples are as dangerous

as you say, I am in your debt."

A large, genuine grin spread across Mannix's stubbled face. "Hoy, that's more like it! Now, you must be starvin'—you're practically skin and bones. Let's go eat!"

CHAPTER 5

Hours later as the sun set in the west, all four of their dragons lounged against a rocky outcrop, their bellies full and bodies tired from a long flight. Zero fought hard to stifle yawns. Jaxson and Mannix, along with the other two riders Salvia and Tephra, were seated around the fire, and were much chattier.

"And then Nalla tried to roar, but it only came out as a screech," Salvia said through her laughter. "Tephra, you and Yammer never moved. And that just made her angrier! Man, she was so mad you let him take her spot."

Tephra looked up from the wood he was whittling long enough to nod. "I remember."

"Your dragon wouldn't dare mess with Nalla now, though."

"This was before I met you two?" asked Mannix.

"Well, before. I don't really recall how long ago, but the dragons couldn't have been more than a year old then. So, we would have been what…eight or nine years old?"

Mannix whistled softly. "That long ago?"

Salvia's eyes grew big, and she threw an empty bowl at Mannix. "I'm not that old! About ten years or so I guess."

Jaxson leaned back, and let their voices slide to the background. He had eaten more during that evening meal than all the previous week's meals combined. His eyes were getting heavy when Zero interrupted his snooze. *What do you think of these people?*

I don't know yet. They seem…normal, but they did attack

us. Not sure I'll ever trust them.

Brunt, the older dragon, told me that it was the only way to save us. The Temples of Skree do not allow anyone to leave. Maybe they did us a favor, replied Zero.

Maybe... How are the other dragons? They seem trustworthy?

Zero took several long moments before he replied. *I sense no deception in them. The two smaller ones that the young riders are bonded with are half my age and defer to Brunt in all things. He is older than even his rider and has seen much, so they say.*

"He is a strong one though. Took everything Nalla and Yammer had to turn him. You said his name is Zero?" asked Salvia.

Startled, Jaxson tried to remember what the others were talking about. "Yeah, that's his name."

"He is a brute. So big and deceptively quick. If Nalla hadn't been able to talk sense into him, I don't think we could have kept him from the temple."

"Speaking of the temple, can any of you tell me what is really going on? I don't understand how going inside definitely means we won't ever come out."

Mannix sighed and held up a hand to keep Salvia silent. "Look Jaxson, we don't know much about what goes on inside the temples. All we know is once you go in, you are never seen again. There are many rumors as to what is in there or why you don't come out. Each is as crazy as the rest."

"But how do you know any of it is true?" pressed Jaxson.

"Grant and his dragon, Easton, didn't just disappear!" said Salvia. "He is stuck in that—"

"Of those that have entered, none have ever come back out," interrupted Mannix. Silence grew as twilight settled over the group. A chill ran up Jaxson's arms as he watched Tephra continue to whittle at the small piece of wood. He couldn't make out if the young man was making something or just passing the time.

"Look, we aren't going to babysit you forever. We have somewhere to be. When we leave in the morning, you can go in the temple if you choose, but at least we warned you. That may be all we can do."

Again, the empty silence returned, broken only by the crackling of the small fire. Jaxson, unsure of how he felt about his "saviors", bid all a good night and rolled into his blanket. He could decide in the morning what he was to do. If the temples were a dead end, he could either return through the portal back home or… do something else. He was too tired to work it all out tonight though. His last thoughts before drifting off to sleep were of his friends a half a world away, Tam and Aleera. Then his father's betrayal came back to the front of his mind, and in that instant, he knew he wasn't returning without the information Forsetti had sent him to find.

CHAPTER 6

"Where are you all going?" asked Jaxson as Mannix, Tephra, and Salvia packed up their camp in the predawn glow.

"I've told you twice already, boy. South. We are going south," replied Mannix.

"What is south of here?"

Mannix stifled a yawn. "Many places that you don't know anything about, but the *where* isn't as important as the *what*."

Jaxson cocked his head and kept his gaze on the older man. "And that would be?"

Clanging pans and plates followed by a loud curse interrupted their conversation. "For the tiny gods' sake!" spat Salvia. "Mannix, just tell him and get it over with. He's either gonna go with us, or he's not. And you, Tephra, quit laughing."

Tephra chuckled once more then resumed his packing. Jaxson looked back and forth between Salvia and Mannix, hoping one of them would tell him what was happening. When neither seemed forthcoming, he reached out to Zero. *Have the other dragons mentioned where they are heading?*

No. Yammer and Nalla have only said they're excited to be going back home. Do you wish me to pry?

With a deep sigh, Jaxson replied, *I guess not. What do you think we should do?*

If the temples are truly a dead end, I think we have few options. Either go back through the portal without what we came for, or follow along with this group. They know this land and its hazards better than us.

"So, you want me to come with you?" Jaxson asked, looking straight at Mannix.

"Well, you see, we are going to the Dragon Trials, and we need one more rider to compete. And your dragon is strong and fast… We could use the help."

"You're going where?" asked Jaxson.

Salvia rolled her eyes and kept packing. Mannix moved closer to Jaxson before explaining, "The Dragon Trials are a tradition older than… well, I can't think of anything, but they are old. There are three separate trials that teams compete in, culminating in a team race. The winner gets the glory among other things."

A loud snort came from Salvia. "Like a meeting with the oracle you mean?"

Mannix scowled at her. "Well, we have to get there first."

"How many teams are there?" asked Jaxson.

"There are usually four or five teams. It only happens every seven years, and I missed the last one because of an entanglement," Mannix said with a thin smile. "I don't think there is a set number. However many receive invitations, I guess."

"I see. And you were invited?"

Tephra, who had been hovering at the edge of the conversation, quickly walked off. Salvia looked uncharacteristically sheepish, her cheeks turning red as she looked to Mannix for his reply.

"We will be," Mannix answered. The robust man finished stuffing his bag and walked over to his dragon, Brunt. Jaxson's head was spinning with all the new information. He stared across the dunes until Salvia placed a hand on his shoulder.

"Pack your stuff. Where else are you gonna go?" she asked.

Jaxson gave a quick nod in response and set to packing his meager possessions. Salvia was correct. He didn't have anywhere else to go.

CHAPTER 7

Weeks passed as the group of riders and their dragons made steady, if slow, progress south. They did not seem to be in any hurry, stopping well before sundown to set up camp and leaving after a hearty breakfast and the rising of the sun. Each night was filled with laughter and stories from Mannix, mostly about former Dragon Trials and the winners. Jaxson learned of Germain the Great and his dragon Grolloff, who set the single rider record in the diving competition. Mannix told tales of the sisters from the Isles of Creptin that, hundreds of years ago, dominated the competition for thirty-five years through speed, grace, and ruthlessness. So many tales that Jaxson's head began to spin with his own desires for glory.

Each time he tried to pressure Mannix for more detail on how they were to obtain their invitation, Mannix would change the subject to strategy for the most popular of the trials or of another champion's heroic conquest. Jaxson was learning much about the Dragon Trials themselves, however. The mysterious hosts, known only as the Council of Heirs, put on the tournament in a different location with different competitions each time. Some of the places and trials had been repeated over the years, but it was rare. This year's Dragon Trials was to be held near the sleepy, coastal village of Gulf Springs, much farther south than Jaxson ever dreamed he would travel. Even after all the distance covered since they began their journey, the group was still several weeks of daily travel away from arriving at their destination.

Shortly after midday, Mannix raised a single clenched

fist from the riding harness on Brunt's back. Salvia, who had been riding near him all morning, fanned out wide right and began a slow descent to the ground, scanning for a favorable spot for Mannix's unusual break. Jaxson and Zero were the last to land and were greeted by vivacious laughter.

"Just one? You, the great Mannix of the Thorn, drink just one ale?" Salvia said through the mirth.

"I use that more as a figure of speech than an actual count of the number of flagons I'll take tonight," replied Mannix, a huge grin splitting his face. He had a twinkle in his one good eye that Jaxson recognized as pure happiness.

"Hmph. One barrel more like," said Tephra from over near his dragon, Yammer.

Mannix and Salvia exchanged a glance then both burst out with renewed laughter. Salvia, bent over at the waist, tried several times to comment but could not get the words out.

"What's this all about?" asked Jaxson.

"I think it's high time we took a night off for some rest and revelry," replied Mannix. When Jaxson did not respond, he continued. "We are gonna stop at this tavern and inn I know of just a bit farther south and eat some good food and drink some good drinks."

"And bathe," said Salvia. "You boys are truly ripe."

Everyone laughed this time, even Jaxson. Mannix boasted that the tavern was an epicenter for all the area's greatest warriors and adventurers, and served the best ale anywhere. Sleeping under a roof with a full belly sounded like a great idea to Jaxson, and though his father had never let him try ale before, a taste surely wouldn't hurt.

****

To the west Jaxson pointed at a sheer, tall cliff with ancient, crooked trees on top. Mannix moved Brunt closer to Zero and yelled to Jaxson, "That is known as Devil's Crown. Bad place.

Close to where we are going, though. Think we will steer farther to the south."

Then Jaxson saw the dusty, one-lane road and the lone mountain well before any buildings came into view. After his time in Esther's capital, he found the small, one-dragon town to be underwhelming. Small, wooden buildings were scattered haphazardly about the large, two-story inn near the center of the town that sat just below a sheer cliff. All along the cliff face, caves of varying sizes led deeper into the mountain.

While you and the other riders rest, I will seek out a comfortable cave to sleep in, said Zero.

You need to find something to eat and get some rest. I think we are going to pick up the pace after this.

What makes you say that? asked Zero.

Just a feeling, nothing more.

The dragons flew for the caves after dropping off their riders just outside of town. Mannix whistled, and Salvia laughed and joked. Even Tephra had a smile on his face as the group approached the tavern. A ragged sign above the door identified it as The Fields of Lefter and depicted two dragons flying. Being well before sundown, Jaxson expected to find the barroom empty, but he was wrong. A minstrel was singing near the fireplace to an assorted crowd of farmers, mercenaries, and rougher looking fellows. Three serving girls wove in and out of the tables and bodies with precision, carrying large mugs and even larger pitchers to the eagerly awaiting patrons.

Jaxson's nose wrinkled at the smell of sour ale and sweat. He looked over at Mannix, who was grinning wildly. The big man took a large breath and said, "Smells like a good time! Let's get a drink."

Tephra found them a table in the corner as far away from everyone else as possible. It wasn't long before a serving girl dropped off some stoneware mugs and a pitcher of water before asking what they needed. Mannix didn't waste any time in ordering a round of ale for everyone else and two for himself, along with some fresh bread and anything "ready and hot". Jaxson objected to his ale but Mannix and Salvia waved him off. Salvia even said something about finally getting hair on his chest before she and Mannix erupted into laughter.

CHAPTER 8

Each time Jaxson looked in a new direction, the world spun ever so slightly. He was on his third ale, and although Mannix described it as "lowly pig swill", Jaxson found it to be quite fun to drink. Tephra had retired to a soft bed long ago, and Salvia had ventured over near the bard that had just started playing beside the large, empty fireplace. He had a grin on his face that he could not quite make go away. When he reached out to Zero, he could feel the dragon roll his eyes as he admonished him *not to consume too many and be careful.*

Mannix returned to the table with three more glasses filled with frothy ale and offered one to Jaxson. He declined and Mannix shrugged, then put one mug near Salvia's seat and the other two in front of himself.

"We haven't talked about you much at all," said Mannix out of the blue. "But we are getting closer now, and I need to know something."

Jaxson had started when Mannix spoke, as he was focused on the bard's slow tune about a grasshopper's love for a butterfly. "What do you need to know?"

"Well, it's time you told me what's been bothering you, and if it might be a problem for us."

His head tilted and his brow furrowed. "Whatever do you mean?"

"When you first started stirring the day after we stopped you from entering the temples, you were thrashing about and mumbling a lot. During your nightmare, you talked enough that I got the gist of your problem," said Mannix as he locked eyes with Jaxson. "So, if it's your da or whoever that wants to hurt Zero, they aren't coming here and causing problems for us, right?"

"No, we are a long, long way from that danger," said Jaxson. "Why have you taken so long to ask me about it?"

The older man scanned the crowd and sighed. "I had hoped you would open up to us sooner rather than later, but we are running out of time. I need you with us at the trials, but I can't have any trouble following us there."

Jaxson laughed. "Other than knocking me out, you have been nothing short of good to Zero and me. I wouldn't put you, Tephra, or Salvia in any danger that was preventable, but I also don't know what else to do. I wasn't given much information before coming through the portal to search for an ancient dragonrider's book."

Jaxson looked back to Salvia, who was singing along to a lively jig about a farmer's wife falling in love with their donkey. He shook his head, and his smile returned. He glanced back at Mannix, who stared off into nothing, and the silence stretched on. Just when Jaxson thought perhaps they were through with their conversation, Mannix spoke quietly.

"There is a tale I heard as a boy about such a book. It was a long-winded affair but basically boiled down to the only way to locate the sacred book is through the oracle."

"Do you believe it?"

"I don't *not* believe it, if you follow me," replied Mannix.

Jaxson finished off his third ale, and Mannix pushed another toward him. As Jaxson grabbed the handle, he launched into his tale starting with the storm at the Bend and ending with his father's betrayal that led to his use of the portal. Mannix was unusually still and listened intently. Jaxson's shoulders sagged as the last of the words left his mouth. He felt tired, more tired than he had ever felt, but also relieved to have finally told his new friends about himself. He hadn't exactly been keeping secrets on purpose, but he had kept them all the same.

"Sounds like you could use some friends like us, for sure," said Mannix finally. "Tell you what, you help us win the Dragon Trials, and I promise we will help you find the book that you seek."

Zero, I think we are gonna be all right, said Jaxson.

I never doubted it. But now you need to rest, replied the dragon from inside his cave.

"That sounds perfect, but first before we win races and find mythical books, I think I need to find a bed," said Jaxson.

Mannix smiled and pointed to the stairs on the other side of the room. "Up those stairs, then fourth door on the left. Try not to wake Tephra. See you in the morning."

Jaxson just nodded and stumbled toward the stairs. He waved and smiled at Salvia on his way to the room. He wasn't even sure she saw him, but it felt like the right thing to do. The last thought he could remember was she sure looked pretty with her long hair cascading down her back as she sang and danced in front of the fireplace.

CHAPTER 9

As Jaxson awoke, a boulder rested on his head, or at least, that's what it felt like. He cracked his eyelids and immediately shut them again. Even the meager light of early morning coming in from the small window was too much for him to handle. He wanted to remain in bed but between the whole room spinning and his mouth tasting foul, he decided getting up was the wise choice. His feet hit the wooden floor with a thud. Surprised, Jaxson looked down and noticed he had not taken his boots off the previous night. He knew one thing right away—he was never drinking ale again.

Zero, are you up and about this morning?

Ha! I am. Surprised you are, however. How are you feeling?

Jaxson, still seated in bed, rested his head in his hands and took a deep breath. *Not really enjoying this inn as much this morning as I did last night.*

Get some breakfast. The other dragons are still in the cave but I intend to stretch my wings, and perhaps explore south where we are headed. Brunt told me Mannix is unlikely to stir before the midday meal.

Eating does not sound fun at all, but some fresh air might help. Stay within shouting distance, said Jaxson. Zero's affirmative reply came before he attempted to rise off the bed for the first time. He was finally successful on his fourth attempt.

He stumbled to the wash basin and rinsed his face. Mannix snored lightly behind him, and across the room, Salvia slept face down on top of the blanket. Jaxson scanned the rest of the room looking for Tephra. The only other bed was made and looked unslept in. *He must've gotten an early start*, thought Jaxson as he looked in the polished brass mirror. His hair was a mess and needed to be pulled back, but he could worry about that later. Right now, he felt stifled and needed some air. He opened the door to the hallway and was met by the point of a long, curved knife.

The pimply-faced, scrawny man holding the knife did not make sense to Jaxson. His brain, still foggy from last night's escapades, could not understand what he was seeing. He tensed and attempted to call out. Before the words left his mouth, a fist crashed into his nose. Blood erupted on his face and down his shirt. He stumbled backward and landed heavily on his rear end.

One of the thugs was beside Salvia's bed holding a short sword on her before she could move. The blanket on Mannix's bed flew into the wall as the stout man, dressed only in his undershorts, sprang to his feet. One hand gripped a small boot-knife that Jaxson had seen Mannix use to peel many apples.

"What in the tiny gods' names is going on here?" screeched Mannix.

The pimply-faced man responded, "You just drop that knife before my friend there sticks steel in the pretty one's belly."

Mannix dropped the knife onto his bed and held his hands up. "Take whatever you like. My sword and my money are on that belt there hanging behind the door." The thug snorted. "We aren't here for your money, are we, boys?"

The other three men in the room laughed. One still held Salvia in check with his sword. Another was advancing on Mannix with a sword drawn. The last had moved behind Jaxson. A blade pushed down on his shoulder. Still seated, he wasn't in position to do anything other than what the thugs wanted.

When none of the room occupants responded, the thug continued, "You three are coming with us…to your dragons. With a knife at your throat, they will be easier to handle."

"Not a chance we are taking you to our dragons!" yelled Salvia. She had managed to work her way into a sitting position against the wall, although she was still in bed.

The man holding her jabbed lightly with his sword. Salvia yelped and grabbed her arm as a tiny rivulet of blood streamed down. Quickly, she was out of bed scrambling away from the attacker. A sharp pain lanced through Jaxson's shoulder as his assailant applied enough pressure to pierce his shirt and skin.

"Enough. Let's go," said the pimply man, who seemed to be the leader of this ragtag group.

"Fine, we'll come along. Mind if I put some britches on first? You don't want any extra attention, and me parading around town more than half naked will draw some, be sure," said Mannix.

"Go ahead. Keep a close watch on 'im, Rodney," said the leader. "And in case any of yous think to be letting your dragons know we are coming, don't bother. We have that way of communicating blocked."

Jaxson reached out to Zero and was immediately pounded with worry coming from the dragon. He sent reassuring calm back but knew that would only hold Zero at bay for so long. Jaxson did not want his dragon barreling into this situation before he knew exactly what they were up against.

The thugs roughly pushed them in the direction of the stairs. They sheathed their swords and drew knives that they pressed to the smalls of their backs. Jaxson took the stairs down as quickly as possible. Near the bottom step, Jaxson looked up to see Tephra with a shocked expression on his face just coming in the front door of the inn. He recovered quickly and sat at the nearest table.

He made eye contact with Jaxson. Jaxson furiously tried to think of what to do. Finally, he mouthed the words, *Devil's Crown,* but Tephra wasn't looking at him. Jaxson needed to get his attention in some way. Just before they passed him, Jaxson took a step to the left, directly into a chair. He stumbled away from the chair into the thug in front of him, sending him out the door. He fell hard right at Tephra's feet. As he recovered, he whispered, "Devil's Crown. Zero."

Before Jaxson could regain his feet, the thug that had been holding him kicked him in the stomach. He retched the full contents of his stomach on the boards near inches from his face.

"Get up, you lout!" bellowed the thug as he cocked his foot back for another blow.

Jaxson struggled away and used the wall to stand. Zero blared in his head, *Jaxson, are you all right?*

I've been better. Find Tephra. I sent him to the Devil's Crown. Come back and get us, said Jaxson.

I'm coming now! howled Zero.

No! We don't know what we are up against.

The thug grabbed Jaxson and shoved him out the door. He stumbled again, but this time he did not have a wall to help him up. Sprawled out in the dusty road, he made one more plea to Zero. *Find Tephra. Make a plan and come save us quickly. I'll tell you more about what we are up against as soon as I can.*

CHAPTER 10

"Get up, lizard rider," said the pimply thug.

Jaxson struggled to his feet, coughing on the thick dust swirling around him. He thought about his bow all safely tucked into his harness on Zero's back. Their captors had relieved them of any weapons back in the room. Their only hope of escape was through Tephra and Zero.

He was shoved roughly again and stumbled once more. This time, however, he kept his feet. He looked back over his shoulder to see Mannix and Salvia being herded along behind him. Just as Mannix went through the doorway, he pivoted and rammed his shoulder into his captor. The thug went down hard but pulled Mannix with him. Both cussed and called each other vile names Jaxson had never heard before. Salvia's captor stepped forward and whacked Mannix on the back of the head with the flat of his sword. Mannix went back down in a heap of clothes, sweat, and blood.

While his captor came to his feet, a chain with a silver medallion fell out of the front of his shirt. Jaxson's eyes bulged. The sigil that had been branded and cut into the flesh of captured dragons back in the kingdom of Esther, a flame with wavy lines transecting it, hung from the chain. These men were part of the Demon Lizard Death Cult!

Zero! It's worse than I thought. They aren't here to rob us. It's the DLDC. They mean to take all of you. Find Tephra and give him my bow. Come get us!

We will not hesitate. I think I have already spotted Tephra sprinting to the Devil's Crown, replied Zero.

"All right you soggy lot, let's get moving. And no more

funny business," cried the leader.

Jaxson looked to the lone mountain with the caves. It was only a short walk of perhaps fifteen minutes. He wondered if that would be enough time for Zero to get Tephra and head their way. If not, he would be forced to distract the DLDC from taking the other dragons, or worse yet, branding them with the magic sigil that forced the dragons to obey them. He looked to Salvia and saw her face drawn, lips pressed tight. Mannix was white and did not seem to understand exactly what was going on anymore. *His head must still be ringing.* If Zero was to have any advantage, it would be up to him to provide it.

****

The first thing Jaxson noticed as they approached the caves was the sickly, tingling sensation he had only ever experienced one other time. Back in Esther when he saw the sorcerers of Creptin performing the blood magic on Soaren, the dragon he had helped escape, he had felt this same overwhelming shock of evil magic. He attempted to reach out to Zero but found it impossible. He could still feel his dragon and knew he was nearby, but he could not talk to him. Each step forward brought them closer to the caves and made the magical tingling stronger. His stomach threatened to empty its contents again onto the dirt path. Blurry vision crept in on him as they entered the mouth of the cave.

The three dragons, Brunt, Yammer, and Nalla, stood off to the left just inside the opening. They were surrounded by a dozen thugs each holding long spears with black, metal tips. In front of them on the ground was a strange rock. It looked dark black at first, then gray or charcoal. The color kept shifting. It took him a moment to realize the stone itself was black, but some kind of writing in red and gray swirled on its surface. This stone was causing all his discomfort and uneasiness. It was probably what was keeping him from being able to talk to Zero as well. He didn't have time to think about the rock any further. He, Mannix, and Salvia were unceremoniously thrown down with a sword held at each of their throats.

From behind the dragons came a clicking laughter. All three dragons shied away but kept their eyes locked on the creature walking around to stand in front of the riders. Although fully robed, Jaxson saw the being's arms were too long for its body, and its elbows did not fold like a human's. Instead, the creature's arms swung loosely at its side. A three-clawed hand reached behind its back, bending at an impossible angle, and pulled a long, serrated dagger from a hidden sheath. The other hand held the fire and waves sigil Jaxson knew to be used to control dragons through vile blood magic. The being was a sorcerer from the Isles of Creptin, and terror pierced Jaxson's heart. Even Dreknoxious had feared the dark sorcerers.

"Now, dragons, we have your riders," clicked the sorcerer. "Attempt to fight or flee, and they die first."

"No, you don't!" yelled Mannix as he struggled to his feet. Before he was even halfway up, a club smacked him in the back of the head, and again, the big man went down.

"That was unnecessary," said the sorcerer. "If we can all sit quietly, our business will be concluded quickly with as little pain as possible."

The sorcerer pointed at Nalla, Salvia's dragon. The thugs with the spears started forcing her to move away from the other two dragons to the center of the cave. Salvia started to rise but was forced back down with a rough slap and a shove. Silent tears streamed down her face. Jaxson locked eyes with her, and he knew he needed to do something, *anything* right that moment.

He rocked back slowly, then shoved off the thug with the sword at his throat, causing him to tumble backward. Jaxson sprinted to the color shifting rock with his captor recovering quickly and following. The paint on the rock was still wet so he jumped on it, attempting to smear the spell away.

The thugs wrangling Nalla to the center of the room broke off and advanced on Jaxson. The paint was not coming off the rock. He tried to scrub harder with his hands, his shirt, but nothing affected the spell. His head was spinning, and his stomach could not hold back any longer. He vomited on the boots of the men that grabbed him roughly and drug him back to the others. Jaxson heard the sorcerer's bug-like, clicking laughter again.

"Silly boy! A blood spell is not so easily wiped away," said the sorcerer. "You have no—"

The sorcerer's words were cut short by a tremendous roar filling the whole cave. Everyone—Jaxson, Salvia, Mannix, all the DLDC thugs, and even the sorcerer—covered their ears with some falling to the ground, clutching their heads in agony. There, blocking the entrance to the cave with Tephra on his back, was Zero.

CHAPTER 11

Neck extended and wings flat on his back, Zero sustained his roar for a long time. Tephra fired arrow after arrow from his back. Jaxson admired how quickly Tephra was able to release an arrow and nock another. The accuracy of the shots, however, left much to be desired. Salvia was the first to recover on the ground. She sprang to her feet above her captor and issued a hard kick to his face. She quickly scooped up his sword and cut her bonds. Next, she was by Mannix doing the same and yelling for him to get up. The three dragons inside the cave were biting and slashing, forcing the DLDC thugs to retreat right to Zero's waiting jaws.

Some of the thugs turned back into the cave seeking an alternate escape route. Jaxson got to his feet and started toward Zero. Mannix wobbled around brandishing a sword, but finally found the cave wall and leaned against it. The thugs were too busy avoiding the dragons to worry about any of the riders. By the time Jaxson made it to Zero, Tephra was out of arrows and had jumped from Zero's back. He efficiently used his long, curved blade to keep any thugs that got around Zero from escaping out the cave mouth.

Blood dripped from Zero's mouth as Jaxson approached. In all the tight spots he and Zero had found themselves in, Jaxson could not remember one where Zero looked so fearsome and savage. His dragon seemed focused only on destroying the thugs instead of escape.

"ZERO! Look at me," Jaxson yelled and waved. It took a while before the dragon turned to look at him. "Allow them a way out, or we'll have to kill them all!"

Zero scanned the whole of the cave for the first time. He seemed to realize he had forced them to either fight three dragons or attempt to escape by him. He backed slowly out of the opening of the cave. The remaining thugs, backs pressed firmly to the far cave wall, slowly inched their way out of the cave before sprinting down the sloping terrain. Jaxson threw up his hands and yelled in victory. He rushed out to Zero and hugged his front leg. He had another bout of vertigo when he realized how close he was to Zero but still couldn't "talk" with him.

Thoughts of the spell on the color shifting rock brought Jaxson back to the task at hand. *Where did the sorcerer go?* He looked around and even ran to check some of the bodies strewn around the cave, but the sorcerer was nowhere to be found. He asked everyone, but no one had seen what became of the robed creature. Jaxson could not recall seeing him after Zero's arrival.

Mannix slowly shuffled over. "What in the tiny gods' tears was that all about?"

"I have seen similar before," said Jaxson. Tephra and Salvia were both back by their dragons, and Brunt strode toward Mannix. "They were going to bind the dragons with dark magic into their service."

"Don't think I've ever heard of such a thing," replied Mannix. After a long moment's pause, he asked, "Can you still talk to Zero?"

Jaxson glanced at Mannix. The large man's eyes were cloudy and his shoulders slumped forward. "No. I could before we arrived at the cave, though. I think that spell rock is the problem. If we could have talked with the dragons still in the cave, those thugs could never have controlled us or them."

Mannix looked back to Brunt then softly told Jaxson, "It is so uncomfortably quiet in my head. I feel hollow."

"Me too. Let's fix that," he said to Mannix. Then to Zero, he said, "Want to help me get rid of that rock?"

Zero nodded and walked in to retrieve the foul stone. Jaxson told Mannix they would be back after dropping the stone in a hole somewhere. The old man told them of a lake, deep and isolated, just to the southeast. A perfect spot for the spell rock to be dropped.

Jaxson hopped onto Zero's back and waved at the other riders, letting them know they would be back soon. Zero sprang into the air, and Jaxson had to struggle to hold onto the harness. He yelled at Zero to take it easy. It felt very different to ride Zero without their constant communication, some of which he hadn't been aware they shared until this moment. He knew the hollow feeling Mannix had spoken of earlier. Jaxson never wanted to feel this way again.

CHAPTER 12

Days passed by slowly as Mannix, Salvia, and Yammer recovered. Yammer's spear wound had closed but was in a tender spot under his wing. Salvia, bruised and scraped, did not want to wait around. Mannix, however, stumbled about without any balance. Each morning, Jaxson thought it would be time to move on, but it was obvious Mannix wasn't ready. On the sixth morning, just a day's flight away from the village from where they were attacked, it seemed they would finally get to fly south again.

"So, what happens next?" asked Jaxson. All of the dragons except Zero had flown off before sunrise in search of a big meal.

Mannix looked up from his plate of breakfast stew and said, "We are off to Beauxgrand Castle to get the invite we need."

"A castle? That sounds interesting," said Jaxson. "Will we get to meet the king?"

Salvia snorted, and Tephra chuckled quietly. Mannix said, "No kings on this side of the sea. There is an emperor, though he doesn't mess with us much this far away from his capital city. Just a former duke in charge of the land around his castle for the emperor."

"I see." Jaxson sighed—meeting a king would have been grand.

"It's not all that bad," said Salvia. "There is a ton of stuff to do. They have a great training yard for sword and spear work. Also, an archery range with targets ranging from a few steps to almost out of sight. Maybe you could show Tephra how to shoot a bow?"

Tephra's ears reddened, but he gave no other indication he heard Salvia poke fun at his inaccurate shooting in the cave. Salvia continued, "The dragons will be well fed without having to hunt. Oh, and their blacksmith is second to none! I am gonna have them sharpen all my blades and maybe even commission a long dagger."

"And most important of all, the duke will have an invite to the trials," said Mannix.

"He's just going to give it to you?" asked Jaxson.

"I happen to have…quite the rapport with the duke."

This time it was Tephra that burst out laughing while Salvia just grinned ear to ear. They both looked away when Mannix focused a withering stare their way. Then he smiled as well.

"Good may be a bit of a stretch, but he does owe me a favor after that business with the harpies."

"What is a harpy?" asked Jaxson.

Salvia waved him off, still snickering. "A half-buzzard, half-human, but that's not the point. The point is," said Salvia as she pointed at Mannix, "the duke will not have forgotten how you almost set fire to his prized library!"

"That was all overblown," said Mannix with a wry smile on his face. "Besides, that old room needed some renovations anyway."

"I hope the duke sees it that way."

"He won't," said Tephra.

The three old friends exchanged glances, and then all burst out laughing. Jaxson could not help but smile himself. Suddenly, he had an idea.

"How old is the castle?" asked Jaxson.

"Tiny gods… I have no idea. Older than the empire, which has reigned for over a thousand years," replied Mannix.

"And the library has been there the whole time?"

"I assume."

Jaxson's smile grew larger. An old library was likely to have old books. Perhaps the book he searched for would be there as well.

The dragons landed by Zero near the edge of the ridge. Tephra doused the fire, and they all rose to join their dragons and resume the journey south.

Salvia and Tephra were on their dragons and in the air before Jaxson even made it over to Zero. Mannix started to climb up Brunt's back but fell. When he attempted to rise, he hit the dirt once more. Jaxson, followed by Zero, rushed to Mannix's side.

"You aren't any better?" asked Jaxson.

"It don't matter. We need to be headin' south," replied Mannix.

Jaxson and Zero exchanged a knowing look. "We aren't going to make it far if you keep falling off your dragon. Now hold still."

Jaxson placed a hand on Mannix's head, and Zero moved close to the large man. Zero sent energy through Mannix and into Jaxson. He waited until he felt he was bursting with it. Then he let it flow back to Zero through Mannix, slowly at first then in one large push. Mannix yelped, and Jaxson sagged down beside him.

Mannix, open jawed, stared at Jaxson then at Zero. His mouth moved but no words came out. Finally, he managed, "What in the unicorn's horn was that?"

Jaxson rose to his feet followed by a sure-footed Mannix. "Just a little help from Zero and me."

Mannix scrambled up Brunt's back with no issue. He smiled at Jaxson. "Whatever you did, thank you."

"It is no problem. Just keep it between us for now, all right?"

The one-eyed man just nodded and leaned over Brunt's neck. The dragon coiled and sprung into the air. Jaxson mounted Zero and followed. It was time to go see a castle on this side of the sea for the first time.

CHAPTER 13

Their arrival to the castle was met with little fuss. It was a large building made of coal black bricks, and a huge wall stretched around the castle, the keep, the dragon's keep, and a large orchard of citrus trees. Almost as soon as the dragons' feet made contact with the smooth and dry floor within the keep, they were met by handlers offering the dragons fresh food and water. After working hard for every meal for weeks on end, Zero was looking forward to an easy meal and some lounging in the shadows of the spacious rooms within the dragon's keep. He told Jaxson as much as the riders started down the stairs.

As soon as they exited the stairwell into the dazzling sunlight, Salvia took off straight for the blacksmith. She had asked Jaxson to come along with her, but after several stammered replies, she just left on her own with a giggle and a wave. Tephra said he was going to the training yard, although he mumbled something about visiting the archery range later in the day. Jaxson looked to Mannix with a raised eyebrow.

"I have to go see a man about house drake, but if you want to come along, I can show you around as we walk," said Mannix.

"Is there any chance we are going near this library you mentioned?"

Mannix laughed and tapped a satchel at his side. "I'd say there is more than a fair chance we will end up in the library or a cell before this day is done."

Jaxson shook his head but smiled and followed Mannix toward the castle. Every direction he looked, he saw well-maintained grounds and buildings. The grass was trimmed, and all of the flower beds were weeded and lush. He hadn't so much as seen a roof tile out of place on the buildings. He was about to comment on how beautiful everything was when Mannix held out a hand to stop them on the stone path leading to the castle. Coming out of the side gate, which they were bound for, were a dozen armed guards in full armor surrounding an important looking gentleman of the court.

"So much for sneaking in quietly," muttered Mannix. Then directly to Jaxson, he said, "Keep your mouth shut. I'll do the talking, you hear?"

Jaxson nodded as the guards came to a stop directly in front of them. Long moments passed where neither the guards nor Mannix approached each other. Jaxson's palms were sweaty, and his nose itched. Though he dared not scratch it. His eyes darted from Mannix to the guards to the court gentleman and back again. No one moved a muscle until finally two of the guards parted the formation simultaneously. The gentleman in the lacy clothes with the tall hat stepped forward and greeted them.

"Ho there, sir. And welcome to you and your friends," said the man with a flourish of his hands.

Mannix simply bowed his head slightly and relaxed his shoulders. The tension seeped out of Jaxson's body as well, as it seemed they were not immediately bound for the prison.

"The duke has been expecting you, sir."

"Thought he might be," mumbled Mannix.

"If you will follow me, I shall lead you to him," said the gentleman.

"Caffer, is the duke still upset with me after my last... visit?" asked Mannix.

Caffer laughed, and Mannix's expression soured. "The

duke is most eager to see you as soon as possible, sir. Perhaps you shouldn't have been away for as long as you have been."

looked at his feet then nodded to Caffer. "Lead on then."

Caffer spun on his heel and entered back into the box formation of guards. It wasn't until both Mannix and Jaxson were surrounded that the guards started to march into the castle. Jaxson eyed Mannix, who just winked at him and shrugged his massive shoulders. Jaxson had no idea what was happening, but Mannix did not seem worried. *The old man must have a plan,* thought Jaxson as they entered the castle where more guards, dressed in armor with the insignia of the duke's house, took over escorting the court gentleman and them through the stone halls of the castle. Jaxson admired the design, a dragon arching out of the pages of an open book. It was all black on a field of burnt orange. Again, he thought the book he sought just may be here.

After several flights of stairs of varying height and straightness, and after many twists and turns, they finally arrived at two large, ornate doors. Again, the sigil of the house appeared. This time it was carved into the great doors with precise detail. The book spanned the bottom of both doors. Out of its open pages sprang forth a roaring dragon, surrounded by flame and smoke. Jaxson did not have long to study the doors as their escort quickly went through.

Two rows of armed guards lined the way to a small, wooden chair that stood on a raised dais. After the intricate and beautiful design on the door, the plain chair looked out of place. Jaxson had expected a sprawling throne of gold and silver with a big, red cushion. Not a chair that could be found in any commoner's house. He was deep in thought when the duke entered and stood before the chair. Jaxson's mouth fell open.

The duke, a tall and large man, was recently shaved clean—and had both of his eyes. But other than those small details, there were no other differences between him and

Mannix.

"Hello, Sir Rushing," said the duke.

Mannix bowed his head and prompted Jaxson to do the same. "Sire, Duke of Beauxgrand, thank you for having me."

The duke remained still. Jaxson's neck ached as he waited for some sign he could straighten up. Finally, the duke laughed and said, "Rise, brother, and welcome! It has been too long!"

Jaxson and Mannix stood straight. The duke continued, "Follow me to my study where we can be less...formal."

CHAPTER 14

Only a short walk down a narrow hallway behind the raised platform brought them to the duke's study. Mannix and the duke immediately took seats in high-backed, plush chairs near the large window behind the desk. Jaxson stood in awe as his eyes took in all the shelves. From floor to ceiling and in every available space there were shelves, and every one of them was loaded with books. Some were huge, easily twice the width of Jaxson's outstretched hands. Others were so thin they could only hold a couple pages each. A woody, earthen scent filled Jaxson's nose as he stared around the book-filled room. He was swept away in the possibilities of all the adventures and knowledge within the bindings on the shelves. His father had always brought home new books from his travels. Jaxson had consumed every single one of them. Laughter from Mannix brought him out of his revelry.

"You still with us, Jaxson?"

He looked over to the two brothers and smiled. "I am. Just…I have never seen this many books in one place."

Both brothers chuckled this time and exchanged a glance. The duke indicated for Jaxson to take a seat. "This is a fair number of my favorite histories as well as family lineages of all the great families in the empire. There are also a few books on geography that I find most interesting."

Jaxson blurted out, "Have you read all these books?"

The duke shook his head slowly. "Not every page of every book, but most of them I have read."

"You always did have your nose in the crease of a book.

That's why you could never best me with a bow or a sword," said Mannix. Jaxson raised an eyebrow.

"My brother here speaks true. He has always been the more physical of us while I am more academically inclined," said the duke. "Now, before we get further, who is this lad you have with you?"

Mannix held out a hand to Jaxson, so Jaxson introduced himself. "My name is Jaxson, sire. Jaxson Alpine. I have been traveling with Mannix for weeks as I do not know my way around this part of the world."

"Don't know your way around, huh? Must not be from around here then?"

"Definitely not. I am from the Dragon Spine Mountains across the sea."

The duke's eyes bulged and his mouth dropped open. Mannix roared with laughter and said, "See here Jaxson, my brother fancies himself a scholar and has read all manner of books about your side of the world. But he has never met someone from there."

"I have not! This is remarkable. People stopped traveling in numbers across the sea before I was born. All I know of your homeland, I have gathered from dusty travel journals. You will make time to answer my questions as soon as I can figure out which to ask first," said the duke.

Jaxson bowed his head. "It would be my pleasure."

The duke turned his attention back to his brother. "As for you, I assume after the last incident in the library you would not be brazen enough to come here seeking my invitation to the Dragon Trials."

Mannix gave a half smile and shrugged his massive shoulders. The duke rolled his eyes and laughed. "Of course you did."

"I also wanted to see how my baby brother is prospering," said Mannix.

"Right…"

"And before you make any rash decisions, I have something for you," said Mannix as he reached in his satchel. "This should help relieve some of the sting from my last misadventure in the library."

Mannix held out an old, brown leather tome with elegant silver script sprawled across the front cover. The duke did not immediately reach for the large book, and Mannix was left holding the book out in the air. After several moments, he had to put his other hand under the book to keep it from falling to the ground.

"Might want to grab this thing, Kent," said Mannix. "It's quite heavy."

"Is that a copy of *Aristarmy's Logic*? There are only three known to exist. Actually, two since you burned my copy."

Mannix looked at his feet, and the duke grabbed the book from his hands. Mannix looked up to his brother's face. "I am truly sorry. I was drunk and showing off for Larissa. *Trying* to show off, at least. I never intended to do any damage to the library."

The duke, busy thumbing through the thick book, barely acknowledged Mannix. He seemed lost in thought. Finally, his head snapped up. "This isn't a copy of *Aristarmy's Logic*, is it? It's the original! How in the Fields of Limpoor did you get your hands on this?"

"Original, you say? That's why the reagent was so upset he lost it," said Mannix.

"Lost it?"

"Let's just say the reagent may be a wonderful strategist on the battlefield, but he is a lousy four card roll player." Mannix laughed.

The duke sneered. "I see. Well, no matter. This book deserves a good home with an owner that would never gamble it away."

"I thought you might like it," said Mannix. "Now, to other business..."

The duke held up his hand, then grabbed a tiny bell off his desk. There was a soft tinkling sound followed by the immediate arrival of a servant. "Frend, please inform those at the library a page is needed to acquire this volume. They will know what to do with it. Young Jaxson, would you like to tag along? If you think my private office has many books, the library will astonish you."

"I would love to see the library. Can I read the books as well?"

"Of course, my boy. After all, books are written so they can be read," replied the duke.

Jaxson fell in behind Frend with a large grin on his face. If the book he sought was indeed here at the castle, the library was the most likely spot.

CHAPTER 15

Jaxson had to run from time to time to keep up with the long, purposeful strides of the servant, Frend. They left the castle proper through a different side door than what he had entered. Having to concentrate so hard on keeping up with his guide, he was almost at the marble base of the library before he realized it. Seven steps ran the full length of the large building, leading up to the large columns in front of two tall, dark wooden doors. On either side stood a stone dragon three times Jaxson's height. The first had horns similar to Zero's, separating in a half-moon before coming back close enough to almost touch. The second had a single horn that was long and straight. It reminded Jaxson of the fabled creatures known as unicorns. Above each dragon was a different word in a language he did not recognize.

As they approached the front doors, he asked Frend about the inscriptions.

"The dragon on your left with two horns is named Vigilance, and the other with the single horn is named Patience," said Frend without slowing.

"What language are the words written in?"

Frend sighed deeply as he reached for the door handles. "It is unknown. In fact, it is actually only legend that names these old stone dragons. The library predates the castle by hundreds if not thousands of years."

Jaxson opened his mouth, but before any more questions came out, Frend held up his free hand. "Any other inquiries will need to be handled by our head librarian. He is the expert in such matters after all."

Jaxson nodded and passed through the open door. He found himself in a small room with a desk and two high-backed chairs behind it. Frend pressed a large coin into his palm and quickly departed before Jaxson could make sense of it. He looked around at the bare walls and then approached the desk. The only item present was a small bell with a note that read, *For Service, Ring the Bell.*

Jaxson lightly shook the bell and before he had replaced it on the desk, an old man appeared from a doorway to the right. Bent and stooped, the librarian shuffled toward the desk at a determined but slow pace. A long coat with fur around the shoulders dragged along the floor behind him. Jaxson attempted to peer through the open doorway, hoping to see where the old man was waiting to have appeared so quickly. All he saw were bookshelves neatly packed with rows and rows of books. The old man stopped behind the desk. He reached out a wrinkled hand and raised his eyebrows.

"Oy, you must need this coin Frend gave me," said Jaxson, extending the token forward.

"Let's have a look-see, shall we?"

Deceptively nimble fingers whisked the coin from Jaxson, and with a flourish, he bounced it up and down along his fingers before it landed in his palm. He squinted at the coin briefly and handed it back to Jaxson. "A guest of the duke, eh?"

Jaxson nodded. The old man continued, "You have a name?"

"I am Jaxson Alpine, sir."

"Pleased to make your acquaintance. My name is William, and I am the head librarian. I assume you have been made aware of the rules of the library?"

Jaxson looked side to side and tried to remember if he was told any specifics on his way. Frend had been evasive about the library, although he did point out many other pointless details such as the origin of the stones of the keep. "Uh, no. I don't know the rules."

William chuckled and patted Jaxson's back as he guided him through the door into the main book room. "I am not surprised. Frend does not talk much about nor stay very long in the library after his fiasco in one of the study rooms with Mannix. No matter. The rules are quite simple. First and foremost, open flame is not allowed in the main room here. There are candles provided in each study; I only ask you do not remove them from their holders. The high sides are designed to contain the fire should the candle fall over. The second rule is nothing leaves the library with you that you did not bring in. Other than that, do you require assistance, or are you just here to meander?"

Jaxson stared at row upon row of neatly lined bookshelves leading to stairs that climbed to the second and third floors with balconies overlooking the first. Finally, his eyes caught the skylight high above that sent rays to waiting mirrors illuminating the whole building. It was a wonderfully imaginative setup that Jaxson did not fully understand. Even if the book he sought was on these shelves, it would take a lifetime of lifetimes to find it on his own.

"Well..." Jaxson started, trying to collect his thoughts. "I would like to learn about the history of the dragonriders of old."

William again laughed softly. "You seek old knowledge. It will take some time to gather the histories by Gallau, Kingsley, and others."

"I don't really know how long I have in the library or even at the castle for that matter."

"In the meantime, do you have a more contemporary subject you would like to research, or perhaps a witty exposition on the current political climate?"

"How about something on the Dragon Trials? I know

little about them," replied Jaxson with a shrug.

"Of course. I could tell right away you were not from this corner of the empire," said William as he winked at Jaxson.

"Is it that obvious?"

"Your accent is strange but could pass as a Willington Isles inflection. It is the feather in your hair, from a bee bird I assume, that gave you away. It is not a color or pattern I recognize, and I know most of the birds from this continent. Persail is the exhaustive resource on the subject and his work sits on my private desk all the time."

Reflexively, Jaxson grabbed at the feather woven into his hair. It was so easy to forget it was there, especially since he had not felt the presence of bee birds or any strange desires since coming through the portal. He had just assumed there were none of the birds nearby.

"Also, unless it is a huge coincidence, you have your feather braided into your hair in the fashion of the western elves not native to this continent," continued the old man.

"Are you knowledgeable about the elves?"

"As much as books can tell me. But you have to be careful and discern the truth, for even the greatest historians can contradict each other about ancient times or faraway places," said William. "Now if you will retire to that study room there, I will bring you several great books on the Dragon Trials covering both results and a history in general."

"Thank you."

Jaxson waited patiently in the plush chair for the books he requested. He didn't know how to ask for the book he sought. Maybe there would be a mention of it in the histories the librarian was providing. Meanwhile, it couldn't hurt to learn more about the Dragon Trials he had volunteered for. At a knock on the door, he looked up to see a young boy, perhaps eight to ten years old, come into his study room balancing a stack of books taller than himself.

"Where would you like them, m'lord?"

It took Jaxson a moment to realize the boy was talking to him. "Right, put them on the table there. And I'm not a lord."

After expertly transferring the stack of books to the side table, the boy turned back to Jaxson. "Yes sir, m'lord. If you need anything else on the subject, please ring the bell."

And as quickly as he had appeared, the boy was gone, leaving behind a plethora of reading materials on the Dragon Trials. *At least I won't be bored,* Jaxson thought before grabbing the book on top of the stack and settling in to read.

CHAPTER 16

Jaxson looked back and forth between two of the many open volumes on the table. He shook his head and grabbed a dusty blue book and quickly thumbed through it until he found the desired passage. As he read, he threw his hands in the air and shot to his feet. *It just doesn't make sense. Why is there so much inconsistency about the early Dragon Trials?*

Perhaps no one you are reading now was there to record it personally. They are only writing the history as they have heard it, said Zero.

Maybe, thought Jaxson. Then with a jolt, he asked Zero, *How long have we been talking? I didn't even realize it.*

Not for long. But it is very late, and you must be tired.

It's late?

Jaxson stretched, and with it, his knees popped and an ache developed in his back. He had no idea what time it was or how long he had been reading. At first, he enjoyed reading about the trials and their results. The different events, ranging from races to strength tests to accuracy of riders' archery, were exciting and fun. The most recent trials were chronicled in great detail in several different books, but the older trials, although mentioned in many texts, were vague and the accounts differed wildly.

It is close to midnight, Jaxson.

Wow. I don't even know where my room is located. Where are you staying?

There is a large cavern just north of the castle. The other dragons and I are holed up there at the steward of the castle's

198

direction, said Zero.

Jaxson stretched again and started to get feeling back into his legs. He looked out of the study into the eerie darkness of the library. *If I can't find anyone to tell me where to go, I'll come to you.*

I'll come get you. Just let me know.

He left the books open and spread out across the table with hopes of returning the next morning to pick up where he left off. The only light in the cavernous main library came from the two far ends with just a sliver of moonlight streaming in from the skylight. Just as he stepped into the gloom of the larger room, the boy that delivered his books earlier in the day materialized in front of him.

"M'lord, will you be needing an escort to the exit?"

Jaxson jumped and raised his hands before realizing it was only the boy. "You scared me. And yes, I would love help getting out of the library."

"Follow me then, m'lord."

The boy turned on his heel and started a brisk walk toward the exit, hugging the wall of the library. Jaxson fell in behind him, but his mind was still on the books left behind in the study. "Will the books I was reading remain in the study overnight?"

"If that is your wish, m'lord."

"That would be perfect. And my name is Jaxson. You don't have to call me my lord."

"Yes sir, m'lord. I mean, Jaxson," said the boy, glancing at Jaxson out of the corner of his eye.

"That's better. Do you enjoy working in the library?"

"I do, m'lo—Jaxson. William, the librarian, treats us well. He taught all of us that work with the books to read," replied the boy.

"Do you ever get a chance to read?"

"Loads. My room is just below the main floor here, and

William allows us two books in our room at all times."

"William seems like a great man."

"He is. If the duke knew we had books down there…"

"Would he be upset?"

The boy again glanced at him briefly before he responded. "Yes sir. Ever since the fire, no one is allowed to remove books from the library at all. It's hard for most people to gain access to the books at all."

"Well, I feel lucky then," said Jaxson as they approached the exit to the library. "Will you be here tomorrow?"

"I will be around m'lord," said the boy with a grin. "Just ask for me."

"I would, but I don't know your name."

"My name is Mika, m'lord. Goodnight," said Mika before he scampered back into the library, leaving Jaxson alone in the front room where he had met William hours earlier.

Jaxson wondered at the coincidence of meeting two boys in two towns separated by a large sea and both being named Mika. He shook his head. He would need some rest and maybe something to eat before contemplating such wild chances. Right then, he needed to focus his thoughts on finding a place to rest. As he stepped out into the cool night air, he was again greeted by a familiar face.

"Shall I escort you to your quarters, sir?" asked Frend.

"Have you been waiting here the entire time?"

"Heavens no. I have entirely too much to do to be loitering around the entrance to the library all night," replied Frend.

"Then how did you… Never mind. Yes, I would love to get some rest. Lead on."

CHAPTER 17

Jaxson awoke the next morning in a small but comfortable room with the sunlight streaming through the open window. He wiggled deeper into the down mattress, the first one he had ever slept in. *This bed alone was worth coming to the castle for, let alone the library,* Jaxson said to Zero.

I am glad you rested well. I think we are going to have a busy day, replied Zero.

What do you mean?

It seems we are going to have a training day. From what Brunt said this morning, it is not a sure thing for the duke to give Mannix the invitation. There is another group that it may already be promised to, said Zero.

Jaxson forced himself out of the warm embrace of the luxurious mattress. No sooner than his feet had hit the floor, a knock sounded on his door followed by Mannix's large body bursting in.

"Good, you're already sunny side up," barked Mannix. "I was afraid I was gonna have to pry you out of bed. Get dressed and come to my room for breakfast. Third door down on the left."

Mannix wheeled around and was out the door before Jaxson even had time to reply or ask any questions. *You must be right. Mannix seems anxious to get the day started.*

I'll see you soon. But first, I am going to stretch my wings for a bit.

A large yawn and a huge stretch kept Jaxson near his bed. He brushed his fingers across the soft fabric and shook his head. No time for laziness. He had to see what Mannix needed and try to get down to the library too. He dressed quickly and was out the door in no time, headed toward Mannix's room and a big, hopefully huge, breakfast.

****

After a giant belch, Jaxson was able to keep up with Salvia and Tephra as they jogged out of the castle gates toward a large open field. Zero said that all the dragons, as well as Mannix, were already waiting for them on the far side. He could not remember a time he felt fuller. He had eaten the normal staples: eggs and bacon along with some small, diced potatoes. But there had also been some hash with peppers and some biscuits with a spicy cheese mixed in that were delicious. He should have stopped after his first plate but definitely after his second. He reached down to his pocket and felt the bulge of biscuits waiting to be consumed later and smiled. They were so good.

The siblings did not know what they were doing any more than he did. Mannix had left them shortly after Jaxson had arrived to his room with orders to eat and proceed directly to the dragon training field. Salvia speculated they were going to start preparing for the trials although what that would consist of, she had no idea. Tephra just shrugged and continued on not worrying about things outside of his control. When Jaxson asked if they might be leaving early because of tensions between Mannix and the duke, Salvia laughed. She explained those two were always arguing about one thing or another for as long as she had known them.

"No, we aren't leaving. I'm not sure exactly what Mannix is up to, but I imagine it is about the trials," said Salvia as she hurried across the field.

Tephra simply nodded so Jaxson asked, "Maybe it's about getting the invitation the duke has?"

"Won't know till we get over there. Do you see the

dragons yet?"

The field was crowned ever so slightly so the group of riders could not see the distant side until they had traveled halfway across it. From the center, they spotted the dragons resting another few hundred yards away. All of them except Brunt. He was flying low to the ground with Mannix on his back, swerving in and out of large poles standing in a haphazard pattern. Jaxson admired how the large man stayed low to his dragon's back and moved and swayed with each turn and alteration Brunt made as they darted through the poles. As they approached, Jaxson saw it was more than poles. A whole obstacle course of dragon-sized rings, poles, walls, and bridges were set up over the acres of land.

Brunt landed in front of them, and Mannix slid off with agility, surprising Jaxson that he could do so with his girth. Salvia clapped, and even Tephra smiled and whooped.

"Brunt seems in great form! You two were blasting through the course," said Salvia.

"It felt good for sure, but we don't have time for cheering. We have work to do," replied Mannix. "As you can see, there is a full obstacle course for you and your dragons to master. Brunt and I have some stuff to do, but we'll be back before the midday meal. Make the most of your time."

Salvia grinned and bounced softly on the balls of her feet. Tephra rolled his head and stretched his arms, getting limber for his first flight on the course. Jaxson laughed. This was going to be fun.

Come and get me. Let's give this course a run, said Jaxson to Zero.

Zero shot off the ground. Within two great beats of his wings, he was before Jaxson. *Yes. Let's fly.*

CHAPTER 18

Hours later, Jaxson's chest heaved as he stood beside a winded Zero. Even after several attempts, they had not been able to complete the obstacle course straight through, but they were getting closer.

Zero had mastered winding through the poles, angling his body and turning rapidly to snake through the jagged line as quickly as possible. Jaxson leaned close to his back and moved with his dragon best friend without conscious thought. Next came the rings that required a reverse loop to go through each of the six hoops without steering off course. Jaxson had not been prepared the first time Zero attempted the maneuver and had nearly slipped out of the harness, causing Zero to veer off course. By their third run at the rings, Jaxson had it figured out.

Once out of the rings, the course turned down into a deep trough riddled with rocks and obstacles. Again, it took Jaxson and Zero several runs to find the optimal line through the dips and turns while avoiding boulders and trees. And doing all that while maintaining a high speed kept both of them concentrating and working hard. It was after the canyon near the three bridges and lone tower that the duo could not seem to find the correct path and speed to stay on course. It was the final section of the route, which so far seemed insurmountable.

I just don't see how we can make it under the last bridge and then shoot up quick enough to go over the tower, said Jaxson.

Zero, still breathing hard, took a moment to reply. *It is obvious trying to scale the western side of the tower will not work. Perhaps we need to pass the tower and corkscrew our way to the top?*

That could work. Here comes Nalla. Let's see how her and Salvia's run went.

Salvia sat atop her small, gray dragon as they slowly descended to land softly in front of Jaxson and Zero. Her hair, secured in a long ponytail, hung down the side of her face, partially obscuring one dimple caused by her huge smile. Jaxson's face heated as he extended a hand to help her off of Nalla. She laughed softly before grasping the offered hand and slipping down the dragon's smooth scales.

"That canyon run is amazing! Nalla shot through it this time," said Salvia as she lovingly rubbed behind Nalla's ears.

"Have you tried the bridges and the tower yet?"

"No, we struggled with the rings," said Salvia. Then in a mock whisper she continued, "I couldn't stay in the harness at first. Nalla has never done that type of flying before, and I was a little shy."

"Glad you have it straight now. How is Tephra doing? I haven't seen him all morning."

Salvia sighed and looked out toward the course. "He and Yammer breezed through the course on their first run. They have been at the front trying different routes through the pillars ever since."

Jaxson glanced back to the beginning of the training course. Yammer was darting in and out of the pillars before rising high above. As he watched, the dragon circled slowly and then started flying in their direction.

"Looks like he is on the way over here now."

As soon as Yammer's feet touched the soft grass, Tephra slid off pointing back toward the castle. Both Salvia and Jaxson turned to see several men on horseback galloping to meet them.

"Wonder what this could be about?" asked Salvia.

The three riders met the approaching horsemen halfway. Jaxson noticed Caffer, the dignitary that first greeted them upon their arrival, and Frend were leading the way. There was not a single smile in the group of men as they brought their horses to a stop in front of them.

"What is happening?" asked Salvia.

Caffer finally smiled, though it didn't reach his eyes. "The duke has asked for you to return to the castle immediately."

"Why?"

"It is enough that he wishes for it, but if you must know, the duke and his brother have had a disagreement. I believe you will be leaving upon your return to the castle," replied Caffer.

Salvia's mouth moved but no words came out. Frend moved his horse forward and said, "It may not be as serious as all of that, but your presence at the castle is required. Please mount one of the available horses. Your dragons can return to their caves at their own convenience."

"But..."

"Let's go see what all of this is about," said Jaxson before Caffer could speak again.

Salvia nodded, and all three mounted a horse. Frend turned his mount around toward the castle. Without another word, they rode for the castle stables, leaving the training yard behind before midday.

CHAPTER 19

Once at the castle, they were quickly ushered through the stone hallways. In short time, they were herded into the duke's office where Mannix and the duke stood on opposite sides of the large desk. The men were staring at each other. Mannix's neck and face were beet red, and a slight sheen of sweat clung to his brow. The duke looked equally agitated with a scowl locked onto his face. The two brothers did not seem to notice the new arrivals.

"I don't care why you thought it was a good idea to confront William! There was no reason to have an open flame near the books!" shouted the duke.

"Quit going back to what happened months ago. You are just using that incident as an excuse. You knew I wanted the invitation to the trials, and you gave it to someone else!"

The duke looked down for a brief moment then back at his older brother. "I did. I wanted someone that would represent this castle with dignity and respect. A true dragon knight, not a drunkard with a flying lizard!"

Mannix's face darkened from red to crimson. His fists balled, and his whole body shook. Before he could respond, Frend interjected. "Gentlemen, guests have arrived."

Both the duke and Mannix turned quickly to Frend, and then finally noticed their arrival. The duke blushed, and Mannix let out a large breath. The one-eyed man seemed to cool considerably in a short time. Salvia approached Mannix and said, "We knew it was not a guarantee."

"It should have been," replied Mannix as he glanced at

his blushing brother.

"After you meet Knight Tallyverse, I think you will agree he will carry the banner of Castle Beauxgrand with honor," said the duke.

Mannix completely unwound. His shoulders slumped and his chest deflated. "So, you are not going to kick us out this time?"

"Not just yet," said the duke with a small laugh. "The knight should arrive this evening. We will celebrate before sending him and his team off for the Dragon Trials. You and your friends are invited."

Mannix began to respond, but Salvia cut him off. "Thank you, Duke. We would be honored."

Frend approached the group and directed them back into the hallway. After giving them instructions to be prompt for the dinner celebration, he told them to resume whatever activities would keep them away from the duke. Mannix attempted to object, but Frend wouldn't let him.

"The duke's mind is decided. Arguing will only widen the gap between you two. For now, be the good brother and support the duke's decision. It is not the last Dragon Trials of all time, you know?"

"I can't support the decision, but I will keep my mouth shut until I meet this so-called dragon knight," replied Mannix before storming off. Jaxson started to follow, but Tephra stopped him. Mannix turned the corner of a hallway and was gone.

Frend sighed. "Do you three require any assistance?"

"No thank you, Frend," said Salvia. "Tephra and I are going to the archery range then back to the dragon obstacle course. Jaxson, are you joining us?"

Jaxson thought for a moment. "No, I think I'm going back to the library."

****

Jaxson's return to the library was uneventful at first. He was greeted by William in the vestibule again. As the head librarian escorted him to the private study he had previously occupied, Jaxson finally asked about the book he sought.

"Have you ever come across an old book about training dragonriders?"

William glanced at him out of the corner of his eye but kept shuffling forward. "I have heard tales of ancient texts written by the dragonriders of old for their students. However, I have never seen one."

Jaxson was quiet for a moment. "Do these tales say where one could be found today?"

"If they once contained that type of information, they do not now. These tales mostly mention the *scoutians*—that's the word for book of knowledge in the old tongue, in passing only."

They arrived at the study, and Jaxson thanked William for the escort and the information. "And by the way, where is Mika today?"

"He is around. He has too many duties for too many people, I am afraid," replied William before turning and beginning the slow walk back to the front of the library.

The study remained as he had left it the night before. Jaxson dropped into one of the padded chairs circling the table and grabbed the closest book. Within seconds, he was sucked into the telling of the one hundred and eleventh Dragon Trials. He noticed nothing else around him as he experienced the daring come-from-behind victory of Atlan and his dragon Bravo.

CHAPTER 20

Jaxson's fingers clenched the cover of the book as Bravo skirted the falling rocks of the canyon. Then Atlan threw a magic pulse shattering an outcrop of jagged stone. Atlan was the favorite coming into his third trials but had fallen behind early in the final race. Jaxson eagerly consumed the words on the page in anticipation of another Atlan victory.

"Sir. Sir!" interrupted a servant.

Jaxson started slamming the book and nearly fell out of his chair. He collected himself and sat straight in his chair before acknowledging the young man.

"It is nearly time for the celebratory dinner hosted by the duke," said the servant.

Jaxson's stomach rumbled at the mention of a meal. He had not realized just how hungry he had become. When was the last time he had eaten? He could not recall. "Right, of course. I just need to change my clothes. I smell of dragon and sweat."

"As you say, sir. Shall I escort you?"

Jaxson waved him off as he stood and stretched. "I can manage on my own. Thank you."

"Do hurry, sir. You do not want to be late. The duke frowns on tardiness," replied the servant before turning on his heel and disappearing into the halls of the library.

Jaxson left the library at a jogging pace. He turned left away from the castle. If he went the shorter route through the grounds, he would be forced to navigate through the many halls and stairwells before making it to his room. He chose to run around the outside of the castle to the smaller gate near the gardens and right beneath his rooms. He would be winded upon his arrival but would save much needed time.

Almost to the gate near the giant wall that surrounded the castle, Jaxson spotted Mika skulking out of an alley with a huge pack on his back. Before Jaxson could ask him what he was doing, he spotted two men in dark clothes peel away from the shadowy alley wall and tail the young library page. The men were large and the dark cloaks did little to conceal the bulge of their armor and weapons. Instead of calling out to Mika, Jaxson decided to follow and look for a more opportune time to intervene.

As Mika approached a small hill that hid a stream on the other side, the two stalking men picked up their pace. Jaxson knew it was time to act. He sprinted around the hill and made it to the small bridge spanning the stream just as Mika came over the hill. Jaxson grabbed the boy and shoved him roughly under the bridge

"What are you—" started Mika before Jaxson gestured for him to be quiet. "M'lord?"

"You are being followed," said Jaxson. He expected Mika to be surprised or scared or both.

The boy simply asked, "How many?"

Jaxson smiled. "I only saw two."

"Tall and dressed in black with big swords?"

"That's right. They should be coming over the hill any moment," said Jaxson as he pointed in the direction Mika had come from.

At that very instant, four men—not just the original two anymore—dressed in black cloaks crested the hill. They stopped short of the bridge and looked about. One of them, clearly their leader, gave orders for the other three to spread out and keep going. He turned and went back the way he had come.

Jaxson and Mika waited in silence until there was no sign or sound from the dark cloaked men. Mika gestured for Jaxson to come close. "We must be quick and quiet. Follow me."

Mika bounded up onto the bridge and trotted silently to a cross street. Jaxson expected him to head toward the castle or double back and run to the town. Instead, he entered a small shack butting up against the exterior wall. Once inside, he immediately led Jaxson downstairs into a dirty and cramped basement. Mika shoved some barrels away, revealing a secret doorway.

Jaxson followed Mika into a narrow passage and then up a ladder into another storeroom at ground level. "Where are we going?"

"Shhhh!"

"But—"

"Not now. Quiet!" Mika whispered urgently. Mika peered out of a dusty glass window for a while. Finally, he said, "Think we lost them."

Jaxson moved in close to Mika to peer out of the window as well. The castle was not in sight. In fact the only thing he could see was a ragged inn and an old, bricked-up gate. Mika led them out into the street and then entered the dilapidated inn.

Once inside, Mika did not stop or speak to anyone. He went directly to the backroom and pushed aside more barrels, revealing yet another secret tunnel. After several twists and turns and one ladder climb, they arrived in a long but narrow room. Men and women were sitting at desks that lined the room writing as fast as they could. Before Jaxson could ask any questions, a knife appeared at his throat.

CHAPTER 21

Jaxson's heart pounded as the sharp edge of the blade moved slightly on his neck. A tiny rivulet of blood ran down to his shirt. He didn't know if Mika set him up, or if this was even worse and the cloaked men were already here. Zero suddenly intruded on his thoughts.

I am on my way! Tell me exactly where you are, said the dragon in Jaxson's head.

I'm not sure exactly where I am. Near the high wall surrounding the castle, replied Jaxson. He looked around the room again searching for clues to their whereabouts. There were no windows or any other doors. It was simply a long, straight, stone room. Then it hit him. *We are in the wall. The room Mika led me to is in the castle wall.*

I will tear it down if I must.

Voices from behind Jaxson caught his attention.

"So, Mika, did you lose them then?" asked an old voice.

"Yes sir. And I have the requested books in my sack," replied the young boy.

Even through his fear, Jaxson could not understand why Mika was taking books from the library. And that voice... He felt like he should know who it belonged to. He just could not quite put his finger on it. Mika began passing out the books from his sack to those seated at the desks all around the room. Some pushed their papers aside and started copying the new book on clean paper. Others continued scribbling away as fast as possible without even appearing to notice Mika had dropped a book on their desk.

The voice talked louder as Mika moved away from him. "Good, good. But it appears you have been compromised."

Mika shrugged. "Maybe. I don't see how I could have been. Maybe they just got lucky."

"Perhaps. It is possible it was by accident they started on your trail. They could have been looking for someone else altogether," said the voice. Jaxson still could not place it. "Now, what are we going to do with you, young Jaxson?"

The knife dug into Jaxson's neck as he stammered an incoherent reply.

The voice, getting closer to Jaxson now, said, "Calm down now. It's not all that serious. Vernan, put the knife away. See, Jaxson, we mean you no harm."

Jaxson's mouth gaped, and he made small noises, again unable to speak. This time it was the shock of seeing William standing before him, the voice belonging to him.

"But I do need your assurance that you can keep our little secret we have here," said William with a small smile.

Jaxson looked around at all the people at the desks. He didn't understand. Were they just copying books? It did not make sense to him, but finally, he spoke. "I cannot promise to keep your secret completely until I know what it is. I have no idea what is going on here."

William laughed. "Of course, let me explain."

Hiding knowledge was the term William used to describe the duke's actions, making the library inaccessible to most people. It had not always been that way, but increasingly over the years as the duke's fascination in old books turned to obsession, he became possessive of the books and in turn, the knowledge within. The old librarian had tried to reason with the duke, had begged him to reconsider and allow access to the library. But nothing could alter the duke's mind. He was convinced the knowledge was too dangerous for most people.

"Too dangerous?" asked Jaxson.

With a heavy sigh, William responded, "I am afraid so. He does not believe most men can handle the power of books, or more specifically the knowledge within, give them."

Jaxson frowned. "I don't understand."

"I'm not sure I do either," said William. "But the fact remains that the duke limited library access to only those at his invitation. The religious sects are banned. Almost every historian has been turned away even though this library has been the center of historical writing for over a century! I had to do something."

"So, you are taking books from the library and copying them? Then what?"

"Then the ever more difficult part. Getting books to those that need them without tipping off the duke. It is quite an intricate problem," said William. "One which we have not completely solved just yet."

When Jaxson looked around the narrow room again, he focused on the piles of books and paper instead of the people. There was organization to the chaos. Books stacked neatly near the door ready to go back to the library. Piles of finished copies on bookshelves waiting for their covers. It was quite the process they had going here.

"I see no reason to tell anyone about what I have seen here. Though, I must say, if asked directly, I do not know if I would be able to lie about this," said Jaxson. The librarian's eyes furrowed so Jaxson continued quickly. "I get why you are doing it, and I even agree. My time spent in the library has been amazing, and I think everyone should get that opportunity. But if the duke asks me directly, I'm just not sure I could be dishonest."

William sighed. "Then, I am tasking you with ensuring he does not ask you about what is going on here. Avoid conversations with the duke, and if you get caught up with him, steer the topic of conversation away from books as best you can."

"I do believe I can promise you that," replied Jaxson. "But can I ask a favor of you in return?"

"You can certainly ask."

Jaxson thought for a moment. "I was sent to this land in search of knowledge contained in a book myself. A book that helped the dragonriders of old become the mighty forces they were. Could you help me find it?"

William took several steps away from Jaxson and stared across the long room. Long moments passed, and Jaxson began to wonder if William was going to answer him at all.

"I do not believe a book such as that exists. It may have long ago but no longer. I have researched the ancient dragonriders thoroughly, and the one thing I can say for sure is there is no way everything they had to learn could fit in one book...maybe not even one library," said William.

"So, you think it is a lost cause? My search for this book?"

"I think, young Jaxson, the book you seek is within you. You just need to let it out," said William. "Now, I must be going, and so should you. You have a dinner celebration to attend, do you not?"

Jaxson's eyes grew wide. He had completely forgotten about the duke's party to celebrate the arrival of the dragonriders he was sending to the trials. Mannix was going to be furious with him.

"I do need to leave, and fast," said Jaxson. He looked around, trying to gain his bearing. "Though it would help if someone pointed me in the right direction."

"Mika here will escort you back to familiar territory, but if you don't mind me saying, you should probably freshen up a bit before dinner even if you are late," said William with a smile. "You look as though you have spent a week on the back of a dragon without a bath."

CHAPTER 22

Dusk had come and gone as Mika pointed Jaxson to the shortest route to his room. Jaxson rushed, knowing even with running he was going to be extremely late for dinner. Hopefully, dessert was still on the table by the time he arrived.

In his room, he splashed water on his face from the basin in the corner and threw on a clean shirt. He talked to Zero explaining all that had transpired with Mika and William. Zero was interested but also seemed distracted.

What is going on? asked Jaxson.

I am not sure. There is some type of commotion outside our keep. I'm sure it is nothing to concern us, replied Zero. *Now, you need to get to that dinner.*

I certainly do. Leaving my room now.

He was running, not concerned about castle etiquette, trying to get to the grand hall as quickly as possible. He was only a few turns away when he crashed into Tephra with Salvia right behind him. As soon as Salvia stopped laughing, she helped both of them off the floor.

"Why aren't you two at the dinner?" asked Jaxson.

"We were just there. Didn't you hear?" asked Salvia.

"Hear what?"

"The dragon knight, Sir Tallyverse, finally arrived late, but he was all bloody and beat up," said Salvia. "The duke kicked everyone out of the hall immediately."

"What happened to him?"

"We're not sure, but before the duke sent everyone out, I

heard Knight Tallyverse shouting about being attacked. The group of dragonriders that were with him for the trials were all captured...or worse."

"Captured? Or worse? By who?" asked Jaxson all at once.

"I don't know," said Salvia. She glanced to her brother, who just shrugged. "Does the who really matter as much as the *attacked the group of riders with four dragons and kicked their butts part?*"

"I guess you're right. Though I wonder if it's the same group that attacked us?"

Again, Tephra shrugged, and Salvia didn't have a response.

"Where is Mannix?" asked Jaxson.

"He was right behind us. I don't know where he went off to," replied Salvia. "Maybe up to his room or out with the dragons?"

"I'll ask Zero," replied Jaxson. *Is Mannix with you dragons?*

No, but there is a new dragon here. She is injured quite severely. Come to me.

"Knight Tallyverse's dragon is hurt. I'm going to help Zero," said Jaxson. "If you see Mannix, tell him where I am."

"For all the tiny gods' love..." groaned Salvia. She looked at her brother, who nodded. Salvia turned back to Jaxson. "We are coming with you."

Jaxson and the siblings rushed to the dragon keep as quickly as possible. A small, reddish-brown dragon lay at the entrance. Blood soaked the surrounding straw and puddled in the corner of the keep. If the dragon was breathing, it was slight.

To me, now! shouted Zero in Jaxson's head.

"I'm here. Where do you need me?"

On the other side of her chest. The laceration there looks to be the most severe, replied Zero.

Jaxson positioned himself precisely where directed and placed his hands on the smaller dragon's scales. She was cool to the touch, too cool. *I think we need to hurry.*

Yes. Are you ready?

With a nod, Jaxson braced for the influx of magic Zero was set to deliver through the injured dragon. His fingers tingled for a moment, then grew more intense. Soon, he was flooded with Zero's power. He held it as long as he could, filling himself up to the bursting point. At that moment, Zero stopped and immediately Jaxson knew it was time to send it back through the injured dragon to him.

As the last bit of magic slipped down the tips of his fingers, the injured dragon finally raised her head and gave him a weak smile. Jaxson smiled back and slumped down to the floor. He was sweaty and tired down to his bones but was glad he and Zero had been able to help. Without knowing the true extent of her injuries, he could not say if she was fully healed, but she was certainly better. And that was good enough for right now.

I believe she will recover now, though it may be a bit of a process for her. There are many minor injuries that will linger, said Zero.

"That's great to hear," replied Jaxson. "Do you know her name?"

No. And now she needs to rest, not talk. Look, she is already asleep.

"I wouldn't mind a nap myse—"

Before Jaxson could finish, Mannix came bursting into the keep. "We need to fly, now!"

Salvia stepped away from the wall. "Why the rush, Mannix?"

Their large, one-eyed leader held up a folded piece of parchment. With an impish grin, he said, "Cause there's no need to give my brother a chance to find this. The invitation to the trials, I nicked it."

CHAPTER 23

Salvia gasped loud enough to startle both Jaxson and Zero. Then she said, "You did not steal the invitation!"

Still smiling like a drunken fool, Mannix shook his head. "Sure did. Now, let's get in the air."

"But Jaxson may not be able to fly right away."

The grin on Mannix's face slowly slipped away as he looked around the keep. His eyes first found the other dragons huddled along the wall watching the sleeping dragon in the middle of the floor. Then he followed the small river of blood slowly inching toward the keep's entrance. Finally, he locked eyes with Jaxson.

"What in the tiny gods…?"

Mannix did not finish the question. Instead, he stammered and glanced around again, his mouth gaping open. He shook his head and finally asked, "What happened here?"

Salvia gave a brief recap of the previous hour starting with running into Jaxson and concluding with him slumping over after healing the new dragon. Just as she finished and before Mannix could respond, Knight Tallyverse burst into the keep. He was breathing heavily and drenched in sweat.

"Ellandy! Ellandy, are you well?" shouted the haggard knight.

Tallyverse ran straight to the injured dragon's head. She lifted her eyelids briefly before closing them again with a

221

large sigh. Jaxson attempted to rise but stumbled. He was more sure-footed on his second attempt.

As Jaxson approached the knight, Tallyverse crumpled to the ground at the injured dragon's head. He sobbed and mumbled and then sobbed some more. Jaxson could not decipher what the knight was saying, but it soon became obvious it was a chant of some sort he was repeating over and over. With a great cry of anguish, the knight jumped to his feet.

Careful, Jaxson. She will recover, but it looks like he has lost it. Fear can cause good people to act irrationally, said Zero in Jaxson's head.

Maybe he will be better once she wakes, replied Jaxson.

Tallyverse wiped the tears from his face. "I am so glad to have made it before... Well, at least she won't have to die alone!"

Tallyverse jerked his sword free from the scabbard and placed the edge along his own neck. Jaxson's eyes widened as he realized what the knight meant to do. Before he could try to stop him, Salvia jumped onto the knight. Both crashed to the ground and the sword clattered away on the rocky floor. Tephra darted forward to secure the blade before the knight could harm them or himself.

"Why did you stop me? I am nothing without my dragon," cried Tallyverse.

"You won't be without your dragon, sir," said Jaxson.

"Boy, I saw the severity of her injuries those thugs with their sorcerer caused to sweet Ellandy. No, there is no chance she will survive, and I have nothing to live for without her," said Tallyverse as he gained his feet. "So, if you don't mind, I would like to finish what I started."

The knight reached for his sword that was still firmly in Tephra's grasp. Salvia jumped in front of him. "She is not going to die, you dolt! She is recovering from her injuries because of Jaxson and Zero's help."

Tallyverse paused, staring at Salvia with a blank look on his face. After several moments, he shook his head. "She is not going to die?"

"No! That's what Jaxson was trying to tell you. He and his dragon helped her!"

The knight looked to Jaxson who could only shrug and say, "The worst of her injuries have been knitted. I think she will recover with some rest."

Again, Ellandy opened her eyes and moved her head closer to Tallyverse. He dropped to his knees and embraced her, tears streaming down his face as he laughed. "You are alive! I don't believe it, but there you have it."

"Yes, yes. Your dragon will be in the air again in no time," said Mannix. "As for us, we need to get going now."

Salvia rolled her eyes and cut Jaxson off from replying. "As I have already told you, Jaxson is in no shape to fly even if Zero could handle it. We will have to wait until morning."

"But what if my brother—"

"Then it'll be your own fault for 'nicking' the invitation," said Salvia. "Now, Jaxson, do you wish to go back to the castle and rest?"

"No, I think I'll just go lie over there with Zero. I don't think it will take me long to fall asleep," said Jaxson.

Mannix, again flummoxed, stuttered and started until finally he said, "Fine. We will all stay out here with our dragons. But we leave at first light I tell ya, and not a moment after!"

As Jaxson settled down against Zero's warm side, Zero covered him with a large wing. He could hear small bits of the conversation between Salvia, Mannix, and Tephra. Something about how Mannix didn't appreciate being talked to like a servant after all he had done for her and her brother since they had been no taller than pygmy dragons. Tephra laughed, and Salvia, for her part at least, appeared to apologize.

Rest, Jaxson. Seems we start a long journey in the morning, said Zero.

"Yes, I think I will. You should too," he replied.

I shall, do not worry about me.

The last thing Jaxson noticed before the sweet darkness overtook him was the laughing, joyful sobs of Tallyverse and the humming of a lullaby from Ellandy. The tune was familiar from his distant past. Perhaps his dad had played it on his lute, or maybe his mother had sung it to him when he was small. He wasn't sure. He simply knew the melody made him feel warm and safe…and loved.

CHAPTER 24

"TO YOUR DRAGONS! To your dragons!" shouted a familiar voice through the predawn fuzz of just waking. Jaxson could not immediately place it.

He wiped the sleep from his eyes. "Is that Frend?"

Zero responded quickly. *It is. And something is very wrong.*

Jaxson's nose wrinkled as the overpowering smell of smoke assaulted it. Combined with Frend yelling and Zero's worried insistence, Jaxson jumped to his feet. His heart raced and sweat blossomed on his forehead. "What—"

A half-naked Mannix stormed up from the back of the dragon keep. "What's going on over here? Better yet, what is going on down there?"

Frend moved in front of the large, one-eyed man. "Nothing to concern you, sir. Now, everyone mount their dragons and fly. I would suggest south as a good bearing to take."

Jaxson, Salvia, and Tephra started to pack and ready their dragons for a flight. Mannix stood with his hands on his hips and stared at Frend. Significantly calmer than before, he said, "You spill it, or I'm marching down to the castle right now to find out for myself."

Frend sighed. "Your brother, the great man that he is, made some enemies. Hold now!" He held up his hands to stop Mannix from dashing toward the exit of the dragon caves. "He is safe and away from any hostility. He just seeks the safety of his brother and his brother's friends."

"I'll bet he does!" screamed Mannix. He started to push

forward again before Frend continued.

"He knows you have the invitation to the trials."

Mannix stammered at this revelation. He shuffled his feet and rubbed one hand through his long beard. "Well... umm..."

"Your brother loves you and knows why you seek to win the trials," said Frend. "He wishes you well on your quest."

Again, the large man could not respond, so Frend continued, "You and your dragons should already be a mile south by now."

Mannix looked from side to side. Suddenly, he announced, "You heard the man. Let's ride!"

Everyone scrambled to finish preparations. Tephra finished harnessing his dragon and moved on to Salvia's. Salvia stuffed shirts, blankets, and anything else close into her sack. Mannix dressed quickly and tossed biscuits to everyone telling them to eat up as there would be no stops for some time. Jaxson was the first on his dragon and took to the air. Several dragons were weaving in and out of the smoke rising above the fields to the north and west of the castle. The castle itself was unmolested, so it did stand to reason the duke had managed to find safety.

Mannix and his dragon joined them as Tephra and Salvia trailed behind. They set a quick but not wing-tearing pace south and a little east. Mannix was redirecting the group more south when Tallyverse appeared in the middle of them.

"Where are we going?" Tallyverse shouted.

Mannix shook his head. "What in the tiny gods' kingdoms are you doing?"

The dragon knight shrugged. "Along for the ride," he said. Then he pointed back to the castle. "There is nothing left for me back there."

Jaxson watched Mannix carefully, gauging his reaction. After several long moments, Mannix threw his hands in the air and laughed. "Can your ol' girl keep up with her injuries?"

Tallyverse patted his dragon's side. "We can manage."

"That's fine then," replied Mannix.

****

The warm wind blew on Jaxson's face as the group of dragons and their riders flew south well past midday. Mannix and Tephra alternated doubling back to check for any pursuit, though it became increasingly unlikely with each passing moment. When Mannix had determined they were safe, he motioned for everyone to land in the next clearing.

As soon as everyone was on the ground, Mannix barked orders about a quick meal, watering the dragons, and getting back in the air as soon as possible. It was clear that Ellandy was worn out, and the knight hovered near her while the others ate. Salvia, mouth full of cold cheese and bread, nodded toward the new duo. Everyone shuffled over, even Mannix though he did so with a grunt and an eye roll, to give Tallyverse some rations. After everyone had their fill, the conversation increased.

"So, what in the underworld happened back there?" asked Mannix.

"I have no idea, but it did not look good," said Salvia.

"Perhaps the duke has ran afoul of the emperor in some way. It does not take much to incur his wrath these days," replied Tallyverse.

Mannix shook his head. "I just can't see that. My brother is a louse. Of that there is no doubt. I wouldn't want him watching my back out in the wild, but politics is his game. And he is a master."

No one said anything to that and the silence stretched on. Until the knight said, "It could have been the same group that attacked me. That cult. What was their name?"

Jaxson's eyes grew wide. It seemed they were everywhere. He knew he was right before he even said their name. "The Demon Lizard Death Cult?"

"That's it! I have no idea what they were after other than our dragons," replied Tallyverse.

"I don't think they are after anything," said Jaxson.

"All right you lot, back in the air. Let's put a little distance between us and whoever they are," said Mannix.

Jaxson shook his head and then smiled. "How long until we make it to the trials?"

"It'll take a couple of weeks at a nice, leisurely pace," said Salvia. "Shorter if Mannix drives us like this the whole way there."

As the dragons pushed off from the ground, Jaxson noticed Ellandy had trouble. He wasn't the only one either.

"Set an easy pace, Mannix," said Salvia. She pointed back to the knight and his dragon.

Mannix snorted. "Why is he even here?" At Salvia's scowl, he backtracked. "All right, all right!"

Mannix led them higher to soar on the big winds where the noble ones always glided. They would be easier to spot, but it would also be much better for Ellandy to not have to pound her wings constantly.

They stopped well before dusk and settled down for the night near a loud stream and a huge rock outcropping. Even with all the excitement of the day and the revelation about the DLDC being everywhere, all Jaxson could think about was the rapidly approaching Dragon Trials. He fell asleep curled up next to Zero recounting some of the famous riders' heroic deeds.

CHAPTER 25

It had been a short flight the final morning of their trek down to the trials. The sun had not yet reached its midday zenith as Jaxson stretched and rubbed the top of Zero's head. It had been a long two weeks of flying, though more steady than urgent after putting some distance between them and the duke's castle. Jaxson started toward Mannix, Tephra and Tallyverse as they talked quietly just past where the dragons rested in the green field.

Before he took two steps, Salvia jostled him as she rushed to join the group. Jaxson's face reddened when she turned and smiled at him, giving him a little wink as well. Mannix scowled, and Tallyverse guffawed loudly.

Salvia moved beyond the group to get a closer look at the large tents and waving flags.

"You two have been spending significant amounts of time together, I have noticed," said Tallyverse to Jaxson.

"So? What of it?" replied Jaxson.

Again, Tallyverse laughed. Mannix's face appeared as though he had just eaten a bad berry.

"Oh, no reason," said Tallyverse. "Just thought it was worth mentioning, seeing how you are redder than an overripe spritemelon after she nudged you just now."

Mannix shook his head. "Enough of that dragon dung, Tallyverse. Come on, we need to present our invitation. And I could use something to eat that didn't come from a camp pot."

The large man spun on his heel, aiming for the biggest

tent Jaxson could see. He fell in behind Tephra and Tallyverse as Salvia jogged over to join Mannix at the front of the group. The closer they were to the tent, the more activity of all sorts increased. Many brown-robed men and women bustled about carrying platters of food or stacks of scrolls. They swarmed around the tent like stirred-up ants. Additional robed men were setting up another tent directly behind the main tent while some were breaking down smaller ones on either side.

Mannix led the group to a grand, ornate wooden desk long enough for three men to sit and work comfortably behind it. All three men were small and slight with pale skin and wispy hair. Mannix addressed the one in the middle, though it was the older one on the left that accepted the invitation.

"This all looks to be in order then. You may move along to the refreshment tent straight down the hill," the little man said in a high-pitched voice. "Someone will be along to escort your dragons to their keep."

Tallyverse and Salvia started down the hill until Mannix raised his hand. "We will get our dragons settled ourselves I think, before we seek to fill our bellies."

"As you wish. Riley will escort you and your dragons to your shared keep with…" He scrambled through some papers before saying, "Ah, the team from the Hidden Lakes region."

"Shared?! What in the tiny gods' sake is this?" erupted Mannix.

The small man tilted his head but offered no other reaction to Mannix's outburst. The official in the middle responded, "Yes. You are one of the last teams to arrive, and what's more, a staggering number of teams have answered the call this year. Many more than all of the most recent trials."

Jaxson had to jump to the side to allow Mannix to pass. Salvia indicated they should follow as Mannix stomped back to the dragons where an even smaller robed figure stood waiting.

Riley introduced herself as their guide to the dragon keep. Then she told them about how the food tent worked, as well as times to get the freshest meal or coldest drink. She said the last part with a wink to Mannix, who smiled for the first time since talking with the officials. As the riders and dragons followed Riley, she pointed out items of interest such as the unassuming tent of the oracle and the blacksmith's temporary forge. She warned them not to go to the south and east as those areas were strictly off-limits.

She did not stop talking even as they arrived at the stables. "And the opening ceremonies will last all day tomorrow. Other than the trials themselves, it is the greatest day ever. Keep your dragons here. My Sharim doesn't mind them but most of the horses are scared of them."

Jaxson looked at Mannix as Riley entered the wooden structure. The one-eyed man sighed and rubbed his hand through his hair. He wasn't used to not being able to get a word in.

A shiny, white horse-like creature trotted out the double doors. It had long folded wings tucked against its body and one long silver horn mounted on its head. Jaxson's eyes grew wide while his mouth dropped open.

"What is that?"

Salvia giggled. "What does it look like, mountain boy?"

"Well, I guess it looks like a unicorn, but unicorns haven't been seen in thousands of years. And they didn't have wings," said Jaxson. When Salvia just nodded, he continued, "So a pegasus then, but those aren't supposed to have a horn."

Salvia's grin grew. "So…"

Jaxson had a thought, but first he asked Zero. His dragon rumbled with laughter even before he finished telling him.

I don't think that is the correct answer, said Zero. *But you should say it anyway.*

Jaxson sighed. "Is it a pegacorn?"

Everyone, even Riley, erupted in laughter. Jaxson could even feel the other dragons joining in at his expense.

From the ground where she fell laughing, Salvia said, "A pegac—"

But she couldn't finish as another round of intense laughter took over.

Riley was the first to calm down. "Sharim is a cerapter from the high desert above Beourte. Though pegacorn is about right, it's just a silly word. Now, mount your dragons and follow us...or at least try!"

CHAPTER 26

Hours later, after the dragons had been tended to and their bellies were full, Jaxson, Salvia, and Tephra talked quietly in the keep as Mannix and Tallyverse were "seeing a man about a drake" down in the makeshift city. Jaxson had thought about it since they had left and still was unsure exactly what they were going to do. Obviously, they had no interest in an actual drake. Maybe?

A steady rhythm of metal scraping stone came from Tephra as he systematically sharpened first all of his knives then his short sword. Jaxson sat very still watching with unblinking eyes as Tephra raked his short sword down the gritty stone. When he suddenly stopped, Jaxson jumped.

Tephra smiled. "Would you like to learn how to use a sharpening stone?"

"Absolutely," replied Jaxson.

Jaxson took the supplied stone Tephra pulled from his pack. He copied the way Tephra held it at an angle down and away from himself. As he slid the blade of his knife down the stone, he noticed the sound was different. He tried again following the young man's demonstration. Still, the sound from his stone was different than that of Tephra's.

"Loosen your grip on your stone," said Tephra. "That will keep you from moving it. Only the blade should move at a steady pace."

This time his stone sounded more like Tephra's but still just not right.

"Spend some small coins next time we are in town

and have it done right," remarked Salvia from her lounging position across the small table. "You sound like you are dragging a cat across it instead of a knife."

Tephra frowned. "Don't listen to my sister. She does not have the patience to perfect the use of a sharpening stone."

As Jaxson was about to respond, all the dragons snapped their heads to the entrance of the keep. Jaxson covered his ears as loud screeches filled the cavern. Following the shrill noise, in flew long, four-winged dragons with their riders atop. With their slender bodies, they landed smoothly side-by-side. Salvia and Tephra did not move, but Jaxson rose as the riders slid off their dragons.

The riders, all of which were young women, were each suited with leather armor and had bows slung across their backs. Their hair was pulled back with a headband, a gemstone dangling from it to rest against the center of their foreheads. Immediately, three of the riders started taking care of the dragons while one walked toward them.

"They told me at the big tent that the girls and I were gonna be splitting this keep, but I was starting to think y'all weren't gonna make it in time," said the new rider. "Folks call me Gemma cause my real name is too hard to pronounce."

Gemma reached out a hand, and Jaxson shook it as Salvia and Tephra rose to their feet. Jaxson replied, "Nice to meet you. I'm Jaxson and this is Salvia and Tephra. We only just arrived this morning."

Gemma smiled, revealing one dimple on her round cheeks. "Cutting it close. We have been here almost a week practicing."

Salvia rolled her eyes. "We will be ready. Don't worry about that."

Gemma giggled and waved her hand. "I'm sure. It's only our first time. How many trials have you completed?"

The look in Salvia's eyes reminded Jaxson of when

Mannix had spilled the last of the stew at dinner before she got a bowl. Jaxson spoke up before she could respond. "It is our first time competing as well. I'll be honest, I'm not really sure what to expect. I have read about the infamous Dragon Trials, but I think it'll be different once I am actually competing in them."

With a deep, throaty growl, Salvia turned on her heel and marched deeper into the keep.

"Welp, guess I should get to it. Big day tomorrow," said Gemma. "See you around, Jaxson."

With that, she too turned and walked away, leaving Jaxson with his thoughts. Gemma was not beautiful in the traditional sense with her round face and big ears, but Jaxson found her to be confidently captivating. He didn't have long to ponder this, however. Mannix and Tallyverse returned from the makeshift city with strange news that kept them talking long into the night.

CHAPTER 27

The opening ceremonies for the Dragon Trials had always been a grand affair. During Jaxson's time in the library at Castle Beauxgrand, he had read of the great spectacles, of stunt-flying dragons and drakes, and even amazing, exploding lights in the sky. Tallyverse called them firecracks or fireworks. While the group of riders were huddled together near the dragons, Mannix told them that this year was to be no different. If anything, this particular ceremony was rumored to be the biggest and most extravagant in living memory. Wild speculations flew as the riders settled down simply enjoying each other's company.

It was a foreign experience for Jaxson, who had spent most of his lifetime in the mountains with only Zero and his father sometimes. He smiled as Salvia and Mannix argued over the likelihood of gnomes riding pygmy dragons. He agreed with Mannix that an event like that would be great fun.

"I have never seen this many cerapters in one place," commented Tallyverse. "They have to be involved somehow."

"That would be a first. Cerapters are proud creatures. Doubt they would allow themselves to be paraded around for show," replied Mannix.

"It would be beyond amazing to see," said Jaxson.

"Magic," said Tephra quietly. "With this many teams here and the cerapters around, there has to be magic involved."

Mannix nodded sagely. "Could be. It's said the right

person can harness the vast magical power of a cerapter and use it at will."

"That's dragon dung," said Salvia. "But we are close to the sea. Maybe we will see a water dragon during the ceremonies. I've never seen one."

"Nor have I," added Tallyverse.

Jaxson, still smiling, said, "I'm not even sure what a water dragon looks like."

Everyone nodded. Spotting a water dragon was a rare event. Mannix looked around the group and the rest of the keep, then said softly, "There have been some strange happenings here at the trials city in the last couple of weeks."

"Strange happenings? What does that mean?" asked Salvia.

Tallyverse and Mannix exchanged a glance before the dragon knight responded. "Seems two different riders have died in training accidents."

Salvia snorted. "That's not all that strange. Riding a dragon is dangerous after all."

"Those two deaths alone would probably not raise an eyebrow. But considering everything else that's been going on..." said Mannix.

"Such as what?" asked Jaxson.

Mannix sighed deeply. "Dragons being hurt in their keeps in the middle of the night, for one. Riders and dragons not being able to communicate. Lots of small things that, if isolated, wouldn't mean a thing. But all together? That paints a different canvas."

Jaxson scanned the other riders. Tephra hung his head low. Salvia stared at the entrance of the keep into the darkness of the night. Mannix and Tallyverse both seemed anxious fiddling with a stick and running their hands through their hair. Finally, Jaxson spoke up. "Some of that sounds too familiar for comfort."

Salvia and Tephra both nodded. Mannix replied, "Reckon it's the work of the same group that we have encountered a couple of times now."

The conversation, so light and merry only minutes ago, turned dark and fearful. There was much discussion about the Demon Lizard Death Cult and all they had heard about them. No one was sure where they came from or why they did what they did. But it was obvious the DLDC was strong, widespread, and evil.

"With all of that said," Mannix said finally, "one of us should stay here at all times with the dragons."

There was no argument from anyone in the group. So, Mannix continued, "Even during the opening ceremony tomorrow."

All the agreements turned to groans.

"Shouldn't the dragons come with us?" asked Salvia.

"Not this year. Only riders are allowed at the opening," said Tallyverse.

Tephra stood. "Better safe than sorry. How do we decide who stays behind tomorrow?"

"I think the fairest way is to simply draw straws," said Tallyverse. "Shortest stays back to help look out for all of our dragons."

After ensuring everyone agreed with the importance of the task and the method of choosing, Mannix picked up a stick and broke it into five pieces. Then he turned his back to them. Once he faced them again, his fist held the small sticks. They were even and spread out. Tephra was the first to step up and grab a stick. It was several inches long, and he let out a relieved sigh. Tallyverse went next and was equally relieved with a long one. Next up was Jaxson.

As soon as he pulled his selection free, Jaxson knew he was not going to be watching the opening ceremonies. In his hand was a nub of the stick barely longer than his fingernail. Salvia patted him on the back as she pulled on one of the two remaining sticks. It was the longest yet. That left only Mannix. He opened his fist and confirmed Jaxson's fear. He would be in the keep while the others watched the festivities the next day. Sleep that night took a long time to come.

CHAPTER 28

The cheers easily reached the mouth of the keep as Jaxson sat with his back against the rough stone looking out over the city. The opening ceremony was taking place just out of sight behind the keep. It was frustrating to hear the excitement of the gathered riders and spectators but not be able to see why it was so exciting. Jaxson threw tiny rocks at a boulder just below the entrance. Each time a rock hit the mark, a satisfying crack sounded. He was so engrossed in throwing the stones, he did not hear Zero approach.

At least we will get to compete tomorrow in whatever trial is set before us, said Zero in Jaxson's mind.

You're right, replied Jaxson. Another round of rowdy applause echoed to them. *But just listen to those shouts! Whatever is happening must be amazing.*

For a while they sat in silence that was only broken by the distant, thunderous applause.

Do you wish to tell me what is truly bothering you? I know you are disappointed in missing the ceremony, but you also seem…conflicted, Zero said.

Jaxson, staring out over the empty city, took a few moments before he answered. "I just don't know anymore."

Zero tilted his barrel-sized head. *Don't know what?*

Jaxson flung the remaining pebbles all at once and grunted. "Anything! I don't know anything. Why is my dad working with the DLDC? And this book we are supposed to find, we haven't even really tried. But how do we do that? It's not like we were given specific instructions."

There is a lot to consider there, but I still think those things are not what is truly bothering you.

His shoulders slumped. "I feel guilty."

How so?

"I know we should be doing more to find the book. It's supposed to be really important," said Jaxson. "But I like having friends. And Mannix treats me the same as he does Salvia and Tephra. I like it."

There is no shame in that. It's natural to desire kinship.

"Maybe you are right. But for so long it was just you and me, and I've even been ignoring you," replied Jaxson.

Zero butted Jaxson's shoulder. *We are linked, Jaxson. There is no way for you to ignore me even if you tried.*

"I hadn't considered that," said Jaxson. He turned to the entrance. "The ceremony should be over soon."

"I believe it just concluded," said a voice from above them, causing Jaxson to jump to his feet.

Gemma poked her head into the keep's entrance from above. Her single braid dangled down. She flashed her one-dimpled smile at Jaxson before swinging out away from the wall and flipping down to the ground. She landed softly and gave Zero a little wink.

"Oh, hey. What are..." Jaxson stammered.

Gemma laughed, and Jaxson could not help but stare. Zero, for his part, acted quickly. The dragon excused himself to go "stretch his wings".

"Zero! Mannix doesn't want any of us to go out alone," yelled Jaxson as Zero circled higher and higher above him.

I'll be fine. I won't leave sight of the keep.

Jaxson turned back inside and almost jumped. Gemma stood right behind him. He looked down, shuffling his feet.

"Sounds like you have quite a bit on your mind, dragonrider," said Gemma. She twirled her braid absentmindedly with her left hand.

"Oh, you heard all of that?" asked a pitiful Jaxson.

"I couldn't help but hear. Your docile tone carried well out of the keep."

"I'm sorry for disturbing you. But why aren't you at the ceremony with everyone else?"

Gemma paced around Jaxson slowly, and his eyes followed her as best they could. "I was, but if you've seen one magic dragon and cerapter show, then you have seen them all."

"A magic drag—"

"Besides, this seems to be more fun," said Gemma, cutting Jaxson off. She stopped directly in front of him and started to move closer.

Jaxson blushed, and as he took a quick step back, he fell hard on his bottom. The giggle that escaped the young woman seemed more playful than mean to Jaxson. This only made his face burn hotter. Luckily, he was saved from further embarrassment at Gemma's hands. His friends appeared at the mouth of the keep.

Tallyverse looked back and forth between Jaxson and Gemma, then to Salvia. Mannix let out a raucous laugh but was subdued immediately by a withering stare from Salvia. Jaxson scrambled to his feet and moved to join his fellow dragonriders until Salvia focused her stare on him. For the second time in as many days, Salvia brushed by him without a word.

"What did I do?" whined Jaxson to no one in particular.

Tephra shrugged, and Mannix chuckled softly.

"The ways of women are a mystery, but you, my good sir, are simple," said Tallyverse. "A simple stone head."

"What?"

Mannix nudged the group to follow Salvia. "Never mind all that. We have an early rise ahead of us. The trials start tomorrow!"

CHAPTER 29

Steam rose from Zero's back on the unseasonably chilly morning of the first trial. Though it was not as cold as Salvia had been since the previous night. Jaxson had attempted to talk with her at breakfast. And again when they walked back to the keep to mount their dragons. Nothing. Not even a biting retort. So, as he stood beside Zero and waited for the beginning of the race, he was not thinking about the prize of talking with the oracle or even the trials themselves. Instead, he was wondering how things had changed so quickly with her.

"All right you lot, we don't have to win this thing. We just need to finish in the top half," said Mannix.

"I've never heard of them eliminating teams like this," commented Tallyverse.

Mannix shook his head. "No, but I've never heard of so many dragonriders answering the call to the trials before."

Jaxson examined the egg and the cradle used to carry it. The egg, though not a dragon's, was still immense, and he had no idea what kind it could be. The contraption it was resting on resembled an oversized sling, like one he had used as a small boy to fling rocks at targets though rarely hitting them. It was going to be cumbersome at best.

It should not be too much for us to handle, said Zero. *Brunt, Yammer, and Nalla are all fit and eager to do something besides sit around the keep. As am I.*

"Has Nalla said anything about why Salvia is so angry with me?"

No, and right now, I do not think that should be foremost on your mind, replied Zero.

"You are right, of course," said Jaxson. "It's just so frustrating."

Focus. I have a feeling this will be anything but a simple race before the morning is up.

The sun had risen fully above the eastern horizon, and trumpets sounded loudly. The signal to prepare for the race caused a flurry of motion all around them. The teams were stretched along the bank of a slow river. Jaxson counted six teams to their left, one of which was the women riders from the Hidden Lakes region. There were at least twice that to their right. The sky could easily become crowded with so many wings pumping hard. Mannix had a plan for that, however. He assumed most teams would shoot straight south, climbing as they went. He decided they would go high up first and avoid the crowd. It was a calculated gamble, but at least it should keep them from getting tangled up with another team right at the start.

Jaxson took a deep breath. Mannix and Brunt were set to lead them, with Salvia and Tephra riding their dragons in the middle. He and Zero were going to be positioned at the rear. Mannix had stressed over and over how important it would be for Jaxson and Zero to keep their eyes sharp. The team did not need any surprises coming from behind them.

Two abrupt trumpet blasts echoed behind them. It was time to mount the dragons. Zero grasped the rope connected to the egg holder and tensed, preparing to leap into the sky. Jaxson felt the immense power his friend possessed, and suddenly, every worry or fear he had been envisioning melted away. He didn't think of Salvia and her cold demeanor. He was no longer concerned about the futility of his quest to find a book filled with dragonrider knowledge. He wasn't even worried about his father and his duplicity. His only thoughts were for the task at hand, flying with his dragon to compete in the Dragon Trials.

Jaxson gripped the soft leather throng connected to the harness he rode in. He closed his eyes for a brief moment and let out a long, slow breath.

At the blast of the trumpets, they sprung into the air. The Dragon Trials had begun at last!

CHAPTER 30

Straight up they flew. As agreed upon earlier, Zero and Brunt supplied most of the power as the two small dragons needed to save their strength. At Mannix's lead, they started south toward the beach. Two other teams used the same strategy, but at least both were plenty far away to not cause any issues tangling with each other. The same could not be said about those down below.

A mass of dragons and riders were all wrapped and tangled up in each other's ropes. Several teams had already struck the ground and were thus disqualified. A particularly large, gray dragon roared and spewed flames in the air out of frustration. He looked south to scan the remaining majority of the teams. He spotted the four-winged dragons of their keep mates staying low to the ground and making good time. Behind them were the redheaded lava dragons. Jaxson didn't know much about them, though he had heard Tallyverse mention their riders were crazy.

Two green and two blue dragons to their right caught Jaxson's attention. His mouth dropped open in shock. They represented the team of the Demon Lizard Death Cult. He was sure of it now. The insignia on the dragons' armor was the same he had seen a continent ago. They veered into another team while attempting to slash the ropes.

Jaxson shook his head in disgust. Seemed the DLDC would take any advantage possible, which shouldn't come as a surprise. They were ruthless and cruel. He still didn't know what they wanted other than the eradication of all dragons as their name suggested. There had to be more going on with them than what was first noticeable.

Zero dipped suddenly to accommodate for a shift in the wind, and Jaxson was forced to refocus on the task at hand. They were picking up speed. Over one third of the distance was behind them already. And though they were still following the leaders, they were in a great spot. Jaxson smiled and patted Zero's side.

"Looks like we have a real shot at advancing," said Jaxson.

Too early to tell, really. We should stay vigilant. Carrying this egg makes the winds this high up treacherous, replied Zero.

Zero was right; they should stay on mission. Jaxson checked behind them and nearly fell out of his harness. A wall of steam drakes, small and black with glowing red eyes, were bearing down on the competitors. Riders on cerapters seemed to be herding them or at least goading them forward. Jaxson had really had enough of steam drakes for two lifetimes.

"Watch out ahead!" shouted Mannix. "Tephra, be ready to disengage and fend off an attack."

Jaxson turned to the commotion in front of them. Huge serpent-like drakes with water dripping from their wings were flying directly at them. With their size, and soaking wet, they could only be leviath drakes. Normally, leviaths were not dangerous, docile even, spending more of their time swimming lazily in warm currents of the sea. Except when on land protecting their nests. Then, they were one of the most dangerous beasts known to man. Jaxson took a closer look at the egg Zero and the other dragons were carrying in the giant sling. If that was truly a leviath drake egg as he suspected, they were in big trouble.

The leviath drakes careened forward, though none flew as high as they were. As they reached the leaders of the race, several of the drakes roared so loud it hurt Jaxson's ears even from this height. He watched in horror as a rider clutched his ears and screamed as he fell off his dragon. Another team dropped their egg and fled parallel to the beach to avoid both the steam and leviath drakes. Jaxson snuck a peek over his shoulder and was glad to see the steam drakes were not closing on them as fast as he had feared.

Most of the leviath drakes passed the riders below and circled around. As they flew, they made a strange clicking sound. When a drake quit making the sound, it honed in on a team and attempted to take their egg. Mannix spurred them forward, going faster now than was safe for dragons, riders, and the egg nestled below them. Another thunderous roar sounded below. When Jaxson dared look, all he could see was the huge eyes of the leviath drake as it shot straight at them. The mother drake had found her egg.

CHAPTER 31

"We have to get out of here!" yelled Salvia. Mannix looked down, then to Tephra.

"Distract it," Mannix called to Tephra. Then pointing at Salvia and Jaxson, he ordered, "You two, dive! We'll lose it amongst the others."

Tephra leaned in close to Yammer's neck. The dragon shivered then inched higher and to the back, almost over Jaxson and Zero. Yammer let out a quick roar and released the rope. Zero banked slightly and caught it as they started their descent into the chaos below.

Even with the wind in his ears and the roars of the leviath drakes, Jaxson could still pick out the screams of the terrified riders all around him. Over twenty teams had started this race, and now after the jumbled mess at the start and the arrival of the leviath drakes, Jaxson could only count eight. Their keep mates were still leading, and as of yet, had not attracted the attention of a drake. The DLDC team was also still airborne carrying their egg. But with so few teams left, speed was not as important as just making it to the beach in one piece.

Tephra and Yammer jerked up and out of sight, but the drake wasn't right behind them. Jaxson wasn't sure what they were doing to distract the monstrous beast, but it must've been working. Mannix leveled them out just above the tree line. Below, two of the remaining teams were weaving in and out of the trees to avoid being mauled. As speed was their ally now, Mannix urged them to move faster.

Then out of nowhere, Tephra was back and in front of

them. His eyes were wide and face pale. The three dragons holding the egg sped up even faster at Tephra's urging. The beach was finally in sight; they were well over halfway through the race. Jaxson smiled.

"We're going to make it, Zero," he told his dragon.

Before Zero could respond, they were drenched as water from a leviath drake above rained down upon them. Large teeth in a giant, gaping mouth were all Jaxson could see. The drake focused her attention on the smallest dragon holding her egg: Nalla. There was no way she would ever let go of the rope and drop the egg, but there was a slim chance she could avoid being attacked.

"Tephra, to me!" shouted Jaxson.

What are you doing? asked Zero.

"We have to help her. I don't think the leviath drakes like fire, and you have the hottest dragon's fire by a bunch," replied Jaxson.

Yammer swooped in with Tephra clinging to his back and grabbed the ropes. The whole group sagged when Zero released his rope to engage the drake. As Jaxson and Zero climbed, Zero released his fire to get the drake to alter her course and focus on them. It worked, but the drake did not flee. Instead, she circled higher and started another dive attack. She was not going to leave her egg.

Zero roared his dragon's fire again and again. The large drake would recoil and circle above them and try again. The other dragons struggled with the egg as they slipped closer and closer to the sandy earth. They'd hit the ground before reaching the beach if Zero did not help carry the load, but his dragon's fire was all that was keeping the leviath away. They needed to singe the beast and make it flee.

I am almost depleted of fire, said Zero.

Jaxson looked around for any help. Finally, he said, "Try and get closer! Let's send her back to the sea."

As they swooped nearer to the drake, Zero let out his final flame. The drake backed away but did not retreat. They needed the fire to burn her to make her flee, but Zero was exhausted.

Jaxson screamed in frustration. Zero's fire grew hotter, burning white. The flames licked at the drake's face. He pointed at the beast and a sphere of Zero's flame shot out just as Zero could no longer hold the fire. The fireball struck the drake on the neck and spread down its belly. She roared in anguish and rushed past them to plunge into the sea. Jaxson slumped over Zero's neck. Both he and his dragon were fatigued more than the physical exertion could account for.

With no time to celebrate or wonder what happened, Jaxson and Zero rushed back to the team and grabbed the rope. Slowly, they gained altitude as they pushed forward. The beach lay so close now. While they made their descent onto the sandy shore, Jaxson took stock of the scene below them.

Five teams had landed safely carrying their eggs. The DLDC team celebrated near the water. A team of longneck dragons were roaring their approval of completing the race. Cerapters patrolled both on the ground and in the air. As soon as the dragons touched the sand, they were greeted with cheers from all those around. Then another team landed, and everyone cheered for them as well.

Jaxson jumped down from Zero's back, and Mannix immediately crushed him into a giant bear hug.

"Don't know what you did, my boy, but it was excellent," said Mannix. Tephra thumped him on the back and smiled.

"Thanks. I'm not really sure what happened either," replied Jaxson. Then, he was stumbling backward as Salvia crashed into him. They both fell in a heap on the sand.

"Thank you, mountain boy," said Salvia with a huge grin. "Thank you for saving us."

Jaxson stammered a reply, more focused on her arms

wrapped around him and her body pressing against him. "I-it was—"

"Shhh. Just enjoy being the hero."

"I'm no hero. Zero did most of the work," said Jaxson. As they were getting to their feet and dusting off the sand, their keep mates landed. The leader Gemma and her dragon were both lathered with blood. Gemma did not so much slide off of her dragon as fall.

Jaxson rushed to her side, calling for Zero to follow him.

CHAPTER 32

"What in the tiny gods' gardens happened? A leviath catch up to you?" asked Jaxson as he slid to a stop in the sand.

A tall rider with the same braided hair as Gemma answered, "Those lowlife eels did this to her."

Salvia and Zero arrived next, followed closely by everyone else including Tallyverse and his dragon Ellandy.

"And who is that exactly?" asked Salvia.

The tall rider pointed at the riders of the DLDC. "Slammed their brutish dragons with that foul armor into her for no reason."

Over his shoulder, several of the DLDC pantomimed being struck and then collapsed onto the sand. They all roared with laughter. But they were a problem for another day. He looked back to the injured rider and her dragon.

The back left wing was impaired, possibly even broken. There was also a nasty gouge that ran the length of the dragon's side along the rib cage. Terrible injuries, but not life threatening. Gemma, on the other hand, seemed to have taken much more punishment. The sand around her was stained red as blood seeped from her shoulder and head. Shallow breaths and a lack of consciousness were also a large concern.

"We can help," said Jaxson.

"How?" asked a skeptical Hidden Lakes rider.

"I don't have time to explain," said Jaxson.

The dragon insists we help her rider first, said Zero.

I think that wise. I hope we aren't too late. Then aloud he said, "Give us some room. Zero, settle in just there."

Jaxson waited until Zero was in position, then he grasped Gemma's small hand. He recoiled slightly at her cool skin. They didn't have much time. He prepared for Zero to send his magic through Gemma and into him, wherein he would gather the energy and send it back. That's the way it had always worked before, but this time was different.

Tingling from the ground and a crackling in the air converged on Zero as he drew magic from both elements. It swirled above Zero's head and wrapped around him from his horns to the tip of his tail. When Zero passed the power to him through Gemma, the magic flowed like living water from Zero's claws into Gemma's damaged body. It flowed over, around, and into her from all directions. The magic coursed through her, searching out her injuries. Then he felt it reaching for him.

Jaxson closed his eyes and allowed the magic to come to him. He swelled with power unlike any he had ever felt. The source of the magic, always mysterious, was revealed. It was in everything, was everything. He breathed the cool sea breeze, felt the rocky permanence of the cliffs beyond within the magic. The freezing cold in the high mountains shocked him until the searing heat of the volcanos of Tipili washed over him. He didn't know how he knew these things or sensations, but he knew them all the same.

He looked at Zero and truly saw him for the first time. The dragon's body glowed with magical power and still more flowed into him. His heart pounded and the magic pulsed to the beat. Jaxson concentrated on that rhythm and soon discovered he could take in even more power. He had no desire to ever relinquish the sensations that filled him, the power that now resided within his body. But Gemma needed his help.

Focusing on the most egregious wound first, Jaxson released the magic back to Zero. It flowed out of his hand

and into Gemma's. Rushing up her arm, it pooled around her shoulder before continuing to her head where it swirled and moved faster and faster. Jaxson squinted as the magic brightened to a glowing bluish white. Still, the magic pulsed and grew brighter until Jaxson released all that he held.

Gemma's wounds began to heal immediately, and Jaxson smiled down at the small rider. When he looked at Zero again, he saw the magic seeping away. He wanted to know where it resided, wanted to find the source. He reached out as hard as he could, and then he was floating with the magic. He was amongst it, a part of the whole. Power coursed through him.

"Zero, you have to try this," said Jaxson. His smile faltered when he didn't get a response. He looked down at his friend, and to his shock, he saw his body lying on the ground by Gemma.

He scrambled and thrashed at the air, trying to get back into his body but to no avail. Salvia shook his shoulders, but Jaxson did not feel it. Her mouth opened in a scream, but Jaxson did not hear it. Then the magic wrapped itself around him, and he couldn't see the ground anymore. He couldn't see anything. He was in the void...again. He spiraled away into the nothing.

CHAPTER 33

His eyes snapped open, and Jaxson inhaled a sharp breath. He looked side to side, not yet recognizing his surroundings. Panic blossomed in his gut. He had been floating within and intertwining with streams of magical power. Peace and comfort were all he had experienced as the magic current flowed and ebbed like a river. Always moving. Knowledge, not that of books but of a more fundamental element, had filled him. He understood his place in the world better, but more importantly, the role of dragons and their magic had been revealed. But with each waking moment, that knowledge slipped back into the void. His heart raced as he tried desperately to cling to the revelations revealed within the nothing.

Calm now, Jaxson. You have been...away for quite some time, Zero murmured in his head.

Jaxson turned and even in the dark, he recognized his best friend and companion's face. "Yes, I was in the void for a long time. A lifetime."

Zero chuckled. *Not so long as that. Only two weeks.*

Jaxson cocked his head as he contemplated this news. He approached Zero and reached out to stroke the rough dragonhide on Zero's neck. Magic burst forth and flowed from Zero to Jaxson and back again. Even when awake, now he could see the tendrils of magic as they danced.

Has it always been this way? asked Jaxson.

Yes, replied Zero. *You are only now aware of it.*

"Amazing. Is this how all riders and dragons are

connected?"

I am unsure. I can only speak for us.

"You can't see the magic flow between them?"

Zero was silent for a few moments. *No. Can you see the magic?*

"Yes."

He sank down to lean against Zero's side. A comfortable silence settled over both of them. Jaxson thought back to before his most recent foray into the nothing. At first, it was difficult. Everything from before seemed so far away, like he was remembering only echoes of memories. Then, he recalled a beach, Salvia hugging him after they completed the first trial. And Gemma lying in the bloody sand. Gemma!

Jaxson jumped to his feet. It all rushed back to him: Salvia, the Dragon Trials, Gemma's injuries, the fireball he had produced from Zero's flame.

"Is Gemma well? And the trials... did I miss the trials? Two weeks?! How could I have slept for two weeks?"

Zero stood as well but leveled his head with an agitated Jaxson.

First, Princess Gemma of the Hidden Lakes is doing exceptionally well. She was even able to compete in the final two trials, Zero informed him.

Jaxson sighed with relief. "That's great... Wait, you said she competed in the..."

Zero nuzzled Jaxson with his barrel-sized head. *Yes, you unfortunately missed the remainder of the trials.*

Waking to find he had lost two weeks of his life caused Jaxson serious confusion. "What? How?"

Some might say laziness, but we both know that isn't true.

A sound at the entrance of the keep diverted their attention. Holding torches against the darkness, Mannix, Salvia, Tephra, Tallyverse, and many more entered the keep. Mannix shook his head at the sight of Jaxson awake. Salvia beamed. Tephra just nodded to Jaxson with little other expression.

"She was right. She always is," said Mannix.

"Of course she was," said Salvia. She ran to Jaxson and gave him a ferocious hug. "We were so worried."

"I'm fine. Maybe better than fine. But who was right?" asked Jaxson.

Tephra stepped forward. "The oracle. She called us to her tent earlier and told us when we returned you would be awake."

"The oracle?"

"We have much to tell you, but first, let me congratulate you. We, you included, won the Dragon Trials!"

CHAPTER 34

"We should celebrate," said Mannix. With a quick motion, a robed servant appeared. "Food and drink for everyone. And maybe some tables and chairs."

"As you wish, Champion," replied the servant.

The smile on Mannix's bearded face couldn't get any bigger. "And some ale!"

The servant nodded once. "Yes, Champion."

They scurried out to fulfill Mannix's request. "I could get used to that," Mannix said.

"I am not sure I ever will," said Tallyverse.

Accommodations arrived quickly. Their dusty, dark dragon keep transformed instantly into a formal dining area complete with lit candles, lacy tablecloths, and a bard in the corner strumming his instrument. Wine and spiced mead arrived before the food, but Jaxson abstained having just woken up—and from his last experience with the ale. He stuck with refreshing, cold water.

Their keep was crowded as more people packed in, which meant more tables were set up for them. Jaxson recognized several of the faces including the riders from Hidden Lakes, Gemma amongst them. After giving him a little wave, she leaned over and whispered to the three young boys seated next to her. The oldest, maybe twelve years of age, looked at Jaxson with wide eyes while the other two snickered. Next to them were the riders of the ginormous northern dragons. Jaxson had not met them personally, but they seemed nice enough now. Many more people filed in and sat or congregated near the spiced wine barrels.

Mannix motioned him toward an open seat between himself and Salvia. Tallyverse and Tephra both sat across from them. Salvia nudged his shoulder when he joined them.

"Seems like I missed quite a bit," said Jaxson.

The group erupted in laughter. "You could say that," said Mannix. "And I would guess you'd like to know what the blue blazes is going on."

Jaxson nodded quickly. "Absolutely."

"Well, what do you remember last?"

Jaxson looked around the room, stalling for time. He did not think this was the time to talk about magic or the void. So, he said instead, "I was kneeling on the beach with Zero trying to help Gemma. Then, it all went blank until I woke up tonight."

"You remember the beach? Good, we'll start from there. As you can see, Princess Gemma has made an outstanding recovery," said Mannix.

"When did we find out she was a princess?" asked Jaxson.

Tallyverse answered first. "Shortly after she was taken from the beach, an entourage attempted to make her return home, but she wasn't having it. She still wanted to compete. And besides, she had to show her three little brothers how to be brave."

Jaxson smiled. "What about the second trial?"

Mannix laughed. "Right to it, then. Well, we couldn't compete with only three riders, so Tallyverse here stepped up and took your spot before the second trial. There were only nine teams left after the brutal encounter with the leviath drakes, so the field was much reduced."

"Which made the next challenge more daunting," said Tallyverse. "A giant game of tag on a playing arena bigger than some countries made for an exhausting day of flying at breakneck speed and attempting to hide on barren rock."

"How did you all do?" asked Jaxson.

Salvia reached over to pat Tallyverse's hand. "We did not fare so well."

Mannix waved it off. "It doesn't matter. All the second trial did was seed us for the final. And you already know we won that one."

"But how?!"

"You have heard of the game capture the flag?" asked Tallyverse. When Jaxson nodded, he continued, "We played that on our dragons, full contact allowed. It was an epic battle. But for the third time in three trials, Tephra and Yammer proved their worth and showed their courage."

"Tell me everything," said Jaxson eagerly.

Just then, the food arrived. Fresh fish grilled to perfection, crabs boiled with spicy sausage and corn, an assortment of fruits both sliced and whole. So much food. Everyone filled their plates and dug right in. In between bites, Jaxson asked again, "Is anyone going to give me more details?"

Mannix said through a mouth of flaky fish, "Too much to tell. I could write a book about the last two trials alone, and there are many other things to discuss."

Jaxson did not pressure them further. He was enjoying the food; he hadn't eaten in weeks after all. As his stomach filled and his pace slowed, he looked at his friends. They all seemed the same as before, but he knew they were different. He didn't know how yet, but it was a truth he did not doubt.

"Tephra, I have to ask, what is going on with the robe?" asked Jaxson. He had wanted to question him on the dark brown robe he wore earlier but had been overcome with news of the Dragon Trials.

Tephra smiled, though it did not touch the rest of his face. "It is quite exceptional really."

"He was 'touched' just yesterday," said Salvia.

Jaxson glanced between them, hoping for a more detailed explanation. No one was forthcoming. "And that means...?"

Salvia rolled her eyes. "You are dense sometimes. The oracle made him an acolyte of her order."

Everyone nodded their heads solemnly. Jaxson had no idea what that meant, but he was positive that it was a revered position even if Tephra seemed to not like it. "You all have met with the oracle then? Tell me about it!"

CHAPTER 35

Salvia blushed and looked down at her hands in her lap. "I had a question in mind to ask the oracle before I went into her tent, specifically about what happened to our parents and how we ended up in an orphanage."

"I would want to know that as well if I were in your shoes," said Jaxson.

"Instead, I asked about my future," said Salvia with a glance to Jaxson. "I was hoping for one answer, but the oracle gave me another."

Jaxson knew better than to ask exactly what the oracle said to her. That was an extremely private and personal experience. The fact she was sharing so much astounded him already. "Are you happy with your future then?"

Salvia laughed. "I have no idea, but it's going to be one great adventure!"

Mannix jumped in. "Salvia has been asked to join the Katsu. It is an old and revered group of dragonriders that explore and seek adventure over the whole of Kealqua."

"That sounds so exciting!"

Salvia nodded. "It is exciting, and I am honored. We depart in the morning for the eastern marshes. There is rumor of an ancient treasure the Katsu seeks out there."

Mannix beamed. "With your help, they will find it in a fortnight."

"What of you, Mannix?" asked Jaxson.

Mannix cleared his throat and stood. When he did, Gemma and her three little brothers stood as well. Mannix walked around the back of the table to stand behind the boys. "I have been given the honor to train the young princes of the Hidden Lakes. Jaxson, I would like you to meet Shua, the eldest. He rides a prickly dragon named Weste. This young man is Bash, and his dragon, the fastest of the lot, is called Spetten. Lastly, this gangly young fellow is Benja. Though the youngest and the skinniest, Benja and his dragon Raja can out fly his two older brothers two out of three times."

"He is going to be the royal dragonrider advisor as well," said Gemma. "My mother, Queen Carrie, is looking forward to his counsel."

Jaxson grinned. "You'll be a great teacher, Mannix. You already were for us."

"Thanks. I think we will see great things from these three in the future. Maybe worthy of ballads and tales remembered for generations," said Mannix.

Tallyverse then stood abruptly. "The post was to be mine until I met with the oracle. Now, my mission is simple. I go where you go, young Jaxson. I will follow you and Zero to the ends of the world if I must."

Jaxson, really confused for the first time, said, "But Tallyverse, I intend to return across the sea to my home. Will you leave all you know behind?"

"With a light heart, I will."

"I'd be honored to have you with me as a friend but no more," said Jaxson. "You owe me nothing."

Under his breath but still loud enough for Jaxson to hear, Tallyverse mumbled, "But I will. We all will."

At that moment, a cerapter landed at the mouth of the keep. Down jumped a familiar robed figure. Riley left Sharim outside and hurried in to find Jaxson.

"My heart sings to see you awake, Jaxson," said Riley with a small smile. "But I have been sent to fetch you as soon as possible."

"Fetch me?" asked Jaxson.

"The oracle wishes to see you. Now."

There was a moment of stillness finally interrupted by Mannix. "Go, boy! You shouldn't keep the oracle waiting or she may curse your future. You may end up a toad, or worse yet, married living on a farm."

Everyone laughed. Everyone except Jaxson. He hadn't been sure that he would be allowed to see the oracle, so he had not really thought about what he wished to ask her. There was so much he desired to know. He wanted to understand the portals and Zero's mysterious past. Then there was the DLDC's plans, or asking if his dad was really a traitor.

She summoned you, said Zero. *I'm not sure you will get to be the one making requests.*

Jaxson replied silently, *But if I am given a chance?*

Go with your gut. It has mostly kept us out of trouble.

"To the oracle then," said Jaxson. Everyone cheered as Jaxson mounted Sharim right behind Riley.

She looked over her shoulder. "Might want to hang on. Zero is fast, but Sharim is faster."

CHAPTER 36

The burning incense tickled his nose and irritated his eyes as Jaxson sat on the soft carpet. Riley flew Sharim low and fast, and they arrived at the oracle's tent in short order. Now he sat amongst the brightly colored pillows and frilly blankets awaiting to meet one of the most powerful people in the world. The oracle did not have a kingdom or an army, but if needed, she had them all. She could safely pass any border and enter any land. None would dare wish to incur the wrath of one that sees and shapes the world in the future.

"A coin for your thoughts, good man," came a voice from behind Jaxson.

He turned and tried to rise from his seated position at the same time. The result was him sprawled on the floor wrapped in blankets and pillows flopping around like a fish. He looked up to see a young woman, much younger than he had expected, smiling down at him.

"Madame Oracle... Your excellence, I am sorry," stammered Jaxson.

"No need for formality and titles, especially those that are grossly wrong," said the oracle. "You may call me Broocke as that was my name once."

"Broocke, then. Thank you for seeing me," Jaxson said.

The oracle waved a dismissive hand as she sauntered to the bar on the far wall of the tent. After pouring herself a dark, thick liquid, she turned with the glass in hand to face Jaxson.

"This meeting has been inevitable since you and Zero

first entered the Taufan. It has been foretold for much longer than that, though it could have gone either way before," said Broocke.

"I'm afraid I do not understand."

"No, you don't. And you won't understand much of what we discuss here tonight for quite some time," said the oracle as she sat near to where Jaxson had finally freed himself from the soft bonds. "If you ever do fully understand them at all."

Jaxson paused for a moment, then asked, "If I'm not meant to understand, why did you send for me?"

"Are you always in such a rush?" asked Broocke.

Jaxson shrugged. "It's not every day I talk to someone that can literally change the course of my life, the course of the world, with just a few uttered words."

"That is true. I am old, Jaxson, really old. I know I do not look it at all, but I am only allowing you to see what I want you to see," said the oracle. "This illusion makes the experience smoother for both of us, I think."

Jaxson nodded and tried to look relaxed. He stretched his feet out and lounged on several overstuffed pillows, but he was too tense. He sat back up quickly.

"Why did you tell Tallyverse he needs to follow me?"

"Tallyverse?" The oracle laughed. "Oh, you mean Danny! Is he calling himself that ridiculous name?"

"It is the only name I have ever known him to go by," replied Jaxson.

"Quite a mouthful. It's almost as if he made up a name and was intent on changing it one day. Then he just never did."

"I still wish to know why you told him he needed to stay with me," said Jaxson.

"I am sure you do. You wish to know many things no doubt. The truth about your father's betrayal, perhaps? Maybe to understand how the gates work, or learn something of Zero's clouded past? Hmmm," Broocke said in between sips of the thick liquid. "Am I correct?"

Jaxson simply nodded.

"Of course I am," said the oracle. "I will be honest now and speak plain just this once. You will learn none of those things in this tent tonight. Though you will learn all of them and more before too long."

"What am I to learn tonight then?" asked Jaxson.

"This and only this. You have already experienced and seen everything you will need in order to bring down the rotting disease that is spreading across not only your land but all lands," said the oracle. "The battle against the Death Cult will intensify, but they are just the muscle. You must cut out the heart after you deal with the muscle. And to deal with them, you will need to raise an army. That will get expensive."

"An army? Again, I don't understand."

"Not yet. I'll tell you what, our time is nearly at an end. So, here is more plain talk for you: You, Zero, Danny, and Ellandy should be at the port at sunrise. There you will board the ship *Consequences,* and set sail back to your lands. That is all you need to know at this moment."

"Wouldn't it be quicker to take the portal back?" asked Jaxson.

"The portals are no longer safe. In fact, they never were," said Broocke. "Heed my advice and return to your lands via the sea. You have friends there eagerly awaiting your arrival."

"I would like to see my friends again. Tam and Aleera, even Dreknoxious. But why are they so eager for me to return?"

"You ask so many questions." The oracle sighed. "Things are darker in your native lands now. War is coming, and they will look to you and Zero to lead the way to victory."

"War?"

"It is as terrible and daunting as it sounds, but you are up to the task," said the oracle. "You have to be."

Jaxson stared at nothing. After several long moments, Broocke continued, "One last item. A boy by the name of Mika came in search of you but, once seeing your condition, returned from whence he came. He left a message that will make sense only to you."

"What does the message say?"

Brooke handed him a folded piece of paper with the seal of Head Librarian William burned into it. Jaxson smiled. At least the old librarian had survived whatever had happened at Castle Beauxgrand. Jaxson went to put the paper in his pocket, but Broocke indicated he should go ahead and read it.

"He also wanted you to know that all is well with William and the duke. And of course, the books all escaped harm," said Broocke. "He is a very brave boy. Most would not talk to me as he did."

"He is something," said Jaxson absently. He opened the note quickly.

Dear Jaxson,
I hope this message finds you well. I have discovered the
book you seek. Seems it was closer to home than you ever could
have imagined. Last known location is the Red Dragon Castle
within the Dragon Spine Mountains. Good luck.
William, Head Librarian

"I do not know how this will fit in with all the other tasks you must complete, but I feel it is important," said the oracle.

Jaxson just nodded. "At least I know where that is."

CHAPTER 37

Everyone had come to see him off. Salvia had given him a lingering embrace with tears in her eyes. She was already dressed in the lively colors of the Katsu. They were set to depart that very day as well. Tephra kept his distance and looked at Jaxson more as a curiosity than the friend he had become. Mannix's smile was huge as he and the three princes each said their goodbyes. Gemma gave him a quick hug with a whispered thank you in his ear. Tallyverse was already on the ship ready to depart before Jaxson even made it to the docks that morning.

Jaxson spent the next two-and-a-half-week sea voyage contemplating all that the oracle had told him. He could not understand how a war was coming. He didn't even know who he was supposed to fight, never mind the fact he had no army. Zero grew weary of his constant circular thinking and had told him so. As Jaxson looked out over the sea knowing that day he would reach his homeland, he finally made a decision on a course of action.

Zero's head wrapped around him as they watched the shore come into view as a dark line on the horizon.

Are we going to find Tam or Dreknoxious? Maybe go find the book? Or do you have something else in mind?

Jaxson sighed. A coming war that not only was he to lead but finance weighed heavy on his thoughts.

"If we are going to pay for a war, I think our most prudent action is to get the funds," replied Jaxson. "We need to get back to the cave with the dragon glass."

Zero nodded and became silent.

A course had been set in Jaxson's mind. He hoped it was his idea and not placed there by the oracle. Even she had been at the docks the morning of his departure. When she spoke, it was barely above a whisper. "Confrontation, even against those you once held dear, is coming. One seeks to take everything from you. And you must not let that happen at any cost."

He could think of nothing worth more than his dragon, Zero. And no one was going to separate them.

CHAPTER 38

Almost as soon as the ship made port, Jaxson had Zero and Danny with Ellandry in the air. They flew straight west, stopping only to eat and sleep at night. It took less than a week to make it to the forest at the base of the Dragon Spine Mountains. They had encountered few people after leaving the port. Their ship's captain had provided them with food and provisions, so they had not even had to stock up before departing.

"It may take some work to get into the cave. Last time I saw it, Dreknoxious had brought half the mountain down in front of the entrance," Jaxson said.

"I'm not scared of a little work," Danny replied.

It was work too. They spent the better part of two days, dragons and riders alike, trying to clear the entrance. Still, they seemed to be getting nowhere. Jaxson decided they needed to regroup. He asked Danny to fly to Tam's old village and purchase shovels and then something to carry the dragon glass in once they were inside. Danny had reservations about leaving Jaxson out in the wild alone.

"I'm not exactly alone," said Jaxson. "Zero will watch my back. Besides, what could happen out here?"

By noon the next day, Danny was already gone and Jaxson was hot and sweaty from trying to move a particularly stubborn rock. He had dug under it and was using a long, strong branch Zero had found to attempt to pop it out of its hole. There wasn't much room on the little ledge so Zero had been flying larger rocks a ways before dropping them on the mountainside. The dragon was on a return trip when he warned Jaxson.

Movement below you, Jaxson. I count at least seven coming at you from the forest.

Jaxson slipped behind a large rock and peered around, trying to get a glimpse of those coming up the mountainside. *Who are they? Can you tell?*

I cannot. But at least one has a sword drawn, and they are moving slowly and deliberately. They seem to know where they are going, replied Zero.

Jaxson swore under his breath. His bow was on the other side of the little ledge, but to get to it, he would be completely exposed. *Stay in the air. A surprise from the sky may be all that saves me.*

Zero circled higher but not so high as to lose sight of Jaxson or those stalking up the mountain. The first man crested the ridge, and Jaxson's worst fear was confirmed. On the soldier's breastplate was the symbol that had been etched into the dead dragon's armor so long ago. The Demon Lizard Death Cult had been hunting them, and now they had been found.

How did they find us? asked Jaxson.

I am not sure. It's too late for me to come grab you without being seen. Can you sneak down the other side? asked Zero.

Jaxson looked left then right. In each direction, soldiers were cresting the ledge. Jaxson had an idea. It was crazy, but maybe their only shot of getting away without all out fighting for their lives.

Zero, once all of them have come out of the forest, land behind me and produce the hottest dragon's fire that you can.

You have a plan?

Distract them with fireballs, and maybe I can reproduce what I did in the trials. Then, I'll jump off the far cliff and you catch me, replied Jaxson.

Seems like a lot of risk with little chance of success.

You have a better idea?

When Zero did not respond, Jaxson smiled. *All right then, let's do this.*

CHAPTER 39

Just as the last man stepped into the clearing in front of the entrance to the dragon glass chamber, Jaxson signaled for Zero to initiate their plan. Jaxson did not see any heavy archery equipment of any kind, so Zero should be in the clear, and if Jaxson was fast enough, he would be as well.

The soldiers started shouting and pointing as soon as Zero started his descent. His dragon landed with a roar and blew dragon's fire as far and hot as he could. It was nowhere near striking the men, but still they retreated to the edge of the clearing. All was going well thus far until Jaxson spotted a ballista that other soldiers were rolling up the hill. It would take them several moments to set it up, but then Zero would be in grave danger.

We need to go now! shouted Jaxson in Zero's mind.

With the dragon's fire burning hot, Jaxson attempted to cast it forward as he had done during the trials. Nothing happened. He desperately tried again, but still, no fireball was produced.

I can't do it. I'm gonna make a run for it. Be ready, said Jaxson.

Just as he stepped clear of his boulder, soldiers pointed and started toward him. That's when Jaxson saw him. Standing just to the left of the ballista, seconds away from hurling giant arrows at him and Zero, was his father.

Alan locked eyes with Jaxson and shouted. Jaxson couldn't believe it. His whole time on the far continent, he had hoped his father had an explanation for joining with the enemy. He had let them go after all, but if he was here now, he truly was a traitor to all dragons.

You need to run, Jaxson!

Soldiers advanced. The ballista was locked and loaded and swinging in Zero's direction, but Jaxson could not move. His father, the man that had brought him Zero as an egg, had turned his back on everything Jaxson knew. He could not comprehend it.

With a deep roar, Zero landed between Jaxson and the soldiers. Arrows flew in his direction and men charged with swords and pikes drawn. The ballista swung into position and released a fatal arrow in Zero's direction. It was now Jaxson's turn to scream. His father started tussling with another soldier, probably because the first ballistic arrow missed.

Zero blew dragon's fire in every direction, and Jaxson lost all conscious thought. He willed the fire to strike the soldiers. And fireball after fireball flew at lightning speeds. He locked eyes with his traitor father and sent one last fireball hurtling his way.

He knew it was a good strike even before he saw impact. He was already jumping on Zero's back and urging him into the sky. They circled the deadly clearing one time to see nothing but smoke and devastation below. They had survived a well-organized ambush, but the costs were high. Jaxson screamed into the wind as Zero set a course to nowhere in particular, as long as it was far away from here.

Still, Jaxson screamed.

EPILOGUE

Wind blew through his long hair as he rode the back of the ancient petri drake. One thing Tam had admired about Jaxson was his long hair, so he had let his grow since the night of their escape so many months before. He would never be a dragonrider, but with his affinity for talking with animals, he had convinced Grog to take him on this particular adventure.

If someone had told him back in his small, rundown town that he would very soon be at the heart of the rebellion against a new, tyrannical empire, he would not have believed it. But fighting against that evil was not really a choice. The enemy had swept into the coastal kingdom of Midden Gual, destroying any that opposed them. Their dragon knights were brutal and efficient and no traditional army could withstand them. They spread their hate throughout the continent including the kingdom of Esther where the DLDC had softened any defense. The only reason Esther did not fall within days was the rebellion's inside man. Dreknoxious, the de facto leader of their group, had placed someone within the ranks of the DLDC: Alan, Jaxson's father.

With any luck, Jaxson will have already made it back and had a joyous reunion with his dad, thought Tam.

Dreknoxious told him to meet at the cave with the dragon glass that he and Jaxson had discovered a lifetime ago early this morning. But Tam had been delayed with Grog, who was acting grumpier than normal. He was almost there now just after midday.

Smoke rose from the clearing in front of the cave's

entrance. *Oh no. That cannot be good.*

As Grog landed with a thud, Tam jumped from his back, rolling on the ground and drawing his short sword in one motion. Enemy soldiers lay strewn about with severe burns. There were remnants of a heavy weapon or two as well, all destroyed. Tam called for Jaxson and Zero to no avail.

"I think they have been here and already departed," came a familiar voice behind Tam.

Strolling out of the cleared entrance of the cave came a white-haired man with a long staff. Dreknoxious.

"Did you see him? What happened here?"

"I did not see him, no. And I could only guess what happened here, though it doesn't seem to be that big of a mystery," said the old wizard.

"Well…"

"Ambush. Jaxson and Zero were ambushed and had to fight their way free," said Dreknoxious. "Before entering the cave, as I had moved the final stones to clear the path."

"So, he didn't get any of the dragon glass and just left?" asked an incredulous Tam.

"It would appear that way," said Dreknoxious. "On a more disturbing note, I found Alan's cap over near the wreckage there. Seems he was here as well, though…I do not believe he survived Jaxson's fury."

"What?" screamed Tam. "This couldn't get any worse. We need him to turn the tide of this war!"

"We do need him, yes," said Dreknoxious. "But we need him to be of sound mind and focus. I am not sure that would be the case right now."

"So, he just left after being ambushed and maybe killing his dad?" When Dreknoxious nodded, Tam continued, "And he didn't take any of the dragon glass?"

The wizard shook his head.

"But that is the most valuable stuff in the world," said

Tam.

"It is valuable, no doubt," said Dreknoxious as he looked out over the wild forest. "But for Jaxson, if what I believe occurred truly happened, it is worthless. At least, worth less than Zero to be sure."

"What do we do now?" asked Tam. "All of our plans rested on a true dragonrider leading us."

"What do we do now? That is truly a marvelous question."

RESOLVE EQUAL TO ZERO

PROLOGUE

Fifteen Moons Later

A drop of sweat left a trail on Jaxson's dirty face as it fell down his nose and clung on the tip. From his crouched position in the dense fern, he didn't dare wipe it away and give away his hideout. He looked around using only his eyes and not turning his head. The jungle, normally alive with bird calls and the rustling of leaves by smaller animals, seemed to hold its breath in anticipation of... something. The sweat droplet tickled his nose causing Jaxson to close his eyes and think about anything but the discomfort.

But discomfort is all he had known the past nine moon cycles since he'd slipped away from Zero in the dead of night in search of the Living Scroll. He needed to find it; it was the only way to set right what he had made wrong on that cliffside so long ago. Zero just did not understand why it was so important to him.

Another drop of sweat beaded on his forehead. He moved his hand to swipe his face clean, but just as his hand slid down over his eyes, a twig snapped behind him. Frozen, not with fear but with prudence, Jaxson remained blind and crouched. Moments later, a loud whistle came from his left followed by a noise from all around him as people walked in from all directions and stopped right in front of him. He dared to move his hand down just enough so he could see. Seven warriors from the jungle tribe, Haglund, had appeared from nowhere and congregated. They spoke loudly and with many exaggerated hand movements and gestures. Although he did not understand their language, he caught the gist of their conversation. There was an intruder in their land. The short-handled spears and compact bows would be more than enough to end any threat, and an intruder was definitely a threat. The biggest problem for Jaxson—he was indeed the intruder.

After the animated conversation, the leader, or at least the one with the most tattoos, barked some orders. Silently, the warriors melted into the jungle in a direction opposite of Jaxson's course. He finished wiping his face and then sat on his haunches. Even though it was still morning, he was already exhausted. The strain of avoiding the warriors while keeping an eye out for the various types of wildlife that could cause him serious harm weighed heavy on his shoulders. But if the rumors from Taverny were true, this particular tribe's shaman had a propensity for healing spells. Such a skill could be the product of the Living Scroll. Since the Haglund's did not view outsiders favorably, he had been forced to sneak into their village and check for the scroll instead of just asking them for it.

He shook his head. Sitting in this palm bush sulking about how tired he was would not get him the scroll any faster. He needed to move. First, he checked to ensure all of his gear was still in place after the hectic escape-and-hide. He patted his side and felt the long knife sheathed there. His bow and quiver were still over his shoulder. Both wristbands that held some interesting contents were still in place. The small pack hung across his chest holding the meager amount of food and odds and ends such as flint and a tin cup. Satisfied everything was in its place, he stepped out of the palm bush and snuck up a game trail in the opposite direction of the warriors. He didn't have to pull out the map to know he was close to the river, and from there, it was a short hike up into the dense hills to the village.

He wondered how he was going to get the scroll or even how he was going to know for sure it was even present with this particular shaman. But he put those thoughts aside—that was a worry for a later time. Now, he had to evade capture and arrive at the village unseen.

With a brisk pace, it was not long before he heard the roaring of the river masking any other sound. The path in front of him was clear, and there was a small pool of calm water. His eyes widened; he was so very thirsty. He picked up the pace, but then the hairs on the back of his neck stood up and a tingling shot down his back. His next move put him back in a palmy bush. Eyes wide, he tried to see what had spooked him. It looked quiet in front of him; the path showed no signs of footprints, but still, he felt something was off. So, he waited. As his breathing slowed, he continued to try and figure out what had made his skin crawl. Over the last several months, he'd learned to trust his instincts more and more.

Sticking his head out of the bush slowly, he peered down the path to the cool pool that looked so inviting. The nagging in his gut that something was off did not go away even as his throat yearned for the fresh water. This would be the perfect place for an ambush, he thought to himself. He felt around his feet for a large stick and hurled it as far as he could into the jungle away from the path. Nothing happened for a moment, and Jaxson was about ready to believe he had made it all up in his head. There had been nothing to worry about after all. Then, a shrill whistle sounded. A moment later another whistler answered it. Two warriors, both carrying short spears, jogged up the path from the direction of the pool and slipped into the jungle near where he had thrown the stick.

He trembled. That had been a close one. The warriors never came back out of the jungle, and without knowing where they were, Jaxson chose to wait it out for a bit. *Patience allows the eagle to soar*, he thought to himself. He frowned;

that was something his dad had said to him a thousand times over the years. His dad was why he was in this jungle after all. He needed to talk to him, needed to apologize, so therefore, he needed the Living Scroll. Again, he decided that sitting around wasn't going to get it done, so he crossed the path and plunged into the jungle. He would travel along the river without coming out to it for a bit. Maybe later, he could sneak to the riverbank and get a drink, but now it was too dangerous.

Taking a quick sip from his water pouch without stopping, he moved quietly through the jungle. The noise from the river would cover up any noise he made but also would keep him from hearing anyone approaching. It was a chance he had to take. By midday, his waterskin was dangerously low. He finished it off and tried to find a path down to the river to refill it. He moved slower now, weighing each step carefully. A tangle of river trees with their long and jumbled roots blocked his final way with only a few steps to go. He crouched down and crawled under them until his hands and knees splashed each time they went down. He drank his fill and filled the skin. Then, he drank some more. Finally, he turned and made his way out of the dense roots back to the relatively open jungle. As soon as he stood, three warriors stepped out from behind the trees with spears pointed at him.

Jaxson sighed and put his hands out in front of himself. No need trying to outrun them at this point. Those spears looked sharp; he didn't want to give them an excuse to use them. Not yet at least. The warriors screamed at him and motioned for him to get down. One leg at a time without taking his eyes off his captors, he got down on his knees. All three of them were still in front of Jaxson, and he did not see nor sense any others around. Three of them weren't enough to hold him. He just needed to wait until the perfect moment.

With both arms fully tattooed, the middle warrior

stepped forward brandishing his spear. He barked another order, indicating with his hands that Jaxson should lie flat on the ground. The other two warriors began separating to get on either side of him. That's what he needed. It would be easier to go through one of them than all three. Again and louder, the leader yelled at Jaxson.

"What? I don't understand," replied Jaxson. He slowly inched his hands closer together. When he didn't lie on his belly, the leader planted his spear, tip down, into the soft soil. Reaching over his shoulder, he pulled out a short, thick machete. Brandishing it in front of Jaxson's face, he spoke again. This time he was quiet and calm. Another chill ran down Jaxson's spine. He looked into the eyes of the warrior and knew instantly to disobey would be death. Still, he inched his hands closer together to where they were almost touching.

As he placed his hands on the ground in front of him and leaned forward, he used his left thumb to open the tiny pouch on his other wristband. He closed his eyes and cleared his mind, entering the nether with ease after so much practice the past few months. While keeping his eyes closed but before going fully prone on the ground, he lifted his right hand and spilled the contents of the wrist pouch into his left hand. He blew the black powder and mumbled a word from the nether.

"Fenwa." A word that means deep night soul combined with the powder from a sorceress from Taverny created quite the effect.

Quicker than a blink, darkness fell over them all. Not a nighttime darkness where the stars and moons provided meager brightness, but instead, a complete absence of light filled the space all around them. He heard the warriors gasp and knew it was time to act. Knowing not to open his eyes because they would be useless, Jaxson relied on his other senses. He could smell the lead warrior approaching. He sidestepped and allowed the larger man to stumble past him. Then, he jumped forward, grabbing the spear the warrior had left behind. He could hear the warrior to his left swinging his spear back and forth wildly. So, he opted to go to the right.

With his shoulder lowered, he rammed into the unsuspecting warrior causing him to tumble away screaming. After a few steps toward freedom, Jaxson spun on his heel and went the opposite direction. He hoped to confuse their efforts to track him if only for moments. Then he ran like he had never ran before. He let his need for distance between him and his would-be captors outweigh the need for silence. He kept pushing until he was back in the midday light and still farther. It wasn't until he stumbled into the edge of a creek off the main river that he slowed. When he did, he heard the sounds of people nearby. It wasn't the warriors but the village he sought. He had made it this far at least.

****

After finding a hidden spot on a little rocky hill overlooking the village, Jaxson studied the layout below. The circular village of mud and wood buildings culminated in the center with a long, low hall. Children ran around everywhere with little oversight from the mostly women adults. The men, most of whom were apparently in the jungle looking for him, were either old or injured. He had a difficult time discerning what each building was used for and specifically which one housed the shaman. So he waited and watched all afternoon and into the evening which led to twilight then darkness. Still, he waited.

When the warriors returned back to the village several hours after dark, his patience was finally rewarded. Emerging from the long, low hall was a person to whom each other villager stopped and bowed their head as the person passed. With a headdress and long, multicolored robes,

Jaxson had no doubt this was the shaman rumored to have the healing ability that could only come from possession of the Living Scroll. He knew where he had to look now. He shook his head as he thought that of course it had to be in the only large building that happened to be right in the center of the village where all eyes could see him trying to sneak in.

He rummaged in his pack and pulled out some hard cheese and a piece of stale bread. As he chewed, the warriors below grouped up in front of the hall and shaman. The warrior that Jaxson had knocked down stepped forward. At this distance, he could not even hear the strange language but with the exaggerated pantomiming the warrior was doing, Jaxson had no difficulty understanding the warrior was telling of his disappearance. When the warrior threw his hands in the air and then covered his eyes, the rest of the warriors recoiled. They were scared of magic. Perhaps, he could use that to his advantage.

The shaman raised one hand, and the warriors fell silent. From around her waist, she pulled out a small pouch. After sweeping the ground with her foot, she dropped to her knees and emptied the contents of the pouch onto the bare earth. The warriors started chanting, at first very slowly and then with greater speed. As the tempo of their song escalated, the volume rose as well. The shaman twirled her hand over the spilled objects too small for Jaxson to see exactly what they were.

The warriors were in a frenzy, not only chanting but jumping up and down as well. Some individual warriors broke away from the group and tossed their spear over the small buildings into the jungle before rejoining the group, dancing, rocking, chanting. The shaman threw her head back and screamed. It was a shrill, piercing cry that caused the warriors closest to her to recoil, and a few fell over, passed out. Even at this great of a distance, Jaxson shut his eyes tight and covered his ears from the scream that seemed to be coming from in his head rather than the shaman in the village below.

Then, silence. Deep, thick silence covered the village, the surrounding jungle, and his little, rocky hiding place. No warrior made a sound or dared to even move. The insects that had provided a steady drone of noise fell silent. An invisible blanket had descended upon the area, stifling all sound.

Jaxson finally peeked through his fingers back down at the village below. Nothing moved, nothing stirred. The shaman, still on her knees with hands raised and head tossed back, appeared as still as a statue until quick as a thought, she pointed directly at Jaxson hiding in the rocks.

Wide-eyed, Jaxson stumbled away, tripping onto his backside. Before he could rise, the shaman appeared right in front of him. She did not climb onto the rocks; she did not jump up from the jungle. She was not there, and then she simply was. Jaxson held his hands in front of him and attempted to talk, but only a few stammered words escaped his lips before the shaman smiled.

Again and for the final time that night, a chill ran up Jaxson's spine. He was in trouble, big trouble.

The shaman smiled and then spoke the word that meant night soul from the nether, "Fenwa!"

Jaxson's world slipped into darkness, and he saw nor heard no more.

CHAPTER 1

Five Moons After Cliff

Even from heights above the clouds, Zero followed the path of the River Ural with ease. It was a wide, slow river whose headwaters were in a distant land. Rolling grassland dotted with the single large trees or the occasional stand of smaller scrub bushes stretched out in every direction for as far as his dragon eyes could see. To the north, a large herd of bison grazed. To the west, the direction they were traveling from, a sheet of heavy rain led up to dark, ominous clouds rolling to the south. The east and, eventually the Jasmine Sea, though it could not yet be seen, lay in front of Zero and Jaxson as they soared on a favorable wind.

I know it's not even midday yet, but if you see a favorable spot to rest and maybe even eat, go ahead and stop, said Jaxson in Zero's mind.

The dragon could not help but smile. Jaxson being hungry was a great sign as the young man had not been eating well lately. Zero could sense the boy's hunger now though, ravenous. *There is a bend in the river we should reach before the sun is on top of the sky. There is a copse ahead. If it is similar to the last two groups of trees on the riverbank, there will be persimmons. I know you like those.*

I do, replied Jaxson as he turned in his harness to grab his pack. *I haven't tried the new fishing reel I picked up in that coastal town. It is so light; I still don't know what type of wood it is made of.*

Going to try and catch a fish for dinner?

I could use something fresh. This dried pork is tough. What about you?

Zero's barrel-sized head turned one way and then the other. *If you could spare me for a bit, there is a herd of gazelle-shaped creatures not too far to the south. Can you see them? I might go visit them for a fresh meal of my own.*

I can't see them with my eyes, Jaxson said. *But I can with yours.*

Zero felt the comfortable presence of Jaxson inside his mind. Since the Dragon Trials and Jaxson's connection with the nether's magic, he and Jaxson's connection had only grown stronger. He knew Jaxson had been troubled with depression right after causing the death of his father and then obsessed with obtaining a way to speak with his father's spirit. But today, Jaxson's mind was more focused and less clouded. There was a playfulness to their interactions that Zero interpreted as Jaxson's happiness.

Hang on, I'm going to start going down.

After an uneventful landing, Zero gulped down the clean, cool water of the river. Behind him, Jaxson gathered the honey-sweet persimmons. Then, after removing the harness from Zero's back, they sat under the sun, relaxing in the warm breeze. Just before Zero could doze off, Jaxson rose and startled him.

"Think I am going to see if there are any trout along the edges," said Jaxson. "You should go get a meal. You haven't eaten in weeks."

I'm not starving, but I could eat. Please, be careful and pay attention to your surroundings.

"I'll be fine. Besides, we haven't seen any of the Empire soldiers for days," replied Jaxson as he assembled the pole and attached the reel.

Still, they have become more and more... dangerous after

their defeat near the Laguza Sea.

"Get out of here," said Jaxson with a smile as he pushed at the dragon's side. "You'll scare away all the fish."

Zero chuckled before springing into the air. The absence of Jaxson's weight did not affect him, but without the harness, he felt less constrained, freer. He shot straight up in the air with five strong thrusts of his wings. The trees below swayed and flailed around even as he leveled out and began a wide circle. A couple of loops just to be sure Jaxson was in no danger and then he would go hunt.

Keeping his eyes focused on the ground as he circled out and away from Jaxson, Zero did not see any threat. After three revolutions, he cut straight over Jaxson to head toward his meal. Jaxson was shin-deep in the river holding his fishing pole out in front of him. He pulled back and the line flew behind him. After a pause, he thrust his arm forward and the line followed. Zero waggled his wings to say good job. Seeing Jaxson fishing again after so many months, an activity the young man had always enjoyed, made Zero think that perhaps the darkest days were behind them. Jaxson had mourned his father's passing long and hard. It was time for them both to move forward.

And Zero did. He caught his gazelle and returned to camp with a full belly to see Jaxson cooking a fresh trout over a small flame. Both of them were full that night.

CHAPTER 2

The sun rose the next morning despite the evidence to the contrary. It was not raining, but dark clouds spanned the sky from horizon to horizon. Before even opening his eyes, Zero stretched his wings then stood with only his back legs and extended his front legs out resembling a cat more than a dragon. When his head finally came up and he opened his eyes, he was surprised to find that Jaxson was not still asleep.

Where are you?

The reply inside Zero's head came quickly. *Downriver about two hundred steps. There is a little pool here, and the trout are thick. I've already caught two.*

Excellent. Will you be back soon?

Depends. I would like to have a dozen filets or so. That may take a bit. Feel free to stretch your wings though.

The dragon paced around for a bit shaking out all of the early morning stiffness. A light drizzle began just as he launched himself into the sky. He decided the gazelle from the day before had been so tasty that he might need just one more. Even though he could go days without a meal with no adverse effects, there was no telling how long it could be before he ate again. He circled once to locate where exactly on the river Jaxson was set up and to also check for any possible dangers. Satisfied everything was as it should be, he angled toward where the herd had been yesterday and leisurely flew in that direction.

It did not take long for him to single out one of the

gazelles. After his meal, he quickly took to the sky to return to Jaxson. Although the boy was clearly acting more himself, Zero still worried about him. There had been weeks when all Jaxson would speak were ten words. Then other weeks he chatted nonstop about finding a witch that communed with spirits or the location of the fabled Living Scroll. A one-day turnaround did not completely assuage his worries about the boy's well-being.

As he approached the camp, a thin tendril of smoke rose from the stand of trees. Zero landed a distance away to not disturb Jaxson's cooking fire and approached on foot. Jaxson wrapped fish filets in longwood leaves and put them to the side before starting to cook more.

Fishing was productive, I see.

"I could've kept catching them; I left 'em biting," said Jaxson.

They'll still be there tomorrow, said Zero as he settled down opposite the fire from Jaxson who kept rearranging the pan on the hot coals.

"Maybe, maybe not."

What about us? Are we going to be here tomorrow?

Jaxson studied the crackling trout filets in the pan for a long time. He flipped them and then said, "I'm not sure."

Do you think it is time to go look for Tam or even the wizard?

Jaxson's lip curled up and his fists clenched. A second later he was back to his relaxed demeanor. If Zero had not been looking for a reaction, he would have missed it.

"Where would we even begin to look? We know Tam was with the bulk of the army that defeated the Empire on the coastline, but would he still be with them? There has been fighting all over the Kingdoms."

There is one true way to find out. We could be there in two weeks and it is hard flying, three if we take it easy.

Jaxson looked up to the sky and sighed. He rolled his head and his shoulders with his eyes closed. Quietly, he muttered, "Fine."

What did you say? asked Zero because he was sure he had heard, maybe not out loud but still heard, the word "whatever."

But a smile on Jaxson's face as he stood and stretched calmed Zero's suspicions.

"Fine, but I do want to go along the river for as long as possible. I had forgotten how much I really do like to fish."

Later that afternoon at Jaxson's request, they took to the sky and continued to follow the river looking for their next stop. Two eagles joined them for a time, darting in front of Zero and under him. Jaxson laughed, so the dragon engaged the noble ones in an air game of tag. When they turned south towards the distant hills, Jaxson urged Zero back to the river. That is where they saw the band of goblins camping near the riverbank.

Why do you think they are so far from their caves? asked Jaxson in Zero's head.

I cannot say for sure, though many appear to be injured. The party also have many goblin spawns which is odd this far away from the mountains. And not a good sign.

Why would you say that? Goblins aren't evil. Most battles or encounters with humans have been the humans' fault! said Jaxson.

Though they may not be evil per se, they are easily bought and have been known to do evil things for coin, replied Zero.

We should just avoid them. There are still hours left before sunset. Let's put some distance between them and our next camp.

Without responding, Zero gained some elevation and spurred them forward at a greater speed than they had been using. Just before sunset, the river split with the smaller stream going to the north. A decent-sized pool formed just past the division on the larger section of the river. Zero could sense Jaxson's excitement at the fishing opportunity below.

Even before setting up camp, Jaxson grabbed his rod and new reel and trotted down to the river's edge. Zero took the opportunity to stretch out and catch the sun's last remaining rays. Before the sun fell beneath the horizon, he fell asleep and remained that way until the next morning.

CHAPTER 3

Even through the fog of sleep and closed eyes, the world was lit up brighter than the midday sun. Thunder crashed. Zero leapt to his feet, his wings lying flat across his back and his teeth bared. Huge raindrops splashed on the ground all around him one at a time for a few moments until a sheet of rain drenched him and the campsite. Tension left his body as he realized it was just an overnight storm. It was common this far south to encounter these gales at any time.

The wind whipped the small stand of trees, pushing the tops to the ground before they sprang back into position. The dead campfire did not even produce a wisp of smoke. How long had he been asleep?

Jaxson, how can you sleep during this tempest?

When the young man did not immediately answer, Zero thought he must be exhausted. Much had happened recently and healing took so much energy. Jaxson had taken the death of his father hard and even more so because the boy knew he was the one that caused it. In the last few days, Zero had been pleased to find Jaxson climbing out of the depths of depression. Quietly, he moved over to the boy's bedroll and extended a wing, shielding the spot from the worst of the rain.

Zero could not believe he had slept from the late afternoon and through the night. He looked to the east and even with the storm clouds and rain, the horizon was brighter. It was morning.

Lightning struck again. A flash of the world around

him brighter than any daytime sun revealed little streams of rainwater coming down the slope directly at the slumbering boy.

Time to rise, Jaxson. I don't think you can swim while sleeping, said Zero. Again, the boy did not reply. With his front foot, the dragon nudged the bedroll. The soft blanket moved without resistance. Jaxson wasn't there.

Zero cocked his head to the side, taking a moment to realize what the empty bedroll meant. Perhaps Jaxson had gone to the river to fish before Zero had woken up. He turned to the small stump where Jaxson had piled his pack the day before. The boy's rod and new reel were on top of the old leather bag.

Something started growing in the pit of Zero's stomach. He could not identify the sensation at first. But it grew, spreading up his spine and causing his wings to shudder all the way to his head. Jaxson was missing. With that thought, the panic that had started in his belly reached his head.

Jaxson! Where are you?

Of course, no reply came back to him. He stalked around the campsite looking for any indication of where the boy had gone. The rain had washed away any track or sign. Zero ran to the riverbank looking around wildly for the boy. Again, the rain foiled his attempts. He could not see more than a dragon's length in any direction. With a roar, he took to the sky. He stayed low as he flew in a small circle around the campsite. Flying faster and faster, he expanded his search. Lap after lap did not produce any results.

It was as though Jaxson had disappeared into thin air. But Zero knew that to be impossible. The rain lessened and sight lines increased, so Zero gained some elevation. His eyesight allowed him to spot his friend at a great distance even from this height.

Thunder rumbled as the storm continued on its way.

Daylight from the midmorning sun pierced the clouds. How long had he been looking for Jaxson? No more than an hour surely. The sun should not be that high in the sky. Why had he slept for so long?

He blew dragon's fire in his frustration as he screamed Jaxson's name. He reached out with his mind, attempting to locate the boy through their connection. He could sense him, but the link was weak. Too weak. He could not identify anything about Jaxson's condition or whereabouts, only that Jaxson lived. He made another circle, which revealed nothing, so he landed back at the muddy campsite.

Taking a deep breath, he closed his eyes and calmed himself. Frightened panic would not be helpful. Focus and alertness was what he needed. He stuck his nose in the sodden bedroll. The only smell was that of Jaxson. No clue there. He used a claw to clumsily move the pack around. All of Jaxson's stuff, the frying pan, his quiver with arrows, the rod and reel were all present. His bow was missing however. Instead of flying in circles, Zero decided to walk the perimeter searching for any clues.

Near the riverbank to the north, he found Jaxson's shattered bow along with one broken arrow. There were no tracks around, but one of the small trees had a gash in it like it had been struck by something sharp. Had Jaxson been attacked and captured by the Empire? No Empire troops had been seen for days, still he knew they were looking for both Jaxson and himself. But surely, he would have spotted them either the day before or this morning. It was hard to hide from his dragon eyes with all of the armor and horses.

He had spotted no one. No one except that gob of goblins. The goblins! They must have Jaxson, expecting to get a ransom or to turn him in for the reward coin the Empire was offering. Zero's nostrils flared, and a tiny bit of dragon's fire slipped out. But he was definitely going to get him back.

CHAPTER 4

The goblin band left behind an easy trail to follow from the place they had been the day before. Even while staying high in the sky to prevent being spotted, Zero had no trouble following their path. The sun slowly sank toward the horizon when Zero began circling their campsite. He needed to know where Jaxson was being held before dropping in to save him. He didn't want to accidentally hurt him.

Not many of the goblins were armed. The sentries scattered around the camp carried bows. Several male and female goblins had short swords at their waist and wore ill-fitting armor. Zero found it odd how many little ones scampered around from tent to makeshift tent as they played tag or some other game. In the center of their camp, a large fire blazed, and many of the goblins were near it, drinking out of skins and eating fish straight from the pan.

As it grew darker, torches were lit from the fire and placed throughout the tents. It was when the older goblin shuffled over to a large tent just outside the fire's light that Zero noticed the guards. Stationed outside the dark-colored tent, two guards with the best-looking armor of all the goblins stood watch. Jaxson must be held within that tent.

Stars shone down on the camp, and Zero still flew above it. He had not been noticed even as he descended to get a better view. He reached out to Jaxson again. Although he could sense the boy, Jaxson did not answer him. Zero grew concerned as it was a weaker connection than before. He made one more pass before deciding to go rest for the night.

He needed to be sure Jaxson was in the tent being guarded before he attacked.

Zero found a spot just upriver and to the west. A large hill with three out-of-place boulders overlooked the grasslands below. Zero wedged between the two largest rocks and attempted to sleep. Every so often, he would reach out to Jaxson, and each time, he failed to connect. Before the sun even rose, the dragon was in the sky hoping to catch a glimpse of his friend so he could rescue him.

Without the light, Zero circled the campsite lower than yesterday. Smoke from the low-burning fire obscured his view. Most of the torches had burned out overnight, adding to his lack of sight and frustration. From what he could see, little was different, though it was quiet. The tent he thought Jaxson was in was still guarded, though now four goblins with armor and swords stood out front.

The sun peeked over the horizon forcing Zero higher into the sky if he wished to still maintain his surprise advantage. As more and more goblins left their tents, it became obvious to the dragon that a battle had occurred. Many goblins were heavily bandaged and others used sticks as canes to help them walk. Some of the younger and still fit goblins moved around with waterskins and plates serving those that struggled to get around on their own.

Even if Jaxson had put up a fight, he wouldn't have caused this level of destruction without getting away or dying himself, thought Zero before he reached out to Jaxson again. No response, and the connection felt weaker yet. Zero began to worry Jaxson was dying in that tent.

Horns blasted from down below. Goblins scurried everywhere. Some started ripping tents down while others gathered whatever arms they had and moved to the edge of the camp. Little ones were herded together and pushed toward the river. Two goblins began dousing the fire, first with water then dirt. Finally, they stomped at any remaining embers as another group of goblins brought a large wet blanket and smothered even the smoke. The campsite was a hive of activity. Zero knew this was his chance. Enter in the chaos, retrieve Jaxson, and be back in the air before anyone was the wiser.

With one great downstroke of his wings, Zero climbed and then turned his nose back at the ground. His legs were pulled in tightly to his back as he started his descent. Another mighty wing beat, then his wings folded neatly onto his back. He was straight as an arrow as he raced to the goblin camp. Just before striking the ground face-first, he pulled up, using his wings to soften his landing. The wind caused the blanket to fly off the dying fire, and smoke and ash filled the air.

Goblins scattered in every direction. An older goblin outfitted in outdated armor dropped his sword and ran along with most everyone else. Two goblins, however, came at Zero from the same side. Patiently knowing their short swords were little threat, Zero waited until they were too close to turn around and jumped toward them, ramming them with his shoulder. They landed in a head of leather armor and tangled legs outside the tent area. A high-pitched scream pierced the air as a goblin female tried to stop a little one that was running toward Zero.

Having no desire to crush the tiny goblin child, Zero sidestepped and headed straight for the tent he thought Jaxson to be held in. None of the goblins tried to stop him. Several adult goblins holding infants dodged out of his way as he thundered forward. His plan was to rip the tent from the ground exposing what was hidden inside. Jaxson could then jump on his back or Zero would pick him up. Either way, they were leaving together.

One of the four armed guards slipped into the tent, but the other three, obviously well trained, pulled their weapons and spread out. One had a long spear that Zero had not seen before, one had a short sword in one hand and a small iron shield in the other, and the final goblin had a bow with a quiver full of arrows. He wouldn't be able to take them all at one time like the other two that had rushed him. Zero would need to eliminate the archer first. A well-shot arrow to his face or wings could spell trouble.

He turned his body to not allow the spear wielding goblin a clear shot to any vulnerable areas and stepped toward the archer. The goblin with an arrow already clear of the quiver and on the bow did not back down. Zero bobbed his head just as the arrow was released causing it to sail high of the intended mark. The sword goblin attacked, but the dragon simply batted him away with his large front leg. The spear raked down his back scales but did little to no damage. Zero pulled his head back, preparing to loose dragon's fire onto the archer who had already nocked another arrow. He took in a deep breath and—

"STOP!"

The booming command made him freeze. He turned to see the old wizard, Dreknoxious, emerging from the long tent. The wizard held his staff aloft and the sword, bow, and spear flew out of the goblins' hands. When he lowered the staff, Zero's mouth shut involuntarily.

"Zero, what is the meaning of all this ruckus? And where in all of creation is Jaxson?"

CHAPTER 5

When the goblins saw that Zero was no longer attacking them, they immediately went back to breaking down camp and packing it away. Zero turned his head from side to side, looking at the chaos around him, then back down to the wizard. Nothing around him made sense.

What are you doing here?

"You didn't answer my question," replied Dreknoxious. "But give me a moment in the tent, and then I'll explain all. Why don't you go to that hill just over there? I think the rest of the Solostire Clan would appreciate the space."

Zero nodded and began walking away. The wizard ducked back into the tent just as Zero made it past where the last row of tents had been only moments ago. The goblins assembled near the river in the opposite direction from which he was headed. As he arrived at the hill an hour later, he realized if he would have flown, he would have been there in a fraction of the time.

He was not surprised when he saw the wizard sitting atop a boulder waiting for him.

I'll answer your question before you ask again. I don't know where Jaxson is right now. He disappeared two nights ago, and I thought the goblins had taken him for ransom.

Dreknoxious scratched his neck under his long white beard and looked to the sky before replying. "That is... unfortunate news. But before we talk about Jaxson, I imagine you wish to know why I was with the clan of goblins, yes?"

To be honest, I hadn't even considered the why. I am solely focused on finding him. Our connection is weaker now than it has ever been regardless of distance.

The wizard laughed. "But you can still feel him, then? That's excellent, excellent. But about the goblins, it seems the Empire is running out of soldiers so they are capturing goblins, giants, trolls, and humans to fight for them."

How is the Empire getting them to fight? I can see getting captured but never fighting for those that wish to just take or destroy.

"They also enslave anyone one the captured warriors care about. They fight so their loved ones may live," said Dreknoxious. "In all fairness, that is precisely why most wars are waged."

Still doesn't explain why you are with these goblins.

"Ah yes, of course. I was simply in the area and saw their plight. Their king was in the tent, gravely injured. He slowed them down. I lent a hand to get him back on his feet again," said Dreknoxious with a smile. "King Leonity and I go way back."

Zero shook his barrel-sized head. *You are friends with the goblin king?*

After standing and puffing out his chest, Dreknoxious replied, "I am a friend to many, which is no concern of yours. It was fortunate I was present as many goblins would have died by your claws for no reason today."

Looking down at the ground, Zero nodded an agreement. *I was prepared to roast every goblin in that camp if I thought it would save Jaxson.*

"As any good dragon would do for their rider, of course. Now, we have much to do, and I'm afraid time is not on our side," said the old wizard. "So, could you come near the boulder please?"

Doing as he was told, Zero pressed up against the rock.

Dreknoxious hopped onto his back with a little grunt. "Now, do you have any supplies or such to gather before we depart?"

No. But where are we going?

"To find Jaxson, where else?" exclaimed the wizard. "I do have a stop or two to make as well."

That's fine, but really, where are we going? I don't even know where to begin looking.

"Whoever took him—if in fact he was taken—has long departed this area," said Dreknoxious. "Let us check on the Three Kingdom's forces. They are expecting an update from me anyway. There may even be a familiar person or dragon or three with them that would be willing to lend a wing to the search for your missing dragon rider."

With a powerful downthrust of his wings, Zero took to the sky, and after flying due north until midday, the wizard told Zero to angle toward the Dragon Spine Mountains, Jaxson and Zero's home.

But I thought the army was near the coast.

"Oh, it is. But first, we have a slight detour."

The Dragon Spine is not a slight detour. It's at least three days' flight and then the same again just to get back here, replied Zero even as he turned in the direction Dreknoxious had indicated.

"I don't think we will have time to stop at your dragonling home if that is what you are worried about," said the wizard as he slapped Zero on the back.

And for three days, Zero flew in the direction that he had spent most of his life.

That was until he saw the Empire's army in the foothills.

CHAPTER 6

"We will approach the outskirts of the Dragon Spine shortly," said Dreknoxious as he mounted Zero.

Just the foothills. It is another day's flight to get back home.

"Ah but we aren't going back to your and Jaxson's valley. Our destination is much closer," said the wizard in between bites of hard cheese.

Without a fire the previous night, the wizard had not cooked anything. Thus far the old man had survived on water, cheese, and the occasional wild fruit. Zero had not been able to eat since Jaxson had disappeared but was growing hungry now.

Wherever we are going, if I see a meal on the way, I'm gonna get it.

"Of course, you are still a growing dragon after all."

The wind crossing the plains had been warm and dry. But now as they approached the mountains, a distinct chill filled the air. Zero took in a huge breath and rose higher into the sky. It had been some time since he had smelled the crisp mountain air. But there was a scent mixed in that shouldn't be there. Ahead and to their left, smoke rose gently before being ushered away on the wind. The fire was too large to be a single campfire and made Zero curious. It was the wrong season for wildfires, though a lightning strike could spark a fire at any time if there was no rain. The wizard did not object when Zero altered their course slightly to get a better look.

As they approached the smoke, Dreknoxious said, "Turn

back. I do not wish for us to be spotted."

Spotted? Who is it?

"From the individual fires, I would put their numbers somewhere near a full division," said Dreknoxious.

How do you even know it is the Empire? I can't see anything yet.

"Look below. Do you see the wheel ruts? Notice anything different about them?"

The dragon scrutinized the path below. It took a moment before he blurted, *There are three ruts. That is weird.*

"The Empire used a three-wheeled wagon pulled by teams of horses. That is the only thing that could make tracks such as those," said Dreknoxious.

They shouldn't be this far inland!

"Although the overall war is going well with the Kingdoms keeping the Empire from gaining a permanent foothold, the Empire has vast numbers. And they travel in a way that we do not yet understand," said the wizard. "Hence why I would like us to go undetected."

From the other side of the smoke that was getting closer each moment, two large dragons with mounted riders took flight. They were both pointing directly away from Zero and Dreknoxious. Zero's back bristled. Dragons fighting for the Empire did not sit well with him.

"Easy now, Zero. Perhaps, it's best to avoid them."

I could take them.

"Surely, but there would be no way to avoid detection if you dispatched two of their dragons," said Dreknoxious. "We should turn back."

For several wingbeats, Zero did not alter his course. He knew he needed to trust the wizard. He started a wide turn then dove straight now, skimming the tops of the tall evergreen trees. With the dive, he gained speed and banked harder. In a matter of seconds, they were flying in the direction they had come. Dreknoxious gave him some directions for the long way to the destination he had in mind.

Just before dark, after a long day of flying and staying vigilant, they arrived at the camp. It sat up a small rise with a sheer drop on the other side sandwiched by a vertical cliff. Across the small canyon the Dragon Spine Mountains rose straight into the sky. As far as defensive positions went, it was as good a spot as any. The tents were huge and easily able to house twenty to thirty people each. It wasn't until after Zero landed and was quickly surrounded by warriors carrying spears as long as he was that he realized why the tents were so large. Dreknoxious had brought him to a camp full of giants.

CHAPTER 7

With a quick thrust of his wings, Zero could be in the air and, with any luck, avoid all the jagged spearheads pointed at him. He told the old wizard on his back his plan, but Dreknoxious strongly suggested that he wait.

Pulling his hood off his head and standing on Zero's back, Dreknoxious announced his presence. "I am Dreknoxious of the Fifth Path, Great Wizard of the Three Kingdoms—lay down your weapons and let your leader know I seek his counsel."

No movement from the giants. A quick count revealed there are seventeen warriors encircling us with many more just behind. I don't think they were impressed.

"Apparently not," whispered Dreknoxious. "Let's try something a little more dramatic."

Shrugging off his coat, the wizard pushed the sleeves of his robe up. He put one foot forward and bent his knees slightly, balancing on Zero's back as the dragon turned slightly to face the biggest portion of giant warriors. Dreknoxious started chanting words that sounded like nonsense to Zero. The giants nearby whispered to each other, and several with weapons began backing away.

He threw his hands in the air and began swirling them around. The clouds above began to move in a lazy circle. The very daylight around them dimmed. As the wizard's voice rose, so did the nerves of all the surrounding giants. All except the young male giant that took two large strides and stood in front of Zero with crossed arms.

"Stop!" commanded the giant.

Dreknoxious clapped his hands together and said, "Pop!"

Without blinking, Zero noticed the clouds stopped moving and the light was normal. The wizard, defying his age, hopped off his back and landed lightly directly in front of the giant chieftain that had stepped forward. Although it had been years ago and Zero had only seen him from the sky, he had no doubts this was the giant that had defected from the Goat Head Warrior's side to the Princess's army. The wizard stood before the giant, the top of his hat barely making it to the giant's chest. After a tense moment of thick silence, both let out a laugh. Dreknoxious's laugh sounded like water running down a rock bank, and the giant chieftain's laugh clapped like thunder. They embraced, and the surrounding giants finally put away their weapons.

When Dreknoxious and the giant started walking toward the cliff near the back of camp, Zero followed. The wizard turned and motioned for Zero to stay. With them chatting and the other giants doing anything but engaging with him, Zero simply sat and looked around. His nose caught the scent of cooking beef before his eyes, and he was drawn to three large fires cooking whole sides of juicy meat. He ambled over, transfixed by the flames and the intoxicating scent. The giants manning the large spit-roasting sticks that the meat was skewered on did not flinch when Zero approached.

Instead, they offered him a side of beef they had just pulled from above the red-hot coals. Without hesitation, Zero gulped down the meal in one motion. Wide-eyed, the giant closest to him clapped. "It good?"

Zero smiled as only a dragon can and bobbed his head. The giant laughed and clapped again as another side of beef was skewered and placed over the coals. Trying not to seem greedy, he turned and walked slowly toward the tree line. It was there that Dreknoxious caught up with him.

Still in the company of the giant chieftain, the wizard launched into the plight of the giants. He explained how the Empire had captured some of their kin and were now trying to wear the rest of them down. If they could capture more of the giant warriors, it would be a huge boon to their army.

"And of course, you have seen many of these giants before. This is Dane, Chieftain of the Broken Cliff Tribe. He was at the battle against the Goat Head Sorcerer that you and Jaxson aided the Princess with," said Dreknoxious.

I remember him, though we never met, replied Zero. *Are we finished with our detour now?*

"I know you are eager to find Jaxson," said Dreknoxious. "But Dane was wondering if you could help out a bit first. If we could somehow neutralize the Empire's dragons, the giant warriors would make short work of the remaining Empire soldiers."

I see.

"Shouldn't take us more than a day or so to plan," said the wizard, pointing at Dane. "He already has a wonderful strategy laid out. He just needs some help neutralizing their winged attackers."

Zero rose and started walking to the edge of the camp. He moved with purpose, putting one foot in front of the other, looking only straight ahead. The wizard and Dane exchanged a glance before Dreknoxious started following the dragon.

"And just where are you going?"

Zero did not answer and did not alter his path except to avoid a couple of giant craftsmen working on studded leather armor. He did not even look back to acknowledge the old man had spoken.

"Now, hold on just a moment, Zero!"

He was past the last of the tents now in the last open area before the tree line. His knees bent and wings flattened as he prepared to leap into the air.

"Jaxson is still alive and his situation has been unchanged for days now. You can still feel him, I know you can. He will most likely still be there in two days wherever he is," said Dreknoxious. Zero turned, facing the wizard, with nostrils flared and a tiny stream of smoke rising up from them. "But these folks here won't be."

Zero's eyes darted over the wizard's head and took in the camp again. Giants worked on weapons over a makeshift forge. Others manned the cooking fires. Several giant children were coming up the hill carrying huge urns filled with water. Some of it splashed on the smallest child's head causing him and the other with him to burst out laughing. He saw how the mother of a small child couldn't keep her eyes off of the little one playing. And how each time the wind blew, every warrior looked up to the sky as they raised their spears, anticipating an attack from above.

"They are barely holding on and just need a bit of help. We can be that help," said Dreknoxious softly as he stepped up to Zero's head and placed a hand gently on the green snout.

What if Jaxson is hurt? What if he is in serious trouble?

"You could probably help him if that is the case. But there is no doubt, absolutely and fundamentally no doubt, you can help these." Dreknoxious raised a hand and swept it around in a circle. "You can make a difference NOW. You just have to resolve to do so."

Zero turned away from the giants. The thought of Jaxson being in trouble was almost too much to bear. He reached out to his rider and could sense his presence though weak. It was unchanged—weak but there was no sign of any additional distress. Or any distress at all. Jaxson was simply there, but he had no idea where there could be. He closed his eyes, and his head dropped slightly.

So, what is the plan to take care of the Empire's dragons?

CHAPTER 8

Zero, Dreknoxious, Dane, and an assortment of different giants planned and schemed long into the night. Zero realized early on that the others, including Dreknoxious, had no real ideas on how to deal with the aerial threat of the two enemy dragons. One giant advisor wanted to build a catapult, but that was quickly dismissed as being too time consuming. No one knew the proper way to build one anyway unless the wizard was holding out. The prevailing battle theory that Dane was most enthused about was for the giants not to leave the relative safety of the tall pine trees. The forest would at least keep them safe from above.

"But dragon's fire doesn't care if you are under a tree. It burns everything with equal prejudice," said Dreknoxious as he threw his hands in the air. The wizard turned around mumbling about thick headed, boulder-like creatures.

"Trees better. Wide open, dangerous," replied Dane for the sixth or seventh time.

"The Empire's army isn't foolish enough to follow you in there. The dragons will simply burn around the edges until you are forced out. We need to take the fight to them and not wait for an attack up on this hill," said Dreknoxious.

We should take the battle to them. Stop the dragons before they ever get off the ground, said Zero to Dreknoxious.

And how do you propose we accomplish that?

"Dragons away. Distract," said Dane.

"That is an idea worth exploring," replied Dreknoxious.

Drop a rock on their wings or something.

Or... we could go fishing! Throw a large net over them, and I could anchor it down. It would take them too long to cut the dragons free.

That could work, but where would we get a net that is strong enough? asked Zero.

"Oh, Chieftain Dane, do you have many here that are good at weaving or sewing?"

Dane cocked his head to the side and grunted, a sound Zero took to mean yes. "Why?"

"Perhaps we could use the tents, if they are properly cut and sewn, as a giant net to trap their dragons on the ground," said Dreknoxious. "Then, you and your warriors go down there and take the fight to them. They will be running away before the sun even rises."

A rumbling sound akin to two large boulders rubbing together came from the chieftain. Dane bent over, grabbing his side. "Might work. But funny."

All the giants listening laughed, but after a couple of moments, Dane flicked his wrist and all started moving. Tents were pulled down and gathered; all the ropes were placed next to the dense fabric. Zero watched in astonishment as the giants, within an hour, had a giant net made, folded, and ready to be dropped on the unsuspecting dragons. Even the wizard seemed surprised at their quick craftsmanship.

I need to rest. Half the night is gone already, said Zero.

"I agree. With all of this noise, I'm not sure how much sleep we can get."

Let's go under that clump of trees. It is far enough away to rest but still be ready with a moment's notice.

Zero used the largest pine tree as a scratching post, taking care of an itch between his wings. He circled the area twice and lay down. Dreknoxious sat near Zero's large front claw and leaned his head back. His eyes closed, and he was snoring before Zero even laid his own head down. He needed to rest, but he couldn't keep his thoughts from Jaxson. He reached out to him again. Jaxson was there, Zero knew that, but the boy did not respond to him. He laid his head on the cool mat of pine straw, and his eyelids started to close.

Then, dragon's fire lit up the night, and the screams of the giants filled the air. Zero's head shot up and looked back to camp. Soldiers were marching steadily toward the bonfires as one of the dragon's laid down a line of fire to keep the giants contained.

The wizard sprang onto Zero's back. "We have to eliminate their dragons or Dane and his people don't stand a chance!"

Do you have a plan?

"No, but we will come up with something. Now, let us get in the air," said Dreknoxious.

Launching up and out, Zero stayed low to the ground and then slipped over the edge of the canyon. He flew below the fray for a few moments, staying silent. Surprise was still their best weapon.

I just really wanted to do some fishing. The net idea would have worked.

"Fishing can be fun, but so is hunting. Let's go hunting for some Empire!"

The air down in the canyon was warmer with no top wind coming down off the mountains this low. Although it was still hours before dawn, moonlight illuminated his flight path as Zero flew straight ahead.

"We need to find their other dragon. The brown one spitting all of that dragon's fire is simply there to contain the giants. The other dragon is the most immediate threat," said Dreknoxious.

I can come out of the canyon over the hills behind the camp. That will keep us shrouded in darkness for as long as possible.

Banking first to the right before diving slightly then pointing straight up and to the left, Zero climbed out of the canyon and over the high rocky foothills. To their left at a significant distance, the glow of the dragon's fire lit up the sky like the coming of the day. Zero climbed higher still, scouring the sky for any sign of the other dragon. Slowly, he turned back toward the camp and the battle that should be in full rage by this time. Still, there was no sign of the other dragon.

Gliding so high, the camp came into view quickly. A solid line of dragon's fire, the canyon, and the sharp cliff hemmed the giants in on three sides. Empire soldiers set up a defensive line along the other side but did not attack. The brown dragon with his rider flew over the fire, adding to it occasionally as it would die down slightly.

What are they waiting for? Why haven't they attacked?

"Excellent question. I think the answer must lie with the other dragon. Have you managed to spot it?"

The skies as far as I can see are clear, said Zero as he scanned left to right. *Wait a moment, yes! There, next to the river by the top of the falls. It's a blue dragon on the ground. The rider is still in the seat. They are waiting for something.*

"A signal to attack most likely. Perhaps they are attempting to get the giants to surrender. It would mean more giants fighting for them if they don't have to fight now."

What should we do?

"We still have the same goal: neutralize their dragons. The blue one is probably waiting for the giants to engage so he can come in behind them."

Any idea how we can stop them?

"I have a thought... How do you feel about long odds

with very little chance of success? But if we succeed, it'll serve more than one purpose?"

That's too much to consider right now. Just tell me where to fly and who to attack.

"Easy enough. Slip back down into the canyon, but hurry, time is not on our side."

CHAPTER 9

Just before Zero and Dreknoxious flew back into the canyon undetected, Dane managed to get his warriors to rally, forming a defensive line in front of their young and old. If the wizard was correct, the blue dragon was intent on separating the two groups holding the defenseless hostage. Everything happened so fast, and Zero did not understand the little of Dreknoxious's plan that the wizard had conveyed. Still, any plan was better than his, which was nonexistent.

Flying silently and with haste, Zero approached the camp and then the line of dragon's fire from the brown dragon. "Remember, we need to get this dragon's attention without alerting the blue one on the hillside."

With the wizard on his back, Zero came out of the canyon just past the line of dragon's fire burning brightly. He stayed low to the ground watching the brown dragon flying above the line of flames away from him. Zero slowed down, waiting on the brown dragon to turn and add more flames to the growing line. Just as it tilted in the air and started spewing more flames, Zero rose and shot his own flame directly at the brown dragon. He was too far away to cause any damage and still low enough that he hoped the blue dragon would not be able to differentiate the two different dragon flames.

As the wizard had hoped, the brown dragon and its rider saw them and moved to intercept. Zero banked hard, completely turning around. He stayed slow, waiting on the brown dragon to get behind him. When it was in place,

Zero sped up and lowered himself to just above the rocky terrain. When they arrived at the canyon, Zero dove straight down, but instead of flying either up or down the canyon, Zero altered his angle and stopped abruptly, clinging to the canyon wall. Moments later the brown dragon flew overhead. Dreknoxious held up his staff and chanted softly. Down the canyon in the opposite direction of the blue dragon, flames erupted.

The wizard continued to chant, and the fire curled and grew before extinguishing in a flash. The brown dragon took the bait with a roar and a blast of its own dragon's fire. When it rounded the corner out of sight, Zero pushed them off the wall and back into the canyon.

"Now, go grab the net."

I hope it hasn't been singed or all of this has been for nothing.

"We will find out when we get there. But again, we should hurry!" shouted the wizard.

Gliding quietly in the canyon alongside the camp, Zero judged their progress to be about correct. He turned up and flew out of the canyon, staying low to the ground again. The net was still neatly stacked in the camp away from the defensive line formed by the giants. The Empire soldiers had not yet attacked, giving Zero hope they just might pull off their stunt. Without landing, he reached down with his large talons, grabbing the rope handles the giants had attached to the pile of netting. He grunted; it was heavier than he had assumed but not so heavy that he couldn't manage. The net started to sway beneath him as he accelerated.

"Steady there, Zero. Slow is smooth, and smooth is quick. Make no mistake, we need to be quick," said Dreknoxious. Even though the wizard did not shout and did not communicate via the dragon thought, Zero heard him loud and clear.

I dare not move my head; I'm just trying to keep this heavy net steady. Is the blue dragon still on the ground?

"Yes, yes, we still have time. Now, swing around so we come at both dragon and rider from behind. They will never know what hit them."

Zero did as he was told and swung wide and then climbed up over the foothills. He angled their flight back toward the camp and the blue dragon that they could not see from this vantage point. When he was at a point that was as straight a shot as possible, he began to gain speed. Their good luck and element of surprise was bound to run out eventually. No need in lollygagging until that happened. Without turning or accelerating wildly, the net stayed suspended beneath them relatively in place. The ground beneath them rolled past quickly.

Just ahead and slightly to the left, Zero saw the blue dragon. It was on its feet now, wings pushed back ready to leap into the air. In mere moments, their plan would be shot.

Do you see—

"I see them. Hold very still," said Dreknoxious. The wizard stood on Zero's back and waved his staff and free hand in the air. "Get ready to drop the net!"

It's too early!

"Now," shouted Dreknoxious loud enough for the blue dragon and its rider to turn toward them. Zero let go of the net. Unfurling as it fell, Zero knew it was going to miss the mark. He told the wizard it was too soon. The blue dragon tensed, preparing to spring into flight. A wind from behind them pushed the net forward, and before the blue dragon left the ground, the net slammed into him. Dreknoxious continued waving his staff and shouting. Roots shot out of the ground and wrapped themselves around the net, making it impossible for the dragon to shrug it off.

"There. That should hold it on the ground for a bit," said

the wizard.

What is our next move? asked Zero.

The wizard never had a chance to answer. With a crash, the brown dragon slammed into Zero causing Dreknoxious to slip off Zero's side and plummet to the ground. He didn't have time to search for the wizard, however. He was distracted, fighting for his life.

CHAPTER 10

The enemy dragon, though much smaller than Zero, was still large enough to cause problems to Zero's flight when it wouldn't let go of him after ramming him in midair. The rider shouted at the brown dragon in a language that Zero was unfamiliar with but still understood to mean, "Hang on!"

His left wing throbbed with each beat, bleeding near where it met his body but also shredded in a portion of the thin membrane near his wingtip. Each wingbeat caused more damage, so Zero angled toward the ground where his superior size would be an even bigger advantage. As they approached the ground at alarming speed, the brown dragon realized what was happening and attempted to disengage from Zero. It was an expected reaction, and Zero twisted in midair, grabbing the smaller dragon and forcing it under him. With a thunderous crash, they bounced and rolled along the rocky ground.

Sliding to a stop, Zero rose to his feet and turned back to the brown dragon, expecting an attack. But the smaller dragon did not stir from its sprawled position. Halfway between the two dragons, the rider lay face down. Zero knew without checking that the rider would not rise again, but the brown dragon's back swelled with breath. Cautiously, Zero approached the injured dragon. It wore armor, mostly plated steel, that covered its chest and exposed sides leaving only the neck area vulnerable. As Zero circled to the side where the dragon's head rested, his eyes grew big. Etched into the dragon's skin were the jagged signs of blood magic used by the Sorcerers of the Isle of Creptin. Some of the lines were fresh, wounds still open. Yet others were nearly healed. Even thin lines of scars could be seen in between and amongst the tortured scales and flesh.

I did not expect you to crash us into the hillside, said the brown dragon. *But I am glad you did.*

Why? Why would you be happy? Your rider is dead, and from the looks of it, you will be soon as well, Zero growled.

My rider? the brown dragon said as its head rose; its eyes, black as a moonless night, locked onto Zero. The larger dragon took a quick step back. *My rider? My captor, not my rider.*

Zero sighed. *I see. And now you are... free of his imprisonment?*

Now, I am free.

The not-so-distant sounds of giant war calls seemed muted as Zero moved in closer to the brown dragon. *Be free. Soon your wings will carry you over the clouds to join our family in the Mountains of Ramphirion. Rest easy.*

With a small flutter, the brown dragon's eyes closed as a small final breath escaped its lungs. Zero threw his head back and blew dragon's fire straight into the air. He held it, the flame reaching higher and higher, lasting longer than any fire he had ever produced. When he finished, he flopped onto the ground. So much was wrong. Dragons being forced with vile magic to do the bidding of cruel riders. Giants and goblins and others being rounded up to fight in a war they did not believe in. He was still no closer to finding Jaxson than he had been the morning he awoke to find him missing. He did not know if he had the strength of will to keep going.

"It is truly horrific the lengths man and some others will go for power," said Dreknoxious.

Zero turned his head to see the old wizard standing

near him, perhaps leaning on his staff more than usual but other than that looking the no worse for wear. He thought he should be surprised to see the old man, but somehow, he could not muster the strength even for that.

"And there will be a time to mourn and a time to lament, even a time to scream into the ether, but now is not that time, young one," said Dreknoxious as he placed a wrinkled hand on Zero's neck.

I don't know how to keep going. Jaxson is who knows where. Dragons are being tortured. It is too much. Zero closed his eyes again as he laid his head back on the rocky ground.

Below them, the giants issued another war cry and charged at the Empire army. Arrows loosed from behind the line of armored men. Several giants stumbled and one fell but most pushed forward. Before they reached the enemy line, the soldiers from the other side turned and ran leaving behind only some upset barrels strewn out across their retreat. As the giants approached, archers from the Empire loosed another volley, but this time, the arrows were tipped with fire.

Whoosh! Flames flew up from the ground when the arrows ignited the contents of the emptied barrels. The giants were forced to watch their enemy retreat without being able to put an end to them.

Zero raised his head to watch the scene below. *Why are the Empire soldiers retreating so quickly?*

"I imagine they anticipated the dragons they control to do most of the work today. With them not in play, there stood little to gain in dying at the hands of the giants because that is all that would have happened."

What are you going to do with the blue dragon? We can't let it go right back to the Empire.

"Yes, the blue dragon," said Dreknoxious. "Let's go have a look-see, shall we?"

C. H. SMITH

Without responding, Zero rose to his feet. His wing screamed in agony as he folded it along his back. As they approached the net holding the dragon in place, the dragon rider suddenly jumped up, dropping the short sword he had been using to cut at the ropes and nocking an arrow.

"Hold if you value your life," said Dreknoxious. The rider just laughed and loosed the arrow. The wizard sighed and swiped his hand. The arrow fell harmlessly to the ground.

Seeing his arrow pushed aside so easily, the rider turned tail and ran after the rest of the Empire soldiers. Zero moved around the netting until the blue dragon could see him.

Easy friend. I don't want to hurt you, said Zero.

The blue dragon strained against the netting, hissing and spitting out weak flames of dragon's fire. Zero tilted his head then looked at Dreknoxious.

"I made the net heavier and resistant to flames," the wizard said as he shrugged his shoulders.

We can't free him.

"The same armor the brown dragon wore is on this one. We can assume the same vile sorcery has been etched into its scales," said Dreknoxious.

Growling, Zero looked down the hill to where the rider still ran after the remaining soldiers. Springing off the ground, Zero flew after him. Each beat of his wings sent an agonizing thrill up his back. It didn't matter. This evil needed to be stopped. Dragon's fire, hot and red, billowed out of his mouth, incinerating the rider and leaving nothing but ash.

Zero landed and trudged back up the hill to where Dreknoxious had removed the side plate on the blue dragon, revealing the deep gashes of the blood magic.

"I believe I can alter this enough to make it powerless, and as the dragon heals, it will be gone completely," said the wizard to Zero. "But there will be a large amount of pain."

326

The blue dragon continued to strain against the ropes but without any real force. *Free him, Dreknoxious. No one should be a slave.*

CHAPTER 11

The silence draped over Zero like a shroud. It had taken him all afternoon and into the twilight to work his way up the side of the biggest hill. He was tired, sore, and his wing hurt worse than anything he had ever felt, but he was glad to be away from everyone. The giants celebrated their victory over the Empire with gusto; everyone singing and dancing and shouting and laughing. But Zero could not join in the merriment with Jaxson still missing and dragons being abused. So, he had climbed the hill to escape the bluster and noise. Now, as the stars started twinkling, he took a deep, chilly breath, exhaling slowly. For the first time since Jaxson's disappearance, he slowed down enough to properly think.

And think he did. Though he was tired, his brain would not allow him to sleep. So, he didn't. Instead, he tried to relive the last few months leading up to the morning Jaxson disappeared. It had been a dark time, real dark with days on end without Jaxson saying a word. He had only eaten if Zero asked him to, and he had never laughed or even smiled. His obsession with finding the Living Scroll had consumed him and put a wedge between them. Jaxson knew Zero thought they should be in search of the book a continent away that Dreknoxious and the ancient dragon had sent them to find. There they had found friends, glory, and a hint from the Oracle, but no book. But that had search ended before it had even started on the day Jaxson had defended both himself and Zero against an attacking enemy.

His father had led the enemy group. Jaxson did what he

had to do, but more than his father died that day—a part of himself perished as well. For several moon cycles, Jaxson had been in disbelief, then the anger came. With the abandoned search for the dragon rider book all but forgotten, Jaxson had heard a tale of an ancient text that allowed a person to commune with the spirits of the dead, and the need to find the scroll had consumed him for several moon cycles.

Zero sighed. Several moon cycles ago, he had begun to lose hope. Several times their connection was interrupted, similar to the way it was muted now. But about that same time, the boy had started climbing out of the deep well of depression. Jaxson had mentioned he wanted to go fishing. He had started eating better and even slept more than an hour or two at a time. Zero had thought the worst was behind him. Now, he was beginning to suspect that was the true beginning of their current predicament. It was a thought too horrible and complex to fully form in his mind, and Zero did not want to entertain it. But he could not ignore the fact that he now thought Jaxson had left him voluntarily.

He has somehow blocked our connection and is out there, alone, seeking the Living Scroll, Zero thought to himself as the horizon slowly started to glow with the coming sun. Who knows what kind of trouble he could be in?

"Whatever trouble young Jaxson finds himself in will be his doing and his doing alone," said Dreknoxious as he climbed up the hill. When the old wizard finally reached the top, he turned to face the same direction as Zero, settled some of his weight onto the staff planted firmly in the ground, and stood in silence.

The sun finally peeked over the horizon, and the trees at the edge of his vision began to dance. The wind, following the path of the sunlight, danced its way along the valley, past the creek, and into the giants' camp, causing the fires to sputter and flare. The large pines swayed first one way and then the other and still the wind moved toward them. Zero closed his eyes just before the breeze struck him, sending a chill down his spine.

His trouble has always been my trouble, said Zero as he stood. He flexed his wings, extending them out before wincing and drawing them back in. *But that was always because we were inseparable. Or so I thought.*

"The winds of change blow. That is the only thing in this world that stays constant."

Where do I go from here? The ancient text Forseti had tasked us with finding is still unaccounted for, and Jaxson has no desire to search for it.

"That is a decision you and only you can make. The book by the dragon riders of old still needs to be found," said the wizard slowly. "But I do believe you already know the real answer, though it may not be what you ultimately choose. I, for one, must be on my way."

And where are you off to?

"I have some business to see to in Crystal Forge before stopping in on the Kingdoms' Army," said Dreknoxious. "I am quite certain we will see each other again soon."

But will Jaxson be with me?

"That's the rub, isn't it? You will seek him; I can see it in your eyes," said the wizard. "Just please, don't lose yourself on a quest to find him."

What do you mean?

The wizard huffed and turned away from Zero, walking back down the hill. With each step, the old man faded a little. Just before he disappeared completely, he called over his shoulder. "Much is yet to be done, and I must go. And you, my friend, must also be on your way. Whichever direction that may take you."

CHAPTER 12

Sitting in the afternoon sun after contemplating all the paths he could take, Zero narrowed down his choices to only two. He could continue to look for someone that did not want to be found, or he could, alone, pursue the task the ancient dragon had bestowed upon them and find the dragon riders' book. It was an impossible choice.

Still, he knew he could not move forward without at least trying to find Jaxson. But where to begin? If Jaxson had thought this out—and all that had transpired made it seem he had—the young man could be anywhere. He had no idea where to even start looking. For the innumerable time, he reached out to Jaxson via their link. And again, Jaxson was there, weaker than ever, but no communication flowed in either direction. He thought back to Jaxson's sudden shift in mood. The darkest days had been just before they had met the caravan of traders headed across the Kingdoms.

Jaxson had spent most of a day with them while Zero waited out of sight. When his friend returned to him, they had an argument. The traders had supplied Jaxson with a new lead on the Living Scroll, and Zero did not want to pursue it. What was the place the traders had told him the scroll was rumored to be? Aisgamer? Seascape? If Zero would have kept his head better and not become so emotional during their argument, perhaps he would be able to remember the conversation more clearly.

It was Taverny. I remember thinking we were just going in circles if we went back there, Zero thought to himself.

Taverny, after all, is where their ship landed after their sea voyage from the distant continent. At least, he had a destination in mind now. Though when he arrived, he had no idea how to get information from a city full of people. That was a problem for another time, however.

He glanced around and stretched his wings. Pain flared from the wound again but not nearly as intense as this morning. If he stayed on this hilltop for a couple of days, the wound would heal nicely. But he didn't have the time or patience. He coiled and sprung into the air. Hard wing beats sent pain dancing across his body, but he made it to the friendly coasting winds. As he sailed along the sky, his comfort rose because the piercing pain faded to a dull ache. He couldn't fly fast, but he could fly. And he would rather be looking for Jaxson slowly than not at all. Only a five day flight, Taverny was bound to have the answers he sought. He was one step closer to Jaxson—he could feel it.

CHAPTER 13

Two weeks since departing the serenity of the hilltop and still he had not yet arrived at his destination. The wound, which was manageable while cruising up high where only the noble eagles soar, made taking off and landing difficult. He needed to rest more, especially after pushing too hard on day three and reopening the jagged cut where his wing met his shoulder. Forcing himself to wait two days after that particular setback still rankled him.

But he had moved forward every single day. The days he couldn't fly, he ran. If he couldn't run, he walked. Luckily, there had not been a time yet he couldn't walk. So, it was on a clear morning still a few days' slow flight to Taverny that he spotted the Empire soldiers massing along the edge of the ancient forest of Viana, home of the elves. More enemy soldiers than he had seen at one time were strung out over quite a distance. The tents and campfires along with the piles of firewood made it obvious this group of soldiers had been there for some time.

Thrusting his wings downward with minimal pain, he turned his body and angled neared the enemy camp. No dragons flew patrol, and he did not see any on the ground. He was safe as long as he stayed aloft.

As he drew closer, a group of soldiers unaware or unbothered by his presence stood in formation facing into the trees. As one, they started a slow and steady march into the forest. The heavy foliage of the tall and wide hardwood trees made it impossible to continue watching their advance.

Just as Zero turned to continue on his journey and leave this particular problem behind him, shrill cries of terror reached him even at his current height.

Suddenly, a soldier shot out of the forest, flying twenty feet and landing in a crumpled mass of limbs and damaged armor. More of the soldiers that had just entered the forest came running back out, all showing signs of a struggle. Most were bloodied or worse with several holding onto stumps where an arm or hand had been only moments before. A roar, not unlike a dragon's call, filled the air and all of the nearby Empire soldiers moved farther away from the forest.

The elves, and whatever creatures that were helping them, kept the invading forces out of their forest, and Zero could not be happier about it. Filled with a renewed spirit knowing the fight against the invading forces continued, Zero realigned himself to his destination and continued on at a quicker pace. Unfortunately, the Empire soldiers below him were not the only ones he came across over the last three days of his flight.

A make-shift prison camp had been erected by the Empire. The prisoners worked digging a trench, creating their own prison. Goblins, a giant, and humans were all shackled as they moved their shovels in and out of the dirt. Two dragons rested on either side of the camp, so Zero was forced to alter his flight to avoid detection.

The day before arriving on the outskirts of Taverny, patrols of enemy soldiers on horseback scurried along the low hills. Most stuck to the roadways, but several groups had ridden through the tall grasses that swayed in the breeze. It was clear to Zero, they were searching for something or someone. Thoughts of Jaxson filled his mind as Zero worried whether it was him they were after. But he had no way of knowing if it was, in fact, his friend the soldiers searched for, so he kept going.

As he landed gently next to three giant palm trees

on the banks of the Hurline River just north of Taverny, the futility of his mission settled on him. He had been so focused on arriving at Taverny, the place he thought Jaxson may have been headed, that he had not considered what he would find once he arrived. He couldn't land in the town square and ask anyone if they had seen Jaxson. First, if he landed, unannounced, in the center of town without a rider most people would flee in terror. Second, and probably more importantly, he couldn't speak with anyone to question them anyway. His only hope was if a dragon in the area might know something of Jaxson's whereabouts.

Zero sighed as he used the rough back of the tall yellow oak tree to scratch the back of his neck. The likelihood of finding a dragon willing to talk was slim, and one that knew anything about Jaxson's location was even more unlikely. Still, he had flown all this way because it had been his best lead. He just needed a way to find out if Jaxson had been here.

He thought about the problem as morning turned to midday and midday to evening. He drank deeply from the river and tried to sleep, though it was not a restful respite. As he stared at the glittering stars, his heart grew heavy. He still did not have a way to get information out of Taverny. A chill ran up his spine; the trail for Jaxson was cold.

In the very moment that Zero lost hope, he was flooded with intense anger that threatened to block out all reason, all sanity. Even with eyes wide open in the dead of night, all he could see was red. His breathing became heavy and his claws clenched and unclenched. Throwing his head up into the air, he blew a tremendous flame of dragon's fire. It was not his rage pulsing and racing through his veins. Somewhere to the west, the direction he had come from, Jaxson's anger boiled over and spilled past whatever protective wall the boy had set between them and filled Zero to the bursting point.

As quickly as the all-encompassing red rage had engulfed him, it left, leaving only an echo of anger behind.

A night bird called out on the wind. Another answered from across the river. The stars, which moments before had been blood red, sparkled white and blue once again. Collapsing onto his belly, he waited until his breathing resumed its normal cadence before trying to figure out what had just happened. The sun peeked over the town of Taverny at his back, but he was focused in the other direction. Toward Jaxson.

It didn't matter what the tremendous rage meant, not yet. What mattered was that Zero knew Jaxson was in that direction, and with the sun slowly creeping up, it was time to fly toward him.

CHAPTER 14

Wind rushed past his face as he moved toward the fading sense of rage left behind by Jaxson. With each passing moment, the feeling faded, but it was still there like a signal fire on a hillside at night slowly dying. With speed he had not used since before the encounter with the Empire while helping the giants, Zero shot through the air.

As fast as he traveled through the sky, his mind worked faster. He wondered what could possibly make Jaxson so angry. Had he been captured? Was he injured or worse? No, not worse. He could sense Jaxson on the other end of their connection, but like before, it was now walled off where there could be no communication. Still, the lingering rage was there and Zero followed the trail.

Late in the afternoon after flying the previous day and night straight through, he spotted smoke on the horizon. His stomach fell. He was flying straight to that devastation, though he didn't know exactly what he would find. Certainly, Jaxson was not to blame. But in his heart, he knew nothing good had occurred.

A small village appeared. The single-story wooden buildings on the outskirts were primarily residences. A long, low earth and wooden hall dominated the center. It was surrounded by farmland on three sides but no workers were in the fields. On the farthest side from him sat a ruined stone building which had once been a temple, the large golden seven-pointed star giving it away. The smoke rose from the ashes and crumbled stone. Whatever had destroyed the temple had done so quickly and completely. As he studied the devastated ruins, rage boiled over him again. It was not fresh, simply a strong echo from two days ago. Jaxson had been in the temple as it was destroyed.

Zero had to get down there and try to pick up Jaxson's trail. Starting his descent, he did not take his eyes off the smoking rubble. When he was halfway down, he heard Dreknoxious in his head. *Zero, land outside of town. These people do not need another shock.*

Dreknoxious? What are you doing here?

"Same as you, I suppose," said the wizard. "I will meet you out past the former Temple of Renewal just where the forest begins."

Is Jaxson down there? asked Zero, though he already knew the answer.

"He was but no longer," replied Dreknoxious. "Now, no more questions until you land. There will be time then."

Altering his course with just a tilt of his wings, Zero landed in tall grass next to a distinct tree line. Though these trees were not nearly as old as those of the Viana forest, they were closer together and offered no view of what they held beneath their branches. Dreknoxious, long gray beard thrown over his shoulder, hiked up to him using his old wooden staff as a crutch.

What happened here? asked Zero as the wizard stopped in front of him and leaned on the staff heavily.

"In a single word: Jaxson. I do not have all the details but enough to surmise the most recent events."

And?

"The details are not important, but Jaxson came here in search of the Living Scroll which was rumored to be housed in the temple. When told there was no scroll of that name here, Jaxson lost control. Whether he believed they were lying or he was just frustrated, I do not know," said

Dreknoxious. "I do know it was he that laid waste to the temple from the inside. The villagers said he walked out of the smoldering rubble and then simply vanished."

Wha... Vanished? What does that even mean? And why did he destroy the temple? Was he attacked?

"I'm afraid I have as many questions as you and with very few answers," said Dreknoxious.

Well, let's go have a look. Maybe there is something over there that could tell us why he did this or where he is going?

The wizard's shoulders slumped and his head fell. With his chin on his chest, he said, "I do not believe that to be the best course of action."

Why not?

"Jaxson destroyed more than a temple here," said Dreknoxious as he looked up into Zero's eyes.

What does that mean? asked Zero, though he already had a pretty good idea, and it was not good, not good at all.

"The blood of the innocent stains Jaxson's hands now. You do not have to witness the results of his anger to know it is bad," said Dreknoxious. "Beyond bad, really."

I'm going down there, replied Zero as he started walking toward the temple ruins.

"Stop," said Dreknoxious gently. Something about his quiet, somber tone made Zero check up. "You will see horrors in this life, of that I am sure, whether you wish to or not. I strongly recommend you do not intentionally search for them. Jaxson is creating his own horrors now, and I'm not sure what you could do to help him in any meaningful way. Sometimes lessons are learned the only way possible, through pain and mistakes."

Zero trembled with energy. He needed to do something, not just sit here talking. Jaxson was obviously in pain and making poor decisions. Poor decisions could lead to disaster.

I cannot do nothing.

With a large smile the wizard replied, "I would not expect you to. There is much to get done. For starters, you could deliver me to the Kingdoms' Army. I need to have a chat with Tam about where we stand with the war."

Without knowing what else to do, Zero agreed. Moments later, the wizard was on his back, and they were in the air. Away from the ruined temple, away from Jaxson's rage, they flew, but Zero could not help but think they flew away from Jaxson as well. And he was not really sure how to feel about that.

CHAPTER 15

The following days passed by in a blur. Up before the sun, in the air until after the sun had set. There was little of note on the ground and even less conversation between himself and the old wizard. Zero had many questions, such as: Where did Dreknoxious think Jaxson had gone? Why had Jaxson destroyed that temple? And many more. But he dared not ask them for fear of the answers he would receive. He was glad the old wizard had kept him from entering the village. Though he had seen atrocities before, not one caused by Jaxson, a person to whom he is attached.

The horizon brightened through a blanket of thick clouds signifying a new day starting. The wizard climbed onto his back, and Zero finally asked a question that was easy to answer. *Where are we going exactly?*

"To the Kingdoms' Army of course. And to see an old friend or two of yours," replied the wizard.

Zero did not immediately respond. He simply pointed his nose at the rising sun and flew. Once they were at cruising height, he followed up his first question. *And what are we going to do once we locate the army?*

"Now that is a much more complicated question! You offered no time reference, so I could say in the moment directly after locating the army, we would alter course so we could land. Or I could say something like a hot meal sounds like the best thing to do upon arrival," said Dreknoxious. "Furthermore, I could infer that you meant for the foreseeable future taking into account all the variables that could come into play and say all sorts of things. If we arrive during a battle, we may fight or help the retreat or form a defensive position. If we arrive at night, we may seek to wait until daylight to make ourselves known. I could keep going if you like?"

No. And that wasn't very helpful information.

The wizard threw his head back and laughed. It was a deep laugh, full and merry, that forced Zero to smile despite the heaviness of the topic.

"I gave a full and open-ended answer to your question and you do not like it? Perhaps my answer was not at fault. Instead, it was your question that lacked substance."

Zero thought for a moment. *That was not the right question. I guess I really want to know if I should give up looking for Jaxson.*

"Ah, I expected several more jabs before you went for the knockout punch, but good for you, getting to the point quickly. I've always said you are wise beyond your young years."

Thank you, I think.

"As for the answer you seek, it is not one I can provide," said Dreknoxious. Zero bristled beneath the wizard. "Calm down now. I didn't say I wouldn't offer counsel; I just can't answer that particular question for you."

Zero's nostrils flared. *And what counsel do you offer?*

"Only this: I know you will never give up looking for him as do you. However, I think looking for him while he so desires not to be found would be futile. You can do other things while keeping an eye out for Jaxson until something changes."

That feels like giving up on him.

"Yes, it could be interpreted that way. But you know you will never give up on him. There are just some places he can go that you can't follow," said Dreknoxious. "Nor should you even attempt it."

Why shouldn't I attempt it? I am not scared.

The wizard scratched his chin. "I expect you are not. But I fear you seeing Jaxson in a state that you could not unsee."

I don't understand.

The wizard laughed again, though this time not quite as fully. "You will in time. Or you won't. Either way, I strongly believe that you should focus your efforts on helping with the war for now. They could use your skills and bravery now more than ever."

Not willing to concede the point but also not wanting to push any harder, Zero changed the subject. *Speaking of the army, I think we may have found it.*

The thick cloud cover and patchy rain finally subdued. In the distance and to their right slightly a long and wide river flowed coming from out of sight to the north and winding south as far as Zero could see. On the near bank, a vast and sweeping army camped. Large and small tents were erected in various clusters. Temporary stables made of hastily thrown together wood lined the back of the camp. Far to the north and away from the river, wooden buildings that appeared to be more permanent stood surrounded by guards. To the south and again away from the river, a large clearing had been made next to a rocky bluff. Several dragons rested on the ground. Even with all the activity and all of the soldiers, the camp was clean. Fires burned only within rings of stone. Long tables were placed in rows near several large tents that Zero assumed housed all of the kitchen staff.

The cleanliness and order of the Kingdoms' Army was in stark contrast to the billowing smoke and chaotic arrangement of tents across the river that could only be the Empire's largest force on this continent. However, an earthen wall wrapped around much of their camp obscuring the view of a large portion of the enemy camp. On top of the wall and on top of wooden towers scattered throughout the camp, large ballistas were placed. They were cocked and ready with bolts at least half his length. The weapons were more than powerful enough to take a dragon down from the air.

Patrolling the skies over the Kingdoms' Army were two dragons. It did not take long for them to spot Zero and turn towards him and Dreknoxious.

Where do you wish me to land?

"I believe our first stop should be wherever young Tam is located," said Dreknoxious. "Though he is not the leader of the entire army, his unit of… irregulars always have the best intel."

And where do you suppose we could find him?

"Perhaps it would be better to ask the approaching dragons," said the wizard. "They should be able to assist in locating the young man."

As the closest dragon drew closer, Zero could not help but smile. He knew that little purple dragon. *Soaren, I hope you and Aleera are well.*

Better than you since my rider is on my back and you carry a troublemaker, replied Soaren as she twisted in mid-flight beneath Zero and appeared flying in the same direction on his right wing. *What brings you to the army?*

The troublemaker as you would call him, though I call him a friend, as should you. He was instrumental in your rescue after all.

He took me out of the frying pan and put both me and Aleera in the fire, replied Soaren. *Regardless, our patrol shift is up. Follow us.*

Is that where Tam will be? asked Zero.

The purple dragon went quiet for a moment that Zero recognized as conversation between her and her rider,

Aleera. *He is probably at the Aviary which is where we were headed anyway.*

What is the Aviary? asked Zero.

For now, it is home.

CHAPTER 16

Descending slowly behind Soaren and her rider, Zero saw the entirety of the Kingdoms' Army and then a swampy thicket. Just past the jumble of trees, vines, and thorny bushes another clearing sat nestled next to a large rocky cliff overlooking the river. The Aviary, as Soaren called it, was separated from the rest of the army but was no less clean and organized. A line of tents sat next to one oversized tent just outside of the center where a large fire blazed. Several archery targets and an area for hand-to-hand training stood on the side farthest from the river. As he got closer, Zero identified a couple of goblin tents, darker in color and made from the hides of steam drakes on the opposite side of the fire from the standard issue army tents housing the dragon riders. A cave entrance, partially concealed by a large boulder, peeked out from the cliffside.

Just as he touched down, Dreknoxious slid off his back and landed gracefully on the soft ground. Zero shook his head; there was no way the old man should be able to pull off such an athletic move without hurting himself. The wizard, with Aleera close behind, moved quickly toward several approaching men. The tallest of which waved at Zero, and he bobbed his head in response. So, Tam was here after all.

I suppose you want me to show you around, said Soaren.

If it is not too much trouble, replied Zero. *I'm not sure how long I will be here, but I have a growing feeling it may be some time.*

Soaren snorted but made no comment as she turned

and started toward an open area just before the brambles where several dragons lounged in the bright sun. Both brown dragons lifted their heads at one time as Zero stopped in front while Soaren circled around. When she was wing to wing with them, she stopped.

This is Paullo and Arty. They will be on night patrol tonight so their riders are resting, said Soaren. *This is Zero. His rider is not... here currently.*

Well met, Zero, said Paullo. *Arty was just saying we needed some new wings in the Aviary. You planning on flying with us?*

I'm not sure how long I will be with the army, but if given the chance, I would be honored to fly with you.

Both browns laughed, and Arty stretched her front legs forward, spreading her claws as her hind end and tail rose straight in the air. *He can definitely fly with us—so polite!*

Arty, calm down now. He just said he wasn't sure if he would be here long, said Paullo as she looked sideways at the other brown dragon. Arty, now fully stretched and standing with her wings tucked in tightly to her back, stared at Zero with a smile.

But he is at least pleasing to look— said Arty before Soaren cut her off.

That's enough. Paullo, can you please do something with her? You are the older sister after all.

I'll try, but it is time for her to make her to make her first dwell. You know how it is the first time, replied the taller brown dragon as she too stood. With a nudge of her head, she pushed Arty toward the tents. *Our riders should be up anyway. They've been asleep for hours, and I'm hungry.*

The two brown dragons slowly walked off, offering Zero his first full view of them. Along the younger Arty's side were long, wide scars just now being covered with fresh scales. Zero waited until he was sure they were not turning around before asking, *Was she taken at some point? Is that how she got those scars?*

Soaren snarled but quickly hid it. Her long face returned to her normal stoic face. *You were wise to wait and ask that question though it is still exceedingly rude to ask about another's scars.*

Zero's eyes widened and his mouth dropped. Before he could stammer a reply, Soaren continued, *But yes, she was once a prisoner of the Empire. The troublemaker helped her sister, Paullo, free her some time back. Paullo and her rider have been with us from the beginning.*

Quiet stretched between them as Soaren indicated Zero should follow her. As they started walking to the end of the camp that he had not yet seen, Zero commented, *I am sorry for any offense I caused. It was not my intention. I recently witnessed Dreknoxious relieve a curse from another. It was not pleasant.*

No, I bet it wasn't. Ah, here we are.

Zero looked all around, but the only things visible close by were brambles. *And where is here exactly?*

I want you to meet one of our most secret weapons… Pud.

What is a pd?

Not a pd. That's his name, Pud.

Zero's eyes darted around, and his head turned, but still he saw no one. *Who is named Pyd? What are you talking about?*

Soaren did not reply. Instead, she sat and looked at Zero expectantly. Zero did not know if this was a joke at his expense or if he was just missing something. Regardless, it was clear that he was not in the know of whatever Soaren was playing at. Then, the air in front of his face moved. Blinking rapidly, Zero looked at Soaren. *Did you just see that?*

Soaren chuckled but did not answer. Zero looked back at the space in front of him but everything was normal. The air was just… air. Then, it happened again.

There! You saw it that time surely.

Come on out, Pud. This big, ugly green dragon is actually a friend, said Soaren.

Right in front of his face, mere inches from his nose, a tiny dragon no bigger than a human infant materialized. It didn't fly up from the ground. It didn't fall from the sky. One minute nothing was in front of him, and the next, a tiny dragon appeared. Zero arched his back and his wings flared out, startled.

Soaren no longer chuckled, she cackled. She laughed so hard she couldn't even speak. After she finally calmed down, she said, *And there he is.*

Zero relaxed his back and tucked his wings away. The tiny dragon, still hovering in front of him, tilted his head, staring intently at Zero.

What... Umm... Is he a hatchling?

Soaren scoffed. *No. Have you never met a pygmy dragon before?*

Not until today. Where are they from?

I don't know, replied Soaren. *One day he just showed up. He has not communicated other than his name.*

Zero turned his attention back to the tiny dragon. They locked eyes, and an image floated up in Zero's mind: a tall tree with a huge flower on the ground below. When the flower opened, light shot out in all directions. This was the little dragon's home, Zero knew. As soon as the thought crossed his mind, the little dragon flew around his head and perched on his shoulder. They were connected. He did not know how or why, but he knew all the same.

Zero looked at Soaren and said, *Interesting little dragon. But his name is Pyd and not Pud.*

At that very moment, an alarm rang out from the nearby Kingdoms' Army camp. Zero did not know what the alarm signified, but everyone near him started racing around. Riders ran to their dragons launching into the air. Aleera jogged to Soaren and mounted quickly.

"They are attacking Hurline Bluff," Aleera shouted. "We need to go try and save the town."

Ask her if I should wait for Dreknoxious, Zero said to Soaren.

After a brief moment, Aleera answered. "The wizard is not coming with us. Tam is going to rouse Grog. You can stay or go—your choice—but I'm not waiting around for you to decide."

CHAPTER 17

Zero watched as Soaren coiled low with her head just above the ground. A moment later the purple dragon sprang into the air, wings beating quickly to gain altitude. He looked from side to side. The Aviary was emptying out quickly with most answering the call to save the town just up the river. With a huff, he too leapt into action, rising quickly to catch up with Soaren. He couldn't stay behind in an empty camp when others were risking their lives.

As he pushed harder, he saw several platoons of infantry following way behind a regiment of light cavalry. All were headed up the river to aid the small outpost in the town of Hurline Bluff. Finally, he caught the purple dragon gliding wing to wing.

How far is it?

Only a fifteen-minute flight for us, but it will take the infantry several hours.

Behind them, Grog, the large petridrake, rose with Tam on his back. To his left, Arty and Paullo flew with their riders nocking arrows on short, compact bows.

Where are the dragons from the regular army? asked Zero.

The general rarely uses them for skirmishes. They will probably stay and patrol the line while we do the real work.

Why don't the two armies just fight it out? They are so close to each other.

Soaren looked over at Zero but did not respond. Zero knew she was talking with Aleera privately. *We are not sure.*

We think it may be a mutual destruction thing. They would wipe each other out and no one would win.

Seems a little… odd, replied Zero.

Don't worry about it. Worry about the problem in front of us, not behind. I see four dragons circling the town and a lot of smoke rising.

There are six. The two you didn't notice are much higher and farther back. One of them is huge!

We'll need to keep an eye on them, said Soaren. *But first we need to drive those dragons off so we can start eliminating the ground forces.*

Should we split up? asked Zero.

Again, a pause from Soaren as she consulted with Aleera. *No, they are all flying solo. It will be easier to take them out two on one.*

Agreed. That blue dragon is causing the most damage. Let's start with him. You go low, and I go high?

Agreed.

All four of the enemy dragons were flying low, pouncing on anyone that tried to escape. The town's wall, mostly made of wood and dried mud, had a gate to the north and south which were being battered by Empire soldiers. Two wooden towers flanked each gate filled with archers raining arrows down upon the attackers. The river blocked a quick retreat to the east. The townspeople and the few soldiers were trapped.

Zero climbed, wings beating furiously as he tried to keep pace with Soaren and Aleera who were now beneath him. Paullo and Arty banked left, circling wide. Zero assumed they were going to push the enemy soldiers away from the gates.

The enemy blue dragon swooped down and used dragon's fire on one of the towers with archers still inside. Even as the flames licked up to their lofted position, they loosed arrows until the flames and smoke fully engulfed them.

We need to stop this NOW! shouted Soaren.

Zero leveled off and surveyed the battle below. Paullo and Arty worked in tandem, one swooping to disrupt the enemy ground forces and one flying protection above. Then, they would switch. Two yellow dragons from the enemy noticed and started toward them. The blue dragon, slow to rise after gushing out dragon's fire, flew over the river. The only other enemy dragon, a small black, had turned and was flying toward the two enemy dragons hovering in the distance.

I'm ready. Draw the blue dragon away from the town and keep it occupied. I'll come down from above, hard.

Without a response, Soaren shot forward and then banked to the right, looking to intercept the blue before it could turn back toward Hurline Bluff. As Soaren approached the side of the blue, he finally spotted her and attempted to swerve away. But Soaren was too quick, latching onto the blue dragon's wing with both claws; the purple dragon and her rider dove straight now. Even from his height above the fray, Zero heard Soaren's claws ripping through the thin membrane and the accompanying pained roar from the blue.

Soaren relaxed her claws, releasing the blue dragon and its rider. She started climbing as the enemy dragon struggled to stay in the air with its shredded wing. *Go help Paullo and Arty. I'll catch up.*

Zero turned his attention to the two sisters across the town. Paullo was following one of the yellow dragons, her rider firing arrow after arrow. Arty, however, was being hounded by the other enemy dragon. Blood ran in streaks down her side. Zero immediately altered course and sped up to intercept Arty's attacker. *Arty, I'm coming. Try and gain some altitude!*

I'll try... replied Arty, though her voice was strained. *He clawed my side pretty good. I can't fly full speed.*

Dive now and let the yellow close on you, then pull straight up, said Zero as he knifed through the air toward the smaller brown dragon. *I'll be there when you do.*

What? I'll be as helpless as a hatchling! bemoaned Arty.

Do it now! screamed Zero as he started his dive toward where Arty and her attacker should be in just moments.

Aaarrgggghhhh, growled Arty as she pitched forward and down, tucking her wings in. The yellow dragon hesitated for just a moment not believing its good fortune. Then springing forward, neck stretched out and teeth bared, it attacked.

Just before it chomped down on Arty, Zero crashed into the yellow dragon at full speed. Arty pulled out of her dive and leveled out with Soaren on one side and Paullo on the other. The remaining yellow dragon abandoned the area, and with the Kingdom's light cavalry approaching, the Empire's ground forces were also withdrawing.

Yes! shouted Soaren, celebrating their victory. Then, she saw Zero had not disengaged from his attack on the enemy dragon. They were still joined together and falling. Falling fast.

CHAPTER 18

Blood blurred his vision though it wasn't his. Even so, he knew the ground was rapidly approaching. Zero's chest had crashed into the enemy dragon's side while its wings were folded in. The enemy rider could not hold on and plummeted off of the yellow's back. Zero should have pushed off and flown away at that moment, but he hesitated at the sight of the armor. Knowing that evil blood magic resided underneath, Zero clawed at the thick leather straps that held the armor in place. Before he could relieve the dragon of its armor, his claw became stuck. This gave time for the yellow dragon to swivel its head and bite down with razor-sharp teeth on his right wing just where it joined his body. Zero let out a roar of pain as the two entangled dragons fell.

His vision cleared enough for him to see the individual trees that were getting alarmingly closer with each passing second. He jerked and pulled his snagged claw before the leather strap snapped, freeing him. Zero slashed at the yellow dragon's snout causing more blood to stream up into his face. The other dragon would not relinquish his grip, however. At least it's not the same wing as before, thought Zero as he tucked in as tight as he could just before the soft ground near the riverbank stopped their fall.

Luckily for Zero, the yellow dragon took the brunt of their crash landing. The force of the fall and his own body weight pushed the yellow dragon deep in the soft earth. Mud and muck rained down on them as Zero tried to rise. The yellow dragon's jaw finally relaxed and freed Zero's wing. He stood on shaky feet and bared his teeth at the enemy dragon, but unseeing eyes looked back at him. Zero sighed. The yellow dragon would never rise out of that hole again.

Soaren, with Aleera on her back, and both Paullo and Arty with their riders still in place, landed near the crash site.

Zero, are you alright? cried Arty.

He looked up and saw three dragon heads peering down at him. *I will live, I think.*

"Can you fly?" Aleera shouted the question down at him.

I'm not sure. My wing is pretty messed up, replied Zero to Soaren who relied the response to Aleera.

"Well, we need to find out before..." Aleera trailed off, and all three dragons looked up at the same time.

The two dragons that were watching as well as the two that abandoned the fight are returning, said Paullo.

We are in no shape to battle again, said Arty. *Especially not against that huge red dragon.*

Zero struggled out of the hole, now more of a muddy-brown dragon then green. He turned and followed their gaze to the approaching dragons. There was something about the red that led the charge that was familiar to him, but he could not figure out what. *Let's get out of here.*

Paullo and Arty immediately leapt into the sky, circling once before heading back in the direction of the Aviary. Soaren stood near Zero as he stretched his wings, testing the injury. With a nod, she took to the sky. Zero coiled and jumped, beating his wings. Pain flared along his wound and up his wing, but he kept rising slowly.

You need to pick up the pace, said Soaren. *Or they are going to catch us.*

Go ahead. I can handle myself.

Soaren snorted as she settled in on his left wing. *I don't abandon those that go into battle with me. It is not honorable.*

Staying here and dying will not bring honor to anything, said Zero.

The red dragon with the three other smaller dragons drew closer. Zero peeked over his shoulder and did a double take, his mouth hanging open. He figured out why something about the red dragon was familiar. He knew that dragon. It was Tollison, and Zero knew that if the enemy had control of him, there was no way to win against them. From behind that group of dragons, another group could be seen in the distance. At least three more dragons followed behind Tollison.

We are in trouble, said Zero.

You think? replied Soaren. *Can you go any faster?*

No, but maybe we can use that to our advantage.

What do you have in mind?

First, tell Paullo and Arty to circle around low and slow, said Zero. *I am going to fall back and aggravate the enemy. Timing will be everything, and we will need more than a little luck.*

They are turning around, relayed Soaren. *What else?*

Just don't be late, said Zero as he slowed. *Here's the plan...*

CHAPTER 19

Zero's shoulder ached, but the injury was not nearly as bad as he first imagined. Still, he slowed his pace even more, allowing himself to dip down in between wing beats. Soaren stay closed, constantly checking behind them for their pursuers.

It's almost time, she told Zero.

I'm not going to look, but are Arty and Paullo in place?

Yes, hovering just on the other side of that large swath of trees. You'd have to know they were there to spot them, said Soaren as she again checked over her shoulder. *They are almost on top of us, and I still don't see HIM.*

Me neither, replied Zero. *But he'll be here.*

Show time, said Soaren as she started to speed up.

Do it and tell Aleera to be convincing, said Zero as he allowed himself to tumble a little more before starting to fly straight again. If they had any shot of surviving this encounter with Tollison and the other enemy dragons, the enemy had to believe he was severely limited. It offered them an advantage, though a small one at best.

Soaren fell behind and then shot forward. Aleera screamed for them to fly away and waved her hands erratically. Soaren jerked from side to side and then peeled off to the right, headed toward the sky above the big trees.

All three are following me, leaving you to deal with the big red one, said Soaren. *Oh, and that other group of dragons is about five minutes behind.*

Great but let's deal with one problem at a time, replied Zero as he let himself slip lower in the sky. *Keep them busy.*

Zero banked away from Soaren. In only minutes, she would be in place with the enemy dragons in tow. The last thing he wanted was to give away their plan by watching. A roar from above and behind him brought him back to the task at hand. Tollison was bigger, stronger, faster, and more experienced than him. A direct confrontation would end poorly when he was in top shape. With his wing injury, he stood no chance.

Zero waited until the big red dragon was almost within striking distance, then he tucked his wings and dove straight down. He looked over his shoulder, watching Tollison slowly angle down after him. The gap between them grew momentarily then started shrinking again. Zero smiled. Tollison and his captor did not seem to be in a hurry. He sold his injury well.

Again, he waited until Tollison was right on his tail before banking right and diving down again. He leveled out just seconds before striking the ground. And again, Tollison and his captor slowly angled down, allowing the gap to grow larger. Zero spared a moment to check on Soaren and smiled.

Aleera was still screaming for Soaren to flee. Just as they reached the back of the trees with the enemy dragons closing fast, Soaren suddenly flared her wings and hovered in the air. The enemy dragons shot right past her. The yellow and black banked to the right in a wide circle to come back around. The newcomer, another blue dragon with a rider brandishing a bow and arrow, flared its wings and turned midair to face Soaren then hesitated, looking over its shoulder at the other two dragons. Clearly, it had no intention of battling Soaren alone.

The two circling enemy dragons turned sharper toward Soaren, but just as they started to level out, Paullo and Arty slammed into them from underneath. Soaren sprang forward after the blue that was distracted by the ambush behind it.

A loud roar behind him made Zero look over his shoulder. Tollison closed the gap quickly, and his captor stood in the harness trying to get a better look. Zero feinted left then banked right and pulled straight up. He needed some elevation. The red dragon took the bait and banked hard left, trying to cut Zero off, but he was already climbing and moving away from them quickly. Zero strained harder and harder, flying upward faster and faster. His right wing throbbed, and then he felt a flash of pain as fresh blood poured out of the aggravated wound. He chanced a look over at the other dragons. They were doing well as only the enemy blue dragon remained in the air with all three of his friends.

I'm headed your way when I start my dive, said Zero. *Can you see him from over there?*

I can't, but you are closer to where he should be. We need to come to you, replied Soaren.

Zero grunted with the effort of gaining speed with going up. *First, you have to get rid of that blue.*

He is already fleeing. We are headed your way, said Soaren. *ZERO! Look out!*

Zero glanced down, but all he could see was red. Then an enormous crash as Tollison crashed into him from below. Someone, probably the enemy rider, shouted to "end him."

Tumbling down again, Zero saw his friends on the way as fast as they could fly. Tollison wheeled around in a big arc. Black spots danced across his vision and crept in from the sides. Just before it all went black, he saw a mountain flying in the sky, moving toward him. Not a mountain, a huge petridrake. Tam and Grog had arrived at last.

CHAPTER 20

"ZERO!" screamed Aleera from atop Soaren's back.

Fighting to keep the darkness away, Zero shook his barrel-sized head. Trying to figure out where he was and why his head moved easier in one direction than the other took all of his attention. He shook his head for the second time and still it was easier one way than the other. His vision cleared a little, but instead of making things easier to understand, it complicated things.

The world was sideways and the wind was deafening. He heard his name but couldn't locate the source of the voice. So, he reached out to Jaxson just to encounter the emotional wall. He couldn't talk to him, couldn't ask him where he was. Just nothing. And that's when he remembered Jaxson had left, and he was with the Kingdoms' Army. And the enemy has Tollison. And Zero remembered he was... FALLING!

He flared his wings out to slow his descent, flailing his head around wildly, trying to locate the larger red dragon. Tollison was nowhere to be seen but Soaren was right beside him.

You back with us? she asked as they leveled out and started gliding.

I guess. Where is Tollison, the big red?

He held you high up in the sky until Grog was almost on top of you. Then, he released you and took off. Grog and Tam are chasing him, but they won't catch him unless he wants them to. Is everyone else alright?

Soaren bobbed her head slowly. *Umm… everyone will be alright. Arty took a pretty nasty blow to the head. Paullo is escorting her back to the Av—*

Zero lurched and started falling again, his wing not able to hold his weight. He also felt blood running down his side.

"Get it together!" shouted Aleera.

I have to get on the ground.

I think that is for the best, replied Soaren. *How about on that hill with the two huge oak trees? At least they'll offer a little shade.*

Lead the way, said Zero. His head drooped and each beat of his wings was harder than the previous one. But in a few short moments, he was settling in under one of the oak's long branches that started high in the tree and arched down to the ground before growing up again.

You need to rest. We're gonna go track down Grog and Tam, said Soaren. *Be back to check on you soon.*

Zero did not bother to reply. His eyelids fluttered once before they closed. His chest rose and fell in a slow, steady cadence. Just before the darkness overtook him, he took a deep breath and smiled at the pleasant smell from the flowers on the vines in the oak. It reminded him of the valley in Dragon Spine Mountains that he and Jaxson had called home for most of their lives. It reminded him of peace. It was an illusion.

****

An unseasonably chill wind blew across his ridged back, and the large limbs of the giant oak tree swayed gently. Zero jumped awake not remembering where he was at first. Through a gap in the trees, stars winked in an otherwise empty sky. The bare dirt ground, scattered with leaves and twigs, radiated the heat of the past day onto his belly.

He attempted to stand but fell back down. Swiveling his

head, he saw a bandage on his back leg. He stretched his wings as much as he could with the branches just overhead. They both hurt but in a dull, old way. He knew that Dreknoxious had been here. His wing had been healed.

With extra effort and bracing for the injury to his rear leg, Zero stood and looked to the west. That was the direction he knew Jaxson to be. He inhaled deeply and closed his eyes. The wall that his friend, his rider, had raised between them stood unchanged. Zero pushed against the invisible barrier, wanting to break it down. He wanted to talk with Jaxson, make sure he was doing fine. Ask him to come back or let him come back. Flying with other dragons, helping the war effort were good things. And he should be cautious because he didn't cause the rift between them. With all of that he still didn't care that Jaxson had left him without a word. It still hurt, but he just wanted his friend back.

A small popping sound made him open his eyes. On the ground in front of him, Pyd appeared. Zero cocked his head, wondering what the curious little dragon was doing here with him under this oak tree so far from the Aviary. Pyd stared into Zero's eyes. Lowering his head, Zero held the gaze even as Pyd walked up to him. The tiny dragon nuzzled Zero's large nose, tickling the larger dragon. The same image as before blossomed in his head, the beautiful flower and the large tree. Pyd's home. Zero smiled and his heart was lighter than it had been for weeks.

Sitting straight up, Zero asked, *What are you doing here, little one?*

The tiny dragon mirrored his movements. As they looked at each other, he saw in his mind's eye Soaren flying by and then he was filled with joy and amusement as an old man with a long beard crossed his mind.

Soaren and Dreknoxious sent you? Zero knew the answer was yes. So, he asked another question. *Dreknoxious was already here, wasn't he?* Yes. He saw the wizard healing his wing. *And where is everyone else?* Suddenly, he soared over the Kingdoms' Army then circled the Aviary. *Good, they made it back safely. Why are you here?*

The images that had been crystal clear before now were choppy, just brief flashes. A tall tree burned. Then, heavy vines from thick, stunted trees drooped into brown water. A flash of Dreknoxious's face but, instead of a smile, deep lines creased his forehead and his cheeks were flushed. Smoke rose from the Aviary. Dragon bones littered a rocky hill. A beautiful yellow flower bloomed and closed and bloomed and closed. Jaxson's face was all muddy with a black eye and cracked lips.

Wait. Why are you showing me Jaxson? Why is he beat up? Where is he? Do you know where he is?

Pyd drew back away from the questions, eyes wide. His little head dropped for a second, then he looked up into the larger dragon's eyes. Zero saw a large frog sitting on a patch of floating water grass. Bugs buzzed around, sometimes close and sometimes far away. Still the frog didn't move. The largest fly yet flew by his face. Quick as a thought, the frog's tongue shot out and snagged the bug. One wing slowly spiraled down until it landed in the water. Rings radiated out across the glass smooth water. The frog made a celebratory croak then waited on his next meal.

I need to be patient?

Pyd rose to his feet and circled one of Zero's front claws before settling down next to it. Yes, he needed to be patient, and Pyd was here to help him.

CHAPTER 21

Three Moons Later

Just like each and every morning since encountering the captured red dragon, Tollison, Zero rose before the sun. This day was no different except he was not in the Aviary. Far to the north in the low Crawnshee Mountains, Zero and the rest of the detachment were hunting. Empire soldiers along with dragons and their riders were spotted by Kingdoms' scouts in alarming increasing numbers. Clueless as to why the Empire was sending so many to this area, the Kingdoms' command had dispatched Aleera and Soaren along with Zero and Arty with her rider to investigate.

He turned and faced the south, taking in a deep breath then slowly exhaling. When his mind was quiet, he reached out to Jaxson, focusing all his concentration in the direction he faced. Yesterday, he looked east. Tomorrow would be west. But today, today was south, and Zero concentrated on the familiar feeling: Jaxson, muted, quiet, but still there. It was no stronger than when he faced east. A rustling ended his inner thoughts as Pyd landed from the evergreen tree right behind him.

Did you sleep well that high in the tree?

Zero's head was flooded with soft clouds flowing lazily with the breeze. Pyd looked up to him and cocked his head in a way Zero had learned meant, "Do you understand?"

Good because Arty and her rider are on the way back and she sounds excited. Aleera is requiring me to report to her down in the valley. Looks like there could be combat, said Zero as he stared down at the pygmy dragon. *It would be fine with me if you stayed here in the safety of the trees.*

Pyd did not respond. Instead, he flew up and landed on Zero's back right where his neck started and settled in.

Alright then, let's go.

****

Lying in wait on the rocky ground with his back to the little canyon's entrance with Pyd on his back, Zero thought over their plan again. Arty had come back with news of three enemy dragons, but the best part was they were separated, flying solo. After some back-and-forth, it was decided to try to take them out one at a time. Then, Arty had the big reveal.

That big red dragon, the one you said you knew, is up there.

Tollison.

Zero wished there was some way he could contact Dreknoxious. This could be their best chance to alter the blood magic etched into his side that bonded him to his captors. Zero knew that a deep gash could alter the runes enough to reduce their hold on a dragon but only magic could completely erase the curse. The fresher the jagged runes on a dragon's side, the more magic had to be involved.

But the first dragon they targeted was not him. Instead, it was a small black dragon with a rider dressed in full chain mail. Arty said the rider only carried a sword, no ranged weapons. So, tracking where it was headed, Aleera and Soaren set up an ambush.

Arty was nearby, wedged in amongst some large boulders above Zero. He was backed up against the canyon wall entrance. He wouldn't see the black dragon until it was already past him. He looked up and behind Arty where Soaren floated on the breeze high in the sky. Above her, several noble ones soared. It was rare to see multiple eagles flying so close together.

I have always wondered, why are eagles called Noble? asked Arty.

Once long ago, began Zero, *before the time of the first dragon riders, a great war between dragon-kind and a race of demon-like people known as the Atlafals brought this world to the edge of annihilation.*

Pyd nuzzled Zero's neck, tickling him. Zero chuckled before continuing. *The war was not going well, though most of the creatures and peoples had joined against the Atlafals. It is said that in the final battle, the most noble of all eagles, commander of the skies that directed both eagles and dragons during wartime, sacrificed not only his own life but also his kinds' ability to communicate like we dragons do to end it.*

Zero gasped as suddenly the image of a great eagle almost as large as himself battling a multi-headed wolf with fiery wings. Zero swiveled his barrel-sized head to gape at Pyd.

Zero asked him, *How? Were you there?*

Pyd did not respond at all, but Arty said, *I've never heard that before. How do you know?*

I just do, Zero replied, turning back to the empty canyon. *Sometimes, I have memories—strong, clear memories—that aren't mine,* replied Zero. *Most do not come forth until I have a need, such as this. I didn't know that about eagles a few moments ago, but now I do.*

So, the eagles were like us once? Able to talk, communicate?

I believe the noble ones are just as noble now as they ever were, said Zero. *And that's enough for me.*

That's perfect because here he comes, said Arty. She had the better vantage point from the top of the canyon wall.

Stick to the plan, Arty. We have the numbers; we should use them.

The black dragon drifted right above Zero followed by his shadow which slipped over Zero's head. Just a little longer and Arty would take off to give chase. Soaren would be above to keep him in the canyon, and if he backtracked, Zero would be waiting. It was a solid plan that failed almost instantly.

CHAPTER 22

Silently, Arty, with her rider on her back, slipped into the canyon, giving chase. Staying close to the wall and slightly below the cruising height of the black dragon, she started gaining on their target. Zero readied himself to spring into the air at a moment's notice if needed. He had confidence in Arty and Soaren, and their plan made sense. Still, it was better to be prepared.

The black dragon just had to go a little farther into the canyon where the walls come closer together, and then Soaren swooped down. If the black didn't react quick enough, Soaren would take it to the ground. If it stopped or retreated, Arty would then take her run at it.

Arty closed more of the distance as the bottleneck part of the canyon came upon them quickly. Soaren streaked down from the sky at the perfect moment. The black dragon either had to fight her or retreat. If he tried to bolt forward, Soaren would make easy work of it by driving it straight into the sandy canyon floor.

That was when the black dragon did something completely unexpected. Instead of doing any of the things they had planned for, the black turned straight into the canyon wall and latched on. The rider pointed up, and the black's head followed, looking up at the top of the canyon wall. Then, it roared, and the rider's hands started moving in an intricate pattern. The black dragon's roar grew, and much to Zero's dismay, he could see it. Lines or sound shot up at the top of the canyon wall, and a shower of small rocks rained down.

Arty changed course, intent on crushing the black dragon to the side of the canyon where it was perched. Before she even came close, small boulders from the top fell. The black's rider kept moving his hands, the pattern growing faster and tighter. The falling rocks and boulders changed direction slightly, angling toward Arty and her rider. She dodged and turned up on her side to avoid the larger rocks.

Soaren was forced to pull up, not having an effective angle clear of falling rocks. So, both she and Zero watched as the biggest rock yet struck Arty's left wing.

A sharp crack sounded, bouncing off the canyon walls several times. Arty fell then, one wing unable to keep her aloft. When she struck the canyon floor with a loud thud, dust flew into the air halfway up the canyon wall. Before the dust had finished rising, Zero launched himself into the air intent on taking the black dragon and its rider, or captor, down.

They were distracted watching Soaren and Aleera wheel up and come back down for another pass. The black dragon roared again causing rocks to tumble down the canyon walls, and its rider weaved his hands around directing the rocks toward Soaren. Aleera screamed as a small rock struck her arm, and Soaren pulled up out of the canyon. The black dragon did not move, watching as Soaren circled high and then dove straight down where the rocks would be as likely to hit the black dragon and its rider as them.

But the black was quick. It pushed off the wall and shot across the canyon, perching on the wall opposite from which Soaren dove. The rider directed more of the falling rocks toward Soaren, and again they were forced to pull up. The rider threw his hands up triumphantly. It was the last thing he ever did.

Gaining speed with each beat of his wings, Zero crashed

into the black dragon and rider at full force, pinning them to the canyon wall. Zero focused most of his energy on the rider. The full plate armor crumpled between the wall and Zero's large front claw. When he pulled his front claw away, the lifeless rider dropped like a stone to the canyon floor. The black dragon roared and snapped its jaws at Zero. So focused on eliminating the rider, Zero had left himself exposed. Sharp teeth sunk into his neck; blood flowed down his scales. He pushed away from the wall and fell with the black attached to him. One of his wings was tangled with the black's, so they plummeted at a rapid pace.

With wind rushing past them and the ground getting alarmingly close, Zero clawed at the underbelly of the black dragon, forcing it to release his neck. The armor the black wore ripped off, and where the blood curse was normally carved into a dragon's side, it was unmarked.

You aren't a prisoner?

You killed my rider! We will both die today! replied the black.

Not today!

Zero pushed away from the black and opened his wings, gliding to a rest at the bottom of the canyon. The black also regained flight and circled above ready to dive down at Zero. Soaren came down from above, and the black dragon snorted before flying away. Soaren landed next Arty, and Zero rushed over to join them.

Is she alive?

She is, replied Soaren. *Though her rider is gravely injured, and with her injured wing, Arty cannot fly.*

"We need to get Brazios to a healer and fast," said Aleera before turning to Zero. "Will you allow him on your back?"

It took a moment for Zero to realize Aleera was talking to him. He had never let someone he did not know on his back, and for the most part, Jaxson had been his sole rider.

But he knew he had to help—that was why he had stayed with the Kingdoms' Army, to make a difference. He indicated to Soaren he would be glad to carry Brazios.

Aleera, bracing her injured arm, helped Brazios to his feet and half carried him near Zero. As they were trying to come up with a way to get him on Zero's back without further hurting him, a red shadow, large and dark, passed over them. Zero looked up to see Tollison circling above.

Aleera sighed. "New plan. You distract that big boy there, and let us get Brazios to safety. Arty, can you walk?"

The smaller dragon finally struggled to her feet and though she swayed, she remained upright.

"Good. Go push yourself in amongst those boulders over there," said Aleera as she used her one good arm to give Brazios a shove onto Soaren's back. "Zero, be careful. That red is a beast."

Tell Aleera for me that Tollison is a friend and needs help. Not an enemy that needs purging, Zero said to Soaren.

I'll tell her. But you really do need to be careful. Distract him, and let us get away. Then you come back to us, you hear me?

Zero nodded as Aleera climbed onto Soaren's back and sat behind Brazios who was already slumped over. Zero knew the man did not have much time. With Arty tucked away inside the boulders on the canyon floor as best she could, Zero launched into the air to meet his old friend in battle. He only hoped they would both fly away from it.

CHAPTER 23

Right away, Zero knew something was amiss. Tollison led him down the canyon and out over the rolling hills. Soaren and Aleera had taken Brazios the other direction so they were safe. Arty was still in the canyon, so she was not in immediate danger. It didn't make sense. Still, Zero knew he had to ensure their safety, and Tollison was the biggest threat. So, he followed. Each time he would get close, Tollison would speed up or change course slightly. Zero had to push hard to get caught up. This happened many times over the course of an hour. Zero was getting tired, but that meant Tollison had to be as well.

Zero had accomplished his goal. Soaren and Aleera had escaped with Arty's rider. Arty, herself, was still safe in the canyon. He should just turn around. But something kept him on Tollison's trail. Maybe it was the way the big red dragon snuck glances over his shoulder at him. There was no malice. Or the way Tollison's rider yelled and beat Tollison's side to speed up, and Tollison took his time to comply. Just as when he had first taken to the air, Zero knew that something was... off. Still, if he could swipe at Tollison's side enough to damage the blood spell slightly, maybe his friend could escape the Empire's clutches.

Storm clouds on the not-so-distant horizon brought stronger winds and dulled the sun. Tollison led him directly into the teeth of the storm. Lightning flashed across the sky and then again, this time striking the ground. The red dragon dipped allowing Zero to gain the higher air. The rider yelled and screamed, yanking on the metal-riveted leather straps. Below them, the ruins of an ancient castle, abandoned for centuries, was the only structure Zero had seen all day. And Tollison angled toward them as the clouds finally released their fury.

Through the sheets of pouring rain, Zero backed off of Tollison's trail, comfortably waiting to see why Tollison had led them here. If it was an ambush, he wanted to be able to wheel around and flee quickly. The teeth marks on his neck throbbed, and his wings felt heavy. He was not sure a fight would go his way in his current state. Tollison, however, went into a lazy bank to the right, leaving his side and rider fully exposed. This was his opportunity. With a thrust of his powerful wings, Zero shot forward and down, preparing to crash into the larger red dragon right where the rider sat.

Behind you, said Tollison, startling Zero and causing him to slow down.

When he checked over his shoulder, it was already too late. The little black dragon that had escaped earlier along with a blue dragon and rider were right on his tail. Zero did the only thing he could—he dove straight down, and although that left him vulnerable to attack from Tollison, it was his best chance of flying away from this. The black dragon followed him, but the blue kept its course, cutting off one path of escape. He was running out of options as the ground grew closer with each passing moment. It was that exact moment when Zero saw him. On the top of the tallest remaining tower, a gray robe and long beard whipped around wildly in the air. Staff raised high, Dreknoxious called down the thunder. Lightning struck from several places at once. The burnt smell of extreme heat filled his nostrils as he turned to see the black dragon falling out of the sky. The blue did not wait, turning and flying back the way they had come from.

Zero pulled out of his drive to find Tollison and his

rider right above him. The large red dragon turned his body slightly exposing his rider to Zero. Without hesitation, he swiped with one massive claw, unseating the rider in midair. Before the unfortunate rider had even struck the ground, Dreknoxious had ceased his arm waving and the clouds started to clear. By the time Zero landed beside Tollison on the hilltop that the ruins sat on, sunlight was peeking through the clouds. He was not entirely sure what had just happened or how Dreknoxious came to be here, but he was glad he was here.

What is going on? asked Zero.

Tollison kind of shrugged and looked up to the tower where the wizard still stood. Then he said one word like that would explain it all, *Dreknoxious.*

And it did. The old man always knew more than anyone else, was always in the right place at the right time.

What, so he guided you here?

More than that, he is the reason I have been saddled by that maniacal savage for the past several moons. He told me to get captured and prevented the blood spell from taking full control. Seriously, I do not know why I let him put me in these situations.

But... I just... What?

Tollison laughed then. *Perhaps he can explain it better. Here he comes.*

Relying heavily on his wooden staff, Dreknoxious approached the two dragons with a smile on his face.

"Well met, young Zero. Well met, indeed," said the wizard.

Honestly, I don't know how you do it. How are you always right in the thick of things?

"Really it is all very simple. You see, I start by–"

Zero did not hear the rest. He was not even aware if Dreknoxious was still talking. Instead, Jaxson's voice filled his head for the first time in so long. Zero sucked in an abrupt breath and turned his head quickly to the west. It was a short message, and then Jaxson was gone again.

All that Jaxson said was, *Zero! Find me.*

The wizard also turned to the west. "I heard him as well."

Zero's wide eyes darted from the hilly horizon to Dreknoxious and back. His legs coiled, loading like springs, and his wings prepared to take off. But still, he didn't move. He looked back to the wizard.

"Don't let me stop you. Go."

And go he did.

CHAPTER 24

His fatigue vanished. His injuries were only a distant ache way in the back depths of his mind. Lack of sleep, food, water... none of it mattered. Jaxson called for aid, and Zero answered.

To his back, the rolling hills that surrounded Hurline Bluff and the river it sat on were not visible any longer. The Dragon Spine Mountains appeared on the horizon to his left, tiny apparitions that, as he got closer, showed the reason for their name. Flat grassland lay before him and streamed rapidly beneath.

Fifteen moon cycles had passed since that fateful day by the cave filled with priceless dragon glass. Fifteen moon cycles since Jaxson had used his magic to destroy a threat to their lives but also his own father. Fifteen moon cycles since his life had stopped being normal.

Just over ten moon cycles ago, Jaxson had left in the middle of the night without explanation or warning. The connection between them, the sacred bond between a rider and dragon, was muted. Zero had searched frantically but with Dreknoxious's help, he realized no amount of searching will find someone who doesn't want to be found. Or at least no amount of searching should find someone who doesn't want to be found.

But Jaxson had called out through their bond. It was a desperate cry, one of last resort. Zero knew before their bond was again dulled that his friend was in grave danger, and he knew the direction in which to go. So, he flew through the day and night and then day again. Their connection grew stronger with each beat of his wings. He didn't question why, if Jaxson called him, their connection was again blocked. He didn't wonder what his rider, his friend, had been doing. There would be time for questions later. He would ensure there would be time for answers as well. And that meant he had to get to Jaxson and keep him alive.

Closer.

Even though their connection remained muted, he knew he was getting closer as emotions began seeping through the wall on their bond. Jaxson was scared but not terrified. It was more of an impending doom than outright fright. He was also sad but that was to be expected. There was something else there as well. Something Zero had trouble putting a claw on for the longest time. It wasn't until Pyd repositioned on his back near the spot where the scales from his neck overlapped those of his back. Zero smiled as the tiny pygmy dragon scrunched in close to cut the wind as they flew. Home. That was the other sensation coming from Jaxson. He knew Zero was coming, and it was like he was already going home.

The sun set on another day and still Zero flew. Instead of being worn down, he was invigorated. At dawn, he was getting his friend back.

****

He didn't know exactly what he was looking for, only that he would know it when he saw it. The air, significantly warmer than when he'd departed, hung heavy with humidity rising from the swamp below. A new smell floated on the wind as well. It was the sickly-sweet smell of decay and something else... smoke. And most times, where there was smoke there were humans. He needed to follow his nose. He flew, rising higher in the air, hoping to spot a flicker of flame. The night was at its darkest during the witching hours and a flame would be spotted easily from this height.

He reached out to Jaxson but hit the wall. Something, not Jaxson, had their connection blocked. If it was so frustrating to have Jaxson reach out and then be blocked again, Zero might try and figure out how someone could even do that. But as it stood, all of his thoughts were on locating and rescuing Jaxson.

Checking over his shoulder, he snorted. A white line shone weakly on the horizon. Dawn approached, and he was no closer to finding Jaxson than he was hours ago. He concentrated on the smoke where it smelled thicker, closer to the source. He altered his course slightly to where a river flowed through the thick jungle near a series of rocky hills. With how the hills were aligned down the river, Zero thought they were made by someone long ago. Instead of hills, they were ruins.

An image of a lion stalking a gazelle filled his mind. Slowly, the lion crept until he was mere steps from his meal. He quickened his pace, eager to sate his hunger, but the gazelle spotted him. With two quick bounds, the young prey escaped the lion's hunt.

Patience and caution. Got it.

He rose higher still, and that was when he spotted the shadows dancing against one of the pyramid-shaped hills. A huge bonfire raged near the river, and Zero spotted mud and thatch structures scattered around it. That was where Jaxson was held. That was where Zero would free him.

Swooping down on one of the higher hills across the river, Zero peered into the village. He wanted to get an idea of what he was up against and maybe spot Jaxson or where they were holding him. The sun finally peeked over the horizon and soon the dark shapes and deeper shadows lightened, revealing a more complete picture beneath him.

A huge fire raged with only six warriors dancing around

it. He didn't spot any other people in or near the village. Then, from the jungle just outside the village a shrill whistle sounded. Men, women, and children started coming out of the buildings to start their day. Other fires were made and spits set up to cook meat. Children zoomed around chasing each other and any chicken unlucky enough to be in their path.

It was a normal village of people living off the land. Why were they holding Jaxson prisoner?

Zero shook his head. It didn't matter. Freeing him was all that did. Wish I could get a closer look, thought Zero.

Pyd climbed up the back of his neck to the top of his head and sat down. Zero looked up to see the little dragon's upside-down face looking at him. Then Pyd did two unexpected things. First, he winked. Zero's mouth hung open. He'd never seen Pyd act so... human. Then, the tiny dragon disappeared.

CHAPTER 25

Even perched on the rocky hilltop above the lazy river and thick mire below, the air swam around him in swirls. The sun, finally clear of the horizon, set about its business of burning off the early fog. Zero sat still as the stones around him, staring at the village below.

It was quiet, still.

Activity along the river caught his attention. Several villagers were preparing a flat barge not much bigger than a single horse stable. A pole was fastened in the center and the barge was adorned with flowers and vines. The villagers loaded items onto the barge, but Zero could not tell what they were. Slowly, with his head low, he crept forward to get a better view.

An image of the barge from the other side of the river popped into his mind. Then, it was no longer just a picture. Zero was actually seeing the villagers placing pots and baskets of varying sizes onto the barge. Wood was stacked all around the barge in piles of varying heights. The flowers, far prettier than he could see from up on the hillside, were pink and purple with a splash of yellow here and there. Vines wrapped the pole in the center of the barge reaching all the way to the top where a chain with shackles was attached. As his vision went back to normal, he laid his head down for a moment to fight intense nausea.

That was intense, said Zero to Pyd. *I don't like the look of that barge. Looks like a funeral pyre to me. Can you see any warriors?*

Zero peered down at the village trying to find the tiny dragon. A flock of red and white birds flew between him and the river. Two giant flamingos took flight from the river, flying away from the barge. But he couldn't see his little friend anywhere.

Again, he saw through Pyd's eyes. Villagers were starting their day. Several women were stoking a fire while two men chopped leafy vegetables, preparing them for the pot. Children ran around screaming and playing. Chickens scattered as one particularly rambunctious girl started chasing them. An older man shuffled across the center of the village to sit close to the fire. He pulled out a tiny blade and a piece of wood and began to whittle.

Where are the warriors? Do they have any other notable defenses?

A group of heavily armed warriors were leaving for patrol on the side of the village Zero could not see because of thick vegetation. Other warriors in groups of two or three positioned all around the village set a perimeter. Pyd even showed him several warriors training in a clearing on the other side of the village. There was a brief pause that Zero took to mean Pyd had moved before the images could show up in his mind again.

He saw a baby strapped to a woman's back as she carried a basket of water plants up from the river. Then, two kids, a boy and a girl, holding fishing poles passed her on their way down to the water.

I get it. There are many noncombatants in the camp. Lots of kids, said Zero. *That doesn't change the fact that Jaxson is being held down there and something is blocking our bond. Nothing that is doing that is good. Not when Jaxson was doing it and not now.*

Zero caught a glimpse of Pyd as he moved from the top of one tree to another closer to the village center. A long, low building made of earth and straw ended near three smaller earthen buildings. Pyd started showing Zero what he was seeing yet again.

Warriors coming back from a patrol streamed into the long building. But something Zero had not noticed from his vantage point was one of the three smaller buildings was surrounded by guards. Two archers held arrows at the ready on each of the other small buildings. It was the most heavily guarded spot in the whole village.

That must be where they are keeping Jaxson. I could probably fly down, rip the roof off, and carry him away before they even know what is happening.

Crouching down and preparing to launch himself toward his friend's prison cell, Zero's eyes narrowed. He needed to eliminate one set of archers then turn his back on the other set as he ripped off the roof. Speed and power. His tail swished side to side, a sign that takeoff was only a moment away.

His vision turned dark, and Zero flattened his body. Breathing hard, he tossed his head from side to side but only blackness could be seen. Then slowly light returned. Instead of seeing the village below, a robed woman with a long, flowing headdress appeared, striding purposefully from the river toward the guards. The image flickered, and Zero realized that Pyd was terrified. The woman approached and the guards all bowed their heads. With a wave of her hand the door swung open. She flicked her fingers, and Jaxson, bound and gagged, floated out of his cell. Hovering in front of the witch, Jaxson glared at her with no fear in his eyes.

She complicates things, said Zero. He saw the village from his own perspective again. Pyd appeared in front of him but quickly scurried onto his back, trembling.

Arrows were no longer his biggest concern. The village witch, powerful enough to suspend Jaxson in the air, had to be the reason their bond was not working. She was likely taking his friend to that barge waiting down at the river. Jaxson was out of time, and so was he.

CHAPTER 26

The path down to the river, lined with warriors, was short and straight. At the end, the barge rested half on the riverbank. The warriors all chanted in unison in a language that Zero did not understand though it was familiar in a strange way. The witch walked in front of the still-suspended Jaxson. The warriors, more than Zero had thought the village contained, jumped up and down. Their chanting intensified. The energy in the air was palpable.

Once the witch reached the river, followed closely by Jaxson, she threw her head back and shouted. Turning on her heel, she twisted to face Jaxson. Her hand shot out and struck Jaxson squarely across the upper cheek. Zero growled but still he waited. He only had one chance at this—he needed to be sure. Turning back to the river, the witch called out again, and all the warriors ceased chanting instantly.

Silence draped over the village, the river, and the little rocky outcrop where Zero waited. No one moved, and Zero barely breathed. Across the river, another group of warriors stepped out, all twelve coming to a stop with their toes almost in the river. They were taller than the village warriors with bronze, perfect skin. Each had a weapon in hand ranging from bows on the end to long spears held by those in the center. As one, they turned their back on the village witch. Instead of breaking the silence, their quiet arrival and unified movements only made it more stifling.

The additional warriors were not comforting to Zero, so he coiled again preparing to take flight. He kept his eyes focused on Jaxson. Pyd stirred on his back then flew in front of Zero's nose. Pop! The pygmy dragon vanished. Moments later, Zero got his first close look at Jaxson through Pyd's eyes. His friend did not seem to be in terrible shape. He was too skinny, and his clothes were soiled. A large black gem that sparkled in the sunlight hung around his neck. It was the only thing not filthy. The witch paused and looked over her shoulder toward Pyd. Just as quickly, his viewpoint shifted as the pygmy dragon moved deeper into the thick foliage, cutting most of the warriors from his sight. Zero could really only see the newcomers across the river.

Movement from the thick undergrowth behind the taller warriors caught Zero's attention. Another witch with long, flowing, multicolored robes stepped out. She was older than the village witch but not at all elderly. Her headdress, both larger and more ornate, made her seem tall though she was not. The warriors waited for her to pass before turning to face the village. When the witch made it to the river's edge, she held up both of hands.

His normal vision returned. From his current position, he watched the village witch bow. When the newcomer lowered her hands, the village witch rose and gestured toward Jaxson. After some intense back-and-forth, it finally appeared that the two witches had made a deal. Jaxson floated forward and was grabbed by two warriors near the barge. After lashing him to the post with thick leather straps, the village witch approached again. She waved her hands and the piles of wood on the barge ignited. Zero stood just as Pyd reappeared and latched onto his back. The flames grew quickly but the witch did not move. Jaxson scrambled, trying to stamp out the fires within reach of his boots. The witch grabbed the gem and necklace, snatching it off of Jaxson's neck. Immediately, their connection was restored.

Pain, fear, and confusion flooded Zero's mind from the bond with Jaxson. Beyond the obvious—Jaxson being gagged and bound, strapped to a burning barge, and surrounded by enemy warriors—Zero knew something was off.

Jaxson. Hear me.

No response. Pyd wiggled on his back and then was gone. Moments later, Zero saw bronze warriors sneaking in from behind the village. He had no idea what that meant or how Pyd even knew to look for them there.

Can you hear me, Jaxson?

Jaxson's head rose and he looked around him frantically. *What? I can't see!*

Jaxson, relax. I'm here.

Zero? Am I dreaming?

Zero exhaled, relief washing over him. *No, this is not a dream or even a nightmare. I'm here.*

Where are you?

The flames on the barge grew and smoke obscured Zero's view. *I'm close. Don't turn your head. We need them to think they have won.*

So, you heard me? I was worried you didn't or that maybe you wouldn't come...

I will always answer when you call.

I'm so sorry about leaving—

Zero cut him off. *We'll have time for all of that later. Right now, I need to get you free.*

I couldn't agree more. It's getting kinda hot down here.

Let's get to it then. I have been patient enough. Here's what you need to do, said Zero. He gave Jaxson a quick rundown of the layout of warriors and the two different witches. He also mentioned the warriors sneaking in from the rear of the village. *They are trying to go unseen. Let's change that.*

Yeah, we shouldn't wait. My skin is starting to burn.

Pyd, are you ready? A close-up image of Jaxson floated

into Zero's mind. Pyd was in place. It was time to rescue his friend. *Go now. And Jaxson…*

Yeah.

Swim fast.

CHAPTER 27

The smell of smoke mixed with the sweet smell of decay which was always present in a swamp. The flames on the barge, though growing, struggled to really take off with the wet wood. Two warriors approached the barge and quite gently pushed it off the bank. The barge spun in lazy rotations as the slow current gripped it.

Zero watched all of this from his rocky overlook. He turned away and quietly took flight in the opposite direction. He wanted their first view of him to be awe inspiring. After circling wide, he turned and started toward the village from behind the second group of warriors, flying low and fast over the impenetrable canopy of cypress trees, tall palms, and interconnected vines. The thick air matched the low, dark clouds above. Just before reaching the river, he slowed.

Be ready. I'm about to put on a show, he told both Jaxson (who couldn't see it because he was still blindfolded) and Pyd.

Zero flared his wings just as he came over the river. Hovering in place, he roared. Warriors from the village stumbled back, but the newcomers immediately jumped into action. The warriors closest to the witch surrounded her protectively. The archers on the end nocked arrows but did not fire. The village witch stood locked in place staring up at the huge dragon. Every eye was on him as he unleashed a blast of dragon's fire over the village. Arrows loosed, and though none were strong enough to penetrate his scales, one did get lodged in the thin membrane of his right wing. This made him roar again, louder. Every eye down below was on him or running from him. No one was watching Jaxson as Pyd appeared right beside him and gnawed away at the leather straps restraining his wrists.

So far, so good.

The newer witch started chanting and weaving her hands as she stared up at Zero. He did not want to discover what type of spell she was working up. He ducked his head, becoming horizontal with the swamp below, and took off, forward over the village. Arrows shot up at him until he swooped really low, his belly scraping the top of the tallest building. Warriors dove for cover. Women and children ran screaming, seeking shelter anywhere it could be found. The wind from his wingbeats spread the village cooking fire and scattered their chickens. He flew over the building Jaxson had been held in, and then he was again over the swamp's thick vegetation. He kept his eyes sharp for the target he sought. They had to be here somewhere.

Pyd jumped into his head. Zero saw Jaxson free of the gag, blindfold, and bonds diving into the river. Warriors along the bank pointed and shouted. Arrows started hitting the water where Jaxson had gone under. Finally, he spotted the target he sought.

Turning slightly to get behind the bronze-skinned warriors approaching the village from the unguarded side, Zero sprayed dragon's fire in a long line behind them. He had no desire to hurt them—quite the opposite actually. He angled around and loosed more fire, cutting off any retreat to the north. They had to either go through the village or around it to the river. One last time, he came around and rained fire down in a long, straight line. The warriors had no choice but to go through the village now.

Satisfied that they had no other choice, Zero flew downriver hoping to pull Jaxson out of the water quickly. He flew close to the water until he was almost back to the village before turning around. Surely, he must have missed him.

Jaxson, where are you?

No response. Becoming more frantic with each passing moment, Zero flew ever farther downriver calling out for Jaxson over and over. Once he was almost back to the village, he called out for Pyd. *Do you see Jaxson?*

With no hesitation, Pyd showed Zero what he saw: iron bars surrounding him with a big lock on a chain. The necklace with the large black gem was tied around the cage. Pyd had been captured, and Jaxson was not responding. This rescue attempt was not going well.

All the past moons, days upon days, he had worried over Jaxson. Finally, he had a chance to rescue him, and it had gone bad. He didn't even know what had happened. With Pyd captured, it was a complete disaster. He growled.

But a growl did not cover his frustration. He roared. Those people down there had captured Jaxson and were going to burn him alive. Then, they put Pyd in a metal box to do who knows what with. He wasn't going to have it. He gained some altitude in a hurry.

Pyd, be prepared. I'm coming down there.

Without waiting for an answer, Zero pointed his nose down at the river and thrust his wings. He was on a collision course with those that would harm his friends, and he wasn't slowing down.

CHAPTER 28

Having enough control not to hurt Pyd was his final thought before slamming into the river. Water shot into the air, soaking warriors on both sides. Pyd was on the side with the newcomers, so Zero turned to the village side and released his dragon's fire. The warriors not smart or quick enough to flee were incinerated. The witch, however, quickly threw up a magical shield that repelled his fire. He turned to the bronze-skinned warriors, reaching his neck out even with the pain from the bite days earlier, and snatched a warrior off the ground. He shook his head violently and then released the warrior to crash into several more.

The village witch screamed and started weaving a spell in the air. Emboldened by her fierce call, warriors ran back to her side. Pyd sat in a cage right beside her on the ground. Across the river, the new witch also started chanting and weaving a spell in the air in front of her. Fear that he would hurt his little friend determined his next move. Standing in water up to his belly, Zero turned his back to the village and stalked toward the newcomers.

Spears bounced off his scales and arrows shattered or ricocheted, falling harmlessly to the ground. The witch was the true threat. He drew in a deep breath, preparing to release fire upon her when she cast out her hand toward him. Weaponized air slammed into his face causing his head to snap back. His footing, unsure in the muddy river, betrayed him, and he stumbled sideways. It probably saved him as the village witch released her own spell. Magical arrows of crimson fire shot through the spot he had just vacated, passing into the thick vegetation on the other side of the river.

Keep the witches occupied, said Jaxson.

I'm trying. What are you going to do?

End this. That was all Jaxson said.

Zero regained his feet and sprayed small amounts of dragon's fire, first at the newcomer and then over the head of the village witch. Pyd was still in that little cage at her feet. Then, Jaxson appeared from behind the new witch, short spear in hand, and delivered a fatal blow. The spearhead penetrated the witch below the ribs to the right of the spine. Warriors all around him converged. Jaxson, unable to free the spear, released it and dove into the river. Zero covered his escape with a long stream of dragon's fire.

Jaxson emerged from the water at Zero's side and used a wing to hoist himself onto the dragon's back. "Let's get out of here!"

Not yet. The witch has a friend of mine, replied Zero.

Both turned to see the witch struggling with the cage that held Pyd. Finally, she flipped the latch and grasped Pyd by the neck. Yanking the tiny dragon out of the cage, the witch held a long knife to Pyd's stomach. She screamed at them, but Zero did not understand her language.

"I think she is saying to back up or she will use the knife," said Jaxson.

Shouts from behind the witch diverted her attention. Women, children, and even some warriors were running toward her screaming. The bronze-skinned warriors avoiding the fire Zero had sprayed around them had made it to the village and were attacking any in their way. That small moment was all Pyd needed. Quicker than a cobra, he struck the arm holding the knife. When he pulled his mouth away, it was red with the witch's blood. She dropped him, and Pyd disappeared.

"Where did he go?" asked Jaxson.

A familiar tickle near the base of Zero's neck told him Pyd was already in his spot where he liked to rest while flying.

"Oy, how did he get here?" yelled Jaxson.

It's hard to explain, said Zero.

"Tell me later then," replied Jaxson.

Without another word, Zero lifted out of the water. It was not a rapid ascent, with fatigue as much as the river slowing him down. But nothing prevented them from getting high above the swamp. Zero looked back to try and see what had become of the village witch, but smoke from the swamp fires he had set obscured his view.

"Thank you for coming to get me," said Jaxson. "I don't deserve to have you."

Pyd crawled over to Jaxson and rested next to him.

I will always come when called. Just don't ever put us in a situation like this again, said Zero.

The swamp passed beneath them in a blur as Zero used the last of his energy to put some distance between them and the village.

Did you find what you were looking for? Did you find the scroll?

Jaxson did not answer for quite some time. Then just as the sun touched the horizon, he said, "I did not find the Living Scroll, but I think I finally found what I was looking for."

Oh, really. And what was that?

"My rightful place in this world, and that is with you," replied Jaxson.

Zero smiled. He couldn't agree more.

EPILOGUE

The sun rose on a cloudless, chilly day. Smoke from the camp's fires rose straight up in the air, giving the appearance of skinny pillars holding up the blue sky. Large trees, mostly evergreens this high up the mountain, loomed overhead. The smell of winter, or more like the lack of scent, filled his nostrils; the sky was lying. Snow would fall soon. He needed to be far gone before that happened. He had spent far too long in the Empire's camp already. But he needed to be sure before returning back to his old friend, Dreknoxious.

He tightened the scarf around his neck that he used to conceal a scar that would immediately give away his identity. At least with the chill in the air, the scarf did not look out of place. He started the trek up the steep mountainside attempting to reach the plateau hidden between two peaks above. There was the castle and surrounding buildings that was the center of the Empire's focus. It was an old castle, easily recognizable by those that knew the history of the area. It has been known by many names over the years: Esligoth, Kramen's Keep, Valturez. But now people called it the Castle of the Burnt Stone, though no one really understood why.

He didn't know either.

The high altitude had him breathing heavy when he finally reached the top of the ridge. A group of Empire soldiers marched past on the pretense of keeping watch for enemies. In reality, they were there to make sure the workers stayed on task. And the workers were already busy digging in various spots around the castle. They did not know what they were looking for, only that if they found anything strange to immediately report it.

He kept walking past the excavations, the emblem on his stolen jacket showing the rank of captain allowing him freedom to roam over the entire area. He checked his pocket for the seventh time that morning feeling the familiar crinkle of the map. When he arrived at the castle, nothing had changed from the day before. Men swung pickaxes and long handled hammers at the walls. Each strike created a loud cracking sound that reverberated off the mountains back and forth. But no damage was ever done to the stones themselves. If there had been any type of door, the men might have had more luck breaking in, but there wasn't—just black stone after black stone fitted so snugly together it was often hard to find the seam.

Once around the end of the castle wall, he stopped and pulled out the map. It was old, not as old as the castle, but still old. It showed the two mountains, the castle, several buildings that were no longer there, and then up against the far cliff it showed a strange symbol that resembled an open book that flowed or maybe a waterfall. He wasn't entirely sure. What he did know was that the Empire were not looking there, and he was thankful for that. Still, he needed to be sure. So, he trudged on.

For the better part of the morning, he searched for anything that could be a way into the cliff, a hidden door or a disguised cave. It wasn't until he was about to give up and head back down when he spotted something unusual. At the base of the cliff near the edge of a vertical drop, the cliff wall changed color slightly. He had to back up to make sure he was seeing it right, a shape of a life-sized dragon hidden in plain sight. Dreknoxious had been right. That was the entrance to the temple. That was the place the Empire had been searching for, but they were looking in the wrong place. He quickly tucked the map away and turned to retreat back down the mountain. The intel Tollison had gained while in the service of the Empire had paid off.

"You there! What are you doing over here?" an Empire soldier asked.

"Just making the rounds," he replied as he pulled his scarf up higher. "Checking on the progress and such."

"I don't think I've ever seen you here before," said the soldier.

"Just arrived last week. I'm supposed to provide a status report upon my return," he lied.

"What company do you belong to?"

That was a question he could not answer. Not only did he not know which company the man from whom he'd stolen the jacket in Taverny belonged to, but he wasn't entirely sure of any company name within the Empire's army. He needed to get out of there and fast.

"How many men are working on knocking down the walls?" he asked, trying to divert the soldier's attention as he inched his way around him.

"I asked you a question first," replied the soldier, pulling out his sword. "And I want an answer now."

With his left hand, he reached into the pocket with the map while his left gripped a small knife at his waist. "Here. This should put to rest all of your concerns."

He unfurled the map, and when the soldier came to get a closer look, he jabbed him with the knife in the throat. The soldier fell, and he turned and moved quickly back the way he had come. He had almost reached the bottom of the steep path when the alarm sounded. He didn't wait to see if anyone was looking, he just ran.

Luck stayed on his side, and he escaped the camp without being seen. He crossed a dry stream and went a little farther down the mountain and then crossed back over the streambed. He continued walking for another half hour without incident until he heard a branch snap. He stopped cold in his tracks. His hand reached for the knife again, but before he could draw it, Tam walked out of a thick copse of trees.

"Scared me a bit there, boy," said the man, smiling. "But I'm certainly glad to see you."

Tam returned the smile though it did not last long. "Are the rumors true? Are they close to getting in?"

The man laughed. "They aren't close to getting in, and even if they do succeed, they aren't trying to get into the right place. It's like they are reading the right book but on the wrong page."

"That's the best news I've had all week," said Tam.

"Thought you might like that. Will you let the wizard know?"

"Absolutely. Grog is just over that ridge. I'll be in the air within the hour," said Tam. "But where will you go?"

"I'll go back to looking for Jaxson," said the man. "I am going to find him next or die trying."

"I may have some news on that front," said Tam warily. "But it is only a partial report."

"Don't make me beg," said the man.

"Dreknoxious said that Zero is headed to find to him. That Jaxson had finally reached out," said Tam.

"That is excellent. If anyone can reach him, it will be Zero."

"But you are his father. His father that he thought he killed all those moons ago," said Tam.

Alan smiled. "He'll find out soon enough that I'm still here. I just hope he can take the shock."

Tam did not return Alan's smile. "I'm not sure how he will respond."

"As long as Zero finds him well, we will deal with the rest later."

"I guess," replied Tam.

"He will just have to lean on his dragon and have resolve equal to Zero," said Alan. "I think he will be just fine."

THE PRINCESS KNIGHT

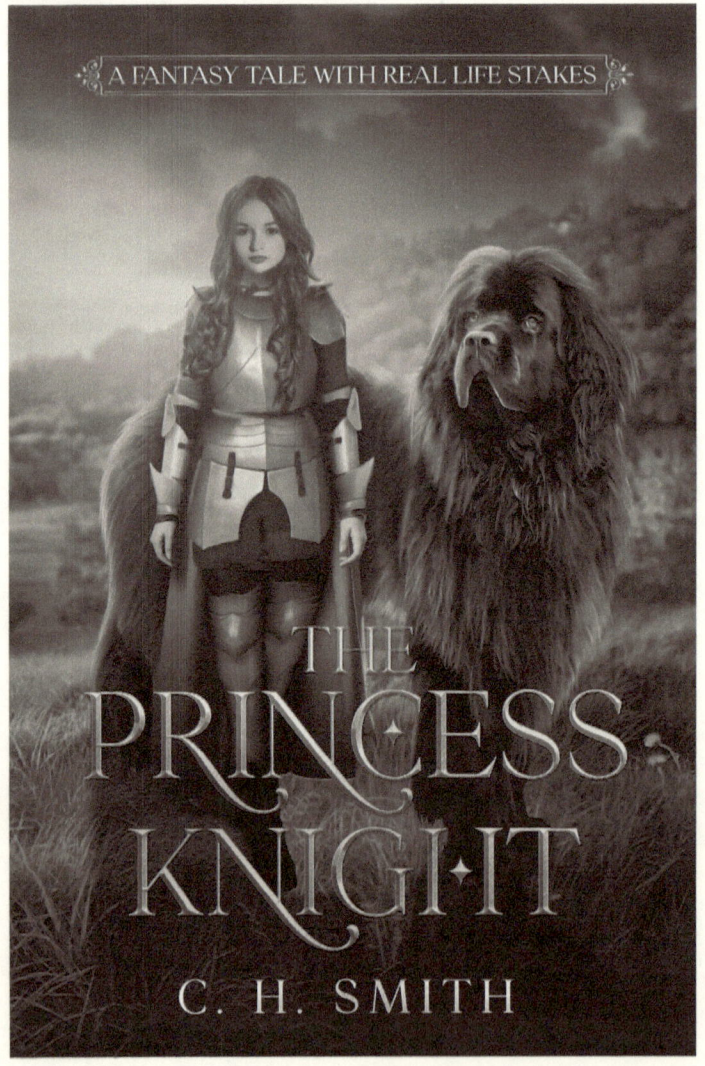

A FANTASY TALE WITH REAL LIFE STAKES

THE PRINCESS KNIGHT

C. H. SMITH

MAP OF CRYSTAL FORGE

CHAPTER 1

I am not exactly sure what answer I was expecting from the quiet, bearded guy a few stools down from me at the bar, but I was definitely not prepared for the one he provided. I had half-expected him to brush me off or offer some noncommittal response. If he was more liquored-up than I had thought, I might have heard a rant about an ex-wife or cheating girlfriend. If he was piss drunk, I would have expected pitiful whining about missed opportunities and regret. His answer did not match any of those.

"How's it going, big fella?" I asked out of boredom.

He looked at me with the wide eyes of a child just caught sneaking into his dad's locked office to peek at something he knew was off limits.

"My princess is gone, and I miss her." Then after a long pause, he continued, "Sometimes, lately, I struggle to remember her face perfectly. And the joy of her laugh, I remember, but not the tone or sound, just the feeling it caused. That's not always enough."

I am a fairly well-read guy for a bar rat and have never met a stranger. In that moment, however, I was at a loss for words. So, I did the only logical thing possible.

"Brandee? Another round for me and my friend," I said, buying some time to collect my thoughts. There is an unspoken rule between most bar patrons. Conversations must pause in front of the bartender, unless said bartender was previously involved, or her opinion would add value in the conversation. The bearded man that had been nursing his beer did not honor the sacred tradition.

"I don't even know why I'm here. I don't drink much anymore, but I couldn't think of anywhere else to be," he said, draining his warm beer and accepting a new one from Brandee.

"Well, I think this is a fine place to be. A few drinks, good conversation, food that won't kill ya," I said with a laugh. "Mighty fine place to be."

The man just nodded and sipped his beer. I thought that was the end of it, so I asked Brandee about her studies.

"Pretty good, Jake," she said as she perched on the bar in front of a large, open history book. "But I do have an exam tomorrow morning, so if I'm a little slow on the pour, just holler."

Again, boredom got the best of me. I slid over a couple seats next to the bearded man.

"What'd you say your name was?"

"I didn't, but it's Daniel."

"I'm Jake. Don't think I've ever seen you in here before," I continued, trying to get the conversational ball rolling.

"Nope," Daniel replied, reaching for his wallet.

"Don't be in a hurry, friend. The old couple at the end there are boring, and I'm too old to hang with the college crowd. But me and you, that's just about right," I said.

This guy had something to get off his chest, I could tell. Daniel paused and looked around the bar. Then he sighed and settled back onto his stool.

"There, that's better. Now, what you do for a living, Daniel?"

"I'm an out-of-work school teacher," he said.

"That's hard. Raising other people's kids, I mean," I told him. "I'm a car salesman, and sales have been good. Let me buy you another beer."

"Maybe after this one is done," Daniel said quietly. "Not sure I'll be up for another one."

"Sure you will be," I said with a smile and took a sip. "What subject did you teach?"

Daniel did not respond right away; instead, he stared at the watch on his wrist. "Subject? High school history."

"One of my favorites! At least better than English lit. Having to read a bunch of stories that didn't make a hoot of sense, written by a bunch of dead folks, never appealed to me," I said honestly, shrugging my shoulders.

"Stories are powerful, though. At least the good ones are, anyway," he said, a vacant look still in his eyes.

I realized I was getting back into strange territory, but now I had to know what haunted him. What made him talk about princesses and powerful stories?

"Do you know any stories like that? Stories with power?" I asked. Daniel nodded, so I pushed on. "We have time. Tell me one."

"I'm not sure about that. The last story I told didn't end well for anybody," he replied.

"Was it about the princess you spoke of earlier?" I asked. My fingers tightened on my glass as I watched for a reaction.

The large, bearded man lifted his head to look me in the eyes. "It was a story I told my daughter, Josie, and yes, it was about the princess I mentioned." I noticed his eyes showed a yearning for something, but I was not sure if it was to tell the story or to forget it.

"I'd hear it if you'd tell it," I said.

"It's not a story I've ever told anyone but her," he said quietly. "And I don't think this is the place or the time."

I watched the enormous struggle happen within him. Daniel's fist clenched tightly, and small beads of sweat appeared on his forehead. The yearning intensified till it burned through him. He needed to tell the story again. He needed it to be heard.

"There is never the perfect time or place for anything," I said, leaning in closer. "There is only now, on that barstool, in this bar. Tell your story. It'll be better than the ending of this massacre of a football game on the TV."

Daniel's shoulders relaxed as he polished off his beer. The intense look in his eyes was replaced with the far-away gaze of a man lost in a memory. A memory replayed so often it was comfortable and inviting between the painful edges.

"Alright, but first, I'll take you up on that next beer," he said.

CHAPTER 2

A long time ago in a land far, far away – or, if you prefer, *Once upon a time* – there was a kingdom known as Crystal Forge. It was a large kingdom, filled with beautiful and wondrous things. Unimaginably tall waterfalls filled crystal-clear pools that fed tranquil streams. Soaring trees in lush green forests were home to abundant wildlife. The cities were regal and pristine each encircled by fertile farmland. To the south, the coast was lined with pink, sandy beaches and blue water. To the north and east, the Dragon Spine Mountains offered protection and unspoiled beauty. Finally, to the west was the Endless Sea of Grass, known as much for its fertile soil as its vastness.

Crystal Forge was a truly beautiful place. It was also quite magical. It was home to the Elves of the Golden Age. The only known colony of water sprites inhabited the two major rivers. Sirens swam in the bay to the south, and dragons soared over the mountains. Even commonplace animals such as deer or squirrels had a touch of magic. Some lived much longer than would be considered natural, others seemed to possess higher levels of intelligence. Though they were rarer, some of the animals could talk! Crystal Forge was both wondrous and mystical. Light causes shadow, as they say, and there was darkness in the Forge as well. This is a tale of one child's quest to fight against that darkness. To fight it at all costs.

There were many castles in the Forge, but only the three

oldest are worth mentioning. The blood-red castle at the base of the Dragon Spine Mountains was said to have been built by the dragon riders of lore. The white sandstone castle on the edge of the grass sea was low and sprawling, and was almost as old as the Red Dragon Castle. Then there was Seascape Castle on the southern coast. It was the newest of the major castles, although no one could remember anyone who would have seen the castle when it was built. Seascape Castle, which was made entirely of coral rock, was home to the Queen, the Princess, and one big brown Shaggy Dog.

Princess Sophia loved to walk the sandy pink beach just below the castle in search of perfect seashells. The perfect shell did not have to be really big, nor did it have to be extremely small. It did not have to be pure white or wildly colored. It did not have to be round or oblong. It could be any of these things or none of them. It just needed to be perfect. The Princess could think of no better way to spend her birthday morning. She loved being on the beach or in the Queen's forest or even the drill yard, as long as she was outside. She felt free and alive, or perhaps merely unencumbered by layers of cloth and frilly lace daily life in the castle required. With her dark hair blowing across her face, she gazed over the sea longingly before turning back to the castle. It was time for her birthday celebration complete with cake and ice cream, but also with dresses and ceremony and oh so many people.

On her way across the short dunes but before the climb up the bluff, the Princess was joined by a big, fluffy brown dog. The dog, which closely resembled a small bear, had long, unruly hair, each strand of which seemed to want to lay in any direction but that of the hair around it. He had a sort of bumbling energy that some might confuse with clumsiness or dimness. Shaggy Dog was far from either of these things, though. In fact, he was one of the animals in the Forge that could talk, although he did so rarely and even then usually only to the Princess.

As he lumbered towards her, the Princess giggled, and her light blues eyes sparkled. Shaggy Dog jumped up eager to embrace the Princess. On his hind legs, Shaggy Dog towered over the Princess as he placed his paws on her shoulders. Hair and laughter were everywhere as these two friends reveled in just being together.

"Shaggy Dog! I am so happy to see you," exclaimed the Princess once her laughter had subsided. Even if Shaggy Dog had wanted to deny how happy he felt, his boat-paddle tail gave him away, swishing feverishly from side to side.

"I'm so glad you came. Are you coming to the castle?" pleaded the Princess. "The party will be awfully dull, but better with you there."

Shaggy Dog's head lowered and the motion of his tail slowed as he muttered, "I'm sure the Queen won't be thrilled, but for you, Princess… anything."

"Oh, thank you! Thank you! This party might be fun after all."

Later, Shaggy Dog sat uncomfortably in the corner of the Grand Ballroom. His eyes took in the immense columns of marble, all three black stone fireplaces, and the vibrant artwork that hung around the room. He had just decided to slip away from all the sneers directed his way by the pompous court attendees when the Princess finally arrived. She was dressed not in layers of lace and ribbon but a simple – if not elegant – green dress. She had a thin smile as she entered to the cheers of all in attendance.

The Queen quickly called her daughter forward to stand before her. "Princess Sophia, let me be the first to say happy birthday this evening. You look quite lovely in that dress."

"Thank you, Momma…. Your Majesty. The dress is rather nice, and I can move so freely. Thank you for it," said the Princess quite sincerely.

"In the Kingdom of Crystal Forge, it is tradition for the Queen to hold an extravagant ball for the Princess's birthday," the Queen proclaimed for the entire room to hear.

The Princess felt the small glimmer of hope about this party slipping away. The rest of the court perked up in anticipation at the mention of a ball.

"However, my daughter is not traditional, and this is her day! So, without further ado..."

The Queen clapped her hands. Suddenly, servants rushed in from all directions. Some set up an archery range in one corner. Another group of servants set up a fishing-net throwing competition. Some started to roast apples in the fireplace while others set up a table laden with biscuits and honey. Other servants set up more fun and more unlikely games and food all around the ballroom. The Princess thought it promised more fun than she had ever had within the castle walls.

And it was, too. She found it difficult to decide what was more enjoyable: climbing the rock wall or casting the nets or throwing knives. Maybe it was watching all the men and women of the court look so silly when trying to play any of these games. Regardless, she was having a great time. Even Shaggy Dog seemed to relax a bit, laughing at the courtiers in their discomfort. Evening turned to night, and the Princess was becoming more tired by the moment. She had just finished her third round with the throwing knives when she noticed a commotion at the center of the ballroom.

She made her way to where all the members of the court had gathered. In the midst of the semicircle stood a figure shrouded in a midnight black robe. He was tall and broad-shouldered, but the most striking aspect was the man did not possess a human head. Instead, his dark eyes wreathed with fire peered from a gigantic goat head. The Princess had no clue who he was, but Shaggy Dog recognized him almost immediately. The Princess saw Shaggy Dog's hair stand up and heard a low growl come from his chest.

Shaggy Dog had no love for the one called the Goat Head Sorcerer – none at all. He knew the mysterious sorcerer well, or at least well enough. He knew of the legions at his command. The Ravens of Despair answered to him. Their incessant cawing could drive a person to hopeless depression. The infamous Goblin Army that specialized in millions of tiny cuts to wear a person down were at his disposal. The Goat Head Sorcerer also had the likes of the Snake Oil Witches under his thumb. These vile creatures could place spells on a person and use fake potions or offer fake weapons which all led to false hope and distraction. The Goat Head Sorcerer had many more creatures and weapons to use for his evil purposes. The mere fact that he was here now was ominous.

The silence in the spacious ballroom felt tangible. No one dared move a muscle as the Goat Head Sorcerer raised his hateful eyes to the crowd. As his gaze swept across the room, so did trembling fear and anxiety. His eyes locked onto the Princess, and a wicked grin split his hairy face. In a whisper that, somehow, everyone could hear, he said, "I curse you."

Then he was simply gone. There was no puff of smoke, no bang, or flash of light. The fear and anxiety of the onlookers was now accompanied by shock, sadness, and guilty relief, the only evidence he had ever been there.

The first sound was the anguished cry of the Queen. There were no words, only a primal sound of fear, fury, and loss. Servants rushed quickly to her side to keep her from collapsing. Shaggy Dog sat near to the Princess, staring blankly at the spot the Goat Head Sorcerer had occupied moments ago. The Princess, still quite confused and becoming ever more so, just watched as the crowd broke into small groups, chattering quietly but urgently.

The Queen was the first to recover her senses and immediately ordered everyone but essential personnel out of the room. As the ballroom emptied, a guard attempted to usher the still shocked Shaggy Dog through the doorway. As if waking from a dream, Shaggy Dog bounded around the guard to remain at the Princess's side. The guard looked to the Queen, who waved him off with a resigned sigh. Standing beside her throne, she motioned for the pair to approach.

"My daughter, I am so sorry. If there was anything that could have prevented this curse on you, I would have seen it done." The Queen had become stoic, although her eyes were still full of tears.

The Princess was beginning to understand that this – whatever *this* was – was extremely serious.

"I'm afraid. I'm afraid because you all are afraid. I do not understand what is going on!" the Princess cried out as tears ran down her cheeks.

Shaggy Dog attempted to move closer to her, but he could not get much closer without knocking her down and lying on top of her.

The Queen moved down the steps and placed one arm across her shoulders. "It's quite alright to be afraid, my dear. We all are. You have been cursed by the most evil Goat Head Sorcerer. For what purpose, I cannot begin to understand. But I do know we can fight it. I have already sent for the Benevolent Witch to join us as soon as possible." The Queen looked into the beautiful, terrified face of her daughter. "She will know what steps to take to vanquish this evil."

The Queen, the Princess, and Shaggy Dog retired to the cozy confines of the study, where they found the Benevolent Witch awaiting them. Shaggy Dog thought the Benevolent Witch was difficult to describe. She appeared neither young nor old. She was not beautiful or plain. Her skin sometimes seemed milky white and other times appeared golden tan.

She offered a kind smile to the group, but there was no chit chat or small talk. Getting straight to the point, the Benevolent Witch asked about the encounter with the

Goat Head Sorcerer. She seemed to think no detail was too small. After exhausting the scenario with accounts from everyone present, she focused on the Princess, asking how she had been feeling recently. She asked about her sight, her hearing and taste, and if she had experienced leg cramps or numbness in her fingers. The Benevolent Witch asked scores and scores of questions, and the Princess answered them all wearily. The Princess was beginning to wonder if the Benevolent Witch was really a Raven of Despair in disguise, given all her cawing. But finally, the Benevolent Witch stopped asking questions and stood in silence for a long time.

Shaggy Dog had started to become restless when the Benevolent Witch finally spoke. "Princess Sophia, dear, you have truly been cursed by the Goat Head Sorcerer himself. From what I have learned today, the curse is most vile and if you do not fight it – and *him* – it will surely be your demise. But do not dwell on what could be. Instead, focus your heart on the task that lies before you. For if you are strong and brave, and if you have just a spot of good luck, you will defeat the Goat Head Sorcerer and throw off this vile curse!"

The Princess, although still scared, saw hope in the Queen's eyes, as well as determination in the dark eyes of Shaggy Dog. She knew that with their help she could beat the ol' goat.

"What do I need to do?" she said.

The Benevolent Witch smiled. "You must go on a quest, like the bravest of knights. And you will have many adventures, though I will not promise they all will be pleasant. You will search for the Helm of Knowledge first. It is rumored to be with the witches of Houstonia. Then, with all courage you possess, you will continue on to find your weapon to use against the Goat Head Sorcerer. And, finally, there will be the inevitable battle. There is much I do not know about your quest, but the beginning and the search for the Helm is clear. I, of course, will check on you as often as I

Then, much like the Goat Head Sorcerer, the Benevolent Witch was gone, but instead of leaving fear behind, she left tentative hope.

After only the briefest of moments, Shaggy Dog positioned himself in front of the Princess. He bowed his head low and made a formal request to accompany the Princess on her quest. The Princess was delighted and even the Queen smiled at Shaggy Dog's initiative. It seemed that a nervous excitement was replacing their earlier heavy fear that had fell over the room. The Queen motioned for a servant near the door, and he rolled a tall, shrouded rack into the center of the room.

"Princess, although I give you this gift with all of my heart, I never dreamed you would need it so soon or so dearly," the Queen stated. As the Princess pulled at the shroud, she continued, "This armor will help to protect you from many threats. It is light but durable. It is strong but flexible. The Armor of Love has magical properties as well. For example, it has the ability to mend itself, given time and care. I hope it aids you well on your quest."

The Princess's eyes were wide as she stared at the rose gold armor hanging before her. It was sleek and beautiful, but it was also a stark reminder of the seriousness of her situation. She accepted the gift from the Queen solemnly.

The next morning, the Princess and Shaggy Dog began traveling early. It was a long road to Houstonia though mostly easy riding. The Princess did not push her horse too hard; Shaggy Dog was trotting beside her, after all. She soon began to feel that same nervous excitement as she traveled farther from the castle than she had ever been without a full entourage. In the early morning light, they had passed through the farmland that surrounded the castle and entered the Queen's forest well before lunch. As they trotted through the small clearing that contained the giant, scarred

413

oak, she realized that every inch forward would represent a new milestone. Every step would be one step farther from home than she had ever been. And so, the morning continued through a quick lunch and into the afternoon.

That night, Shaggy Dog found a smooth patch of ground next to tall rocks to act as shelter. There was no need for a fire on this warm night, and enough moonlight crept into their camp for them to see easily. For the most part, the Princess and Shaggy Dog sat in comfortable silence, listening to the sounds of the forest and consumed by their own thoughts. It was peaceful.

The next morning, after a quick, cold breakfast, they made another early start. By mid-morning, the duo emerged from the forest into dazzling sunlight. The forest continued on their left, and off to their right they thought they could see the mountains in the distance – or, at least, they knew they were there, so they *must* be seeing them. Before them were gently rolling hills with the occasional lone oak standing sentry. It was on the top of the fourth hill and under the second oak that they spotted the first tiny town on their journey. Shaggy Dog guessed they would reach the town just after lunch, and suggested they try to find a hot meal. The Princess eyed the tiny town and thought that a hot meal may be a long shot. It was not much of a town, really. But a shot at a hot meal was worth pushing a little harder.

When they had cut the distance to the town by half, they happened upon a woman in distress. She was frantically trying to right a cart still hitched to her mule. As excited as the woman was, surrounded by hundreds of packages and tiny bottles which were the former contents of her cart, the mule was quite the opposite. He was the color of weathered stone and might as well been made of it judging by his lack of movement. As the Princess and Shaggy Dog approached, the woman called out for help. Of course, the duo answered her call. In no time at all, the three of them had turned the cart upright. It took considerably more time to pick up the packages, bundles, and bottles littered all around, not to mention organizing everything. But eventually it was done, and all three sat down for a break.

"You are truly kind to help a lady you don't even know," said the woman. Shaggy Dog and the Princess took in the woman fully for the first time. She was quite striking, with her red hair and pale skin. A spray of freckles across her face did not distract from her beauty at all. In fact, they enhanced her green eyes and charming smile. She was wearing a hunter-green robe and her hair was pulled back in a single tie. She definitely appeared to be frazzled but only in a temporary way.

"It never occurred to me not to help," said the Princess. Shaggy Dog remained silent but alert. "I would assume you would do the same for anyone you happen across."

"Without a doubt, I will always lend a hand to anyone in need. I have made it my life's work, but you and I are in the minority, I am afraid. Most people would go out of their way to avoid helping out. It is the way of the world."

"That is so sad," the Princess lamented. Shaggy Dog looked at her as she continued, "But at least there are people like you that use their entire life to help others. How exactly do you do so?"

The woman swelled with pride and any trace of her disheveled state seemed to melt away. "I am a witch that has dedicated my life to fighting dark curses, using nature as my guide. I have studied from the Dragon Spine to Clear Lakeshire and everywhere in between. I help those who have lost hope, and I educate people before calamity strikes! I have found a cure for most curses that the snobby witches think are beneath them and therefore disregard." She sneered, but quickly her smile returned.

The Princess could hardly believe her luck – here was someone that could help her! Maybe she would not have to go on such a long quest after all. She could get a cure from this witch and be home within a couple of days.

"I think that is wonderful! I could so use your help, Madame Witch. I am actually on my way to Houstonia to seek the help of the witches there, but if you have a cure for evil curses, I won't have to go that far!" All of this came from the Princess in one breath. "I would be so grateful if you could help me."

"Well, it is fortunate I ran into you and your dog on this barren road. Tell me, girl, what type of curse afflicts you?"

The Princess told her all about the Goat Head Sorcerer and the night of her birthday. She told her about the words used so quietly by the vile one. She recounted the aftermath of whispers and fear. Then there was the meeting with the Benevolent Witch. Madame Witch seemed most interested in this conversation and asked many questions. Finally, the Princess told her of their quest, starting with the search for the Helm of Knowledge in Houstonia. She mentioned again how lucky she felt to have met Madame Witch so soon, and how excited she was to get a cure and go home. Madame Witch, for her part, gasped in all the right places. She was attentive and asked informed and probing questions. She had a gleam in her eyes that Shaggy Dog found to be off-putting. He couldn't quite put his nose on it, but something was not right about this witch.

Madame Witch rummaged through her cart and pulled out a large leather bag. She motioned for them to sit and opened the bag. She first pulled out letters explaining they were from people she had cured of one curse or another. The Princess was most impressed with the number of letters. Then Madame Witch pulled out a beautiful necklace and bragged that it was a gift from a wealthy merchant after one of her potions cured his wife. Again, the Princess was most impressed with the beautiful jewelry. Finally, Madame Witch pulled out a short, slender wooden rod. It was covered in writing the Princess did not recognize, and the glow at its tips could have only been gold. Madame Witch explained that this rod could determine exactly which of her miraculous cures would work for the Princess. She waved it over the Princess's head, muttering softly to herself.

"Most difficult... yes... yes. Oh, that is interesting... Most difficult..."

The Princess was on pins and needles until Madame Witch finally stopped waving her wand, closed her eyes, then mumbled as she placed the rod on her forehead. After a moment, her eyes flew wide open, and she shrieked. The Princess and Shaggy Dog both jumped back, startled by the outburst.

Madame Witch locked eyes with the Princess. "Young lady, you have a most serious curse. It will take quite a bit of my resources to cure it, but cure it I will. My magic rod has whispered your ailments to me, and I have divined a cure. It will take time and be very expensive to find all the ingredients needed to complete it. But we can get started right away."

With that, Madame Witch began digging in her cart again. She set up a small table and started unwrapping packages and pulling stoppers from bottles. She was mumbling to herself about how expensive this cure would be, but as a good witch she would help... yes... she would help.

Shaggy Dog stared at the witch as she mixed a potion for the Princess. He noticed she had added drops from the same bottle on three separate occasions. He thought she was just grabbing things at random to add as she muttered about how expensive it was going to be to create a cure. He nudged the Princess, and she bent down close to him. Shaggy Dog whispered, "Ask her what she wants in return for a cure. She does not know you are the Princess, and let's keep it that way."

"Madame Witch, I am forever grateful for your efforts. How can I ever repay you?"

"Oh, young one, I do this out of pleasure to help others. However, if you would like to donate to help me buy supplies... you know, I would be grateful. I would think a girl with armor such as yours would have coin to spare," the witch said with a hungry look.

"I do not have much money with me on this trip, but I could always pay you back," the Princess replied quietly.

Madame Witch stopped mixing the potion and turned to face the Princess. "These ingredients are not cheap! How do you expect me to provide a cure without any money to replenish my stores? Or to live on? How selfish are you that you would steal from a kindly witch?" Her demeanor had changed completely. She began repacking her supplies, then stopped and said, "I could take your armor as payment. You do have a quite serious curse on you, or at least that's what my spell told me."

The Princess looked down at her armor gleaming in the afternoon sun. She did not want to part with the armor the Queen had just given her, but for a cure, she would part with almost anything. She was about to agree when Shaggy Dog gave a low growl.

The witch looked at him nervously, exclaiming, "Control your beast, little one!"

"SNAKE OIL WITCH!" Shaggy Dog exclaimed angrily, baring his teeth. "That is all you are. You said a spell revealed her ailment but you only used your fancy rod and cast no spells! You are lying. You are a fraud and a cheat!"

The Princess was shocked, and was about to protest to defend the witch when she noticed her changing. The beautiful face was melting away to reveal an old hag underneath. The witch's sweet, charismatic voice was replaced with a raspy screech as she said, "I should have gotten rid of you, dog! I knew you were going to be trouble."

Shaggy Dog growled and backed away, beckoning with his head for the Princess to follow. The witch just glared as the duo started away.

"Shaggy Dog," the Princess said, "how did you know?"

"I had my suspicions early on, but I was hoping for a miracle cure. I should have been more level-headed, and she never would have gotten so far. I'm just glad you didn't drink the potion. Who knows what it could have caused?"

"Well, thank you, Shaggy Dog," said the Princess as they trotted down towards the town. "I didn't realize until now how badly I want to beat this curse and go home. Guess I am more scared than I realized."

"You do not have to thank me, Princess, and of course you are scared. We will just take it one step at time. And first of all, we could find something to eat – I'm starving."

"I knew it was serious when you growled. But when you spoke in front of a stranger, I really paid attention. Now all you can talk about is food!"

Shaggy Dog just wagged his tail and kept his rapid pace towards a hot meal.

The next few days were simple and almost happy. The duo traveled by day, taking short breaks to keep themselves from becoming tired out. They stopped early each evening to enjoy each other's company before going to sleep. They told stories and played games, and joked and laughed. Troubles and fears and curses seemed to be far away, or at least someone else's problem. The freedom of the open road, the beautiful scenery, and the excellent companionship made the trip to Houstonia pass quickly. It seemed that they had only just left the Snake Oil Witch when the sparkling gates came into view ahead.

CHAPTER 3

"Shoot! Be right back, guys," Brandee said over her shoulder as she rushed to make drinks for the impatient waitresses at the other end of the bar. I had not noticed how busy the college side of the bar had become.

Daniel had a far-off look in his eyes again, lost in his thoughts.

"Crystal Forge, is that right? Sounds like a crazy and amazing place," I said.

Daniel actually smiled – not ear to ear, but a real smile nonetheless. He pushed the empty bottle across the bar and said, "Truly wonderful."

"That goat head dude though, he sucks big time," I replied, draining the rest of my drink. Brandee rushed back over to us, out of breath.

"Yeah, he sucks. Bad dude, that one," was all Daniel said.

"Why did he curse her? The princess – why her in particular?" I asked.

"I don't know if anyone knows why he did what he did. Some people's lifestyle made it easy for him to curse them. But for her? The curse was just an act of random evil," Daniel said through a rigid jaw as his hands clenched into tight fists.

"I think the Princess was very brave," offered Brandee.

Daniel's hands flattened upon the bar, and he cocked his head slightly. "How so?"

"She barely hesitated. She was scared, but she didn't let it engulf her, paralyze her. Without a second thought, she set off to beat the curse," said Brandee.

Daniel laughed a little.

"Sure did. She didn't complain or fret. She just wanted to beat him. She was so strong."

Brandee brought over another round, even though Daniel shook his head. The older woman who had been sitting with her husband at the end of the bar returned from the restroom and sat one seat closer to Daniel. He did not seem to notice.

"I thought Shaggy was gonna rip that witch apart right at the end," I said.

Daniel's knuckles turned white on the hand that held the bottle. He took a big swig of his beer before saying, "Shaggy Dog was pissed. He was mad at everything, and just the fact someone tried to take advantage of the situation set him off. I don't know how he didn't rip the witch apart. Probably didn't want the Princess to see him do it."

I drew away as Daniel leaned toward me with bulging eyes. Brandee acted quickly, years of breaking up bar fights giving her a sixth sense, and said, "Well, what happened next? Or was that it?"

Tense moments passed until Daniel started talking again. Each word he spoke had a small piece of his pent-up anger attached. Eventually, his shoulders relaxed and his voice calmed.

"Not the end, but it was the end of the beginning, I guess," he said. "The duo arrived at Houstonia and then travelled farther. They met many friends. And the real fight against the curse got started. No, that wasn't the end, not yet."

CHAPTER 4

Houstonia, home to the Witches of Truth, was a true marvel. It was a vast and sprawling place. It could not be described as a castle or a palace because it was simply too big. It could not be described as a city because it was simply too grand. The wall that housed the gates was twenty feet high and bright white. The gates themselves were shiny gold and were almost as tall as the wall. Eight horses could easily walk side by side through the gateway with room to spare. Within the walls, the outer courtyard held a five-level fountain. It was solid black marble, and the water streaming down it changed colors from yellow to red to blue to green. Past the fountain was the inner gate. Although not as tall as its outer counterpart, it was no less splendid. Along each rail of the golden gate were intricate designs. Countless hours had been spent hand-carving each shape and line. Beyond the inner gate, the true wonder of Houstonia was on display. Buildings almost as large as Seascape Castle stood in every direction. The building directly before the gate had more glass windows on the front than most cities had in total. It was here that the duo began their search for the Helm of Knowledge.

As they approached the glass-fronted building, they were met by a handsome witch called Reserio. He informed them that the Benevolent Witch had sent word ahead, so their arrival was expected. During their stay in Houstonia, Reserio was to be a tour guide of sorts. He was tall, with a charming smile and an inviting demeanor. He did not seem at all put off by Shaggy Dog's disheveled appearance, or the fact the Princess had not had a bath in a few days. He seemed only eager to help get them acclimated to all that Houstonia had to offer.

After the Princess had washed up and Shaggy Dog had obstinately *not* washed up, Reserio started to reveal to them the wonders of Houstonia. He showed them a building filled with witches researching and battling minor curses such as lesions on the skin. The next building, also full of witches, was for researching and battling more severe curses, such as curses of the head or bones. Reserio then took them to yet another grand building where the witches were working on preventive spells and potions. Shaggy Dog had no idea there were so many witches dedicated to doing battle with the Goat Head Sorcerer and his minions. It gave him a sense of hope to know that all these smart, powerful witches were working tirelessly for the greater good.

The Princess just felt exhausted. It was only early in the afternoon, but she knew she had to take a rest or she may pass out in the next building. Reserio suggested resting in the shade of an old elm tree which stood on the banks of a swift river directly in front of the next building they were to tour.

As the Princess leaned back against the tree, Shaggy Dog studied the white granite building and tried to guess the wonders housed within its walls.

Reserio asked softly, "Do you see that line of little furry creatures crossing the river on that log?"

"I do not see any creatures," replied the Princess dreamily.

But Shaggy Dog did. They were only about the size of small squirrels, but definitely not shaped long and fast like squirrels. Instead, these creatures resembled oversized, fuzzy peaches with legs, arms, and ears. They waddled out onto the log in a long, straight line that seemed endless. Shaggy Dog could see a hundred, if not more, and the line was moving steadily.

"Just up the river a bit, Princess. Yes, right there. Those are known as the Plumplins, and they are curious creatures to say the least," Reserio said in a tender tone. "Each day, every Plumplin that is able crosses the river to scour for food, eat its fill, and bring back some for those too young or too old to do so. One of the first lessons we witches learn when arriving at Houstonia involves the Plumplins. You see, when one of them falls into the river, that is like being cursed by the Goat Headed Sorcerer. Now, most Plumplins never fall into the river once during their whole lives, but some do. Some of those fall into the still water near the edge, where it is relatively easy for them to climb out again and resume their lives. For some reason, not all that fall into the still water climb back out, and the still water eventually drowns them. Some fall near to that branch, in the slightly swifter-moving water. It is still relatively easy for these Plumplins to reach the safety of the shore, but sometimes their bodies are slammed into the branch on the way down or are pulled beneath the surface by the current. Those Plumplins may still survive but will be permanently injured. Finally, some of them fall into the swiftest-moving part of the river. If we do not throw them a lifeline quickly, they never make it out again. Ultimately, what would be best for the Plumplins is to be shielded from ever falling into the river to begin with," Reserio said, ending his speech quietly.

The Princess was not positive she grasped Reserio's intended message and could not think of an appropriate response. So, she remained silent. She just watched the Plumplins as they marched across the log one after another in a seemingly endless procession. As she watched them, she wondered which part of the river she had fallen into.

The next few days were filled with constant motion

interrupted by frequent and progressively longer breaks. Shaggy Dog was beginning to grow concerned about the Princess's lack of stamina as they traveled through the buildings learning as much as they could. The Princess, for her part, never complained. She walked as much as she could and only took breaks when absolutely necessary. Even those breaks frustrated her. She felt she should be doing more and doing it faster to earn her Helm. Reserio was with them every step of the way and assured them many times that they were on the correct path. He spun everything in a positive manner. If the Princess was frustrated in taking a break, Reserio would use the time to discuss potion application or spell theory. If Shaggy Dog was worrying himself sick, Reserio would point out that the Princess was working really hard to gain her Helm, so of course she was getting tired. Learning and walking. Asking and answering questions. Breaks and more breaks. That was their life during the days in Houstonia, until one morning Reserio met them outside the small cottage the duo had been sharing. Upon his face was a larger than normal grin.

The Helm of Knowledge was ready if the Princess thought she was up to the task. Though the Princess and Shaggy Dog had no idea what the task might be, she gave affirmation after only a brief hesitation.

Reserio led them to a part of Houstonia where they had spent very little time. He called it the 'factory corner'. The buildings here were smaller and more practical. Most were constructed from plain stone and were no higher than three stories. Just like the rest of Houstonia, the factory corner was clean and extremely well maintained. Reserio directed them to a round building in the center of the area, positioned like the hub of a wheel with streets radiating from it. Reserio explained that the building was indeed called the Hub. All the finishing work and fine refinement of all the projects from other buildings was completed here, and it was here the

Princess would finally discover whether she had what it took to gain the Helm of Knowledge.

Shaggy Dog was surprised to find that the interior of the Hub was not smoky and dusty from all the work crafting weapons and armor. As they stood in the center of the circular chamber, they were surrounded by the glinting steel of swords, helms, breastplates, and much more, all hanging on the wall. The room shone brighter than a diamond. Shaggy Dog nudged the Princess and pointed out a collection of gleaming swords attached to the wall from floor to ceiling. There must have been fifty, with all manner of pommels from wood to bone to braided leather. Next to the swords were shields, some painted with crests and some unfinished. Upon the most fantastic of the shields were depicted full battle scenes. Next to the shields, the duo saw the archery section. There were long bows made of wood from the Asperian Forest. There were crossbows as long as the Princess was tall – longer, even. So many beautiful weapons and so much beautiful armor sparked hope in Shaggy Dog's chest. Surely if the witches of Houstonia could create a room that was more beautiful than any gallery in any castle, then creating the perfect helm or even a weapon for the Princess should be no problem.

They were still lost in the grandeur of the circular room when Reserio spoke. "Quite a sight to see, isn't it? And yet, despite all of our knowledge and considerable skill, there are curses the Goat Head Sorcerer uses that still confound us."

He gestured to a hallway to the right and led the way. The simple stone hallway shortly led to a staircase. They went up the wooden steps, Reserio leading, followed by the Princess with Shaggy Dog bringing up the rear. Shaggy Dog was close on her heels, and even Reserio had a little extra in his step as he bounded up the staircase. It seemed she was the only one with a knot of dread growing in her stomach. She could not quite figure out exactly what was causing this fear. Shaggy

Dog was right to be excited about all the amazing weapons and armor the witches of Houstonia had produced. And, surely, Reserio's excitement meant he was positive she would gain her Helm of Knowledge today, so she could not come up with one plausible reason why she felt she should turn around and escape down the stairs. Every step she took up the staircase, the knot in her stomach grew a little more.

Then they were at the top of the stairs facing a lone door, and the time to escape had slipped away. There was only one way forward, and it was through the door. She steeled herself and found the dread in her stomach diminished.

They passed through the doorway into a cozy room with a small crackling fire. Four plush, velvety chairs encircled a small wooden table in the center of the room. The walls were mostly bare except for one painting on the left-hand side, which depicted a boy younger than the Princess. He appeared tired and sore. His clothes were soiled and torn. The scabbard on his belt was empty. The boy appeared to be struggling to climb a steep hill to reach the summit. Waiting at the top, suspended in a pillar of light, was a pair of angel wings. It was a beautifully accomplished piece of art that made the Princess both sad and hopeful for the boy.

Sitting in one of the chairs was a witch that resembled an older, rougher Reserio. He did not smile, nor did he rise from his seat as the group entered. Only when the Princess noticed him did he stand and greet them all.

"Welcome, Princess, to the Room of Choice. My name is Anderserio. And I will be the final witch you must speak with on this visit to Houstonia," he said in a deep, resonating tone.

Reserio rolled his eyes and scoffed, "Drop the theatrics, Anderserio. That is my department!"

"My good brother, whatever do you mean?"

"The Room of Choice? Ha! It's just the sitting room for your workshop, you sot!"

Then Reserio stepped forward and hugged him. Anderserio reciprocated with a hearty laugh.

"Wait, so you two are really brothers?" inquired the Princess.

"Unfortunately, it is so," said Reserio with a smile.

Anderserio chuckled as they all settled into chairs. "Princess, I did not realize your companion walked on four legs or I would have had a more suitable seating arrangement for him."

Shaggy Dog simply leapt onto the unoccupied chair and stared intently at Anderserio with a mocking glare.

"Never mind, then!"

From that point on, there was little in the form of pleasantries, as Anderserio immediately addressed the issue at hand. He explained that the Helm of Knowledge the Princess was to receive was not *the* Helm but simply *a* Helm. There were many, and each was made specifically for the wearer. The Helm was constructed in Houstonia and the final touches were completed by him. Many witches from all different buildings had placed spells upon it, imparted knowledge, and added power to the Helm during the process. Now that it was complete, the Helm of Knowledge would provide the Princess with the instincts needed to battle the curse and the Goat Head Sorcerer himself. While wearing the Helm, she would know which potion to take for the greatest benefit, or which weapon would cause her enemy the most damage. It would not speak to her, but if she listened and trusted her instincts, the answers would be clear.

Then, with a small flourish of Anderserio's hands, the Helm of Knowledge appeared in the middle of the small table. It was quite beautiful. It was the same light rose gold as the Princess's armor, and was smooth all around with ample protection for her head and back of the neck. The face was left open except where it wrapped slightly across the cheek area. The Princess sensed the power humming from the

Helm, and she could not keep her eyes off of it.

"Do you accept these terms, Princess?" asked Anderserio quietly.

"I'm sorry, sir. I was lost in thought and mesmerized by its beauty. I did not hear the terms."

"You may take the Helm of Knowledge and use it for as long as your battle takes. Then it must be returned here. All you have to do is pledge to fight with all your being and to help any others you can in their own struggle. Do you accept these terms that have been laid out for you?" asked Anderserio again, a little more forcefully.

"Of course. I will be honored to wear such a fine piece of armor," the Princess answered. She pulled her gaze away from the Helm to look at Shaggy Dog. He too, was staring intently at the Helm in anticipation, eager to put it to the test and defeat the curse as soon as possible.

"Then the Helm is yours, my Princess," stated Reserio. His brother beamed. "Use it well."

"I don't understand," said Shaggy Dog. "I thought there was a task to complete or test to pass?"

The Princess nodded in agreement. Reserio chuckled quietly then said, "Yes. Sorry about misleading you. We Witches of Truth seek out truth but don't always speak plainly. It has been discovered through the trials of others before you who came seeking help against a curse that focusing on a future task allows us to do our work easier. In each building, you answered questions from witches and passed through revealing spells to help us gain the knowledge needed for the Helm."

"I see," said the Princess. "You could have just told me."

"Perhaps, but experience has taught us different," replied Reserio. "All we want is for you to defeat this curse. The Helm is the best we can do to help you on your quest."

The next morning, Shaggy Dog and the Princess were

set to depart. They had accomplished their first major goal on the quest. Although they were not exactly sure what was next, they knew it would not lie within the walls of Houstonia. They had spent much of the night discussing where to go next. Shaggy Dog had felt that a visit to the salt flats would be good, to help restore some of the Princess's strength that the curse was draining away. The Princess had tried to convince Shaggy Dog that there was a good reason to travel to the Dragon Spine – though in truth her only reason was that she had always wanted to see the mountains. The rest of the night had been filled with Shaggy Dog sleeping and the Princess wearing the Helm and trying to get it to tell her something, until she too fell asleep.

Reserio was again waiting for them outside their building, and he invited them to breakfast, saying that there were several guests they may like to see before they departed.

The dining hall was on the way to the stables and the gate, so the duo brought their travel packs with them, eager to be on the road once more. Shaggy Dog looked a little odd carrying both his and the Princess's packs on his back, but he did not mind. The Princess held her Helm under her arm and was fully outfitted in the Armor of Love. She liked the light clinking noises as she walked, a reassuring sound like little bells, which constantly reminded her of her mother and home. She hoped they could eat a quick breakfast, say their goodbyes, and be on the road soon. She wanted to put the Helm to the test.

As they entered the dining hall, they both noticed there were more people than normal at this hour. All chatter silenced and every eye turned towards them. The silence lingered and seemed to grow. Then, from somewhere at the back, came a cry of, "We believe in you Princess!" followed immediately by an uproar that could have been heard clear across the Forge. The Princess saw the Queen standing amongst the crowd cheering along with everyone else. She noticed through her blurry vision that the Queen had tears in her eyes as well. Even Shaggy Dog looked taken aback: he sat on his haunches with the packs on his back, looking blankly at the crowd with wide eyes. It was a glorious reception.

The Benevolent Witch approached them. Speaking briefly, she told them not to leave without speaking privately with her first. Next were several of the servants from the castle. They wished the Princess well and all agreed she had grown at least an inch since she had been on the road. Everyone was smiling and happy as they congratulated her on acquiring the Helm of Knowledge. Everyone seemed to believe that she was going to beat back the Goat Head Sorcerer and end his curse upon her.

Finally, as the crowd simmered down, the Queen approached. Everyone backed away to create a pocket of space. Even Shaggy Dog edged back. The Princess started to curtsy, but the Queen stopped her with a warm embrace. The tears were no longer contained within her eyes, instead they spilled down the Queen's cheeks as she hugged the Princess tightly. Finally, after what could have been moments or hours, they separated.

"My daughter, I am so proud you have started to meet this threat head on," spoke the Queen gently.

"I never had any intention to do otherwise," replied the Princess in confusion.

"I know, but I was worried that after traveling here and seeing all this: the grandeur, all the witches working tirelessly..." she gestured with both arms out wide, "that maybe... Oh, never mind! I am just so proud of you. Now, let me see your Helm."

The Princess showed the Queen her new Helm. She explained to her the details that Anderserio had revealed. Then, she told the Queen all about her experience in Houstonia and the Plumplins. She bragged about Reserio and the splendor of the buildings. The Queen nodded, gasped, laughed, and asked all the right questions.

Before either of them knew it, the morning had almost entirely passed. Shaggy Dog approached and mentioned in a low voice that perhaps the Princess might like to eat some breakfast before it was actually lunch that she would be eating. All three of them laughed. It was not until the Princess was detailing their encounter with the Snake Oil Witch that any tension filled the room. The Queen immediately wanted to send her off with a battalion of her finest soldiers. No daughter of hers would be bothered by the likes of that Snake Oil Witch in her own kingdom. But the Princess reminded her that this was *her* quest, and besides, that many men in full armor and with wagons for stores would only slow them down.

When it was past time to leave and the duo had said all their goodbyes, Reserio approached the Princess. He gave her several items for her quest, from different witches from Houstonia. These included a dozen or so small potions, and he explained the varied properties of each in turn. There were several packages of blue powder to help ease any stomach-related issues. He also gifted her a supple leather belt with pouches and pockets to hold all these items. He said Anderserio had spent most of the night making it, but that he was too stubborn to present it himself.

Just when the Princess thought he was finished, Reserio reached behind him and brought out a sword.

"This you may have seen on the wall earlier in your visit," he said solemnly.

The Princess did not know if she had seen this exact sword, but it was beautiful. It was small and double edged. The blade was a shiny silver color, and the handle was a rough dark wood.

"I do not recall, but it is quite the weapon."

"I do not believe this to be your *true* weapon, or perhaps it is. Regardless, I feel this sword will serve you well. Its name is Aggressio. It was my father's blade. My brother and I would be honored if you carried it with you on your quest," Reserio said as he passed her the sword and scabbard.

"The honor is all mine," replied the Princess, bowing her head first to Reserio and then to Anderserio, who stood in the corner. Shaggy Dog nudged her impatiently, and again they made a round to say farewells before heading to the stable.

The duo did not spend much time at the stable. The Princess's horse had been fed and saddled by the stable hand and was eager to leave its stall far behind. Once the Princess had transferred the bags from Shaggy Dog's back to their new packhorse that the Queen had insisted upon, they were on the move. They walked quickly through Houstonia, through the beautiful inner gate, across the courtyard with the colorful fountain, and beyond the impressive outer gate.

At the first crossroads they reached, Shaggy Dog looked at the Princess with a questioning glance.

"I'm not real sure which way to go now," she said. Houstonia lay behind them, and the whole world was before them.

"Perhaps you should have spent a few moments with me like I had asked you to," said a voice from behind them.

Shaggy Dog whirled around; teeth bared to defend against a surprise attack.

"I could have set you on the correct track hours ago instead of chasing you for the better part of the afternoon," said the Benevolent Witch.

The Princess had the courtesy to look embarrassed as she said, "I am so sorry. With the excitement of my mother's arrival, Reserio gifting me this amazing sword, and all the people wishing me luck, as well as Shaggy Dog pushing me to the door, and—"

"It's fine, my sweet child," interrupted the Benevolent Witch. "I apologize for sounding so harsh a moment ago. I am here with you now. That is all that matters, after all. Come, let's sit. We have much to discuss, and I know you are both anxious to get on the road to defeating the curse."

The three sat in the short grass under two wide oaks. The sun had crested hours before, but the heat of the day was still on them. The Benevolent Witch wasted little time: she congratulated the Princess on coming this far but cautioned that this was only the beginning. She said that the duo should continue their quest to the east, and must travel to the Dragon Spine Mountains, where there was a canyon that could only be found by those seeking it. Inside, the Princess would find her true weapon, by which she could battle the Goat Head Sorcerer.

"When we get into the canyon – what did you call it? The Canyon of Future Yesterdays? When we get there, will her weapon just be lying on the canyon floor?" asked an irritated Shaggy Dog.

"Why, noble canine, I have not the slightest idea what you two will discover, or how you will uncover it. I just know she must seek her weapon there," replied the Benevolent Witch haughtily.

Shaggy Dog began a retort, but the Princess quickly said, "Then that is where we shall go. To the Canyon of Future Yesterdays."

The Benevolent Witch seemed mollified, and departed from under the trees quickly. Shaggy Dog watched as she disappeared more quickly than would be considered natural even by his standards.

"The Canyon of Future Yesterdays... Stupid-name Canyon, more like it," growled Shaggy Dog.

"It is a rather peculiar name."

"And she called me a canine! I should have... Well, she shouldn't have called me that."

"She isn't wrong. And you must forgive her, Shaggy Dog –

she is under a great deal of strain."

"I don't have to forgive her anything," replied Shaggy Dog. "But at least she gave us a destination."

"And it is so far away. I guess we should get going," replied the Princess as she mounted her horse. She turned her steed east and started off at a trot. They had a long way to travel, a very long way indeed.

CHAPTER 5

Shaggy Dog slowed from a trot to a walk, then stopped completely. His ears perked up and the hair on his back raised as he looked ahead at a densely wooded hill. The Princess stopped her mount next to him. Shaggy Dog had become rigid as his eyes locked on the distant hill, never blinking.

After several moments, the Princess asked what he was staring at, but Shaggy Dog did not answer. His attention never wavered. He remained perfectly still.

Seconds turned into minutes. Just as the Princess about to ask him what he was looking at again, she heard it. The crash sounded as if a full-size tree had been snapped in two, then been hurled away. Shaggy Dog's ears had flattened, and a growl escaped his throat.

"What in the realm could that be?" asked the Princess, she too now staring at the dense woods.

"Nothing good. Let's veer away from there. We can cross the river farther south at Howling Head, or even Biscayne if we have to," said Shaggy Dog, still not moving his focus from the wooded hill.

"But that will add days to the journey!"

"Better to add days than have to face whatever that is, Princess," Shaggy Dog replied.

As they started to move off the road and cross the field away from the noise, the Princess spotted an eagle circling high over the wooded hill.

"That has to be the biggest eagle ever! Look at it, Shaggy Dog," she said, pointing to the sky.

Shaggy Dog tilted his head to look up. "Now what would a noble one be doing mixed up in whatever is going on over there?"

"Maybe we should go and find out," offered the Princess hopefully.

Before he could respond, another booming crash came from the hill.

"Where did the eagle go?" asked the Princess.

"It's almost directly above us. This is getting stranger by the moment," answered Shaggy Dog.

The duo watched as the eagle circled them, then dipped close to the ground only to rise up and circle them again. Each time the eagle dropped, it angled itself towards the wooded hill before rising again and circling.

"I think it wants us to follow it," said the Princess.

"It would seem that way. I'm not sure that would be such a good idea, Princess."

"She seems pretty adamant. Let's go and have a look," said the Princess, already moving in the direction that the eagle was indicating.

Shaggy Dog grumbled but followed along. The eagle still circled high above and still occasionally dipped down just ahead of them, urging them forward.

The wooded hill had not seemed so far away, but it took them over an hour to reach the edge of the forest. The trees were old, and their large trunks supported a massive, interlocked canopy. The absence of underbrush in the dim light under the trees was startling. Now unable to see the eagle, the Princess had second thoughts about this little adventure.

Before she could mention her thoughts of regret to Shaggy Dog, a loud crash shook them both. The trees in front of them were swaying, and the ground beneath their feet was shaking. A massive, oblong boulder came crashing through the trees right towards them.

The Princess's horse bucked wildly to the left, tossing her to the ground directly in the boulder's path. The wide-eyed Princess was rooted in place.

Shaggy Dog leapt to her side, nudging and pushing frantically trying to get the Princess to move. He barked his desire for her to move out of the way of the boulder.

Then the boulder that was barreling towards the Princess came to an abrupt stop.

The boulder made a most un-boulder-like moan.

The Princess's hand came away from her head without a trace of blood. At least she had not struck her head hard... but she was sure she had heard the boulder moan. She glanced at Shaggy Dog, and he shrugged his big shoulders as only a dog is able to do.

The boulder moaned again and began to sit up. It was not a rock at all, but a giant.

The Princess stared as Shaggy Dog renewed his efforts to get her to move. She could not stop staring at the big ears and big nose under the curly brown hair on the humongous head of the giant. She estimated the hulking figure was at least ten feet tall when standing. She was surprised he didn't have a beard. All the giants in stories had long, rough beards.

Shaggy Dog stopped nudging her and instead pulled her by the boot, straining to get her to safety. The giant moaned again and a large tear ran down his smooth cheek.

"Something must be wrong with him," said the Princess.

"That should make it easier for us to get away, then," snarled Shaggy Dog, never releasing her foot as he continued to try to drag her away from the giant. The giant, noticing them for the first time, quickly scooted away striking the trunk of an ancient tree. He cried out in pain this time and more tears flowed. Shaggy Dog, realizing there was no immediate threat, released the Princess's foot and moved to stand guard between her and the giant. The giant's eyes locked on Shaggy Dog, and he became still as stone.

A rustling of leaves behind the duo caused them to whirl around quickly. Perched on a log not fifteen feet away was the eagle that had directed them here. As they watched, the eagle started to grow taller and change. Before even a startled exclamation could escape the Princess's throat, an elf stood on the log in place of the eagle. She was tall and slender, and her dark hair matched her dark skin and eyes. She had two eagle feathers in her hair above her left ear. Her clothing was a natural-colored flexible material that stopped short of her knees and elbows.

She hopped down smoothly from the log, saying, "I have been trying to help this brute for two days. Every time I get close, he starts wailing and thrashing. Then he's off again. I'm not even sure what ails him."

An elf and a giant! The Princess's mouth hung open as the elf approached, stepping lightly without snapping a single twig or rustling a single leaf. Only the movement of the giant brought the Princess out of rapt amazement. The giant had leaned forward and was staring at Shaggy Dog intently.

With the elf only feet away, the Princess encouraged Shaggy Dog to move a little closer to the giant, whose eyes never left Shaggy Dog. Shaggy Dog was halfway between them and the giant when the giant smiled through his tears.

The Princess giggled quietly. "He is a funny-looking dog, but he is a good boy."

The giant's head jerked up in surprise, and he started sobbing again. Shaggy Dog looked at the Princess, then took a couple steps closer to the giant and sat down.

"Have you ever seen a dog before?" asked the Princess gently.

The giant shook his head.

"He has soft, thick fur. It would look nicer if he'd let me brush it every now and then."

The giant's breathing slowed, but his gaze was still focused intently on Shaggy Dog.

"Amazing," muttered the elf.

"I like to pet his coat," said the Princess as she approached Shaggy Dog. "Sometimes I'll pet him until he falls asleep." She reached out slowly to pat Shaggy Dog's head gently. "Do you want to pet him?"

The giant shook his head shyly and said, "Aargh dough."

Shaggy Dog took a few more cautious steps forward. Tentatively, the giant reached out a burly hand and brushed Shaggy Dog's back. Then his face split wide open in the biggest smile the Princess had ever seen. The tears were gone. The elf, the Princess, and the giant were all smiling and laughing. Even Shaggy Dog seemed to relax a bit, his tail swishing slowly back and forth.

Later that evening, after the elf had found a suitable campsite and started a small fire, she left them lounging peacefully to scout the area. She brought back berries and fresh water. They ate quietly, scared to break the peace with their coarse voices.

Finally, the elf said, "I hail from the east of the Dragon Spine Mountains, in the Heart of Viana. My name is too long for most non-elves to pronounce, but you may call me Sasha."

"My name is Sophia, and that is Shaggy Dog. We are both from the coast," replied the Princess.

"I know who you are, Princess. You bear a striking resemblance to your grandfather – not in looks, but in bearing. I knew him and liked him well." The comfortable silence draped back over the group. The Princess busied herself interweaving long blades of grass, and Sasha watched as the giant stroked a slumbering Shaggy Dog.

"That is an interesting dog you have, Sophia," noted Sasha after some time.

The Princess laughed out loud. "He's not my dog, that's for sure. I belong to him way more than he belongs to me. If he was awake, he'd probably say something about nobody belonging to anybody without mutual adoration, or some other nonsense," said the Princess.

"He can talk?" asked Sasha.

"He can. He just holds his tongue around those he doesn't know well."

"He seems to be a loyal companion. Still, it makes me wonder why a talking dog is traveling the countryside with the only heir to Seascape, all alone," probed Sasha.

The Princess looked down at the grass in her hands for a long time before responding. "I was cursed by the Goat Head Sorcerer, and we are on a quest in which speed and stealth are needed." She recounted the quest to Sasha, sparing no details. Once she started talking, it all spilled out. Sasha sat perfectly still and listened intently without interruption. As the Princess's tale approached their current circumstances, the giant shifted.

"Argh Dane!!!" he exclaimed.

The Princess and Sasha exchanged worried glances.

"That's his name. Dane. He says his name is Dane," said a sleepy Shaggy Dog, before putting his head back down and immediately falling asleep again.

Morning came quick and bright. The Princess rose to the rumbling snores of Dane, or at least so she thought. As it turned out, it was Shaggy Dog that had shaken the leaves on the trees with his snores all night. Sasha had left a breakfast for the group but was nowhere to be found. The Princess checked on the horses and busied herself doing small jobs around camp until everyone else stirred. It did not take long for Sasha to return with an armful of leafy plants. Without saying a word, she started boiling the plants over the small campfire. Shaggy Dog rose from his slumber next, and growled about a decent breakfast before setting to it. Sasha probed Shaggy Dog with questions about Dane, as the giant himself still slept peacefully under the trees. Shaggy Dog revealed that Dane had been running for a while, but Shaggy Dog was unsure what had caused him to flee. Shaggy Dog was able to discover the main reason for the giant's thrashing and bashing yesterday was an injury to his foot. Sasha nodded at each of Shaggy Dog's short answers and smiled when he mentioned the foot injury.

"Why do you smile, elf?" asked Shaggy Dog harshly.

"Not because I want to see the giant in pain – I can assure you of that, my four-legged friend," stated Sasha. "I smiled because I noticed his injury last night after he calmed down. I was up before the sun to find leaves of a julerpin palm to treat it. They are boiling over the fire as we speak."

"Hmmph," was the only reply Shaggy Dog could muster.

"He did not give you any indication what he was running from?" asked the Princess.

"No and I didn't press it," Shaggy Dog stated firmly.

"No matter. I will tend to his wound, and you two can be on your way by lunch," said Sasha.

"Fine by me," replied Shaggy Dog, gazing over at the slumbering Dane.

Hours later, when Dane finally stirred, Sasha was able to treat the small wound on his foot with the help of Shaggy Dog keeping Dane still. The Princess understood the giant much more readily this morning, though he spoke less often than Shaggy Dog. Dane's tribe called the hostile northern facing cliffs of the Dragon Spine Mountains home. It was a small tribe but widely known for its ferocity. None were more ferocious than Dane's father, the tribal chieftain. Over two weeks ago, the tribe was offered a position of power from the Goat Head Sorcerer in exchange for certain unnamed favors. The tribal elders were on the ridge about which way to go, but Dane was sure they were going to accept the offer. He saw no benefit in helping the Goat Head Sorcerer, who had never helped them before. So, he spoke out against the Goat Head Sorcerer and the offer. He was forced to flee in fear of retaliation from the Goat Head Sorcerer or his minions. He was lost, tired, and hungry. When he hurt his foot two days ago, he lost control. He felt better now, though, he told them.

The giant's tale lasted well into the afternoon. It was not a particularly long story full of detail, but Dane did not get in any hurry to tell it. Combined with the need to repeat himself endlessly to be understood and charades for words he did not know, most of the day was gone by the end of the telling. He was so tired by the end that he took a late afternoon nap in the warm sun. He was not the only one: Shaggy Dog was right next to him snoring just as fiercely. The Princess found herself alone at the campfire watching Sasha cook a meager supper.

"Do you two plan on leaving in the morning?" asked Sasha.

"Shaggy Dog normally does the planning," replied the Princess, glancing at the slumbering dog. "He'll want to push on."

"Probably wise to push forward and seek the canyon," said Sasha, "but you could stay for a few days and rest. I could teach you how to be more efficient in gathering supplies from the wilderness and maybe how to shoot a bow."

"That sounds great, but Shaggy Dog will want to be on the move," replied the Princess.

"He will, but I will talk to him," continued Sasha. "I think the only way Dane will let me help him further is if Shaggy Dog is close by."

"What are you going to do for the giant?"

"That is up to Dane. I know the people on the other side of the great grass sea, and they would take him in. Or Dane may want to go back to his tribe. He will need help, either way."

"That is so selfless and brave," said the Princess.

Sasha's eyebrows rose and she tilted her head. "Brave? Why do you say that?"

"Well, you're going to do something that could get you hurt, and you know it. But you're going to do it anyway," said the Princess quietly. "I think that is brave."

Sasha laughed. "Well, thank you, Princess. That is why life is so difficult to understand at times."

It was the Princess's turn to be confused. "What do you mean?"

"You said it is brave of me to do something that I know might get me hurt, right?" Sasha asked.

The Princess nodded.

"Some would say it is foolish to do something you know is going to hurt. Foolishness and bravery are very closely linked. That, my Princess, is why life is so difficult to understand."

Silently, the sun started its descent from the world for the night. The evening birds were singing their sweet, sad farewells to the daylight. The crickets and frogs were loud as a gentle breeze swept over the Princess. She stared towards the mountains to the east, thinking, *Yes. Life is difficult to understand.*

Four days later, the duo left Sasha and Dane early in the morning. Shaggy Dog was eager to move forward with the search for the canyon and a way to defeat the Goat Head Sorcerer. The Princess, on the other hand, had allowed the pleasant days with new friends to lull her into complacency. Sasha had taught her and Shaggy Dog how to better scavenge for necessary supplies in the wild. The Princess had learned how to draw and shoot a bow. Dane had gifted Shaggy Dog his bracelet, which Shaggy Dog now wore like a collar, and to the Princess he gave a chunk of shiny rock that, according to him, "Tastes funny." She had so enjoyed their time together, and now felt anxious and nervous as they set off on an easterly course. The road was well worn but smooth, and traveling was easy. Shaggy Dog had little difficulty keeping pace with the Princess on her mount. The rhythm of riding and the beautiful weather helped ease the Princess's doubt and worry. With the wind in her face and sun on her back, it was easy to know that they were on the correct path, and that they would soon find the canyon.

The plan was simple: wake up early, eat breakfast, travel east till dusk, and then set up camp only to do it all over again the next day. On the second day, shortly after breaking camp, Shaggy Dog pointed out a large herd of deer to the north. Later that same day, they quite literally stumbled upon a talking jackrabbit. After many apologies and promises to be more careful, the duo kept pushing east. The next morning, Shaggy Dog became impatient with the Princess. A baby possum had become separated from his family, and the Princess would not take another step till they were reunited. Mama possum seemed grateful... at least, she didn't hiss at them much. After the delay, Shaggy Dog cut their breaks short and pushed the horses hard to make up for lost time.

Shortly after dusk, it happened for the first time. The minions of the Goat Head Sorcerer attacked.

The Princess was tired and asked Shaggy Dog if they could make camp. The day had been hot, and they had traveled many miles after helping the baby possum. Shaggy Dog led them off the road to a patch of trees and what sounded like a small stream coming from a group of rocks to the north. The Princess was eager to shed her heavy armor and relax by a small fire and drinking fresh spring water. As she laid the Helm of Knowledge on the ground she felt, rather than saw, Shaggy Dog tense. Then she heard a twig snap in the patch of trees, and then Shaggy Dog gave a guttural growl. When she looked up, she saw a multitude of goblins streaming towards them. They were half her size, but they were armored with boiled leather and armed with thin, sharp swords. As they got closer, the goblins' battle shrieks threatened to drown out Shaggy Dog's menacing growl. She barely had time to unsheathe her sword, Aggressio, before the goblins were on top of them.

The goblins attacked in unorganized chaos. Several times, the Princess heard goblin squeals of pain that were not caused by her sword or Shaggy Dog's teeth. Her armor absorbed most of the strikes that made it past her sword and Shaggy Dog, who was snarling ferociously, repelling goblin after goblin. The numbers of their attackers never seemed to diminish even as the Princess slashed and stabbed, finding her mark time after time. The goblins had scored small cuts through the creases of her armor and had even made a couple of slashes on her face. Shaggy Dog fought savagely moving in a circle around her but could see the Princess was tiring out.

"Put on the Helm," he growled.

"I can't stop! There are too many," yelled the Princess.

"We need a new plan! Their numbers are too great," replied Shaggy Dog after sinking his teeth deep into the arm of a goblin attempting to strike high on the Princess's back. He backed in close to her as she reached down for the Helm.

As soon as it was snug on her head, she commanded, "Follow me, and keep them off my back for just a moment."

"Done!" barked Shaggy Dog after he tore into the thigh of another enemy. The Princess dug into the pouch at her waist and pulled out a small vial. She hesitated for just a second, then drained the contents into her mouth.

"Get behind me!" she yelled to Shaggy Dog.

He had barely made it before the Princess opened her

mouth and fire billowed out. All of the nearby goblins were consumed, and the rest fled at the sight of the amber and crimson dragon's fire. Shaggy Dog stared in amazement at the Princess, who stood before their enemies and pushed them back defiantly with a weapon that was at once powerful but undoubtably painful to use. Then he saw her sway and fall to the ground from exhaustion. He called her name and licked her face, but she did not respond. He could see her chest rise and fall, so he knew she still lived. None of her wounds appeared to be serious, and the goblins were halfway to the northern mountains by now.

Shaggy Dog stood watch all night without a meal or a fire as the Princess rested.

Birds sang a morning serenade as the soft sunlight crested over the mountains in the east. Shaggy Dog could feel a light north wind dancing across his fur as he stretched out the stiffness of the night. Suddenly, his eyes snapped open, and he looked about frantically for the Princess.

Then Shaggy Dog's shoulders relaxed and his fur settled back down as he saw her lying in the same spot he had left her the night before. Her eyes were open and a small smile warmed her face as she greeted him.

"Good morning, sleepy head," she teased.

"Morning, Princess. How are you today? Do you hurt anywhere? Are you injured? Can you move?" blurted Shaggy Dog, each question rolling into the next.

"Slow down, my champion" laughed the Princess as she nuzzled her face against Shaggy Dog's fluffy head. He seemed to want to inspect every cut and scrape at once, but until she was out of her armor it was impossible.

"I will not. Now, how do you feel?" he persisted.

"Like I was run over by a horse. No, two horses pulling a cart – a *heavy* cart," she replied weakly. "But I don't think there's any permanent damage. Just tired and sore."

"Well, I'd expect so. You were amazing yesterday," said Shaggy Dog, settling down near the Princess. "Where did you learn to use that sword?"

"When Mom – I mean the Queen – is busy with court or some other obligation, I could sometimes sneak to the drill yard. If old Sergeant Rivers wasn't busy, he'd show me some things. Sergeant Gilbert actually let me run through exercises," she said dreamily. After a lengthy pause, she added, "It seems so long ago."

Shaggy Dog raised his head. "What does, Princess?"

The Princess let out a long sigh as she sat up. She gazed to the south, where she knew waves would now be crashing into the pink, sandy beach outside the castle she called home. Her mother would be doing important work for the people of Crystal Forge within those walls.

Long moments stretched out until she continued, "A normal life. As normal as a princess can have, anyway."

Shaggy Dog did not know what to say, so he remained silent. The sun was fully up, and the light dew on the grass was quickly being burned away. The breeze from the north had died down, and the whole world was still. They were both trapped within their own thoughts for the rest of the morning.

Around lunchtime, Shaggy Dog decided to go and fill their dwindling canteen from the stream. The Princess was skeptical but, after some creative maneuvering and strapping, Shaggy Dog set off toward the only nearby source of water with the canteen dangling from his neck. After a small meal and several more trips for Shaggy Dog to fill the canteen again and again, the Princess started to feel stronger. They chatted back and forth about nothing, or at least they specifically avoided discussing the previous day's attack. The next few days were spent this way: Shaggy Dog getting water and the duo eating small meals while conversing about nothing and anything as long as they avoided that particular subject. The Princess slowly recovered, and Shaggy Dog felt the need to resume their search for the canyon. Neither spoke about it, and all was peaceful.

The next day, without any chilly gusts of wind or the sound of thunder rattling in the distance, it started to rain. It was not a spring shower bringing life-refreshing water, and it was not even a fierce summer thunderstorm to cool the land. To Shaggy Dog it seemed like standing under a waterfall and getting pummeled. The Princess could not see five feet in front of her as her horse plodded slowly along, unsure of its footing. It rained for hours, and their progress was minimal. Shaggy Dog struggled tremendously through the muck as they crested a small rise. The Princess hopped down from her saddle, her boots making little splashes as they sank into the mud. As quickly as she could, she rummaged through the packhorse's burden, rearranging as she went. She examined her work from several angles as a dripping Shaggy Dog looked on. She had arranged the packs to support the small camp tabletop in the center. Then pushing down on the table, she created a nest-like structure. Shaggy Dog looked skeptical but remained silent.

"Now you can ride the pack horse," she said.

"Me? Ride a horse? That's ridiculous," scoffed Shaggy Dog. "How would I even get up there?"

"Well..."

"Why would I *want* to get up there?" complained Shaggy Dog.

"So we can make better time! You have to be exhausted sloshing through this stuff," said the Princess matter-of-factly.

"Oh! *I'm* slowing us down? Not as much as this stop is!"

With that, Shaggy Dog marched down the slippery slope, heading east. He made it to the bottom by sliding the last twenty feet on his face. He didn't even take his face out of the mud as the Princess plodded up to stand next to him, but said, "Any ideas how I can get on the platform?"

The duo endured the rain for several more hours. It never slacked off or showed any signs of doing anything but attempt to turn the whole of Crystal Forge into a lake. The Princess could hear Shaggy Dog muttering constantly about "frog-strangling rain" and how they would "need a boat or fins" before too long. She even heard him mumble something about what a "good mucking job" his horse was doing. Dark would come early on a day such as this, so it was no surprise when Shaggy Dog told the Princess they were stopping.

"I know of some rocks just to the south that might offer some protection," Shaggy Dog yelled over the constant thrum of the rain.

"And how would you know that?"

"I haven't lived at or near Seascape my whole life. It might surprise you, Princess, the places I have been and people I know," grumbled Shaggy Dog.

As they approached the rocks Shaggy Dog had mentioned, the Princess saw a sign directing travelers to something called the Ruff Gaming Tavern. Shaggy Dog was pointedly not looking anywhere near the sign as they passed it. Then the Princess noticed a small cave. They both agreed that a dirty and dry cave was better than a muddy and wet anything else.

After getting the horses unsaddled and picketed near the mouth of the cave, the duo was shocked to hear someone call out from deeper within.

"I suppose this cave is big enough for all of us," came a cheerful shout.

The Princess nearly jumped out of her armor, but Shaggy Dog crouched low, the hair on his neck bristling.

"No need in all that, friend-dog! I mean you no harm," continued the voice. "I am going to step forward. Don't bite me, now."

The Princess watched as a man barely taller than herself came around the corner. He was portly, with a long blue and white robe. His hands were extended and open, and there was a wide smile on his face. Shaggy Dog's posture relaxed and his tail swished involuntarily.

"See, it's just old trader Mikaela seeking refuge from the deluge. Much like yourselves, I would presume," continued the man as he walked into the failing light.

"That we are Michael-ah," said the Princess.

"The name is Mikaela, my dear. Both of you are soaked to the bone. Just around the corner I have a nice little camp with a fire, where I am cooking up a delectable stew. Come, get warm." He beckoned for them to follow him.

The thought of being warm and dry overpowered any reservations or suspicions. Around the bend in the tunnel, the cave opened up more than the outside view would lead one to believe possible. Shaggy Dog was glad to see the peddler had been truthful about the fire. As he and the Princess warmed themselves near it, Mikaela put the finishing touches on their supper.

After the small but delicious meal, Mikaela got straight to business. "Since I am such a gracious host, providing both a warm fire and a hot meal, I think it is time for you two to return the favor," he said with a glimmer in his eyes.

Until Mikaela spoke, Shaggy Dog had been sprawled out by the fire, feeling fat and happy. Now his ears lay flat and a quiet, deep growl rumbled in his chest.

"Calm down, Shaggy Dog," whispered the Princess. Then she spoke firmly to the peddler. "What do you have in mind, kind sir? For we can spare little to repay you."

"I seek nothing for free, my dear. I only wish to practice my craft," said the jolly little peddler. He laughed and continued, "You have given me no names, and I have not probed. It is obvious to anyone with eyes that you are on an important quest. Why else would you be out in this weather with such fancy armor and such a fine sword?"

"We *are* on a quest," stated the Princess, "and, as I have already mentioned, we have little with which to barter."

Shaggy Dog had resumed his lounging and was only half-listening. Trading and deal-making did not interest him in the least. Mikaela walked to the far side of the cave and rummaged through his packs. He returned with a sack, within which jostled a number of items.

"Well, let me show you the goods I can offer, then maybe you can think of something to part with," pushed Mikaela. "Maybe the dog's fancy collar? It is of giant origin, is it not?"

"It is not on the trading block, peddler," growled Shaggy Dog from beside the fire.

Mikaela's eyes grew wide and his mouth was agape. Then he bellowed a hearty laugh. "He speaks! I thought you were more than you let on. But I am correct? The collar you wear is of giant origin?"

"It was a gift from a friend," said the Princess. "And yes, he is a giant."

"I knew it! Ha. Not the giant's talisman, then. How about your sword or your armor? Surely with such a fearsome and loyal companion these are of no real use to you?"

The Princess sighed. "I wish you were right, Mr. Peddler, but I have great need of these items."

The peddler's grin slipped for just a moment, but then returned swiftly. "I mentioned my goods before, and here are some items I think you will appreciate. Perhaps after seeing them, you can think of something to trade."

First, Mikaela produced an ingenious saddle device. It had a retractable ramp that folded away underneath a flat, padded seat. He said it had once belonged to a rich prince who had enjoyed riding beside his prized dwarf pig. The pig would waddle up the ramp to sit in his saddle on his own horse. Then the ramp would be folded and stowed under the seat. It would be a serious upgrade for Shaggy Dog. A pleasant aroma assaulted the Princess's nose before the next item was even taken out of the bag. Spiced melons from across the Jasmine Sea – her mother's favorite, although the Princess could not remember the Queen having had any in quite some time. The last item was a purplish ball of soft light in a jar. The Princess heard Shaggy Dog's cry of surprise and looked closer at the jar. The light was actually a tiny forest fairy buzzing excitedly within the large glass container.

"Peddler, why do you have a right to trade such a creature?" inquired Shaggy Dog through tight lips.

"This little fairy had a debt to pay and made a choice in her repayment," replied Mikaela solemnly.

"I don't think that is very nice," protested the Princess.

"Shhh, now..." said Shaggy Dog urgently. He stared intently at the jar for several long seconds. Finally, he said, "The fairy tells me the peddler's explanation is true."

"See, I am but a humble trader and speak nothing but truth," sang the little peddler.

"Still, I don't think it is right," said the Princess sulkily.

"Then let's make a trade so you can set her free! You can balance the scales of this imagined injustice quite easily," relied Mikaela. "And I am so glad you can hear her, friend dog. I was not certain you would be capable, with all that fur."

"I can hear her plain as I hear you. But my friend has already told you we have nothing of value we can spare," said Shaggy Dog, without removing his eyes from the fairy.

"Begging your forgiveness, Mr. Peddler. I need a moment with my friend," the Princess said as she pulled Shaggy Dog to one side.

The peddler hummed and whispered happy sounds to the fairy.

The Princess was convinced they should trade anything not absolutely necessary for the fairy. Shaggy Dog wanted to help but was doubtful they could produce anything from their packs valuable enough to satisfy the peddler. The Princess dug through her bag, inspecting each item in turn.

"Mr. Peddler," she started.

"It's Mikaela, dear," he replied softly.

"Mikaela, then. Would you be interested in some fine silk clothing? I'm sure they would fetch a big price," the Princess said, holding up both of her remaining shirts.

"Although those appear to be fit for royalty and very expensive, I am sure, my clientele would not appreciate the material," said Mikaela.

"Alright. Well, how about this silver dagger?" the Princess inquired, holding up a petite knife.

"Where did you get that?" a puzzled Shaggy Dog exclaimed.

"Never you mind that, Shaggy Dog. Peddler? I mean Mikaela?"

"That is fine work. I think I recognize the craftsmanship. I know a man down south near the pink shores who produces similar weapons. But I am not really in the business of trading arms," said Mikaela.

"Well, other than that... unless you want a hunk of rock that our giant friend said tasted funny, I'm out of items!" exclaimed an exasperated Princess.

"Does your friend hail from the north side of the Dragon Spine?" inquired Mikaela seriously.

"He does. Why do you ask?" replied the Princess.

"No matter. It's a deal," said the peddler with a chuckle.

"What's a deal?" asked a confused Princess. Shaggy Dog tilted his head questioningly.

"I will trade for the funny-tasting rock, of course," replied Mikaela. "Giants love to snack on any rock, and if one tasted funny to your friend, it must be quite unusual. Unusual can mean valuable. I'll take it."

"For the forest fairy?" asked the Princess hopefully.

"Tiny gods, no. For everything I showed you," came the cheerful reply.

The Princess was shocked, but accepted the deal eagerly. They made their exchange, and after Mikaela had helped the Princess mount Shaggy Dog's new riding platform, he slipped off to bed down for the night. The Princess could hear him humming a jolly tune for a few minutes until high-pitched snores filled the cave. Shaggy Dog was still near the fire, talking quietly to the fairy.

"Does she want us to let her out now?" asked the Princess.

"No. She wants to ride east with us for a while. It will take her closer to home," said Shaggy Dog.

"Well, she doesn't have to stay cooped up in that jar," said the Princess.

"I know, and so does she," said Shaggy Dog. "She can actually slip out of the breathing hole in the top any time she wants."

"Then why didn't she ever escape?" asked the Princess.

"I get the feeling she was never the peddler's prisoner," said Shaggy Dog.

"Well, I'll be. This has been one strange day, Shaggy Dog," said the Princess.

"It sure has."

"Maybe Mikaela can point us towards the canyon," said the Princess hopefully.

"Jazzi – that's the fairy's name – says she has known Mikaela a long time, and he probably knows exactly where it is," said Shaggy Dog.

"Great! We can ask him first thing in the morning," said the Princess as she rolled into her sleeping blanket.

"Jazzi says he won't be here in the morning," stated Shaggy Dog. "Princess? Princess?"

But the Princess was fast asleep.

She woke early the next morning eager to ask Mikaela about the canyon, but he had disappeared along with all of his belongings. Outside the cave, the rain continued to fall.

CHAPTER 6

When Daniel paused, I said, "That liquid fire is bad to the bone!"

"What?" he asked over the constant thrum from the other side of the bar.

"I said that fire the princess used is bad to the bone."

"Yeah. Worked well on the goblins," he replied.

"Seemed to take its toll on her too, though," Brandee added.

I looked down at my glass, surprised it was still mostly full, and waved off another round. The TV was showing the post-post-game show, and the college kids were at the tipping point of drunken euphoria and sloshy hell.

"Every time she had to use it, it got worse," Daniel muttered.

"She made a lot of cool friends, though. Did she ever see them again?" asked Brandee.

"Yeah, that big fella and eagle lady elf would be handy in a fight," I added.

Daniel's mouth twitched upwards slightly, but his eyes remained void of any emotion. "The Princess saw her friends again, or at least most of them. At this point in the story, she isn't even finished meeting interesting people yet."

The waitresses were buzzing around, and Brandee scooted off to fill orders. As I watched Daniel push his half empty beer across the bar, I remembered my own drink.

I sipped lightly and stared at the TV, waiting for him to continue the story. He watched Brandee as she poured drinks and then went back to her textbook for a moment. When she closed it with a sigh, he said, "You should keep studying instead of listening to me ramble."

"That's OK. This is way better than the stuff I normally hear from that side of the bar," she replied.

I laughed and winked at Brandee. Then I told Daniel, "She doesn't have to study anyway, not really. She's majoring in art. How hard can that be?"

She flipped a dirty bar rag at me, laughing as she squealed, "Shut up, Jake, or I'll cut you off."

"Art? Like drawing and painting?" asked Daniel.

"Art history. I love to draw, and all forms of art, really. Maybe, one day I'll work in an art museum or something," she replied.

Daniel stood up so quickly that the barstool teetered back, threatening to crash to the floor. By the time it had settled back in place, he was three-quarters of the way to the restroom.

Brandee's eyes were wide as she looked at me. "Did I say something wrong?"

"Maybe, but this dude is on edge. He's raw. Anything could be the wrong thing to him," I told her reassuringly.

She looked toward the bathrooms, then back at me. She bit her lower lip softly, then asked, "Do you think his little girl had cancer?"

"Yeah, or something just as brutal," I said.

Her shoulders sagged. She drew a deep breath and said, "Can you even imagine... You want another one?"

"Yeah, give me one more." Then, after a moment, I added, "And no, I can't imagine."

Brandee reached for the bottle. "How is Janie? She's thirteen, right?"

I nodded my head, smiling. "She is good, good. I don't see her as much as I'd like, but busy, ya know?"

Brandee motioned with her eyes to point out Daniel as he made his way back to his stool. Once seated, he didn't waste any time. "The story picks up from here. Things start to happen fast, but if you are bored..."

"Hell no!" I replied. "I want to know if she ever finds the canyon."

"Alright then," he said. His eyes drifted from me to Brandee, then to his hands. One was clenched tight, and the other massaged it gently. "Let's do this."

CHAPTER 7

Three days later, the group resumed their eastern trek on a soggy but sunny road. It would have been only two days, but a fainting spell had struck the Princess. The Helm's instructions set her right, or at least better, quickly. Shaggy Dog was eager to push forward after he saw the mountains finally starting to take shape. He could even make out the snow caps on the tallest of the peaks. Jazzi chose to stay in her jar – but without the lid attached – upon Shaggy Dog's new platform. The Princess followed behind on her horse, eager to find her true weapon in the canyon.

Immediately, it was evident that the land was sloping up. Every hill they crested had a much shorter descent on the other side. It was on one of these hills, during the morning of the second day after leaving the cave, that they spotted the enemy scouts. At first, Shaggy Dog wasn't sure he had seen anything at all on the next ridge to the north, perhaps just a flicker of movement out of the corner of his eye. It wasn't until Jazzi asked him why the huge flock of ravens was following them that he put it together. Creeping goblins dressed in natural colors were keeping pace with them to the north, while the ravens came in and out of sight to the south. The enemy knew their exact location. Later that night, after their evening meal, the Princess fell asleep quickly due to exhaustion. Shaggy Dog watched as she slept peacefully without her armor or sword.

He had started to nod off himself when suddenly his ears

shot up. He had heard a twig snap nearby. *Just an animal*, he thought. Then a wolf howled loudly, much too close for comfort. Jazzi flew out of her jar and straight to his ear, and whispered, "Quiet now. Wait for the response."

Seconds later, another wolf howled, followed by a third.

"See, they are all to the west of us. If they were going to attack, we would already be surrounded. Get some sleep. I'll stand watch tonight."

"You're probably right," said Shaggy Dog as he shuffled near to the Princess to get some rest, but sleep was slow to come and fitful when it arrived.

Every day after that was the same. The Goat Head Sorcerer's minions kept close watch on them all day. The Princess's fatigue caused by the curse forced them to take more frequent and longer breaks. Every night the wolves howled to each other, or the Princess and Shaggy Dog heard goblins racing near their camp. No one was getting the rest they needed, and it was taking its toll. Minor arguments broke out over things that did not matter. Small talk was all but absent. The traveling was still intense and productive, but at night their camp was quiet and lonely.

The Ravens of Despair attacked without warning on the sixth day since they first saw the enemy scouts. The Princess thought the dark cloud above them could mean another round of rain, until the cloud started cawing and diving towards them. Jazzi was the first to react, flying quickly from her jar to the Princess's shoulder just as the first ravens swooped down to peck at her. She stayed near the Princess's head, protecting her eyes from the sharp beaks and claws. Shaggy Dog felt a wave of uselessness wash over him. He sat frozen on his platform, feeling sorry for himself at just how impossible their task truly seemed.

More ravens came, and then still more. The Princess was almost overwhelmed by the sheer number of feathered fiends that descended upon her. She squealed in pain as a raven nipped at the back of her neck in the gap between the Helm and her armor. The pained sound finally knocked Shaggy Dog out of his stupor.

"Ride!" he yelled, urging his mount toward a stand of trees ahead. The Princess and Jazzi followed quickly. The ravens swirled up into the sky to regroup and prepare for another assault.

Shaggy Dog stopped in the midst of the thickest part of the wood. The Ravens of Despair came at the Princess again, but between the dense limbs and Shaggy Dog's merciless jaws, they soon grew bored and drifted off to the south, cawing raucously as they flew.

The decision to call an early halt to the day's travel was an easy one. The Princess made a small fire while Shaggy Dog stood watch. Jazzi flitted off into the thicket to do whatever forest fairies do in an unfamiliar clump of trees. When she came back, she whispered something into Shaggy Dog's ear.

For the first time in ages, Shaggy Dog smiled. He rushed off after Jazzi, telling the Princess he would be right back. When he came strutting back into camp, he was dragging a loaded branch of temple berries. The Princess could not help but smile as well; temple berries were just the thing to sweeten the bland meal she was preparing. Smashed and stewed, the berries were a delicacy. The Princess was already starting to salivate.

"Thought these would be a good pick-me-up," said Shaggy Dog as Jazzi buzzed past his head. "Fine, fine. *Jazzi and I* thought these would be a good pick-me-up."

"I love them. They're almost warm enough," said the Princess as she stirred the berry paste. "I haven't had temple berry biscuits in such a long time," she continued as she lifted the pot from the fire.

Just before tipping the steaming, sweet goo onto the hard biscuits, the Princess slipped. Temple berry sauce flew everywhere but onto the plate.

"Arrgh! Be more careful," growled Shaggy Dog.

The Princess's eyes grew wide, and her lower lip started to tremble. "I'm so sorry," she said.

"Sorry? That's the first decent thing to eat in days, and you say sorry?" barked the flustered Shaggy Dog.

Tears now filled the Princess's eyes and spilled down her cheeks. "It was an accident," she cried as she tried to mop up any sauce that was salvageable.

"Just forget it. Eat your biscuits and get some rest. We need to make up for lost time tomorrow," growled Shaggy Dog as he stormed off through the trees.

The Princess hugged her knees to her chest and sobbed heavily. Jazzi sat quietly on her shoulder until the sun set, when the Princess had calmed a little. The Princess rolled into her sleeping blanket sore, hurt, and hungry. The Ravens of Despair had accomplished their goal well.

The next morning, the Princess was the last to stir. Shaggy Dog had been up before dawn, scouring the area for something sweet for the Princess. He felt terrible about his reaction to the Princess's dropping of the temple berry sauce, and hoped to find something to help make it up to her. Jazzi stirred as the first light crept over the mountains, the same as she did every morning. Both waited anxiously for the Princess to rise from her slumber, eager to be on the road and away from this miserable place. Though the Ravens of Despair had not returned, the forlorn feeling they invoked had remained in the air like a wispy fog.

When the Princess finally stirred, she felt groggy and out of sorts. At Shaggy Dog's behest, she placed the Helm upon her head to try and find a solution. She dug in her pouch for a tiny clear vial. Almost instantly after drinking its contents, her head cleared slightly. Within the hour, she felt she was up to traveling, so the group struck out east, Shaggy Dog and Jazzi leading the way. Unfortunately, the Princess found herself digging back into the pouch again shortly after their midday meal.

For the next two days, as they traveled east with the mountains looming over them, the Princess used more vials and yet her condition became worse in spite of them.

The group started ascending the first foothills of the Dragon Spine Mountains, and with the help of the Helm and the vials, the Princess was able to manage. However, *manage* was all she was doing. So, on the ninth day since they first saw the enemy scouts, when they discovered that the pass they sought was guarded by two massive trolls, the Princess felt like giving up and just going home. She couldn't have turned around even if she wanted to, though. Wolves had been following them all day, howling even in the daylight. The only way was forward.

They crested a small rise onto a flat plateau. To their right was a steep drop into a nasty-looking swamp. To their left was a vertical ridge towering above them. The wolves, their numbers impossible to discern, howled closer behind them. As Shaggy Dog looked out across the elevated plain, dread filled his heart. Up ahead, blocking the only other way to the mountains and eventually the canyon, was a small army of goblins lined in formation. Shaggy Dog did not bother to count them, as their numbers were too great to matter whether there were eighty or one hundred and twenty.

He heard the Princess moan. "So many," she said.

"Yes, but look," said Shaggy Dog with a wolfish grin. "They are scared to attack. Word of the fire-breathing Princess Knight, menace to all goblins, must have reached them."

Despite herself and despite their dire situation, the Princess giggled. *It feels good to laugh*, she thought as she loosened the sword in its scabbard.

As Jazzi buzzed past her face and towards the swamp, the Princess said, "Where is she going?"

"She didn't say, only something about time," replied Shaggy Dog without taking his eyes from the goblins.

"Little Jazzi couldn't fight these things anyway," said the Princess, looking towards the murky swamp into which Jazzi had plunged. It was probably a better place to be than here with the goblins. "No time like the present," she continued as she urged her horse forward.

Shaggy Dog could see some of the goblins unsheathe their swords and loosen their axes at the sight of the Princess moving towards them, but they held their position.

"Whoa now, Princess," said Shaggy Dog sternly.

"Whoa yourself! What are we waiting for? A miracle?" screamed the Princess. "No, let's be done with this."

Shaggy Dog angled his mount in front of hers and looked her dead in the eye. "Don't go rushing to your death. Hear me out."

The Princess simply nodded, so Shaggy Dog continued, "Here, we have some high ground. The goblins know that, which is why they haven't attacked yet. Smarter than most people give them credit for. And besides, Jazzi squealed something about time, or more time, on her way past us. Let's not rush. We'll have our fight at some point today."

The Princess looked away, then stared at the goblins for a long time. Finally, she looked back at Shaggy Dog. "Fine, we make our stand here."

The sun was almost at its highest point, and the unseasonable warm weather had the Princess reaching for her canteen after only minutes had passed. Still, they waited on the hillside, standing upright in defiance of their fear. Shaggy Dog watched as the Princess stared out at an enemy bent on her destruction. She did not flinch or shy away. He realized how proud he was of her bravery and spirit. After a moment of weakness, she was no longer consumed by fear or intimidated by the odds. She was truly a noble warrior.

The sun passed the midday point and was well into its descent when the goblin army started its slow march forward. The Princess spared a single glance towards the swamp, hoping to see Jazzi returning. She had grown fond of the little fairy in the last few days. But no, it appeared that the Princess and Shaggy Dog would face this threat alone.

The Princess pulled her sword from her scabbard, and the orderly march of the goblins crumbled into an all-out riot racing towards them. A group of ten, perhaps twelve of the fastest goblins outpaced the main group. They were lightly armored with short, thin swords. Their battle cry rang across the plateau as they came within thirty paces of the Princess and Shaggy Dog, who were both still on their horses. They waited stoically with the Princess slightly ahead of Shaggy Dog, grasping her sword loosely.

"We will only have a few moments to dispense with the first wave before the main force is upon us," said Shaggy Dog calmly. "Whatever you do, stay on your horse."

"Are you going to stay on yours?" asked the Princess. Shaggy Dog smiled his wolfish smile again, showing his large teeth, and laughed.

"Guess not," said the Princess.

And then the goblins were upon them.

Shaggy Dog barked, "Now! Back!"

Quickly, the Princess pulled her horse back a few steps as Shaggy Dog urged his forward ahead of the Princess. Solely focused on the Princess as they were, half the goblins were ridden down by Shaggy Dog's horse. The remainder were forced to slow down and maneuver around the results of the carnage. Now the goblins had lost their best tactical advantage: speed. The five remaining goblins regrouped and attacked the Princess's unprotected side. Shaggy Dog watched as she worked the reins deftly with one hand and wielded her sword in the other. The Princess never allowed more than one goblin forward at a time and dispatched each one efficiently. When she wrenched the sword free from the last one, she looked up, expecting to see the main force bearing down on them.

"Why do they wait?" asked the Princess, breathing heavily.

"I don't know. They're within bow range, but I don't see any archers," replied Shaggy Dog. "You did well, by the way."

"And you are still on your horse!" mocked the Princess.

"There was no reason to get down. You had it covered," he said, glancing at her.

"We're not done yet," she said. Then, more loudly, "What are you waiting for?!"

There was a ripple through the lines of the goblin army, creating a gap in the center. The ground shook as a huge troll stormed through the gap to the front of the line. It paused and roared a challenging battle cry to the Princess. Shaggy Dog's mouth hung open as he stared, but without hesitation, the Princess raised her sword high in the air and answered in kind. The next instant, the troll charged. The Princess leveled her sword like a lance and spurred her horse forward, Shaggy Dog right at her heels. The clash reverberated in Shaggy Dog's chest as the Princess's sword shattered against the troll's extended, meaty fist. The troll went down, grasping his ruined hand as the Princess flew from her saddle, landing hard on the unforgiving ground. Shaggy Dog positioned himself between the troll and the Princess as she slowly regained her feet. She swayed as she reached into the pouch, searching for a vial of Dragon's Fire. The troll had struggled to his feet and thrust his bloody fist at Shaggy Dog.

"Move, Shaggy Dog!" yelled the Princess as she tossed the handle of her bladeless sword to the ground. She turned up the vial and drank the bitter liquid quickly.

"As you command," said Shaggy Dog, maneuvering his horse behind her.

The troll charged, malice in his eyes and foam coming from his mouth. When it was only feet away from her, the Princess released the fire deep from within. Her eyes were bloodshot and full of tears, and her whole body shook from the strain.

The troll was engulfed by the searing flame, but it still raised his undamaged fist high to smash the Princess like a bug. The Princess continued to spew flame even as she fell to her knees. The troll staggered one more step, then fell with a bone-rattling crash. Shaggy Dog let out a whoop from up on his horse... but it died out when he noticed the goblins advancing with swords, tiny pikes, and axes drawn. The Princess was still on her knees with her head lowered and her arms dangling listlessly.

The Princess did not stir as the goblins started their advance. As they realized she was not going to repeat the dragon's fire, their pace increased. Something within Shaggy Dog snapped; his ears lay flat on his head as he sprang from the platform into the first unlucky goblin. Before its blood hit the ground, Shaggy Dog was upon another goblin, then another. Vaguely, he was aware that the Princess was struggling to stand, and that she was grasping the small, silver knife. His vision was dark around the edges as he ripped and gnashed goblin after goblin. Blood was everywhere, and he was pretty sure some of it was his, but he was positive that none of it belonged to the Princess. The goblins pulled back in the face of his ferocity, and the Princess staggered over and placed a hand on his heaving back. The red ground was littered with goblin bodies, but there were still too many amassing to charge again.

"Stay behind me, Princess. They won't touch you," gasped Shaggy Dog.

The Princess was too weary to argue that once they were surrounded it would all be over. The goblins were spreading into a half-moon shape, in order to accomplish just that, when Jazzi landed on the Princess's shoulder. She kissed the Princess's cheek lightly, then buzzed down to Shaggy Dog.

"What?" growled Shaggy Dog. Jazzi gestured with both hands towards the swamp. "Will that work? Can you do it?"

Frantically, he glanced from side to side, then saw what he was looking for. "Fine, but you'd better be right!"

"Be right about what?" asked the Princess.

"No time. Jazzi has a plan. When they attack, stay very close," Shaggy Dog replied, still scanning the goblins assembling between them and the swamp.

"I will, but what's the plan?" whined the exhausted Princess.

"Just don't stop. Eliminate anything in our path, but for the tiny gods' sake, don't stop," growled Shaggy Dog.

Jazzi buzzed off towards the swamp again, moments before the goblins charged. Shaggy Dog didn't hesitate: immediately, he sprinted in the direction Jazzi had flown. The Princess saw six of the tallest, meanest-looking goblins she had ever seen right in front of them.

"Umm... Shaggy Dog, what are we doing?" yelled the Princess as she stumbled after him as fast as she could.

"Just keep moving," grunted Shaggy Dog as he approached the goblins.

Wicked, sharp teeth showed through the triumphant smiles of the largest goblins as Shaggy Dog and the Princess approached. An armor less mutt and a little girl with only a knife and no Dragon's Fire remaining would be no match for them. Swords raised, they charged or at least, they *tried* to charge. Vines had grown up around their ankles and tripped them up. They fell face first as the Princess and Shaggy Dog passed them on their way to the steep drop and the swamp. The other goblins saw they were through the lines and quickly pursued them. Suddenly, a wall of vines covered with thorns sprang out of the dirt, blocking the goblins from their

C. H. SMITH

pursuit. Shaggy Dog and Princess kept running right to the edge of the cliff

"Jump!" yelled Shaggy Dog.

"Are you crazy?" asked the Princess with wide eyes.

"Trust me. Jump."

As they sailed over the edge, the swamp raced up to meet them. Jazzi flew alongside them, leaving a little trail of fairy light behind her. Moments before they struck the tops of the trees, vines came shooting out of the canopy and wrapped gently around their bodies, bringing them slowly to the soft ground.

They had escaped the goblin army!

Jazzi buzzed around, checking their injuries, and Shaggy Dog let out a victorious howl to rival the loudest wolf. The Princess smiled at her friends, then sank slowly to her knees. She saw the bright afternoon sun fading as she slowly slipped into the delirium of dreams due to utter exhaustion.

A sandpaper tongue and a scorching pain in her throat were the first things the Princess noticed as she woke. The ground squished under her back and hands as she pushed herself up to a sitting position. The pleasant, damp smell of decay filled her nostrils as she scanned her surroundings. Thick moss hung from gnarled, ancient trees, dragging on the ground like overgrown beards. Sunlight cascaded through the few gaps in the thick branches. She felt warm and sweaty. Shaggy Dog and Jazzi were nowhere to be seen, and she decided maybe she didn't need to sit up after all. She stared at the interlocking limbs above her until her eyes slowly closed again.

The next time she swam out of the deep and opened her eyes it was still daylight, but noticeably dimmer. All she could see was a tangle of black hair and two big white eyes.

"Rise and shine, Princess," said Shaggy Dog quietly.

The Princess sat up with some effort as Shaggy Dog

shuffled to one side gingerly.

"Are you hurt?" asked the Princess.

"I'll manage. I gave more than I got, that's for sure."

"Where is Jazzi?" asked the Princess, scanning the swamp around them.

"Flitting around, keeping the goblins out of this murky hole," said Shaggy Dog with a small grin. "She is quite amazing. The vine thing on the plateau was all her doing, and some of the things she is doing now is beyond my understanding. But it's keeping us safe, that much I know."

As the conversation lulled, the Princess drank deeply from her canteen. Animal sounds and the constant drone of insects were the only noises in the dense swamp. There was no breeze, and the Princess thought the air felt heavy and thick. "It's insufferable here – so hot," she said.

"Don't let Jazzi hear you say that," laughed Shaggy Dog. "When I think of forest fairies, I think of tall redwood glens or elegant willows on the banks of a winding river. But Jazzi says this swamp reminds her of home. She is more giddy than usual, so be prepared."

Shaggy Dog looked at the Princess out of the corner of his eye, and they both laughed quietly. The Princess continued to sip on her canteen, feeling her strength return slowly.

"Is there anything to eat?" she asked, doubtful that there would be.

"Jazzi pointed out some fluffy water-pad things she said were edible, if not good. But all of our supplies are up there with the horses, except for this one bag Jazzi was able to haul down here yesterday," said Shaggy Dog, looking at the single, pitiful bag that housed the two canteens, flint, and hard cheeses.

"Wait – yesterday?" asked a puzzled Princess. "How long have I been asleep?"

"Well, if you don't count the day we launched ourselves

off the plateau," said Shaggy Dog cautiously, "four days."

"Four days!" exclaimed the Princess. She attempted to stand, without much success. "We need to be moving. We have to get out of here and into the canyon!"

Shaggy Dog nudged her gently back down to a wet landing. He cocked his head to the side and looked at her.

"I guess maybe we can rest a bit more," said the Princess. "Just till Jazzi gets back."

Jazzi did not return that day or even that night. When the Princess was roused by Shaggy Dog shortly after dawn the next morning, Jazzi was zooming from side to side and back and forth so quickly that the Princess struggled to keep track of her. The Princess saw Shaggy Dog's furled brow, flat ears, and straight tail as he tried to get the little fairy to slow down.

"Jazzi, just stop, or at least fly in a small circle so we can talk," said Shaggy Dog as Jazzi flew by them again.

"What's wrong with her?" asked the Princess as she approached Shaggy Dog.

"I can't tell. She's not making a lot of sense," he whispered.

Then Jazzi stopped and flew right onto Shaggy Dog's nose. The Princess giggled as Jazzi pointed her tiny finger at his eye, obviously giving him the once-over. Shaggy Dog cleared his throat and, never taking his eyes off the little fairy still perched on his snout, continued, "Correction: Jazzi says she is making perfect sense. Evidently, I am just a dumb, hard of hearing... dog."

Immediately, Jazzi started jabbing her finger at him again and stamping her foot impatiently.

"I am *not* saying that in front of her..." Shaggy Dog said. Then, after a pause, "Alright, I am an oaf, a dumb oaf. Is that better?"

It must have been more to the fairy's liking because

Jazzi resumed her pacing like a hummingbird flittering from flower to flower. Shaggy Dog explained to the Princess that Jazzi had said there was something very wrong with this swamp. She did not know what exactly, but she could not seem to find a way out. She flew due south for one solid day, yet ended up where she started. She waited for goblins to enter the swamp looking for the Princess, and after dispatching them, she followed their trail backwards. The trail simply vanished. When she flew far enough above the canopy, she could see the edge, but once back down here, it disappeared.

"See, she isn't making any sense," mumbled Shaggy Dog as he looked at Jazzi out of the corner of his eye. Then, he sighed deeply when she did not hear him.

"We don't have a choice. We have to get out of this swamp," said the Princess. "I say we walk east – that's the way we were going anyway."

After a meal of spongy water pads, the group started their trudge east. Shaggy Dog missed his horse and platform with every paw-sucking step, and progress was slow. Nevertheless, they were moving again, and the Princess felt better knowing that the goblins could not reach them in here. The prospect of leaving the swamp to continue the search for the canyon was too far off to bother her at the moment. She concentrated on putting one foot in front of the other and not falling into the muck.

When they finally stopped that night, Shaggy Dog and the Princess were exhausted. Jazzi went out scouting and came back to report that the goblins had given up on entering the swamp, but she still did not know how to get out.

The next morning started just as the last evening had ended: mud, muck, slow moving, and frustration with no end in sight. The Princess, in particular, started to lose her cool after a root she hadn't noticed sent her sprawling on the runny ground. She had mud all along her front, on her face, and in her hair. If anyone had been standing on the plateau above, they would have heard her scream of annoyance. When Shaggy Dog plopped over to help, she screamed at him too. Her eyes were wide with rage as she kicked at every plant, stick, and root within reach. She took out her knife and threw it at a swamp rat scurrying past. Luckily for the rat, her anger caused her aim to be off, which only elevated the temperature of her blood until she boiled over. She picked up a hunk of dead wood and was about to chunk it into a tree when she saw Shaggy Dog's slack-jawed expression.

She deflated, and fell back onto the squishy ground. Her tears mixed with the swamp water as her whole body was racked with sobs. She looked at Shaggy Dog after her tears had mostly dried up. She saw only love and worry. He was not angry at her for her outburst. She knew in that moment that rage was not going to carry her through to the end of her quest, or even to the end of this swamp. Rage was not her weapon.

The next morning offered more of the same mud and muck. Shaggy Dog pointed out a particularly odd-looking bent cypress tree, which he thought looked like an old dried-out raider wraith. It was spooky but extremely interesting, a rarity during their monotonous grind. The Princess was tired of eating the water pads and longed for something hot and filling. Shaggy Dog never complained, but on several occasions, he did ask Jazzi where the nearest inn could be found.

Nothing changed until Shaggy Dog stopped dead in his tracks, staring out at the swamp. He said, "It has to be the same one."

Jazzi left the Princess's shoulder to buzz around near Shaggy Dog's head.

"The same what?" asked the Princess.

"There – right there," Shaggy Dog said, pointing with his nose to the right.

The Princess peered in that direction but all she saw were trees and vines and swamp. She was just about to tell Shaggy Dog so when she saw a familiar shape. It was like an old dried-out raider wraith, but it was just a tree. The tree they had passed hours earlier.

The hairs on the back of Shaggy Dog's neck stood up and his eyes narrowed. He stalked over to the tree with large, careful steps. After walking around it and inspecting it from all angles, he returned to the group.

"It's just a tree," he said through gritted teeth.

"Shaggy Dog, are you alright?" asked the Princess, reaching out with one hand to settle the fur on his back.

"I'm fine, just angry. I'm mad at the whole thing, from this swamp all the way back to the Goat Head Sorcerer," he said, calming as he spoke. "Sometimes the anger is all that drives me, but it bubbled over just now. I thought that tree was some kind of sign, since we have already seen it once – or maybe whatever has trapped us here was near to it. But nobody was there, and it's just a tree."

"Just a tree," repeated the Princess.

Jazzi flew onto Shaggy Dog's nose and her speech became very animated, her tiny arms going everywhere as she talked.

"Jazzi says the swamp just told her of another presence nearby. Not goblins, but the swamp doesn't recognize it either," said Shaggy Dog.

"Well, let's go have a look, shall we?" said the Princess.

Shaggy Dog just shook his head quietly, laughing. "Nothing seems to bother you – well, other than that root back there. But seriously, you are handling this so well."

"I just have faith. Faith that we are on the right path set forth by the Benevolent Witch. Faith in those that have helped me. The Queen gave me this armor. Reserio and the witches of Houstonia gave me the Helm and sword, although the sword is gone. Sasha and Dane gave us useful gifts:

wisdom and friendship. Even Mikaela gave us Jazzi, and look how wonderful she is." The Princess nudged the little fairy with her pinky finger. "It's all going to work out, one way or another. I just know it."

"I hope you are right..." Shaggy Dog said. Then he cocked his head. "What, Jazzi?" He listened intently to the fairy for a moment, then stared straight ahead. "Are you sure? I don't see anything. Of course you are. Princess, get behind me. The weird presence thing in the swamp is almost on top of us."

The Princess stepped behind Shaggy Dog and looked intently into the dense swamp. She could hear the presence long before she could see it. It was definitely coming straight for them, and making a terrible racket.

Then she could barely believe her ears.

"Shaggy Dog, is someone singing?" she asked quietly.

"I think so. Something about a fish on a hook wiggling loose. A nonsense children's song," replied Shaggy Dog, relaxing a bit. He recognized the voice.

The owner of the voice struggled through the foliage, splashing right up to them. The Benevolent Witch had returned.

"Well, hello Princess, Shaggy Dog," she said in her high-pitched voice. "And who might you be, little one?"

The Benevolent Witch listened intently to the fairy, then giggled aloud, "What a lovely name – Jazzi! I see you have met my friends, and helped them along, I suspect."

Shaggy Dog was staring at the Benevolent Witch like as if she was an aberration that he could not quite comprehend. The Princess was the first to speak up. "Madam Witch, it's great to see you. But what are you doing here?"

The Benevolent Witch giggled again. "Didn't I tell you I would meet you again at the canyon? I did, didn't I? Well, either way, you all are here, and Princess, you have completed the tests. So, I am here."

"Tests? What tests?" asked a thoroughly confused Princess. "And what do you mean, we are in the canyon? We're right in front of you in this smelly swamp."

"Ah, I see. That is strange. You have completed the tests and the illusion has still not passed? Very strange," said the Benevolent Witch. "Well, where is your sword? I want to see it."

"I am so confused. I haven't found any sword in this swamp," cried the Princess.

"But you have found your weapon. The tests are complete – the canyon tells me this is so," stated the Benevolent Witch matter-of-factly.

The Princess threw her hands up and laughed. She walked over to the old crooked tree and leaned very close, almost touching it. Finally, without knowing what else to do, she closed her eyes and whispered softly to the tree.

"I have faith, old tree. I have faith that however this will end, those around me, love me. I have faith that the world is a good place filled with good creatures. I have faith for the future." By the end of her statement, her lips were touching the bark of the bent old tree. When she opened her eyes, she saw a hole in the tree she was sure hadn't been there moments ago. Without hesitation, she reached in and grasped the handle of a sword.

Shaggy Dog's eyes grew wide as the Princess pulled from within the tree a small, beautiful glass sword. It had a silver rod at its core running the length of the blade from pommel to tip. As the Princess returned to the group, he could see the word *Faith* written on the core. She had found her weapon and with it, her chance to defeat the Goat Head Sorcerer once and for all.

The Benevolent Witch's laughter rang across the swamp. A haze filled the air, and then swamp faded slowly, like fog being burned by a bright morning sun escaping the clouds. The group found themselves in a deep narrow canyon: *the*

Canyon. They had been there all along.

Jazzi chattered away, but Shaggy Dog was not paying attention. All he could see was the defiant smile on the Princess's face. She was ready for the challenge ahead; he just knew it.

The sky was quickly becoming muted, as night fell quickly in the canyon. The group, the Benevolent Witch included, decided to camp where they were for the night. Having a witch around paid off: she provided warm food for the group for the first time in days. They ate until they could not stomach another bite. Then, they ate some more. Anything was better than the fluffy water pads that had sustained them in the swamp. Sleep came upon the Princess hard, but Shaggy Dog was restless. He wandered around the camp, finally settling down near the Benevolent Witch.

"Go ahead and ask me," she said.

Jazzi heard the Benevolent Witch talking to Shaggy Dog and buzzed over, interested.

"Alright, what do we do next?" asked Shaggy Dog.

"I honestly do not have a good answer for you," said the Benevolent Witch in an uncharacteristically melancholy tone. "The results of her skirmishes with the minions of the Goat Head Sorcerer are encouraging. But she seems so tired."

Shaggy Dog agreed that the Princess looked tired, and that she was hurting more than she let on. He pressed on. "But she has her true weapon now. What is the next move?"

The Benevolent Witch sighed deeply, looking first at the fairy and then at Shaggy Dog. "I think she should rest. Maybe even go home for a bit before she has to confront him. If she does it now, I fear she will not be strong enough, weapon or no weapon."

An uncomfortable silence fell across the group. The Princess lay just feet away, sleeping soundly and getting the rest she so needed and deserved. Smoke from the little fire blew into Shaggy Dog's eyes, so he got up to move.

"Don't lose heart, Shaggy Dog," said the Benevolent Witch. "She will need you in the end."

Shaggy Dog just nodded and lay down next to the Princess. However, sleep was a long time coming that night.

The next morning, Jazzi informed the others that she was ready to return to her home swamp. It would not be a long flight, and she was eager to see her family. The Princess and Shaggy Dog both thanked her for her tremendous efforts. In turn, Jazzi thanked them for helping free her from the peddler, laughing as she said it. The Benevolent Witch also departed that morning, but not before telling them where she believed they could locate their horses, if they chose to do so.

The Princess and Shaggy Dog found themselves alone on their quest again. This time, however, it was much different. They had the Princess's true weapon and had proven that the minions of the Goat Head Sorcerer were not unbeatable. Hope grew in Shaggy Dog's heart. The Princess did not have room for hope; she still fought every day to put one foot in front of the other and to soldier on. The curse was making it tougher each day.

Shortly after their midday meal, the duo started the trek out of the canyon. Shaggy Dog led the way around strewn boulders and through cracks and fissures. They talked quietly, debating their best course of action. Neither of them had any inspired ideas, so the conversation went in circles. They rounded a sharp bend in the narrow, high canyon to see a flat expanse in front of them. A brisk wind blew on their backs as they started across the plain. The Princess realized they were much higher up in the mountains than she had thought. The swamp, which was really the canyon, was trickier than she had ever imagined. The air was chilly even beneath her armor, but at least there were no signs of goblins or trolls. The duo did not even see a single raven as they crossed the high, flat land.

With several hours of daylight left, Shaggy Dog and the Princess arrived at the little valley in which their horses could be found, if the Benevolent Witch was correct. The valley was more colorful than anything they had seen in weeks. The leaves on the giant trees were all the colors of the rainbow, from orange to red, and even green and blue and more. The Princess stopped and gazed at their beauty for a long time. Shaggy Dog stopped as well, but all he could see was a bunch of trees and no horses.

"Do you see them, Princess?" he asked, without any real hope.

"Oh yes. They're beautiful," exclaimed the Princess. "We never see trees with this much color at home. Flowers, yes, but not whole trees."

Shaggy Dog smiled and rolled his eyes, his tail swishing from side to side. "Not the leaves, for the tiny gods' sake. Do you see the horses? You know, the big, white animals we're looking for?"

They both laughed, and Shaggy Dog leaned against the Princess. *It really is a spectacular view*, he thought.

Shoulders back and jaw set, the Princess said, "That's it."

"What's what?"

"When this is all over, I know what I want to do," she said.

Shaggy Dog's ears raised and his tail moved faster. "And what is that, Princess?"

She didn't take her eyes off the trees as she replied, "I am going to learn to paint. Then, I will visit all the beautiful places in the Forge in order to paint them."

The Princess looked at Shaggy Dog with wide eyes. He looked back with his wolfish grin and said, "And all this time I thought you were going to be a knight."

"No. The drill yard is fine for me, thank you very much," the Princess said. "I've had enough fighting, even though we're not through yet. I think I'd like to paint so that others can at least glimpse the beauty of the Forge even if they can't see it for themselves."

They stood looking at the leaves. The Princess was picking out her favorite colors while Shaggy Dog was thinking how amazing she was. Despite all that the world and the Goat Head Sorcerer had thrown at her, she still saw the beauty and wanted nothing more than to share it with others.

"Well, we need to find those horses," said the Princess abruptly.

"We do. Let's go." Shaggy Dog started down into the valley, eager to find the horses, but then he felt the Princess's hand on his back.

"Not that way," she said. "Let's climb that ridge. If they're here, we'll spot them from up there."

Shaggy Dog nodded and bowed deep. "Lead the way, Your Majesty."

Sasha would have been proud of them if she could have seen how well they managed to follow the game trail up the side of the ridge. The footing was sure, and the path consistent. When Shaggy Dog let out a yelp of pain as he slipped backwards several feet, the Princess was shocked. She went to his side quickly. Shaggy Dog had been watching an eagle on the horizon, thinking about their last encounter with an eagle, when he had stepped on a loose rock that had slid out from under him. His front paw was bent at an awkward angle and already showed significant swelling. *Broken, for sure*, he thought as he struggled to rise. The pain sent him back to the ground. He hopped the last fifteen feet up the ridge with the Princess directly behind him in case he faltered. Once at the top, Shaggy Dog flopped down in a heap, exhausted and in pain. The Princess started to examine his paw but he snapped, "Look for the horses before we lose the light!"

"Just let me examine your paw," said the Princess.

"The horses!" growled Shaggy Dog.

The Princess recoiled, the shock plain on her pale face.

"I'm so sorry, Princess," said Shaggy Dog, rearranging himself to look her in the eyes. "I'm just mad at my own stupidity. I was birdwatching instead of paying attention to the trail. Idiot."

The Princess ruffled the fur on his head as she stood. "Let me look for the horses. Then you're going to let me check on at that paw."

The ridge offered an excellent view of the valley. The Princess could see trees, then a small stream that cut the valley in half. She could see clear across to the other side where the mountains rose again, steeper even than the ridge they were on. She did not see the horses, though, and was in the process of telling Shaggy Dog the bad news when she spotted something coming towards them.

"Is that the eagle you saw earlier?" she asked, pointing towards the rapidly growing winged creature.

"I think so," Shaggy Dog said, the hair on his back rising. He yelled, "Princess! That's no eagle. It's a dragon. We have to hide!"

"A dragon? Are you sure?" Even as she said it, she knew Shaggy Dog was right. The creature was huge, with a bright yellow belly, and there was no doubt that it was headed straight for them.

"Come on. The Goat Head Sorcerer could have sent it to find us. We have to move!" barked Shaggy Dog, struggling to move quickly towards a pile of rocks near the other end of the ridge.

"Where are we going to go?" cried the Princess as she pulled out her sword. "There's nowhere to hide."

The dragon passed over them at incredible speed. As it banked hard to come back towards them, the Princess saw that it had a dark green back that transitioned to a yellow belly. It swooped down close to their heads, the wind from its massive wings almost knocking the Princess off her feet. Quickly, it dropped to the ground lightly. A boy barely older than herself jumped off the dragon's back, deftly landing on his feet. There was a quiver on his back but no bow in sight. He approached with his hands raised.

"Hey now, don't stick me with that thing. It looks sharp," he said with a perfect smile.

The Princess looked down at her drawn sword, surprised to see it in her hands, but she did not lower it.

"Don't come any closer!" said the Princess, brandishing her sword.

With one hand, the boy indicated the lack of scabbard on his belt. "I don't carry a blade, and I left my bow back there with Zero."

"Your dragon has a name?" The Princess didn't know why, but she was intrigued by this piece of news.

"Of course. Doesn't your dog have a name?"

"I do," growled Shaggy Dog, limping up beside the Princess with his hackles raised. Zero stirred, but a slight gesture from the boy seemed to calm him.

The boy said sagely, "All of the tiny gods' creatures have names. Mine is Jaxson, and I – well, *we* –live one valley over. Zero spotted you and thought you might be goblins, so we came to investigate."

"Goblins? Have you seen any?" asked the Princess in concern.

"Not for weeks. They tend to give Zero plenty of space," Jaxson said with a chuckle.

Shaggy Dog had no choice: he had to sit down, and even that hurt.

"You are wounded. Why don't both of you come to our place? We'll get you all fixed up," offered Jaxson.

"I'm fine, boy," said Shaggy Dog defiantly. "Besides, how can we trust you? We don't even know you."

"Doesn't look like you have much choice. And if I meant either of you harm, I would have used my bow or let Zero have a crack at you. I just don't see many folks up this way. Kind of want to hear why you two are up here, and maybe some news of the world."

Shaggy Dog thought for a moment. "If you want to help us, get your dragon to fly around and find our horses. That would be *actual* help."

It was Jaxson's turn to look down at his hands, suddenly very quiet. "Two white horses?"

"So, you *have* seen them?" the Princess squealed with delight.

Jaxson blushed. "Yep. About three days ago. They were right down in that valley there." With a sweep of his hand, he indicated the valley they were all overlooking.

"Where? Can you show us?" she asked.

Shaggy Dog could see something was off, so he asked, "Where are the horses now?"

Jaxson gave a sheepish smile. "Well, one is probably halfway to Bent Pine by now. The other is at my place. Meat is hard to come by up here."

The Princess stared blankly at Jaxson. Understanding dawned upon her and her facial expression went through a range of emotions. All she said was, "That stinks."

"Guess we could use some help after all, boy," Shaggy Dog said gruffly. Jaxson's sheepish smile grew into a genuine face-splitter. He nodded and beckoned them towards Zero.

CHAPTER 8

"Excuse me. I'm so sorry to interrupt," came a sweet voice said from behind Daniel. The older lady from the end of the bar stood meekly right behind him. "We're leaving. Curt is too far in the cups. I just wanted to tell you I loved listening to your story and would love to hear the end some time."

Daniel just nodded as the woman smiled sadly and went to escort her inebriated partner through the door. The few remaining college kids were paying their tabs. I hadn't realized how late it was. Within minutes, we were alone: just me, Brandee, and Daniel.

"You gonna kick us out?" I asked her.

Brandee shrugged. "I'll lock up when I want to."

"Good. I'm gonna hit the head," I said, pushing myself away from the bar.

On my way back to my stool, I heard them discussing the Princess's weapon.

"Things were dark, but at least there was now a chance," Daniel said.

"Shaggy Dog didn't think so. He's giving up," I said as I sat on my stool.

Brandee's eyes grew large, and her hands stopped making a drink mid-pour. Daniel's next words were barely louder than a whisper. "What did you say?"

Brandee attempted to shush me with her hands, but I continued, "Shaggy Dog's feeling sorry for himself. He got mad over some spilled fruit earlier, and now he's being a jerk. Pitiful, really."

I saw Daniel's eyes come alive. There was no far-off gaze, and he seemed no longer trapped in a memory. Instead, his eyes became twin furnaces barely containing a fire within that promised to consume anything it touched. The hair on the back of my neck stood up, and I thought the big, bearded man was going to crush me.

Brandee came to my rescue by slapping my tab forcefully on the bar. "Sir, Jake here is paying your tab tonight," she said sternly.

Daniel didn't seem to hear her. His eyes remained focused on me, and I pulled back as he said, "You don't have a clue."

He stood and turned away. Without looking back, he crashed through the front door, leaving us behind. I kept my gaze on the dregs at the bottom of my glass, too fearful to meet Brandee's eyes. Just as my heart had resumed a semblance of its normal rhythm, I heard the front door open again. Daniel filled the doorway.

He said calmly, "I have to finish this story."

All I could see were his eyes. The fire was under control, but it was still there, smoldering.

He settled heavily into his seat and said, "I have to finish it. Not for you or you..." He pointed at me then Brandee as he continued, "Not even for me. I have to tell the end for *her*, because I don't think I'll ever be able to tell this story again. And it deserves to be told. She deserves to have it heard."

"Alright, then tell it, and I'll keep my flapper shut," I said.

Daniel nodded.

"Brandee, I know it's late, but can I get one more drink?" I asked.

"It's not late. It's early," she said absently, staring at Daniel. "But sure. Hell, I'll have one too."

Daniel waited on Brandee to finish pouring our drinks, then he looked from her to me slowly. Quietly, he said, "Y'all ready? We have a couple more people to meet before the end, and the end is near. I won't stop this time 'til it's over."

CHAPTER 9

"Where are they?" Shaggy Dog asked for the seventh time. It was well after midnight, but Jaxson and the Princess had still not arrived. Zero just rolled his eyes and tried to go back to sleep. It had been a long day, and he was not accustomed to carrying squirming cargo even on short flights.

"Shouldn't they be here by now?" asked Shaggy Dog.

At that very moment, the Princess and Jaxson strolled out of the woods, talking and laughing. Just as he was about to admonish them for making him worry, Shaggy Dog paused. The Princess was smiling, *really* smiling. How long had it been since she had looked that happy? Shaggy Dog's tail started its rhythmic swishing and a small smile crept onto his own face.

"Everything good?" he asked.

"Sorry we're so late," giggled the Princess. "Jaxson wanted to show me—"

"Hey!" exclaimed Jaxson. "That's our secret."

The Princess looked at him, and they both burst out laughing again. The smile on Shaggy Dog's face grew. It was so good to hear her laugh.

"Let's just say Jaxson thought he was going to show me how to catch fireflies," said the Princess, "but he doesn't know what fireflies look like."

The Princess and Jaxson could barely breathe as Jaxson said, "But the fairy was shocked when I snagged her from that bush instead."

"I think you were just as shocked," said the Princess. "You squealed like a startled piglet!"

Even Zero chuckled as Jaxson started making pig noises and flailing his arms around in mock surprise.

"Anyway, we made it," said the Princess after catching her breath. "Oh! How was flying with Zero?"

Shaggy Dog's smile faltered. "I prefer the horse."

The whole group had another good laugh at Shaggy Dog's expense.

"Let's have a look at that paw," said Jaxson, getting serious.

"It's not much to look at. I think it's broken," said Shaggy Dog.

Jaxson pulled the lantern close as he examined Shaggy Dog's paw gingerly. Each time Jaxson applied pressure, Shaggy Dog flinched. Finally, Jaxson stated, "It feels like a clean break, which is lucky for you, friend."

"Doesn't feel too lucky," muttered Shaggy Dog.

Jaxson motioned for Zero to come over. As the dragon placed his head next to Shaggy Dog's side, Jaxson said, "I think we can help. Try to hold still."

Before Shaggy Dog could object, Jaxson grasped his paw gently. All his breath escaped Shaggy Dog's lungs as he felt a jolt. Then a tingling sensation moved from Zero through him, to Jaxson, and back. Finally, Jaxson released his paw and hung his head. Sweat dripped from his brow, and his chest heaved.

"That's all I can do," he said without looking up.

Shaggy Dog tested his paw, and it still hurt. However, he found that it could take his weight, and the pain was subsiding by the second.

"Amazing!" said the Princess.

"Yes, it is. What did you do?" asked a wide-eyed Shaggy

Dog. Jaxson picked his head up to look at Shaggy Dog and then the Princess.

"It's hard to explain," replied Jaxson. "I don't fully understand it myself, but Zero and I can fix some things. That's all I know."

"Like magic?" she asked.

"If you want to call it that. It's just something we can do. Zero doesn't understand it either. It just feels natural somehow," Jaxson said with a yawn.

The Princess looked at Shaggy Dog expectantly.

"Is there anything you could do about a curse?" asked Shaggy Dog.

Jaxson looked the Princess in the eye. "Zero and I can fix injuries like cuts and bruises. Shaggy Dog's broken paw is the most extreme thing we have ever helped heal. I don't think we could tackle an illness or a curse. Might cause more harm than good."

He led them into his modest house and showed them a bedroom near its rear. They said their goodnights quickly, and Shaggy Dog was asleep before Jaxson closed the door. The Princess waited until she was sure Shaggy Dog wouldn't stir, and then she reached into her pouch and pulled out a vial of glowing blue liquid that the Helm urged her to grab. It was bitter and made her gag, but she was taking three a day nonetheless. She was afraid it would be four tomorrow. The curse brought fatigue and pain that only the vials were able to hold off. Every day was getting harder.

Bitterly cold wind blew in ominous clouds the next day. Jaxson predicted a snowstorm soon, but it was too early for full winter. Shaggy Dog's paw, although greatly improved, was not ready for travel, so the Princess was pleased when Jaxson told them to stay as long as they liked. That night, after a full meal of salted horse, Jaxson told his story. He was sixteen summers old and had been on his own for two summers. His father departed their valley to locate and help dismantle an evil organization bent on destroying all dragons. The Demon Lizard Death Cult, DLDC as they were known, had almost captured Zero as an egg, which is why Jaxson and Zero now lived such an isolated life. Zero hatched when Jaxson was three summers old, and they had been inseparable ever since.

"You have been all alone for two years?" asked Shaggy Dog.

Jaxson shrugged and glanced at Zero. "Yup, just Zero and me."

"Must be hard," replied the Princess.

"It's not all bad. Zero can hunt for food, and during the summer, I catch fish," said Jaxson. "Dragons don't eat as much as you'd think."

"Speaking of your dragon, how did he get his name?" asked a curious Shaggy Dog.

Jaxson laughed. "That's actually a neat story. Come to think about it, I have never told anyone. You see, dragons hatch already knowing their true names. When we connected shortly after he came out of the shell, he told me his name. I was so little I couldn't pronounce it right. 'Zero' was all I could say. The nickname stuck."

"Ahh, that is so sweet," said the Princess. Through the back window, Shaggy Dog saw Zero roll his eyes, and Jaxson made a gagging sound. "And you are one of the only people not to be amazed Shaggy Dog can talk."

"Ha. You recovered pretty quickly from seeing a dragon," commented Jaxson.

"I guess. I have read about dragons and giants and goblins," said the Princess quietly. "Never thought I would meet any of them. I've met them all and more recently."

"I haven't asked yet, but since I told my story..."

The Princess glanced at Shaggy Dog, who gave a slight

nod. She formally introduced herself and told her story. Jaxson listened intently, and Zero started at the mention of the huge troll. Then he tilted his head, looking at the Princess with new respect.

Just as she wrapped up her story, there was a knock at the door.

"Expecting someone?" asked Shaggy Dog. He motioned for the Princess to move away from the door.

Again, a knock sounded.

"Not at all," said Jaxson. He looked out the window to see Zero staring back at him. "Zero never saw anyone coming either. I'm gonna see who it is."

Jaxson opened the door to reveal a beard. There was a man attached to it, but he was mostly just white and gray beard.

"Could I trouble you for shelter from this dismal weather?" asked the old man with the beard as he looked around the room. "Have pity on an old man."

He shuffled inside without waiting for permission. The Princess saw Zero take flight, probably to scout the area. She did not believe any harm could come from allowing an old man shelter from the elements. Shaggy Dog was not so sure. Something was strange about this old man and his crooked walking stick, but Shaggy Dog could not figure out exactly what it was.

The old man sat in the only good chair with a sigh of relief. Jaxson stared at him, convinced that he knew him, or at least that he should.

"Do you happen to have anything to eat?" asked the old man.

Jaxson scrambled to prepare a plate even before he realized he had done it. In between bites, the old man kept the conversation flowing with idle chatter.

In an attempt to learn more about the evasive old man,

Shaggy Dog asked, "And why were you coming from the east?"

"Well, I have business in the east," he replied curtly. "But with all the trouble and unrest, I thought it wise to explore other options."

Shaggy Dog pounced on an opening. "What type of business are you in, sir?"

The old man put aside his empty plate and responded, "Oh, a little of this and that. Right now, I have a mind to search out artifacts of a past age. Good money can be made from the right relics."

There was a twinkle in his eyes and a hint of a smile through his beard.

"There are some ruins to the south that not many people know about. The ones that do give them a wide berth, 'cause they are supposedly haunted," said Jaxson. He was still puzzled over his familiarity with the old man.

"South, you say? That's good, with the north in open rebellion against King Dranger and his puppets, the DLDC. I have no desire to go north without great reason," said the old man.

Jaxson's head jerked up, and he stared at the old man intently.

"Isn't that the group you were talking about earlier?" asked the Princess, addressing Jaxson.

"It is," Jaxson replied. To the old man, he said, "What do you know of them?"

The old man knew a tremendous amount, not just about the DLDC but about everything. He also seemed to like the sound of his own voice. He talked and talked. When asked a question, his answer would fork off in different directions three times. Hours passed, though it seemed like only moments to Jaxson.

When the old man laughed, Jaxson exclaimed, "It's you!

You were there when Dad escaped with Zero as an egg. You used to come by all the time... Dreknoxious! Right?"

"Finally. At your service, Jaxson. Now, where is that pesky dragon of yours?" said the old man cheerfully.

"He scouted the area for a while after you showed up. You know, to see if you were alone. He's out back now," said Jaxson, smiling.

"Is your father about?" asked Dreknoxious.

Jaxson's smile slipped. "No. He left to go find the DLDC years ago. He never came back."

Dreknoxious placed a wrinkled hand on his shoulder and squeezed. "Then we shall just have to go to him," he said, winking.

"Really? Alright – we can leave at first light!" said Jaxson.

"Hold now, boy. This weather will keep us here for at least a day or two," said Dreknoxious. "Besides, our dog friend over there needs to let that paw finish healing."

Shaggy Dog, who had been snoozing, looked up and said, "We don't even know where we are going yet."

"He's right," said the Princess. "Our quest is sort of over, or at least the part we were told about. But it feels like it is just beginning."

Dreknoxious smiled. "Some quests never end, or a new one blends with the old in an unbroken river, forever moving towards its end. And some are over before they start. I happen to know a little something about your quest thus far. I ran into the most bubbly witch yesterday, and she told an amazing tale of a Princess and her companion, one Shaggy Dog. That would be you two, correct?"

The Princess nodded, not really surprised that Dreknoxious already knew about her quest. He seemed to know everything.

"You must fill in the details for me," insisted Dreknoxious.

The Princess told her story again. She felt she was getting quite good at reciting it, out of sheer repetition.

After she had concluded, Dreknoxious said, "Remarkable. You have done so well under such adverse circumstances." Then, quietly, so that only she could hear, he added, "And you hide the pain effectively. But not for much longer, I am afraid. Be prepared. I may have an idea of what you should do next. I will sleep on it, and we can discuss it in the morning."

The Princess bowed her head in respect. "Thank you, sir."

By the next morning, the weather had worsened. The temperature plummeted, and midday brought freezing rain. The Princess asked if snow was making those strange noises she could hear. It turned out it was hail pelting upon the roof. Zero had retreated up the valley to a large cave overlooking the house to stay dry.

Shaggy Dog's paw was almost back to normal. For the most part, the Princess and Jaxson sat with Dreknoxious, firing question after question at him. The Princess wanted to hear about every magical creature in the world. Jaxson sought information and advice about how to take down the DLDC and hopefully find his dad along the way. For his part, Dreknoxious answered all their enquiries patiently, even expanding on many topics, which only fueled the fire for more questions. As the afternoon wore on, the Princess found herself alone with Dreknoxious. Shaggy Dog was snoozing, and Jaxson had taken off to check on Zero while the rain was light.

"Princess, I wish I could break the curse for you, but I cannot," said Dreknoxious. "I believe that in this whole world, only you have that power."

"I know. I think I have always known I would have to face the Goat Head Sorcerer one on one," replied the Princess.

Dreknoxious nodded and sat up straight. "I do think our paths could be intertwined for a time, however."

The Princess looked back without comment.

"I am of the belief your next move should be to travel to the Oracle," said Dreknoxious. The Princess's eyes grew wide. "She is quite real and nothing like the ridiculous stories told about her. Most importantly, I think she can help you with a plan of attack."

"Do you know where she can be found?"

Dreknoxious laughed. "Just like that, huh?" Shaking his head softly, he continued, "I think I might. Last time I saw her, she was up north near Bent Pine."

The Princess's shoulders sagged, and her eyes grew misty. "That is ever farther from home."

"It is. But during a quest, one must go wherever it leads," said Dreknoxious. "Besides, you may get to meet another elf or even see the steam drakes."

"Not that I am ungrateful for all the great friends I have made, as truly I am. I just hurt, and I am so tired," said the Princess.

Jaxson walked back in, soaked to the bone. The Princess went to help him out of his cloak.

Under his breath, Dreknoxious mumbled, "It's almost over now, sweet Princess."

The following day was spent preparing to depart. The Princess cleaned every inch of her armor and suggested Shaggy Dog take a bath. Everyone laughed, Shaggy Dog loudest of all. Jaxson packed two large bags containing all the food and essentials from the house. He produced a clever harness designed to be strapped around Zero's back. Jaxson planned on walking to try and get more information out of Dreknoxious. After a long day's work, the group felt they were ready to depart at first light the following day. At dusk, Shaggy Dog glanced out the window to see Dreknoxious standing next to the biggest bear he had ever seen. Dreknoxious was listening to it intently. Suddenly, he threw his hands in the air and spoke very quickly to the bear. Shaggy Dog was too far away to hear what was said, but it was plain that the old man was agitated. Moments later, Dreknoxious entered the house and settled at the head of the table.

"Is it time to eat?" he asked with a smile.

"Just leave some for breakfast in the morning," said Jaxson. "I don't want to dig in the bags before the sun has even come up."

Shaggy Dog approached the full table and said, "Haven't seen much game in this valley."

"I imagine the sheep and deer can smell Zero," said Jaxson.

"Oh. I was thinking there might be bears or something else," said Shaggy Dog, glancing at Dreknoxious. Dreknoxious did not flinch; he just continued shoving dried meat into his mouth.

"I've never seen one this far up," said Jaxson, his mouth full of winter berries.

Dreknoxious finally spoke up. "Have you decided where you are going, Princess?"

The Princess cast a glance towards Shaggy Dog, then down at the table. "I haven't discussed it with Shaggy Dog yet, but I think we are going north to seek out the Oracle."

Shaggy Dog's mouth hung open, but before he could respond, Jaxson said, "Me and Zero are going north. We can travel together. Dreknoxious, you should come too. Safety in numbers, you know?"

The Princess observed Dreknoxious's sly smile, despite it being partially hidden by his long beard. "I think that is a wonderful idea. I would love to travel with you two young people for a while, if I can keep up that is."

CHAPTER 10

Goosebumps invaded the Princess's arms as she stepped into the crisp, sunny morning. The rain and wind had gone, leaving a bluebird sky and chilly air. She watched Zero circle above, the harness holding all of their supplies. She approached Shaggy Dog and Jaxson as she checked that her new sword was secure in the sheath. It was so light that sometimes she forgot it was even there. Shaggy Dog thanked Jaxson again for setting his paw right, but fell silent as Dreknoxious exited the house. The old man walked over to them with the assistance of his gnarled staff. With his free hand, he offered a tall glass to Jaxson.

"Take one pull from this and pass it on," Dreknoxious said.

Jaxson tipped the cup back, then said, "That's nice. What is it?"

The Princess took the cup and immediately smelled spring. As she took a gulp, she thought of flowers and sunshine chasing away a chill. "That is lovely."

Dreknoxious took the cup and a swig. Then he placed it on the ground for Shaggy Dog. "Just an elixir I worked up this morning. It will provide strength and endurance. The side benefit is the taste," he said, winking at the Princess.

Shaggy Dog circled the cup. The smell of wild flowers and the soil after a spring rain filled his nostrils. He circled it again and glanced at Drekoxious out of the corner of his eye. The Princess and Jaxson smiled down at him. Finally, he drank the remainder of the elixir. Immediately his tail swished, and he felt eager to start down the trail.

Jaxson led them out of the valley and up the next mountain. The elixir was everything Dreknoxious said it would be. By midday, the group had traveled farther than Jaxson thought they would all day. When the sun slid level to the horizon, Shaggy Dog said, "Let's make camp. Five more days like that, we'll be at Bent Pine sipping something refreshing."

Zero landed nearby, and they set up camp in short order. As Dreknoxious stirred the beans, he asked Jaxson, "Your father leave any indication of his plans?"

Jaxson stared at the fire. "No. He didn't tell me much at all."

Dreknoxious scooped steaming beans onto the platters, and the Princess passed them out. "I can only conceive two probable scenarios that would keep him absent for so long," said Dreknoxious in between bites. "One is that he located the DLDC and successfully infiltrated the organization. Now, he is waiting from within their own ranks to bring them down."

Still, Jaxson stared at the fire. "And the other?"

"Not something that is pleasant to discuss," said Dreknoxious. "Let's talk about something else, something fun. Like magic."

Jaxson and the Princess shared glances. As Jaxson opened his mouth, the Princess said, "I wish someone could magic this curse out of me."

Dreknoxious sighed deeply, and he looked the Princess in the eye. "As far as I know, there is no magic that can counter the Goat Head Sorcerer's curse in one fell swoop. On this world, anyway."

Shaggy Dog rolled his eyes. "So, you know everything there is to know about magic, old man?"

A smile crept onto Dreknoxious's face. "Not at all. Certainly not. Everything... well, that is a lot. The basics of magic, though, certainly."

The Princess and Jaxson begged Dreknoxious to tell them all that he knew. Dreknoxious was still for long moments, then said, "To discuss magic, first we must discuss magic's source. The common understanding is that magic is fueled by the fabric of realms. Stay with me, now. The spirit realm, the physical realm and the abio – the realm in between – are woven together by magical power. A user of magic is really nothing more than a conduit of that power. The elves can wield the magic of both the physical and the spiritual realm. Wizards can use both as well, but rely heavily on the physical realm. Dark magic is strictly from the spirit realm, witch magic strictly from the physical. And finally, there are dragonwizards – or at least, there were in a past age – that funnel the energy of the abio as their source of magic."

Jaxson shook his head quickly at the Princess. Then he said, "Me and Zero can talk to each other in our thoughts. Does that count?"

"Not really. That connection, although rare, is more common than a dragonwizard," said Dreknoxious. "Dragonwizards are the most powerful wielders of magic, but they flew too high and almost used too much power for the physical world to withstand. It was them that brought about the Blank Years, and their own destruction."

"Being a dragonwizard sounds complicated," said Jaxson. "Think I'll just stick with my bow."

"It's getting late, Princess," said Shaggy Dog. "We should get some sleep."

The next morning, the group broke camp before the sun crested the mountains and set off downhill. The Princess still felt strong from the elixir she drank the previous day and encouraged by the distance they had already travelled.

As they wrapped up their midday meal, Shaggy Dog

pointed out that they had seen no signs of the enemy, and yet almost immediately there came a crashing sound from a small stand of spruce trees below them. The Princess pulled out her sword, and Jaxson nocked an arrow in his bow. Out of the trees stepped a giant bear, moving briskly towards them. Shaggy Dog was sure it was the bear Dreknoxious had talked to at the house.

"Hold your arrow, Jaxson," said Dreknoxious. "Raze is a friend."

Dreknoxious separated himself from the group to meet the bear. Again, Shaggy Dog could not understand the words he spoke, but it was plain that Dreknoxious was agitated by what the bear told him.

When he returned to the group, he spoke quickly. "Princess, stay the course. Seek out the Oracle near Bent Pine. Jaxson, I am going to ask you to accompany her until I return. With luck, I will beat you all there."

"Where are you going?" asked Jaxson.

Dreknoxious, already walking west, said over his shoulder, "Things are escalating quickly. I have urgent business to the west. Stay the course and do not waver!"

He then disappeared into the trees, following the bear.

"What was that about?" asked the Princess.

"I have no idea, but the same bear was at the house talking with Dreknoxious a few days back," said Shaggy Dog. "I'm starting to think there is more to this old man than I first assumed."

"He disappeared awful quick," said Jaxson as he started walking in the direction Dreknoxious had taken. He followed his tracks several steps past the first tree, but then the trail was gone like Drekoxious had simply vanished. *Disappeared is right*, thought Jaxson as he walked back to the Princess and Shaggy Dog.

Even with the elixir wearing off, the group made good

time after coming off the mountain. The ground was flat and only with sparse patches of trees.

Two days of travel later, Zero let Jaxson know there was movement in the trees to the west. Whatever it was, it was traveling parallel to them. Each time Zero tried to get a closer look, it would disappear into the thicker trees.

Close to dusk the same day, Shaggy Dog heard the cawing of the Ravens of Despair. Zero launched into the air and drove them back. The group was on high alert that night, so it was little surprise when, shortly before daylight, they heard wolves howling behind them. Shaggy Dog noted how familiar it felt to be harassed by the ravens and to hear the wolves calling to each other. The wolves did not get any closer, but going back to sleep was not an option. After daybreak, the Princess could see that the trees were thinning ahead. Jaxson told the group that Zero could see groups of goblins and large cats with riders in the distance. Still, they were closer to Bent Pine and the Oracle.

"Should only be half a day out of Bent Pine now," said Shaggy Dog at their midday meal. "Maybe we should cut today's travel short."

"Why? We are so close!" said the Princess.

"Yeah, that seems crazy," added Jaxson.

"Just don't think it wise to barrel into a place we aren't familiar with, at dusk," Shaggy Dog said. "We don't know what's waiting for us."

The Princess opened her mouth to protest, but then stopped to listen. Battle horns blared to the west. A few seconds later, a reply echoed from the north.

"Princess, Zero says someone is approaching from the south," said Jaxson, turning to look in that direction.

The Princess loosened her sword in its sheath.

"Who is it?" asked Shaggy Dog.

"He doesn't know, but he says they are struggling past the

wolves to get to us," said Jaxson.

Finally, the Princess saw the Benevolent Witch laboring on their trail, huffing and puffing. The Benevolent Witch was almost on top of them before she noticed.

"Oh my!" she exclaimed between ragged breaths. "Finally… caught you."

The Princess smiled and indicated Jaxson. "Hello! This is —"

"No time, Princess, no time," said the Benevolent Witch. She stood up straight. "Dreknoxious sent me to find you."

"Dreknoxious? Where is he? Is he coming back? When?" asked Jaxson rapidly.

The Benevolent Witch's eyes fluttered as she responded, "Yes, yes of course. I am just to deliver a message before he arrives."

She hesitated, looking from Jaxson to the Princess to Shaggy Dog, then back to the Princess.

"Well?" said Shaggy Dog to the Benevolent Witch. "Deliver it, then. We need to decide if we are continuing on or camping here."

The Benevolent Witch's body tensed but her face went slack. She looked at the Princess and said, "The armies of the Goat Head Sorcerer are amassed against you, just a few hours walk from here. Seeking out the Oracle is no longer an option."

"What are we going to do?" asked the Princess, addressing no one in particular.

"There is a simple solution. We turn around and go south. Maybe even home," said Shaggy Dog.

"Zero says we are loosely surrounded. But if we hurry, we can slip through," said Jaxson.

The Benevolent Witch sighed and offered a weak smile. "That may be for the best."

"Jaxson, tell Zero to scout for the best route past them.

Then he needs to fly north a ways," said Shaggy Dog. "The enemy will see him and think we're still moving north."

"Wait." The Princess fiddled with her sword's handle as she bit her lower lip.

After long moments, Shaggy Dog said, "Princess, we need to hurry."

"Wait," she said again, pulling out the glass sword. She thought back to all that had happened, from the initial curse to Houstonia to meeting friends and fighting goblins. She thought about finding her sword and meeting a dragon, Zero. "Faith," she muttered. Then more loudly, "Stay the course."

"Princess, we need to escape!" roared Shaggy Dog.

"Zero says we need to leave now," said Jaxson.

"Jaxson, you and Zero should go. Benevolent Witch, you too. Shaggy Dog, I won't insult you by asking you to leave, but I am moving onward," said the Princess. "I am staying the course."

"Of course I am staying with you," said Shaggy Dog gruffly.

"We are too," said Jaxson.

Tears filled the Benevolent Witch's eyes as she nodded.

"Shaggy Dog, find us a place to rest," said the Princess. "Tomorrow, we will stay the course with faith."

The group stumbled through a clump of trees only to encounter a lively campsite. Seven or eight men were dancing to a lute and a stew simmered over the fire. Immediately, Shaggy Dog growled and placed himself in front of the Princess. One of the men stepped forward and greeted them. The Princess could not stifle a smile as she exclaimed "Reserio! Well met. What are you doing here?"

"Obviously, I am dancing a jig," he said. "Come, join us."

The Princess danced and sang. Jaxson hummed along to some of the more popular tunes. Even Shaggy Dog seemed to enjoy himself, though mostly when he was lapping up the delicious stew. Everyone smiled and danced and ate and laughed. No one wanted the evening to end. Eventually, the revelry faded slowly, as full stomachs led to heavy eyelids. The Princess leaned on Shaggy Dog, and Zero curled around Jaxson. All was perfectly quiet.

"Princess, do you know someone named Sasha?" asked Jaxson suddenly.

"I do," replied the Princess. "Surely I told you about the elf we met. Why do you ask?"

"Well, Zero says she is about to walk into our camp. She just told him so," said Jaxson. "Evidently, she can talk to dragons too."

"Is she? When?" asked the Princess in excitement, standing up.

"Right now," came a voice from the edge of the campfire's ring of light. Sasha and seven other elves stepped into the camp.

"Oh! Sasha! I never thought I'd see you again!" exclaimed the Princess.

Reserio ambled over to see what all the excitement was about.

"How did you find us? Why were you even looking?" asked the Princess as she studied the other elves standing alongside Sasha.

Sasha smiled and said, "Dreknoxious told us what you are up against. I'm not prepared to let you face that alone. I am sad to report that Dane is probably on the other side, though."

"Oh, I was hoping he was with you," said Shaggy Dog. "But it's great to see you nonetheless."

Reserio cleared his throat. "Dreknoxious came to Houstonia and informed us of your situation as well. He even helped us get here."

"And when did he do all this?" asked the Princess.

Reserio and Sasha exchanged glances.

Sasha said, "He appeared to me in a dream four nights ago."

Reserio added, "He was in Houstonia four days ago."

The Princess looked back and forth between them. Appeared in her dream? In Houstonia four days ago? Impossible. Finally, she asked, "Who is he? Really, I mean."

Sasha thought for a moment, then said, "It is not my place to tell anyone."

Jaxson spoke up, "He's not just an eccentric old man, is he?"

Reserio and Sasha both laughed.

"Definitely old, but he is way more than a man. With him on our side, we may defeat the Goat Head Sorcerer yet," answered Reserio.

The Princess yawned despite all the excitement. "I'm getting sleepy," she announced.

"We all should rest," said Reserio. "But first, could I offer a prayer?"

"Of course," replied the Princess.

Reserio moved close to the fire and lifted his left hand and closed his eyes. The only sound was the crackling of the logs. He bowed his head and prayed aloud:

"Let us laugh until we cannot.

Let us love even when we cannot.

Let us be strong until we cannot.

Let us have faith even when we cannot.

Gods, we beseech you,

Let us LIVE until we cannot."

"Well said, witch," Shaggy Dog mumbled. "Well said."

The next morning came quickly. The Princess saw the soft glow above the mountains as she approached the sitting Shaggy Dog. In silence, they watched the sun rise into the sky. Peace before the frenzy.

"I just have to ask, Princess," said Shaggy Dog, "are you sure this is the time to make your stand?"

The Princess uttered a single word: "Yes."

Shaggy Dog stood and faced her. "Stay the course. And I'll be with you. Let's go defeat a sorcerer."

"Let's go," said the Princess with a smile. She looked again at the rising sun and saw a twinkle flash by. "Hey! That looked like a fairy. I miss Jazzi."

Shaggy Dog chuckled. "I liked that jittery little fairy."

Then he too saw a flash, and then another. Soon there were flashes all around them. Jazzi landed lightly on Shaggy Dog's snout and curtsied.

"Well, I'll be," said Shaggy Dog. Jazzi's hands moved around very fast, then she flew to the Princess. Gently, she kissed her cheek and buzzed off to join the other fairies.

"She and her whole family have been here all night," said Shaggy Dog. "The Ravens of Despair tried to sneak into camp six times, but the fairies fended them off. Jazzi says she'll meet us on the field."

"She looks so happy to be back with her family," said the Princess.

A battle horn blared to the east. It was answered from the north by three different horns.

"Time to see what we're up against," said the Princess as she turned back to the camp.

Minutes later, the Princess and Shaggy Dog were on the march. Sasha and the other elves scouted ahead. The Princess saw glimpses of the fairies darting in and out of the trees, and Jaxson on Zero's back circled above. The Benevolent Witch, Reserio, and the witches of Houstonia followed, providing a rear guard. They marched towards the horns. They marched to danger and to the Goat Head Sorcerer.

Ravens of Despair circled above and to the left. A

multitude of steam drakes, each about twice the size of an eagle with a serpentine body and thin wings, circled above and to the right. Directly across the field, at the base of a gentle hill, stood a wall of goblins and trolls. gathered behind them were the Snake Oil Witches and the giants. Another wall of goblins separated the lizard knights on their feline mounts from the rest of the army.

On top of the hill, standing tall and still, the Goat Head Sorcerer surveyed his army. To his left, wolves patrolled the mountain passes. He would not allow surprises nor escape from the battle.

The Princess felt despair bloom in her chest. She had no idea what she had been expecting, but this many against her was certainly not it. Shaggy Dog glanced at her, then back at the field.

The group came to a halt with the witches of Houstonia and the elves in front. Jaxson and Zero patrolled the sky above. Jazzi and her family of fairies remained to the left. The Benevolent Witch stood beside the Princess with her mouth hanging open.

"Princess, I feel sorry for them," Shaggy Dog said, indicating the enemy army.

The Princess smirked. "And why is that?"

"They didn't bring any reinforcements," said Shaggy Dog. "They are in a heap of trouble."

The Princess laughed and loosened her sword in the scabbard.

She jumped when a battle horn sounded directly behind them. Before anyone could react, two platoons of mounted knights streamed out of the forest, led by Sergeant Rivers. They moved to the front of the line and assembled alongside the others. The Queen came out next to stand beside the Princess. She bowed her head slightly, and the Princess gave a formal bow in return. Tears streamed down the Princess's face as she scanned all around, looking for Dreknoxious. He was nowhere to be found.

This was her army, outnumbered and outmatched, but all were willing to battle for her.

Battle horns blared from the enemy side. The first line of goblins and trolls parted to allow the giants to move forward. The Princess's heart sank to her toes. On the front lines stood Dane, carrying a menacing cudgel. A giant in the middle started beating a drum, and the group advanced slowly. As the drumming increased, the giants gained speed. The ground shook, and the Princess's armor rattled.

A battle cry from Dane split the air, and suddenly the giants stopped halfway between the opposing forces. Dane turned to face his brethren. More than half the giants started walking off the field. The remainder followed Dane slowly to the line of the Queen's knights.

"Shagg Doog!" thundered Dane. "Dane help Princess!"

Shaggy Dog's tail swished violently side to side as he weaved to the front lines. The Princess smiled at the Benevolent Witch's puzzled expression.

"He's a friend," the Princess said.

"I see," the Benevolent Witch replied.

They both watched as Shaggy Dog issued commands to the knights, then went out to greet Dane. The giants turned in the opposite direction, and as one bellowed a challenge at the armies of the Goat Head Sorcerer.

The sorcerer laughed loudly. Then, with a flick of his hand, the first wave of goblins and trolls attacked.

The Ravens of Despair swooped towards the Princess's army, and the Snake Oil Witches readied glass jars filled with burning liquid to hurl. The Princess closed her eyes and whispered Reserio's prayer from the previous night. When she opened her eyes again, she pulled the glass sword from its scabbard.

Dane and the giants sprang towards the advancing horde. Jazzi and the fairies flew to intercept the ravens. Just before the clash, the Snake Oil Witches threw the evil jars of liquid fire towards the giants. Reserio and the witches of Houstonia were ready. Before the jars could shatter against the giants, the witches propelled them towards the goblins using magic. Reserio gave the Princess and Shaggy Dog a wink. The jars exploded, sending foul liquid into the lines of goblins. Many fell screeching, and then the giants were among them. Dane and his brethren were behemoths on the battlefield, and not a single goblin nor troll within the first wave survived. The giants pulled back, waiting for the next attack as Jazzi and the fairies chased the ravens into the mountains.

The Princess's confidence swelled. The enemy's armies had taken grave losses, and yet all of her friends remained uninjured. She watched as the Snake Oil Witches scrambled to get behind the next line of goblins, then she smiled as she surveyed the field. Her eyes locked onto the Goat Head Sorcerer. He clapped softly, and her smile faltered.

Then the remainder of the goblins and trolls attacked. Dane and the giants, along with the witches of Houstonia, met them in the middle of the field. Jaxson and Zero swooped down to take out a particularly nasty troll. Before they could ascend back to the skies, the steam drakes attacked en masse. There were so many! Jaxson flung arrow after arrow, striking a drake almost every time, but still there were more. Zero took to the sky and circled, but the drakes persisted. Zero's left wing was gashed and blood oozed from a cut on his back leg. Jaxson only had a few arrows left. He put one to his bowstring, pulled it back, and aimed carefully from Zero's back. As soon as he released the string, he knew the arrow was on target.

The second before it struck the heart of the Goat Head Sorcerer, a pulse shot out from his chest. The arrow shattered in midair. Zero struggled to stay in the air after reeling from the pulse, so Jaxson nudged him towards the safety of the mountains.

The strange lizard knights on their big cats joined the fray. Sasha and the elves met them eagerly, but the lizard knights were very fast. The tide was turning in favor of the enemy army.

Shaggy Dog looked at the Princess, and she smiled.

"It's time, little one," he said gently.

"Stay the course," she responded, then raised her sword and shouted a battle cry.

The Princess's army, emboldened by her courage, fought even harder. The Queen's knights helped the elves drive off the lizard knights. The giants and witches of Houstonia attacked the remaining goblins. The Princess, followed closely by Shaggy Dog and the Benevolent Witch, shot into the battle like an arrow. The fighting was intense, but the Princess and Shaggy Dog cut and bit any minion of the vile sorcerer unlucky enough to get close.

Then the Princess heard Reserio yell, "They are on the run! Advance!"

The giants followed Dane and Reserio, pushing the goblins back. The Princess's army was winning.

Then a terrible thunder erupted. The Goat Head Sorcerer descended from the hill and strode towards the Princess. He waved his hand, producing magic to freeze Shaggy Dog and the Benevolent Witch in place. He uttered a spell and a wall of rock shot up between the Princess and her army.

He towered above her and laughed. "All alone now, Princess," he said. "Just you and me."

The Princess looked at her sword, then met his gaze without flinching. "I will stay the course. I will LIVE without fear! I will live until I cannot," she screamed as she leveled her sword and attacked.

Despite his large size, the Goat Head Sorcerer sidestepped the charging Princess quickly and placed a boot on her back. She flew to the ground, hard. As she struggled to rise, the Goat Head Sorcerer tossed aside his serrated sword and laughed.

Again, she charged, taking the fight to him, and again the Goat Head Sorcerer sidestepped and laughed.

"Fight me!" she screamed.

"In good time," replied the Goat Head Sorcerer. He began to circle the Princess slowly. She lashed out with Faith, but the Goat Head Sorcerer danced away. "I thought when Dane the Giant volunteered to lead the charge, he was eager to show his loyalty. I was wrong about that."

The Princess slashed again and said, "You are wrong about many things."

The Goat Head Sorcerer cackled and reached down for his sword. The Helm of Knowledge urged the Princess to quickly search her pack for a vial of Dragon's Fire. Before the sorcerer was upright, the Princess drank it down, and the Goat Head Sorcerer was greeted with flames directly in his face. He stumbled, one arm, his neck and his face smoldering. The Princess fell to one knee, but she was happy to see her gamble had wounded the sorcerer. He bellowed with rage, and the Princess barely had time to stand before she was attacked. She danced back, blocking and avoiding every thrust and jab he threw at her.

"Neat trick with the fire, but it's over, little girl," jeered the Goat Head Sorcerer.

"Not yet!" screamed the Princess and resumed the attack. She feinted low, then struck high, hoping the sorcerer's wounded shoulder would prevent him from blocking.

The sorcerer parried and stepped to one side, bringing his sword around and landing a bone-rattling strike to the center of her chest. The Princess flew fifteen feet to land in a heap of her own armor. The Helm of Knowledge flew off and her breastplate cracked.

The Goat Head Sorcerer stalked towards her.

Suddenly, the Princess heard a victorious cry from her army.

"We will never stop. I will never stop, and they will never stop fighting you," the Princess said from the ground.

The sorcerer looked in the direction of the triumphant cries and started an incantation. When he closed his eyes and raised his arms, the Princess drank another vial and covered him with searing flame. He let out a bloodcurdling scream and released his unused power.

The world grew fuzzy for the Princess as she tumbled away. The next thing she knew, she was staring into the blue, cloudless sky.

The Goat Head Sorcerer approached, steaming and with one horn broken off. He raised his sword for the final blow.

The Princess's defiant scream rang out as she pushed Faith up to block the attack.

The glass sword shattered on impact, so that only the thin, silver core remained. The sorcerer kicked her in the ribs, the damaged breastplate providing inadequate protection. The Princess struggled but could not rise to her feet. Every breath was agony, and her head throbbed.

The Goat Head Sorcerer raised his weapon and said, "I curse you."

A red shadow passed over the battlefield. The Princess smiled as she looked up. The sorcerer hesitated and looked to the sky. A red dragon twice the size of Zero swooped overhead. It turned and came straight towards them.

Dreknoxious was on the back of the dragon, grasping his staff – except the staff was not gnarled wood; instead, it was golden, smooth and straight. The old man jumped from the dragon and landed gracefully beside the Princess. The Goat

Head Sorcerer watched the dragon wheel and fly over the mountains before he turned his attention to the newcomer.

"You have no authority or power here, wizard," hissed the Goat Head Sorcerer.

"The battle is over," said Dreknoxious sternly.

The sorcerer, still smoking from the Dragon's Fire, laughed loudly. "You are right about that. She is mine!"

Dreknoxious placed his shimmering staff into the ground and muttered a series of strange words. Then he looked at the Goat Head Sorcerer and said, "You are finished here today."

There was a soft click, and then the Goat Head Sorcerer was gone.

The wall separating the Princess from the army fell away. The Benevolent Witch and Shaggy Dog, freed from the freezing spell, ran to the Princess's side. Dreknoxious lowered his head and mumbled to himself, and then his golden staff changed back into the twisted, old wooden walking stick as he shuffled over to the Princess.

"Is she alright?" asked a panicked Shaggy Dog.

"She is still breathing," said the Benevolent Witch. "Beyond that, I am unsure."

The Queen hurried over and asked what had happened. Dane and Reserio approached, followed quickly by Sasha and Jazzi.

"Give her some room," said Dreknoxious. "Go and tend to your wounded. Benevolent Witch, if you please?"

"Yes, right away," she said. She pulled her wand from inside her traveling cloak and waved it.

A large tent materialized around them. Once her broken armor was removed, they placed the Princess on a comfortable pallet. Reserio found the Helm of Knowledge, brought it to the tent, and laid it at her feet beside the remnants of Faith and the shattered Armor of Love.

The Princess breathed softly, surrounded by Shaggy Dog, the Benevolent Witch, Dreknoxious, and the Queen. Her eyes fluttered open. Shaggy Dog was at her side in an instant. Tears spilled from his eyes as he licked the dirt and blood off the Princess's face.

"I thought I had lost you," he whispered.

"Not yet," said the Princess weakly.

"Just rest, little one," said Shaggy Dog.

"I'm not sure rest will help," she said.

"Here, drink some water," offered the Benevolent Witch. "Slowly now. Do you feel up to eating something?"

The Princess shook her head. Dreknoxious came forward and placed a hand on the Princess's forehead. The interior of the tent was eerily still.

The Princess looked into the eyes of the old man that was more than a man and muttered, "Thank you."

Then, loud enough for everyone to hear, she said, "Thank you all."

"You hurt him, Princess. You hurt him bad," said Shaggy Dog. The Princess only nodded, so he continued, "I think we should press him while he is injured. Not this second, of course, but very soon. We need to capitalize on this victory."

"Hush now, you silly dog," said the Benevolent Witch. "The Princess is severely injured. We should seek out the healers of Ranah. Let's get her strong again before we thrust her so quickly into another battle."

"The time to rest has escaped us. We have come too far and sacrificed too much. She has sacrificed too much to stop now," screamed Shaggy Dog.

"We can't go on right now," said the Benevolent Witch loudly. "She needs to rest!"

Shaggy Dog's eyes were on fire as he stared at the Benevolent Witch. "I have been with her the entire way. She is stronger than anyone will ever know."

The two bickered back and forth for long minutes, neither conceding to the other. Dreknoxious was about to intervene when the Princess cleared her throat softly. All eyes turned to her as she said, "I'm not sure what is best. But I don't know that I can fight anymore."

Shaggy Dog wilted and the hardness in his eyes evaporated. "Oh, little one."

"I am so sorry," whispered the Princess.

"Don't apologize to me or anyone else, not ever. You have nothing to be sorry for," he said.

Just beyond the foot of the pallet, near the shattered sword, a shaft of light appeared. The Princess was the only one that did not shield her eyes against its brilliance. From inside the light, music flowed as a form appeared. Out stepped a little man the Princess recognized immediately.

"Peddler? I have even less to trade this time," she said.

"I have played many parts before, and you have seen me as a peddler. Not tonight, though," said Mikaela as he spread a pair of angelic wings wide.

The Princess's eyes darted to Dreknoxious as she said, "No one is who they portray themselves to be lately."

The old man had the awareness to appear abashed, lowering his head in acknowledgement. The Queen and the Benevolent Witch each bent a knee and lowered their heads as well.

"Appearances can be deceiving," said Mikaela with a smile. "I think we need a moment."

He snapped his fingers, and the world around them froze. *This is different than the Goat Head Sorcerer's freezing spell*, thought the Princess. *This is more.* She studied her friends for a long time before adjusting her head on the pillow to focus on the angel.

"I know why you are here, and I am so relieved," she said quietly. When Mikaela did not respond, she continued, "But I am also sad. Do I have a choice?"

"There are always choices, child," said Mikaela, spreading his arms wide. The tent filled with sweet voices rising in song, without words. "Some are just easier to make than others."

Everywhere the Princess looked, an angel appeared. There were tall angels and short ones. Some appeared old and others young. They were all beautiful and all were singing the wordless song.

"Do I get to say goodbye?" she asked.

Mikaela thought for a moment. "Certainly. Shaggy Dog is going to take it better than you think; I know you worry for him. He will try to be strong for you. His trial will come later, but I have an idea about that."

He motioned one of the little angels forward. The Princess smiled at the tiny, glowing angel despite her pain. Her smile was matched by the angel.

"Princess, this is Ariana. She has a talent that is quite special. Whenever her family left on this world is in deep sorrow or missing her more than normal, she paints the sky to remind them of the beauty all around them. Would you like her to teach you how?"

Tears streamed down the Princess's face. "I would like that very much."

Mikaela reached down and grasped the handle of Faith. He placed the tip of the silver rod into the ground and pushed the handle down gently. The handle slid down the silver core, and a shining light radiated out from it. Through the light the Princess saw wings unfurling from the silver core. When Mikaela was finished and the light dimmed, a magnificent set of angel's wings had replaced her sword, Faith.

"Are you ready, child?"

"I don't want to hurt anymore. I gave it all I had and kept Faith. I am ready," she replied.

Everyone was moving again. The Princess turned to Shaggy Dog and locked eyes.

"I stayed the course with Faith," she said.

In that moment, Shaggy Dog knew the fight was over. It was not a bolt of new knowledge, but instead an unveiling of the truth that had lingered in his mind for days. He leaned in close and whispered, "You are the bravest person I know, and it is my pleasure to call you my friend. And I will miss you with all my heart, but I don't want you to hurt anymore. You hid it so well, but I knew. Starting in Houstonia, I knew. I saw the pain the curse made you endure, and later the weariness the dragon's fire caused. But I, also, watched you push on anyway. You are so much stronger than me."

"I am strong because of you," she said. "Let me tell you a secret."

Shaggy Dog leaned in even closer as the Princess continued, "There is an angel here with me – you cannot see her, but she is here. Her name is Ariana, and she has the most beautiful smile. She is going to teach me to paint. Isn't that great? Every time you see a brilliant sunset or colorful sunrise with pink and blue, purple, and orange, you will know I am thinking of you."

Shaggy Dog's voice quaked as he whispered to her. "Little one."

The Benevolent Witch and Queen cried softly. Dreknoxious lowered his head.

The Princess looked at Mikaela and said, "I am ready."

At that moment, everyone in the tent with the Princess, and those outside waiting, heard the voices of the angels sing their wordless song. Shaggy Dog laid beside the Princess for a long time even as she was testing her new wings, and he cried. He cried because she felt no more pain, and he cried because he missed her already. He cried.

CHAPTER 11

The wetness on my cheeks spilled onto the bar. I saw the little splash as a tear made contact with the old wood. The only sounds in the room were deep breathing from Daniel and quiet sobs from Brandee. The fire was gone from Daniel's eyes. His face seemed to have smoothed, having become more gentle in the last few minutes. The deep lines and the scowl had disappeared, revealing a much younger man than I had first assumed.

"That's the story I told Josie, my princess, as she lay in the hospital bed," he said into the still bar.

"I'm so sorry," was all I managed to reply.

Daniel rose from his stool and started for the exit. Without a thought, I fell in step, with Brandee right behind me. The sound of waves crashing politely into the sandy beaches greeted us as we stepped into the gloomy, predawn morning. Birds were just beginning to summon the sun from its slumber as we paused and looked out over the sea. I stood beside Daniel as he gazed across the water.

The fiery red sun was rising through clouds of orange and pink. The sky framed it with a backdrop of light purple flowing to midnight blue. I had never seen a more beautiful sight in all my life.

We stood there together, watching the sun rise on a new day, each with our own thoughts. I thought of Janie, and of time wasted, but also of time granted. I decided right then to make a fresh start with her.

After an indiscernible amount of time, Daniel looked at us and then back at the sunrise.

Finally, he said, "My princess turned into one hell of a

good painter."

SELECTIONS FROM TAVERN TALES

THE PYGMY DRAGON'S GAME

There was always a breeze this high up the redwood tree on the northern rim of the valley. Pyd, the small, gold dragon, felt the familiar tingle cascade down his scales as he waited on the morning sun. The valley was suspended between the night world and the day at this magical hour. The sun crested the mountains, and Pyd saw a large eagle take flight. He admired the efficient grace as the eagle, roughly the same size as himself, soared higher on just the power of the wind. He shook his head and stared down into the valley searching for the star tree through the gloom. The sun twinkled off his shiny scales, but there were still minutes before its rays reached Pyd's favorite tree.

His eyes strained and his wings coiled in anticipation. Suddenly, the star tree exploded with different shafts of colored light streaking in all directions. The air whooshed by his face as he raced to the tree then in pursuit of the blue streak of light. He stretched his neck out tight with his legs tucked to his belly as he shot across the valley. Just like every morning, he knew he would not catch the light as it weaved and raced south, but he loved to dance along the wind with the shaft of streaking light for as long as he could. He slowed as the light's gap grew. Hovering above the valley floor, he watched as it disappeared in the distance leaving only the memory of brilliance and the promise of pursuit the next morning. His chest heaved as he gained altitude before circling back to his tree.

Before he could break the canopy to the open air, the scales on his neck shivered. Slowly, he scanned with his peripherals looking for anything out of place. A smile split his face when he noticed it. Twice as long as any pygmy dragon but thin as a ribbon with wiry wings, a steam drake stalked him. This particular one was the color of burnt wood with glowing red eyes. Pyd had no idea why it was so far from the lava vents in the next valley, but he knew it looked hungry. Pyd widened his circle to allow the steam drake to make up some of the distance. As it started its final rush, Pyd laughed and dove straight for the valley floor. This is going to be more fun than chasing light streaks, he thought.

Pyd pulled out of the dive and angled around thick underbrush with the steam drake in close pursuit. Startled forest fairies no larger than a squirrel flitted for cover. He could hear their admonishing squeals for the briefest of moments before he was passed them, moving west towards the lake. As the trees thinned, the steam drake closed quickly. Pyd waited patiently till it lunged forward with a burst of speed. He banked hard to the right, and the steam drake's momentum propelled it well passed Pyd. The gap widened, and Pyd chuckled softly.

The giant waterfall thundered in his ears as he flew behind the curtain of water then began the slow circular flight back up. The ravenous steam drake let out a piercing cry as it flew towards Pyd. The sirens in the lake below and those sunning on the rocks watched the show with glee. Their large tail fins trembled with anticipation. Again, Pyd waited for the moment of impact and juked away. The sirens below clapped and cheered as Pyd took an in-air bow.

Pain shot up his tail from the sharp teeth of the quickly

recovered steam drake. Pyd jerked and twitched freeing his tail after painful moments. Time for this game to end he thought as he weaved in and out of the boulders along the lakeshore. He angled back to the safety of the trees under close pursuit. Once in the trees, he scanned anxiously looking for a particular plant with a large bulb head. The drake closed the gap again and nipped at Pyd's tail. Finally, he spotted the plant trap he was searching for on the forest floor. He shot straight up and spiraled around the large trunk of a redwood tree. The drake backed off and waited for Pyd to level out. Instead, he dove straight for the large bulb of the plant trap.

His claws rested on the warm fleshy plant as Pyd scanned for the drake. The plant started to stir, and the drake streaked at Pyd from above. He dug his claws into the plant and sprung to the side. The drake, committed to its attack, could not stop when the Plant Trap snapped open its large jaws revealing rows of thorny teeth. It was over in a flash, and the plant settled down to digest its meal. Shows how poor its judgement was to hunt a dragon, and then get eaten by a plant, thought Pyd from his perch mere feet away.

He closed his eyes and thought of all the places he had ever been. With a shrug of his wings, he thought of his morning tree, the giant redwood where he waited for the sun to rise each day. A soft click sounded and when Pyd opened his eyes, he was on his branch overlooking the star tree. He wondered what other adventures awaited him before midday.

THE GENERALS' HILLTOP

The stars faded away, and a thin white line appeared to the east. Only the Twin Sisters, the bright morning stars in the south, clung to the sky in defiance of the coming day. The world below turned to shadow out of the inky void. Shapes materialized out of the gloom. From his hilltop view, General Justyne Lauras could see the soft gray of the rolling fields below. To the north, a darker line indicated the dense forest tree line. The looming presence to the south and east was the Dragon Spine mountains. His keen eyes adjusted, but still he felt rather than saw the swift creek that ran the length of his view. There was not a cloud in the sky or a breeze stirring the air. The world was still.

He reached up and tugged the golden chain around his neck. From under his pristine chest plate of silver-edged leather, a medallion pulled free. It was large, about half the size of his hand. Wrought of gold, it was the crest of the royal family, bestowed upon him by the king himself for services rendered to the crown. As it rested on his armor, it felt heavier than usual. A scuffling sound alerted him to another's approach. Without turning around, he said, "I didn't know if you were going to come."

"I didn't know if I was going to catch an arrow in my back on the way up the hill," said the newcomer. "But here I am. Arrowless and all."

General Justyne eyed the man as he approached. He also wore armor, though less ornate and obviously worse for wear. The stubble on his face held a hint of silver among the black. *I imagine if the sun was up, I'd see more than a hint of silver,* thought Justyne. Then he saw the sword on the man's hip and raised an eyebrow.

"I know you said no weapons, but I couldn't come empty handed. Besides, you are armed," said the man indicating to the ornate sword at Justyne's hip.

"I didn't really expect you would honor that request, General Tyrone."

They both looked out over the field as the sun peeked over the horizon. Tyrone glanced at the sword on Justyne's hip. "You want to see it?" asked Justyne.

"Is it really Toland's Blade? I mean, really?"

Justyne just nodded and pulled the sword from the scabbard.

"Hell, yeah, I want to see it then!" exclaimed Tyrone. As he grasped the handle, his arm twitched and his face tensed.

Justyne laughed. "The first time can be rather shocking!"

"Oy, I'd say so. Do you ever get used to it? The shock and the fact it's a two-thousand-year-old blade?"

"I have grown accustomed to the sensation running up to my shoulder, but no, I am still in awe of the age and legacy of the blade," said Justyne, reaching out his hand.

Tyrone hesitated only briefly, then passed the sword back over to its owner.

"I've heard the same rumors as everyone else—" said Tyrone. The sound of the sword clicking back into the scabbard at Justyne's side was deafening. "But how did you come by such a magical weapon?"

Chuckling, Justyne took several steps toward the sunrise. Without turning, he responded over his shoulder. "That is quite the tale. Too long for the time we have…"

"Come now. We have time for this! Keep it short, but you have to tell me."

Justyne turned and saw the same hunger in Tyrone's eyes that he remembered from their youth. "Fine, but I'll be brief."

The general recalled his first time out with men under his command shortly after his first real promotion. They were north of the Laguza in the Bitter Mountains. It was viciously cold during the day, and even worse during the long nights. Goblins had been raiding and burning along the coast for months. His unit was dispatched to locate them and report back.

"Of course, in my infinite wisdom and experience, I led us straight into a trap," said Justyne as he smiled and hung his head.

"Well, you obviously escaped," replied Tyrone.

"Goblins, smart things they are, wanted us alive to trade or something. They took us deep into the mountain, so deep my head felt like there was a huge weight crushing it," said Justyne. "There was no way we would ever be able to remember the twisting and dark route out of the mountain. The goblins knew it too. They threw us in our cell but didn't worry about us much. When we finally made a break for it, we didn't go out the same way we came in."

Justyne peeked at Tyrone out of the corner of his eye. Then with a big sigh, he continued, "I felt the blade calling to me. The goblins didn't even know it was right there the whole time, but I walked straight up a dark path and pushed on the wall in a curve. The wall crumbled, and I walked straight to the blade, which was resting on a stone altar in the middle of the room. We took a staircase on the opposite side of the room and were free in hours. I haven't been separated from the sword since."

"Don't you think my side should have that sword? Magic and all, you know?" asked Tyrone.

Justyne's face became rigid. "That's precisely why I don't want any in the rebellion to have it," he said through clenched teeth. "I know what this blade is capable of. Still, I despise it so."

Tyrone opened his mouth, and then shut it quickly. He pulled his eyes away from Justyne and looked back over the brightening field. The forest to the north was taking shape, and a hint of stream could be seen on the far side of the field.

"Do you remember that old lady who lived up beyond West Ridge?" asked Tyrone.

Justyne cocked his head and arched an eyebrow. "Wha–? Yes, I remember," he said. He shuffled his feet, and a small grin appeared on his face. "We were convinced she was a witch because of the time–"

"Of the time we tried to sneak into her cottage and fell into that mud pit. We were covered in the sticky mess for days. It didn't matter how much we washed; it wouldn't come off!"

Justyne laughed hard. "And stink! It was two moons before the stench finally lifted."

Tyrone was chuckling as he said, "Why were we even up there?"

"If I recall correctly, you wanted to get a potion to make yourself invisible to sneak into the tavern and procure some cider," said Justyne.

Tyrone's cheeks flushed, and he stared at his feet as he mumbled, "I don't think that was the reason..."

Both men laughed again and looked out to the rising sun. Moments stretched into the fading quiet of a beautiful start to the day. Justyne caught himself just before he reached out to place an arm around his oldest friend's shoulders.

Tyrone felt the hesitation, then the withdrawal. "What happened to you? What caused this anger for the creatures you revered at one time?" asked Tyrone quietly.

Anger flashed across Justyne's face. He reached out with both hands and grabbed Tyrone. As Tyrone struggled to get free, his corded necklace slipped out, revealing a wooden dragon's claw medallion. Justyne stared at the wooden claw with his mouth agape. Both men remained locked in place but stopped struggling.

Justyne was the first to break the silence. "You still have that old thing?"

Tyrone pulled free and took a few steps away. With his back turned to Justyne, overlooking the familiar landscape, he said, "I will keep it always."

Both men watched the sun rise above the horizon. Then to the south, a noble one—a giant eagle—soared up into the sky. Its wings barely moved as it rose on the wind to soar at heights that its kind only shared with the dragons.

"You can't win. Take your army and flee," Justyne said quietly.

Tyrone looked at his childhood friend and said, "I know. But your king, that seal you wear around your neck, is evil. He cannot be allowed to continue destroying all that is magic or different!"

"How many do you number? Two thousand? All human? You can't win this fight," replied Justyne.

"Not all human, but certainly not enough. My scouts tell me you have five thousand in your main force, and there are another two you are trying to conceal to the south," said Tyrone.

"Then why are you still here?" asked Justyne.

Tyrone looked at his feet, then back at Justyne. "Maybe I should just show you."

He reached to the dragon's claw medallion and muttered a few words. Justyne could not understand the language, but he got the feeling that Tyrone was calling out. Instantly, a small, golden dragon appeared in the air above Tyrone's head.

Justyne exclaimed and fumbled for his sword as he stammered back. Before his sword was clear, the pygmy dragon landed near Tyrone and nuzzled his leg. Tyrone laughed and held both hands up calmly.

"Hold steady, Justyne," he said. "I want you to meet a friend of mine. This is Pyd. He is a pygmy dragon."

Pyd puffed up his chest and looked Justyne in the eyes. Although only coming up to Tyrone's waist, he was an exact replica of a full-grown dragon of lore. Justyne recovered his cool demeanor but still did not approach.

"I have never seen one this close," said Justyne.

"Most of his kind stay far away from human contact. This fellow here is just a glutton for punishment, so he hangs around with me."

"How? How did you meet it?"

Tyrone lowered his eyes and scowled. Justyne quickly added, "Him. How did you meet him?"

"Shortly after you left home, before the next festival, I took a job with Razka. You know, the trader, remember him?" asked Tyrone.

"Not him so much, but I do recall the wagon and all the strange things it had stuffed within."

"That's him. Well, he paid me to track down leads on odd items, hoping to procure them," replied Tyrone. "Over the next ten years, I traveled all over the kingdom and beyond. The amazing things I saw! I was returning from up north, crossing the Frostline Mountains, when I slipped on a patch of black ice."

Justyne, wide-eyed and clinging to every word, gasped. Tyrone continued, "I'm not sure how far down I tumbled, or how long I was out. But when I came to, there was a pile of winter berries beside me. Someone was watching out for me, it seemed…"

As Tyrone let the story fade, Justyne exclaimed, "Well! Who was it?"

"It was Pyd here," said Tyrone. "He nursed me back to health. We have been friends ever since."

Pyd circled Tyrone quickly and extended his head nestling into his hand.

"He is magnificent. Can he speak? Can you communicate with him?" asked Justyne as he took one step closer.

"We can feel each other's thoughts—impressions really, feelings. I cannot speak to him like dragon riders of old could speak with their dragons, but we get by."

"Unbelievable," Justyne said. He took another step closer and reached out his hand. Pyd looked at Tyrone, who nodded, then took a step forward to allow Justyne to touch the scales on the top of his head.

"Never in my life would I imagine…" said Justyne. Then he cleared his throat and continued, "Amazing as he is, this does not change anything. My king demands an end to the rebellion. It ends today."

Tyrone shook his head. "Many things will end today, but the revolution is not one of them."

"You plan to meet my army on the field? You will all die."

"If I am to die, at least it will be on a field that reminds me so much of our childhood home, surrounded by my friends," said Tyrone.

"So be it," said Justyne as he turned away from his oldest friend.

****

Hours after the sun had left the sky, General Justyne of the King's Own Army looked over the field of victory but felt nothing. The enemy had fought hard, and almost to the last man, but they had been no match for the superior numbers and provisions of his forces. Something tingled at the back of his mind, however. The battle had almost been too easy, and there had been no magic attacks or magical creatures.

Perhaps they had fled before the king's might, thought Justyne, but he disregarded it just as quickly. He won the battle, but he could not get past the feeling it was a hollow victory.

He looked at the king's crest medallion that hung around his neck—a symbol of power and equality. With a deep sigh, he turned it over. Embedded in the back was a wooden dragon's claw charm. It had taken some time and quite a bit of coin to find a goldsmith that would put it in the back of the king's seal. Still, he had carried it with him since he was a boy, when he and his best friend had whittled a matching pair.

They often told each other that one day they would be great explorers and discover some of the world's old magic to help the world. *The path is never as we think when we are young and know nothing of the world,* he thought before returning to his tent.

****

Pyd flew above General Tyrone's head as they traveled north with the bulk of their army. He could feel the weight of the decisions his friend below had been forced to make. The death of so many soldiers as a gambit to allow the transport of the eggs hung over him. But seven eggs from the dragons of lore were more valuable to their cause than anything else.

"Let's go men," General Tyrone shouted to his army. "The end is in sight. We are almost home."

SPECIAL THANKS

Tara, thanks for letting me continue to pursue this dream. I know you tire of talk about dragons and wizards and KNEP read and sales. My stories and I are very appreciative of your patience and support.

I am so proud of the friendships and life-long connections the world of books, and specifically writing, has produced for me. I am going to list names of those that have impacted the journey. I hope I get everyone, but I know someone will be missed. For that I am sorry. But without further ado:
Makenna, Sara, Carrie, Luis, Katherine, Kris, Ondrea, Wendy, Ashely, David, Chris, Kennon, Getcovers.com, Jasmine, the Inkwellians, and many, many more.

BOOKS BY THIS AUTHOR

The Arrow of His Ways

Even death cannot stop a boy's love for his dog.

When his grandpa gave him a mysterious gift on the worst day of his life, Adam didn't believe it would make a difference. But it did.

Through a dream, he is transported to the magical world of Tipping. With a little, old gnome as a guide, Adam must cross the perilous land in pursuit of his best friend, Arrow. He battles goblins, an evil specterhound, and time itself for a chance to see Arrow before he crosses the Eternal Bridge.

A tale of love, perseverance, and magic.

www.ingramcontent.com/pod-product-compliance
Lightning Source LLC
Chambersburg PA
CBHW020605040726
47498CB00003B/643